As I picked up the gold jewelry box, a shower of papers fluttered down. I gathered them together to stuff them back in, noticing an engraving inside on the bottom.

> *My darling Caity-Cat,*
>
> *Whenever I hear this music, I will think of you and wish we'd made different choices.*
>
> *Yours always, P*

"Wish we'd made different choices." What did that mean? I peered down at the pieces of paper in my hand, the souvenirs of my husband's first wife's life.

I heard my husband call from the bottom of the ladder. I jammed everything back into the box, my heart skipping guiltily at poking into his private love notes, the little snippets of his life before me. "How are you getting on, Maggie?"

Tempting as it was to say, "Feeling more inadequate by the minute," I managed a relatively cheery "Fine."

We sorted through a couple more crates, and despite my best intentions, my mind kept drifting back to the letters in the box. The depth of devotion Nico had for his deceased wife had floored me. Maybe I was just a housekeeper with benefits, rather than a second chance at love.

I realized, with a jolt to my stomach, why none of the keepsakes that fell out of the box resonated with the image I had of Nico. Nico's handwriting had curly capital "I"s and funny tails on the "g"s and "y"s, like little handlebar mustaches.

It wasn't Nico's handwriting.

And if it wasn't his writing, who was engraving little messages on jewelry boxes crammed full with love notes to his dead wife?

Praise for *The Silent Wife*

"A compulsively readable novel about family skeletons."
—*Publishers Weekly*

"A wonderful, poignant, heartbreaking, heartwarming story of families and secrets, of hidden strength and unexpected friendship. Brilliant! Very highly recommended. Cannot wait for Kerry's next!"
—Renita D'Silva, Pushchart Prize–nominated author of *A Mother's Secret*

"A page-turner—full of implied secrets, unraveling family lives, and new family dynamics."
—Bookworms and Shutterbugs

"A compelling, chilling, and heart-pounding read that will take you on a rollercoaster ride you'll never want to leave. Phenomenally written and undeniably powerful, Kerry Fisher has done it yet again." —The Writing Garnet

"A gripping, emotional novel . . . a real page-turner!"
—La Biblio de Cara

The Silent Wife

KERRY FISHER

FOREVER

NEW YORK   BOSTON

Forever
Hachette Book Group
1290 Avenue of the Americas, New York, NY 10104
read-forever.com
twitter.com/readforeverpub

Originally published in trade paperback by Forever in November 2018
First Mass Market Edition: December 2019

Forever is an imprint of Grand Central Publishing. The Forever name and logo are trademarks of Hachette Book Group, Inc.

The publisher is not responsible for websites (or their content) that are not owned by the publisher.

The Hachette Speakers Bureau provides a wide range of authors for speaking events. To find out more, go to www.hachettespeakersbureau.com or call (866) 376-6591.

LCCN: 2018948929

ISBN: 978-1-5387-1810-0 (mass market)

Printed in the United States of America

OPM

10 9 8 7 6 5

To my family

The Silent Wife

CHAPTER ONE

MAGGIE, Brighton Registry Office, January 15, 2016

The words "Would everyone be upstanding for the bride?" made me want to look around for the woman in white.

My wedding day took place on a nondescript afternoon in the middle of January, well away from any big deal occasions like Christmas or Valentine's Day. I was thirty-five and I'd never even lived with a man before. Not because I was the last nun in the convent—too late to pull that stunt with my ten-year-old son, Sam, in tow—but because I was addicted to wrong 'uns. The sort of men who would have dads bundling their daughters into basements and throwing burning oil out of the top window.

But I'd never had a dad, just my mum who saw the good in everyone. The broken, the dreamers, the unhinged—Mum just made cheese on toast and let them park their feckless backsides on our couch. When she should have been high-tailing it for the broom, she grinned instead and said, "His heart's in the right place, love, just a bit wild. He'll grow out of it."

But they never did. And then I met Nico, who didn't need to grow out of anything. After all these years of dredging around in the bargain bucket for the most ridiculous of men, I'd found someone who didn't need fixing. Someone who could get up in the morning, hold down a job, deal with disappointment and frustration without leaving a trail of beer cans, debt and bewilderment in his wake. A bloke who turned up on time, who never smelled of booze or burglaries, who didn't call my son, Sam, "the kid." Plus—big bonus—he thought I was amazing or "*incredibile*" as he sometimes said when he was rocking his Italian heritage.

And instead of him finding me less *incredibile* as time wore on, he'd asked me to marry him. Which for a woman in the Parker family was as rare as knowing for certain who your father was.

So as I walked in on Sam's arm, as ready as I'd ever be to take my wedding vows, I should have felt like a mountain climber finally bursting onto a craggy peak after years of standing at the bottom, asking, "How the hell do I get up there?" Instead I felt more like a failed football manager carrying the weight of the fans' woes upon him.

I tried to catch Francesca's eye as I came down the aisle. I wanted to show her I understood, that it wouldn't be as bad as she feared; that we could make this work. But she refused to look up, her teenage face pointed to the floor, her body locked in a fragile battle between antagonism and anguish.

I wanted to pause, to ask the tiny group of guests to trot off for a minute so I could put my arm around those defiant but defeated shoulders and tell her I was on her side. Once again I wondered if Nico's strategy of getting married, leaving his daughter without any other option but to accept me as a permanent fixture, was the right one.

Too late now.

I squeezed Sam's arm, trying to transmit that I'd made this decision not just for me, but for him. My mum, Beryl, adored Sam, but he was going to need more to make a success of his life than lessons in how to hide from the landlord on rent day.

For the last jolly bars of "Chapel of Love," I tried to block out everything other than Nico. I wanted to savor this moment, when the man who not only complemented me, but completed me, was prepared to make a leap of faith and *marry* me. A first in three generations of Parkers.

I looked at the back of his neck, his dark curly hair still scruffy despite his attempts to tame it, and felt a great surge of delight. For one dangerous moment, I considered finishing off the few meters between me and the registrar with a cartwheel. I decided not to push it on my first day as a member of the Farinelli family. Judging by the look on most of their faces, they'd barely done a subdued skip in their whole feather-dusted lives. I clung to the hope that with a bit of patience and luck, we'd merge ourselves and our offspring into something approximating a "normal" family. Though one man's normal was another man's cuckoo.

Normal "for us" would have to do.

And then, the song clapped to a close, my desire to swing my hips and snap my fingers faded and the big grown-up thing that was getting married took off. The registrar was lisping her way through the ceremony, asking whether anyone knew of any reason we shouldn't marry. I held my breath at that bit, braced for a shrill teenage voice to ring out around the room, loud enough to reach the hotel bar and cause everyone to leave their pints on the table and scuttle in to see what was going on. I tried to block out all the fidgeting I could feel behind me. I didn't want to second-guess the expressions on his family's faces—the sneery distaste pinching his mother Anna's snooty features, his older brother, Massimo, standing with a fat grin on his face as though Nico was off doing something silly...again. I had hoped making our love official would tip them into a grudging sense of rejoicing that Nico was happy and settled after all he'd been through. Instead, for all the joy evident in the "ceremony" room, we could have been gathered for a collective colonoscopy.

I glanced behind me for moral support. My mates from the public housing estate gave me a thumbs-up. I looked away quickly in case they started whooping as though a horse they'd bet on had come up trumps. I'd already seen my soon-to-be mother-in-law eyeing up the cleavages and sequins with disapproval. God knows what Anna thought of my best friend's hat, sitting on her head like a feathery Walnut Whip. Instead, I looked to my mum for encouragement. She didn't disappoint, grinning away, a jolly rhododendron bush in a room full of austere alliums. I replayed her words from earlier. "Hold your head up high, darlin'. You're the best thing to happen to that family. Give his daughter some stability and love."

For once in my life, I wanted to surrender to romance, to believe love was sparkly and special and not something that made you look in the mirror and shake your head at your own stupidity.

While I was taking my vows, I kept my eyes on Nico's, cocooning myself in their kindness and warmth, insulating myself from the rest of the room. But Francesca's stares were drilling into my back, making me stumble over the pronunciation of Nico's middle name, Lorenzo. I imagined the whole family rolling their eyes. Nico squeezed my hand, reminding me we'd discussed how tricky this might be, prepared for it. That, as the politicians liked to say, "we were in it together." But I still felt the prickle of Francesca's opinions swooping between us, looking for a crack or a crevice in which to park her protest, the fermented fury that two years after her mother had died, Nico had chosen to marry again.

Despite my best efforts at getting to know her, she veered between stonewalling and outright rudeness. Sometimes her face lit up when I suggested a trip to the cinema or dinner out, before closing down again as though any enthusiasm for my ideas would be disloyal to her mother. Coming to our wedding would probably seem like a betrayal with bells on it, so I'd suggested to Nico it might be kinder to give her the choice about whether or not to attend. But Nico was resolute. "We want to be a family, not an opt-in, opt-out multiple-choice group. We've got to present a united front. In the end, it will make her feel safe."

But how could your father marrying again be a cause for celebration? For a thirteen-year-old, it must have rammed home the message that her mother's memory was fading further and further into the distance. That her father, the person whose grief had been as acute as her own, had learned to live without her and now Francesca was stumbling forward, alone in holding the bereavement standard aloft.

When I heard the shrieking behind me, my heart leaped for a second, thinking Francesca had finally lost control. Even the registrar paused as a scream reverberated around the room. Light footsteps that could only belong to Nico's seven-year-old nephew, Sandro, echoed on the marble floor. The clack of high heels followed him, then the door banged shut.

I resisted turning around, forcing myself to tune into the registrar, who was working up to the words I'd dreaded, the bit about in sickness and in health. I couldn't concentrate on what we were promising each other, only that Nico would be saying these words for a second time. Had he for one moment imagined the burden of that vow, the reality he might be forced to face? Had Nico really expected Caitlin, with the toned biceps and sleek hair, to cash in the bit about "in sickness," to watch her slip away, a little more, week by week? When he thought about having kids, did he ever imagine sitting at a table set for two, talking brightly to a teenage daughter, trying to ignore the third place where Caitlin used to sit, shocking and bold in its emptiness?

His voice caught on those words. I put my hand on his arm to reassure him I was expecting to bulldoze through the next fifty years without so much as a fallen arch. The way he grabbed my hand made me realize his first marriage would shape his second.

Thank God I'd lived long enough not to expect the fairy tale.

CHAPTER TWO

LARA

A little frisson of disapproval dominoed around the congregation—a unanimous Farinelli family frown—as Maggie walked in, barefoot, clutching a single sunflower. If not exactly dancing, she was close to prancing as she made her way down the aisle on the arm of her son, Sam, as though the very beat of "Chapel of Love" was seeping up into her feet, bringing joy to her limbs.

As Sam did a little shimmy past in his junior-sized top hat and tails, I hoped no one else heard my husband, Massimo, say, "It's like the circus coming to town." I couldn't resist a glance at my mother-in-law, Anna, standing there ramrod straight, her pillbox hat perched like a predatory eagle on her head. Her face was a perfect picture of disdain, as though she was having to concentrate on not shouting, "Will someone switch this racket off?"

With a quiver of hat netting, Anna leaned forward and caught my eye. She was far too polished to pull a face that might be intercepted by anyone else—but I knew the dawn of new daughter-in-law comparisons was gearing up in the starting blocks. I might even have a chance of emerging victorious this time after so many years of "Caitlin got her figure back very well after Francesca was born. But then, you did have a cesarean, I don't suppose that helped." Followed by some suggestions on how a scarf could "help disguise that tummy" and the odd cutting from the *Daily Mail* entitled "Drop a dress size in ten days!" left on my kitchen table. I'd also been found lacking in gardening, cooking and what Anna called "household administration" so I hoped Maggie wouldn't possess a huge array of secret skills to put me to shame.

Maggie didn't give the impression that she cared what people thought of her very much. With the little rose tattoo on her ankle, her bright blue toenails and her corkscrew hair cascading down her back, she looked more like someone celebrating a pagan ritual at a New Moon party than a bride trying to integrate herself into a new family where the obstacles were already piled up against her. She was going to need a whole lot of self-belief to resist Anna's decrees for "Farinelli family behavior."

If I knew Anna, she would have tried every which way to stop Nico from marrying Maggie. "Two years is far too soon, you're still grieving." "It's not fair on Francesca. She doesn't need a new mother; she needs a father to focus on her." "Do you really want to take on some other man's bastard child?" And she would probably have used those very words. Anything that didn't fit with Anna's worldview would be singled out and shot.

But she obviously hadn't managed to put Nico off Maggie. His face was ablaze with emotion, as though he couldn't quite believe this carefree creature had come along to liven up the precise hallways of the Farinelli households. It was astonishing that Maggie was only thirty-five, the same age as me. She wore adulthood so lightly, as though it were a state to be dipped into when absolutely necessary, an interruption to having fun and letting tomorrow take care of itself. With my neat bob, pearly pink nails and the knee-length dresses Massimo loved, I could have passed for ten years her senior.

So despite Anna muttering about the marriage being "doomed," I didn't feel sorry for Maggie. I felt envious. Envious of that burning intensity of new love. Of their optimism. Of their hopes for the future.

I imagined Nico laughing at her singing to the radio, dropping a kiss onto her head as she sat at the table, tucking her scarf into her coat before she headed off to work. I felt a pang of nostalgia for the days when Massimo would slip into my office and sweep all the carefully documented papers off the desk, the minutiae of the accounts I'd been auditing receding, blocked out by the ferociousness of his kisses. The "working" dinners where we'd be so absorbed in each other we'd only tear ourselves away when the waiters started sweeping up. I ached for the connection that opened the door to belonging, to feeling part of a family again.

I wished I'd let Dad come to this wedding. Massimo only had his best interests at heart: he didn't want Dad to become confused by all the new faces, but Dad still loved music and this 1960s song was right up his street. Any recognition from him made my day. And I'd have loved to have seen him in his suit again, smart and smiling, like he used to be.

Like we all used to be.

I turned my attention back to Nico and Maggie as they began their vows, catching sight of Francesca's rigid face as I did so. Despite Anna's doom-mongering, I thought Nico marrying again was a good thing for Francesca. Given that my mother died when I was a toddler and now my dear old dad was fading like an ancient Polaroid photo, I'd have been delighted to have had a warm, jolly stepmother to help me along. Maybe if I'd had someone to talk to, rather than protect, I'd have had a different life altogether.

But before I could disappear any further down that path of then and now, my seven-year-old son, Sandro, spotted a spider scuttling under the chair in front of him. Since our cat, Misty, had gone missing a few days earlier, Sandro was even more sensitive and clingy than usual, his pale face carrying the air of someone who'd read the instructions for aircraft evacuation and was just biding his time until the emergency presented itself. The exact opposite to the little I'd seen of Maggie's son, Sam, who looked as though suppressing a mischievous chuckle was a daily challenge. Sandro started to fidget. He nudged me and pointed. I leaned down and whispered that it was only a little spider, that it wouldn't hurt him, when it suddenly encountered Beryl's shoe and ran straight back toward him. He screamed, clambering up onto his chair.

Anna was turning around, frowning, no doubt clocking up more ammunition for one of her "Lara does her best but she really has no control over that child" speeches. Massimo leaned around me, trying to get hold of him, but Sandro started running along the empty chairs. I chased along the row after him, grabbing his hand and leading him out of the room, glad of an excuse to leave all that Farinelli expectation and accusation trapped behind me. Though I could still feel the opprobrium snaking under the ornate door I'd tried to close quietly behind me. I held Sandro to me, waiting for his tears to abate.

I forced out a calm tone of, "It's all right, it wasn't very big."

"I'm not really crying about the spider, Mummy. I want Misty back."

"We all do, darling. She'll turn up soon, don't worry."

I hoped a seven-year-old wouldn't be able to detect the doubt in my voice.

CHAPTER THREE

MAGGIE

Nico and I managed one blissful night away in a fifteenth-century coaching inn as a "honeymoon." We'd decided to take a longer holiday on our own when the kids were used to their new family life, which, judging by Francesca's behavior a fortnight in, might be at the turn of the next century.

Nico gradually introducing me to Francesca over the previous year hadn't worked. We'd tried to edge toward a family atmosphere, with curry nights in and cinema nights out. I could count on one hand the times when she hadn't made some barbed comment about how Caitlin had been better/thinner/fitter/funnier than me. I could have been the world expert in wing-walking and no doubt Caitlin would have been able to do it on a pogo stick. In the end, Nico had gone for the "like it or lump it" strategy, though we'd agreed that Sam and I wouldn't move in until the week before we got married, as a way of drawing a definitive line in the sand, when, for better, for worse, we'd have to find a way to get along together.

"Do you mind moving into the house where Caitlin lived?" he asked when he proposed, months before we'd set a date.

I'd waved away his concerns, thinking it seemed churlish to have any reservations about moving from the mouse house of a flat I lived in with my mum and Sam to Nico's Victorian terrace house, with its two bathrooms and four bedrooms. I did try to work out how to say, "I don't want to sleep in the bed you shared with her, let alone the one she died in," without sounding like an insensitive cow, but I couldn't.

As though he could see into the crappiest, most mean-spirited part of me, Nico said, "We'll choose a new bed together." He didn't elaborate and I was ridiculously grateful not to have to wonder which side of the memory foam mattress was Caitlin's.

As it turned out, buying a new bed didn't make me feel at home. Two weeks after our wedding, I was still waking up thinking I'd dozed off in the middle of a photo shoot for a glossy interiors magazine. Gray cushions with a turquoise fleck to bring out the weave of the subtly striped chair. Shabby chic wardrobes with ceramic handles that looked like they'd been handmade in Tuscany. And storage for everything. Even the trays had a special slot in the kitchen, rather than shoved down the side of the fridge to slice at your ankles if you banged the door shut too forcefully.

The lack of clutter in Nico's house made it look as though no one really lived there. The complete opposite to Mum's with the overflow paraphernalia of Sam's bike in the hall-way, the houseplants that grew like triffids in the hothouse of the lounge and Sam's hamster taking up more space than all of us put together with increasingly complicated tubes and runs. Whatever situation presented itself—a present to wrap, a fuse to replace, a sunflower to stake—I was quite sure Nico's response would involve the words, "in that drawer." Whereas I'd always favored the lucky dip approach of bur-rowing under the sink like a dog digging out a rabbit hole. I could only assume Caitlin had operated a ruthless policy of chucking out one thing every time something new came in through the door.

I'd been desperate to move out of Mum's flat. Sam and I had been sharing a sofa bed in her lounge for the last three years since I couldn't afford the rent on my own place any longer. With its fairy lights, patchwork cushions and rainbow-colored throws, it was like sleeping in a Moroccan Kasbah. Now, though, the reality I'd lusted after—not tripping over a football boot when I got up in the night, finding a radiator key within five seconds, having the perfect-sized jug for gravy—just made me feel I was a guest in someone else's home, as though I needed to pass through with minimum disturbance, leaving no trace of my stay.

I started to think it might be better for all of us to move somewhere where the memories of Caitlin would be the ones Nico chose to take with him. Not the ones that crept out unbidden; ghostly images lurking around every corner, squeezing in between us on the uncomfortable French sofas. Some days I'd imagine Caitlin's long, elegant fingers closing around the same door handles as me. Or her opening the bedroom curtains, glancing back to see Nico's dark eyelashes fanning out on the pillow, his lips still twitching with sleep. I'd deliberately reach really high or low so that my fingers wouldn't curl around the thick fabric where hers had been. I could run up some new curtains in no time. Probably should. But it wasn't quite like walking into the house that an ex-wife had vacated after an acrimonious divorce and thinking, "Right, we'll get rid of her tatty old crap," renting a dumpster and flinging in the mismatched plates, followed by her old slow cooker and half-used toiletries. Everything I threw out was another little part of her mother Francesca would never get back. Another bit of accepting her dad had moved on, to someone with a different taste in curtains. In crockery. In *life*.

Nico and I had touched lightly on the idea of moving but had decided not to broach the subject until things settled down with Francesca. I couldn't see it happening for the foreseeable future when even the smallest changes led to a right old ding-dong. Just that morning Francesca had done a dramatic sniff of her school jumper and said, "This jumper smells funny. What did you wash it in?"

And I'd felt awkward because I was experimenting with having some principles now that I wasn't so broke and had swapped the usual washing powder for some eco-friendly stuff. I left out the "splashing out on my morals" part and went for a mumble about the impact of detergent on the Natterjack toad. The furious response amounted to an amalgamation of "Mum always used Persil and I couldn't give a shit about toads, newts and *especially* you," as though she was hopeful I might accidentally swallow some Spirits of Salt before too long.

"You're quiet," Nico said, as we all sat down to dinner that evening. He put his hand out to cover mine. "Are you okay?"

I snatched my hand away. It was the weirdest thing—when Francesca was around, I couldn't touch Nico at all despite my whole body tentacling toward him for reassurance.

Francesca sat there, her eyes watchful, her pupils little pods of hate. It was all I could do to stop myself from bursting into noisy tears and shouting, "Never better. What could possibly be wrong? Your daughter hates me. It's going bloody brilliantly." It wasn't quite the mealtime scenario I'd conjured up when I told Sam marrying Nico meant we'd be part of a bigger family.

Right on cue, Francesca tossed her long dark hair back and pushed her plate away. "I don't like spaghetti carbonara."

Nico shook his head. "That's not true. You used to eat it all the time." The "when your mum was alive" hung in the air like words written in sparklers in the night sky.

"I don't like Maggie's carbonara, then."

I tried to ease the moment, praying Sam wouldn't take the opportunity to showcase his own fussy eating. "Next time I cook pasta, perhaps you can help me and we'll see if we can make something you like a bit better."

Francesca looked at me as though I'd suggested we run up a quick spaceman's costume and launch ourselves off to Mars. With perfect timing, Sam sneezed at the same time as having a mouthful of water, splattering half-chewed spaghetti onto Francesca's plate. She slammed her chair back and stormed upstairs. There was a five-second delay before the door banging off its hinges made Caitlin's lineup of pastel jugs rattle on the sideboard.

"Sam! If you know you're going to sneeze you need to put your hand in front of your face and turn away from the table."

But Sam killed himself with the naughty laughter beloved of ten-year-old boys. Little particles of bacon, mushroom chunks and strands of spaghetti all competed to remain within the boundaries of his mouth.

"For God's sake. Close your mouth. That's disgusting." My tone was harsher than normal. I didn't want Nico thinking he'd invited an unruly zoo into his life.

But Nico handed Sam a piece of paper towel and said, "Go and get yourself tidied up, you little tinker."

As Sam went to the downstairs cloakroom to sort himself out, we turned to each other and said at the same time, "Sorry about that," which made us both laugh.

Nico pulled me close to him. "I really am sorry. She shouldn't speak to you like that. But I don't know whether to come down on her like a ton of bricks or to try and ignore it."

Just feeling his cheek against the top of my head banished some of the despair in my heart. I wanted to ask him if he regretted marrying me, if he wished we'd just carried on seeing each other when the kids weren't around. But sitting there with a table splattered with spaghetti strands, and stomping feet threatening to crash through the ceiling from the bedroom above probably wasn't going to serve up the answer I wanted to hear. Instead I relaxed into him, savored the moment, the snatched fragment of time when we could be a couple—touch, hug, love—without filtering ourselves into "strategic steps for building a happy step-family."

At the sound of Sam's X-Box starting up in the sitting room, Nico released his hold on me, picking at the fraying sleeve on his jumper. He'd apologized for his scruffiness when we were first together—"Used to drive Caitlin mad"— but I loved the way he was happiest in faded jeans and old T-shirts. I couldn't imagine being with a bloke like Massimo with his navy suits and shirts with cufflinks.

A couple of loose threads and slightly bigger hole later, Nico finally looked up. His lips were moving as though they were trying to find the right words to arrange themselves around. "I'm not really sure how to deal with this, but it's the anniversary of Caitlin's death in two weekends' time. My mother wants us all to go to the cemetery together and then have lunch at hers afterward."

Never let it be said that my social life didn't rock through the roof. Grooving at the graveyard with the first wife's family.

"That wouldn't include me though, would it?"

"You'd be very welcome."

Yeah. Right. Not to mention it would be a bit bloody weird. I didn't actually need to witness the concrete evidence that everyone, possibly including my husband, was still wishing Caitlin had never died, that their lives had never had to break open and include me. No, I could think of things I'd rather do. Like sniff chili up my nose, mistake Deep Heat for Canesten, sever a limb with a cheese wire.

"I think that would just be awkward. Francesca won't want me there anyway."

The tightness around his eyes loosened. "Thank you for making it easy for me. I know it's not ideal. I'm hoping we'll be able to persuade Francesca to go. She's refused point blank to visit Caitlin's grave so far, but it might, I don't know, reaffirm in her mind she's not coming back and she has to get on with the here and now, stop her from being so angry."

"And what about you?"

He kissed the top of my head. "I've been lucky to get a second chance. I don't feel angry anymore. Just sad for anyone who dies too young and misses out on the life they could have had." He tried to make a joke. "You know, all that quality time with Francesca."

I still didn't know what face to put on when anyone talked about Caitlin. I felt caught between apology and guilt. Though we started going out long after Caitlin died, no one believed us. And it was ironic that I'd only met Nico *because* his wife was ill and my mum had helped out with the cleaning and shopping. And sat with her toward the end.

When I went to pick Mum up, Nico would invite me in if she hadn't quite finished. After the first couple of times when I nearly keeled over with the effort of not asking anything to which the response could be "shit," "crap" or "what do you bloody think?" I texted Mum instead of knocking on the door so I could wait in the car. Mum, though, saw owning a mobile phone as an exercise in battery conservation rather than a vehicle for communication. So with no agenda, Nico and I got to know each other at the worst time of his life until I looked forward to seeing him every day. And nearly a year after Caitlin had died, we'd bumped into each other in town, had a coffee and remembered how much we enjoyed each other's company.

No doubt I wasn't the only one who felt uncomfortable about the circumstances. But I probably needed to knock that on the head sooner rather than later so we didn't creep forward with Caitlin's name seeping between us like an embarrassing smell everyone was trying to ignore.

"Why don't you let me do lunch here for everyone? Make it clear that Caitlin is, and should be, part of our lives and no one needs to feel ashamed of missing her?"

Nico leaned forward and kissed me. "You are so lovely. And I am very lucky. Would you really do that?"

"No worries. I'll get Mum to help. She'll be so pleased to see everyone again. And then you can all concentrate on Francesca without stressing about your lunch burning to a cinder. You'll need something hot. It's so flipping blowy up at that cemetery. Will you let your mother know?"

Nico nodded. "Of course. Or you could nip over the road tomorrow? If you're feeling brave enough? She's friendlier than she seems. I bet she'd be pleased to see you."

I wasn't sure Nico was right about that. In fact, Anna living across from us was affecting how often I wanted to go out my front door. For the first time in my life, I was looking in the mirror before I left the house. And as for popping in, of all the vibes Anna gave off, "Do drop in for a croissant and a cappuccino" wasn't one of them.

It would take more than my shiny new wedding ring to catapult us into the category of family. Anna probably still thought of Mum as "staff," as she had been when she was looking after Caitlin, with Anna firmly in the role of lady of the house and chief instruction issuer. And my little seamstress business wasn't going to impress her when Nico owned one of the biggest garden centers in Brighton: "You'd be amazed how much people will pay for a little bay tree. Plants are a gold mine these days. Makes a fortune." Her real boasting, however, was reserved for her firstborn favorite, Massimo, who could barely walk into a room without Anna rushing over to tell him to put his feet up after working so hard. "He's an accountant, you know, doing so well, at one of the best firms in the country." No doubt Anna saw herself standing at the top of the social ladder peering down at the Parker riff-raff at the bottom, churned up with fury that we'd managed to haul ourselves up the rungs to be part of her life on an equal footing.

But of course, we'd never be equal in her mind. She'd seen me arrive to pick up Mum in my battered old Fiesta. She knew we lived in public housing. It was easy to see how she'd come to the conclusion I'd clapped eyes on Nico, spotted a house with a downstairs "cloakroom" and a utility room and plotted to reel him in.

But I couldn't really blame Anna. Sometimes I wondered whether I'd had a subconscious plan myself. Except, in the middle of all the emotions pecking away at me, whenever I was close to him, everything in me lightened as though I hadn't realized what a huge gap there was in my life until he filled it. And even Francesca's resentment of me couldn't make me wish I'd never met Nico, never fallen for his gentle way of making me feel special without a price to pay. Rashly, I agreed that I'd talk to Anna first thing in the morning.

But I didn't get organized as early as I'd hoped by the time I'd waved everyone off to school and work. The preparations to darken the doorstep of the Scary Mary matriarch herself—plucking my eyebrows, flossing my teeth, searching for my eyeliner, which I found on the handle of the hamster cage—of course—took forever. I'd just popped to the loo by the front door when I heard a rustling and a key in the lock. I registered a rush of embarrassment that I hadn't shut the door and Nico, or worse, Francesca, had come back for something and was now going to catch me with my pants around my ankles. But to my horror, Anna marched in, a swish of black crepe trousers, silk blouse and scarf knotted at the neck in a way that would have made me look like a pirate on a hunt for treasure.

Christ. I expected her to have a key to our house "for emergencies" but unless I'd missed smoke billowing from the roof, this was just an ordinary Friday morning. Anna did a dramatic step backward at witnessing me in mid-flow, as though she'd caught me doing something unspeakable with the hamster.

"Just give me a minute," I shouted.

I probably wasn't as horrified as she was. No one would ever have gotten to work or school from Mum's if we'd all taken our turn in the bathroom one at a time.

Some swift pant-pulling-up later, I found Anna sitting in the kitchen, her eyes flickering to the toast-and-butter bloodbath Sam had left behind, her fingers encountering a little blob of jam and recoiling as though a cockroach had mounted a mating ritual right in front of her. I made a big show of drying my hands so that she wouldn't add filthy non-handwasher to her list of things I didn't do as well as Caitlin.

"Sorry about that, Anna. I was in a bit of a hurry."

I waited for her to apologize for bursting into our home unannounced, but it fast became clear to me that was not how it worked. In fact, by the way her dark eyes were scanning the room, I soon realized this wasn't a visit to see how I was getting on, but an appraisal of my housekeeping skills. Which weren't as obvious as, say, my ability to breathe, or to put one foot in front of the other. She looked so disapproving, I nearly got the giggles.

I readjusted my belt. "Cup of tea?"

"I only drink coffee."

"Coffee, then?"

"No, thank you."

I resisted the temptation to do a comedy sketch of "Nettle tea? Spinach smoothie? Hot chocolate with a shot of brandy?" and put on the kettle anyway. No reason for me to die of thirst. As I picked a mug out of the kitchen cupboard, I chose the ugliest, clumsiest one, the one I was sure Caitlin would never have used. I might start throwing things if she said, "That was Caitlin's favorite mug."

I dug deep for the charm offensive I had planned. If I didn't want to keep scurrying out my own front door like a burglar with a couple of laptops tucked down his trousers, I really needed to get Anna on my side. I'd never be that person gliding about with little trays of almond biscuits and discussions about the best product for dealing with limescale on the taps, but perhaps I could persuade her that I had her son's best interests at heart rather than a beady eye on his wallet.

It was no wonder that she was a bit suspicious of me. Initially, out of respect for Caitlin, Nico and I had kept it all low-key. Plus I'd been waiting for him to say, "Thanks for helping me through the whole dead wife thing, but I'm off to find someone a bit classier/cleverer/thinner," so I hadn't really bothered with the daughter-in-law dance. I'd hardly spent any time in Anna's company before Nico had presented her with the fait accompli: he was marrying Caitlin's carer's daughter. But there was no going back. I'd show her I could be an amazing wife even without the fancy clothes.

I'd love to know what she thought of Lara, her other

daughter-in-law. I hadn't seen much of her yet but she hadn't bowled me over with her warmth and welcome. She always looked so serious, with her precise blonde hairdo and blouses with fussy little bows. I didn't have much confidence she'd be an ally against Anna.

And I was really going to need one.

Instead of winning her over with some old shit about the lovely activities we had planned "as a family" and spinning her some yarn about the progress I was making with Francesca, panic made me trot out the one topic Nico and I had agreed he would handle when the time was right. It was the big no-no, the subject that must be rehearsed and approached with the same amount of tact as discussing cardboard coffins with an elderly parent.

As I made a rebellious mug of soupy tea complete with teabag bobbing about—I burst out with, "Nico and I were talking the other night about moving to another house. We thought it might be good to have a fresh start for us all." I plunged on into the silence with an increasingly desperate monologue about how it might be healthy for us to choose somewhere Francesca didn't associate so strongly with her mother. Still in Brighton, of course, still near the sea, still close to Francesca's school...

With every word I spoke, Anna seemed to become more sucked in until it was like being in the worst job interview ever, when you realize that you've actually said the opposite of what they were looking for but don't have the sense to stop and say, "I might have gotten off on the wrong foot here."

As Anna's fine-boned features melted from an expression of surprise to one of outrage, I stammered to a halt. She propped her elbow onto the table and lowered her chin onto her hand in theatrical slow motion.

"Nico cannot move somewhere else. The Farinellis have

lived here for nearly fifty years. My husband bought our
sons the houses—one each—so Nico and Massimo could
live next to each other, opposite us, for the rest of their lives.
Nico will not be moving. This is his home. There have been
Farinellis in Siena Avenue since 1970, when we moved to
England. We chose it because we are from Siena and the
name felt like a good omen."

Before I could respond, she leaped to her feet. "This is the
problem when people do not treat family as important."

I tried to backtrack. "Anna, sorry, I didn't mean to upset
you. Of course, it's a lovely house and road, but I was just
thinking about Francesca and how it might be easier for her
to accept me if we moved somewhere that was new for all of
us. That perhaps didn't contain so many memories of Caitlin. I didn't mean we'd do it tomorrow, or even next year."

"If you were thinking about Francesca at all, you would
never have forced Nico to marry you."

The last sentence was ejected with a rush of rolled "r"s,
as though she had a toffee stuck behind her front teeth. The
unexpected animosity made tears spring to my eyes. I'd
known of course that Anna wasn't exactly rushing to welcome me. I'd accepted it might take time and that perhaps I
didn't look the part—a little dumpy, my hair on the unruly
side of messy and, however hard I tried, a natural predilec-
tion toward tie-dye, tassels and ruffles. But I hadn't expected
her to hate me. I felt the breath return to my lungs. "I didn't
force him to marry me."

Anna emitted a fabulous snort. "Of course you did.
Maybe not with a gun to his head, but Nico was always easily
influenced. Far too soft. His brother has far more sense. Got
rid of that silly first wife who didn't want children and found
someone who understood what it takes to be a Farinelli."

Any vain hope that Lara might be an ally seemed as

misguided as my brilliant idea of selling up and finding
somewhere new for our funny little mismatched family.
There I had it: the whole deck of cards spread on the table
curling at the edges under the brutal spotlight of the truth.
Anna didn't approve of me. Thought Nico was weak and I
had forced him into marriage, charging in as soon as Caitlin
had deigned to die. Never had I missed a shared sofa bed and
my mum singing into a sauce bottle more.

CHAPTER FOUR

LARA

After nearly a month of searching for our cat, I still couldn't accept that she might have simply found another home with a more plentiful supply of mackerel, or worse, that she was dead in a hedge somewhere. I tried to be brave for Sandro, but I'd had to put Misty's bowls in the cupboard to stop myself from bursting into tears every time I walked past them.

I'd inherited Misty when my dad had gone into a nursing home three years earlier. Every time I looked at her, I saw Dad as he was when I lived at home, his fingers stroking her back while he watched *Question Time* or listened to *The Archers*. Not the confused man who struggled with buttons and whose face paused in concentration before breaking into a smile when I walked into the residents' lounge.

Since she'd come to live with us, Misty had resolutely ignored Massimo's efforts to lure her in with little treats of tuna, fondling her ears, shaking stuffed mice on sticks. On the other hand, she snuggled up to Sandro as though his lap had been tailor-made for her gray bottom. Initially, Massimo joked about it. "That cat doesn't know when it's well off. Ungrateful moggy. Who does she think keeps her in chicken liver? Good job my wife appreciates me."

I'd laugh and tease him that Misty was the only woman who didn't think he was wonderful. He'd throw down the gauntlet, promising she'd love him more than me once he'd subjected her to his irresistible charms.

Every few months or so, he'd take up the challenge, unable to believe that there was a single living thing impervious to the force of nature that was Massimo Farinelli. But Misty greeted every bout of mackerel-waving, wool-whirling, "puss, puss, puss" enticements with disdainful stares, before stalking off to hop onto Sandro's knee.

Sandro even tried to encourage Misty over to Massimo, tempting her with little bits of chicken. She'd perch on Massimo's knee for about five seconds while she gobbled down her treat and then, with a dismissive flick of her tail, she'd be off, leaving Massimo half-laughing, half-cursing, with Sandro secretly pleased there was one thing he could do better than his father.

Now, four weeks after she'd disappeared, I still lay in bed every night, thinking I'd heard the telltale tinkle of her bell through the cat flap or a plaintive cry on the garage roof. I'd tiptoe down to check but find no sign of her. When I slid back into bed, Massimo would stretch out his hand to squeeze mine, pulling me to his chest while I sobbed. I couldn't give up on her: just today Sandro and I had done another round of our neighborhood, pinning up little pictures of her staring into the camera with her gorgeous amber eyes, urging people to search their sheds and garages.

Somehow her disappearance brought all my grief about my dad slowly losing his memory frothing up into a frenzy of feelings I found it hard to control. Every drawing pin I pushed into a gatepost, every poster I blu-tacked into a shop window made me feel as though I was trying to recover myself, not just the cat. It was like offering a reward for the woman I was ten years ago, before Massimo wooed me with his Victorian home, his senior position at work, his desire for children. Back then, as a twenty-five-year-old, living at home in the 1930s semi I shared with Dad, Massimo had offered me a vision of belonging to a new tribe. A family that held impromptu barbecues, popped champagne for the smallest celebration, always had enough in the pot for one more. Nothing like our home with its net curtains, butter knife and Tupperware, my whole outlook constrained by my dad's well-meaning advice: "Don't take on too much."

And part of Massimo's charm had been his insistence that "You're the only woman in the world I want to make babies with."

How flattering, how straightforward it had all sounded.

I hadn't realized that Massimo wanted a specific type of child: robust, sporty and confident, a mirror image of his tastes, his abilities, his intellect. Not, apparently, a son like Sandro—thoughtful and artistic—whose very presence seemed to irritate rather than enchant Massimo.

But now, Misty's disappearance had presented us with an unlikely silver lining. Massimo had become much kinder to Sandro, as though he'd finally started to get the measure of our sensitive little boy. It had been several weeks since Massimo had raised his voice over an errant sweet paper on the sofa or a stray sock on the stairs. Tentative seeds of hope gathered; perhaps Sandro's devastation had reminded Massimo how much he loved him.

And contrarily, I had to fight not to feel excluded as they sat down to build Lego sets together, jaunted off to the cinema or went out for ice cream "to take his mind off it." Massimo never invited me along. Instead he winked and said, "What Sandro needs is a bit of Dad time."

I'd watch them walking down the street, Sandro's slight

frame next to Massimo's muscly bulk, so different in build, gait and coloring. Except Sandro, for once, was walking tall, as though this unexpected attention from Massimo was feeding into his confidence in a way I couldn't. Instead of making himself scarce when Massimo came home, Sandro was seeking him out to suggest films he wanted to see, to mention when he'd done well at school, without looking over to me and saying, "You tell Dad."

And Massimo was the only one who could talk to Sandro about Misty without him becoming hysterical. I tried to avoid the subject in case I started crying myself. The last time Sandro mentioned the cat, Massimo smoothed Sandro's hair back from his face and said, "Listen, son, cats can be funny creatures. Sometimes they just go off for a bit, then come back. And sometimes, even though their own families really love them, they find another family they'd rather live with. And you've got to keep in mind that Misty is eleven. She's had a lovely life. It might be that she's gone to sleep somewhere and not woken up again."

Sandro's lip wobbled. "Misty will turn up. She wouldn't go and live with another family. Even if someone else starts feeding her, she'd miss us too much. Eleven isn't really that old anyway. There wasn't anything wrong with her."

Massimo scooped him up and hugged him to his chest, patting his back. "Don't worry. It's normal to feel upset when someone—or something—you love dies. If she doesn't turn up, we'll get you another pet."

Sandro had managed a tiny smile, grateful for Massimo's kindness. Even in my distress, I'd experienced a little burst of pleasure that Massimo didn't rush to tell him to stop crying and man up, and just allowed him to express his feelings without being told how to manage them. One word of understanding from Massimo, the faintest fatherly compliment, the smallest paternal hint of approval trumped any amount of ego-bolstering praise from me. I forced myself to be delighted we'd reached a turning point where Sandro had matured enough to become interesting to his dad, rather than just a demanding child who diverted my attention from Massimo.

Yet again my naïveté was astounding.

CHAPTER FIVE

MAGGIE

After Anna getting all Godfatherish over my moving suggestion, I waved a white flag and left it to Nico to break the news to Anna that we'd be holding the lunch at our house on the anniversary of Caitlin's death. With an admirable "stick it in your pipe and smoke it" attitude, he'd declared, "Oh for God's sake. Mum is so irrational sometimes. If we decide moving is right for our family, she'll have to get over it. And if she doesn't want to come here for lunch on Saturday, then she'll just have to eat a boiled egg on her own. It's bad enough trying to win Francesca around. I'm not pandering to Mum as well. And you mustn't either."

The anniversary that didn't need to be ringed on the calendar, the twentieth of February, arrived, bitterly cold and overcast. Yet again, I felt apologetic for my very existence, a living, breathing reminder of all that Francesca had lost, without yet persuading her that I could add any value. Although Francesca had inherited Nico's golden skin and dark hair, she was every bit Caitlin's daughter, with her angular features and waif-like build. She'd definitely be on my mum's "needs feeding up a bit" radar. I offered to make her scrambled eggs.

"I'm not hungry."

"You'll need something substantial inside you to keep you warm. It's going to be cold at the cemetery."

"I *know* it's cold at the cemetery," she said, stuffing a handful of Pringles into her mouth.

Nico glanced at me, asking for my understanding. I left them to it. Today wasn't a day to win any wars. My heart ached for Francesca, with her wan face and restless fingers, picking away at her cuticles until they were sore and bleeding.

I was thirty-five and still couldn't imagine a world without my mum, who—thank God—had agreed to help me with lunch. She barreled in just as the entire Farinelli family were gathering at the gate to walk up the hill to the graveyard. She clucked through the group, exclaiming about the gorgeousness of Sandro, how much he'd grown, the chill in the February air, Francesca's lack of gloves—trying and failing to foist her own fingerless mittens on her. She didn't care that they all stood around like skittles braced against a bowling ball; she just rattled on, admiring the white roses Francesca was holding, patting Sandro's head, pressing toffees into his hands.

From what I'd seen of Lara, she'd be swapping those sweeties for some cacao nibs or unsulfured apricots as soon as Mum's back was turned. That poor boy trussed up in a collared shirt and jumper. My neck itched just looking at him, skulking along half-entangled in Lara's mohair poncho. They both pressed themselves into the hedge as a teenage boy came past with an Alsatian pulling on its lead.

Sandro looked so pale and cold. He was only five when Caitlin died. He'd barely remember her. I'd offered to look after him while everyone else went to the cemetery but before Lara could answer, Anna had burst in with "No, he's coming with us; it's a family day," as though there were log flumes and spinning teacups to look forward to instead of a black granite headstone and a swarm of sad emotions ricocheting around the group. I had the uncharitable thought that Anna used their collective grief as another way of excluding me.

It was a relief when Mum bustled in through the front door and I could shut out the Farinellis and the complex tensions cobwebbing between them. She flung her arms around me. "Funny being here and not going up them stairs to see Caitlin."

I shrugged off my irritation that even Mum found it odd that Caitlin wasn't here.

I helped her off with her coat, wondering whether a Mongolian goat herder was shivering somewhere without his shaggy sheepskin. As she turned to see Sam shouting, "Nan!" from the top of the stairs, I quietly hung it up in the cloakroom. Sam nearly knocked Mum over as he launched himself from the last step. My heart twisted at his unself-conscious hug for her. She immediately conjured a Twix out of her handbag.

"Missed your old Nan, have you?"

Sam nodded before whisking Mum away to see his bedroom.

When she came down, she said, "I've always said this house was like a fancy hotel. You should think about taking in guests. That's a lovely spare room with an en suite. I could come in every morning and cook the breakfasts."

Mum saw money-making opportunities everywhere she looked. Mend, make, sell, swap…it was how she survived, often finding things in dumpsters to "sell at a car boot." Unfortunately, as one old sewing machine found a new home, a three-legged stool, deckchair or furry cushion crowded into the flat to take its place.

"I'd love to see Anna's face if we started running a B&B. Are you managing all right for money now we've moved out? I've got a bit put by if you need it."

"Get off with you, lovey. I don't need your cash. Got a new job looking after some poor old soul who thinks the Germans are coming for her and keeps hiding all her jewelry in the porridge. Nearly blew up the microwave the other morning because her earrings were in the bowl."

God bless my mum. She always had a little story, an adventure to recount. Word of mouth kept her employed, with grateful families taking her on to help out with relatives that they didn't have time to look after.

"How's Nico? Have you got used to being a wife yet? Has he got used to having another one?" Mum started to laugh, with a Benson and Hedges cough rushing to join the party.

I filled her in on what Anna had said to me.

"Bloody old bag. Forced him to marry you, my arse. He's lucky to have you. I hope you told her that you come from three generations of single mothers. Never mind the frigging Farinelli family in their 'avenue,' the Parkers have lived in Mulberry Towers public housing for over sixty years without the need for a husband."

She sat back victoriously as though she'd just proved, beyond any argument, that Anna was a total fool. You had to hand it to Mum. Her arguments always had been a triumph of illogical conviction.

I had to laugh. "I don't think parading our family's historical failure to blag a husband is going to win Anna around."

Mum's face softened. "I'm glad you did find a husband though, love. Nico is a nice lad. A bit fancy with his food, but not bad for an Eyetalian."

Mum hadn't yet recovered from the one and only time Nico had invited her to dinner here and he'd served poussin.

She spent the entire drive home telling me how she could
have bought four chickens from Lidl for the price of "one of
them bony little pushions."

"He was born here, Mum. He's British."

"Well, whatever. As long as you're happy." She paused,
her eyes narrowing. "You are happy, aren't you?"

I took a deep breath. I struggled to find my no-nonsense
voice, didn't want Mum to think I'd lost my Parker grit and
gone all soft now I was a "wife." "Of course I'm happy! Nico
is really lovely. Just need to win over the rest of the Mafia
now and we'll all be riding off into the sunset on fat little
ponies."

My mum patted my hand. "Oh pet. It's early days. Francesca's had two years without a mum but Caitlin was ill for
nearly a year before that. It's a lot for any child of her age,
poor little mite. Give her time. She'll come around."

I nodded. "I hope so."

Mum sniffed. "And don't worry about that Anna. She was
all for standing there wringing her hands, but I never saw her
roll up her sleeves when there was puke to clear up. None
of the women were any cop. That daughter-in-law, what's
her name, Lara, didn't help out much. Just left it to me to sit
with her and tell her that Francesca would be fine, she'd done
enough, she could go peacefully."

I felt a twinge of shame for cringing when I'd heard
Mum say "Hello, duck" to Anna; for wishing that she'd get
her weight under control; for frowning at the wooly hat that
made her look old. The ability to be kind, practical and stoic
was worth so much more than any amount of draping skill
with a scarf.

"Was Nico really distraught?" I wanted to take that question back as soon as I'd asked it.

Mum frowned. "Don't get yourself into a 'Who did he

love more?' competition, Mags. I know Nico loves you. He did find it hard at the end. Everyone did. She was so young. Nico relied on his brother a lot, though; Massimo was always popping in to give him a break. Made me feel guilty that you'd never had any brothers or sisters for when I go."

"Oh God, Mum, let's not even go there!"

I cut off the oxygen to that conversation by sticking my head in the fridge to find the vegetables for the soup. We soon fell into an easy rhythm of peeling and chopping, while Sam dashed in and out, telling Mum how he was goalie in the school football team, how Nico was going to take him to a proper match, how he was enjoying walking to school now that we lived nearer.

As the soup bubbled away, I laid the table, wondering whether Anna would faint onto the floor if I put out paper, rather than cloth, napkins. Mum was buttering bread rolls, with Sam giving her chapter and verse about the cars Sandro had for his Scalextric next door. "I like the Ferrari best, which is an Italian car. I'm half-Italian now, aren't I?"

I kissed his head. "It doesn't quite work like that. Still, it's nice Lara's happy for you to go around there and play with it." Although I found the way she delivered exact timings so uppity: "Would Sam like to pop around at three-thirty? Till five o'clock?" On our housing estate the kids just wandered in and out of each other's houses until the parents called them home for tea.

"She likes me going because Sandro hasn't got the hang of the Scalextric Massimo bought him yet. Every time he goes around a corner the cars fling off and I help him sort it all out. She said I couldn't go when Massimo's there, though."

"Why not?" Mum asked.

Sam shrugged. "Dunno. I think he finds me too noisy."

"Surely not! A little mouse like you!" Mum said. "Mind you, anyone would seem like they were making a right racket after their little boy. Never seen a child so quiet."

I was just about to ask her what she knew about Lara when we heard the front door open. I wiped my hands on a tea towel. "That was quick," I whispered to Mum.

It didn't seem right to fly out into the hallway and say, "How did you get on?" all cheery, as though they'd been on a little outing with tea and scones, so I waited in the kitchen.

I heard footsteps clattering upstairs, then Nico came in, his cheeks red with cold, his face pinched and weary.

"Are you okay? Where are the others?"

"Still there. Francesca had a meltdown at the entrance to the cemetery, started stamping on the roses and crying." He sighed. "She just can't accept Caitlin's not coming back. I thought it would help her but maybe it's still too soon."

Conscious of my mother looking at me as though I should be whipping out some wifely magic to make everything better, I hugged him. As he sagged into my shoulder, I wondered whether I'd ever stop being the one who came "next," if "Nico and Maggie" would trip off people's tongues in the same way that "Nico and Caitlin" had.

"Shall I go up and find Francesca?" Mum asked. If anyone could talk around a hysterical child, Mum could.

Nico nodded gratefully, as though he was clean out of coping. As Mum went out of the kitchen, Nico said, "This is bloody awful. I don't know what to do. I feel as though she's stuck in no-man's-land. Caitlin would have known how to handle this; she was much better at all this stuff."

Yet again my stomach lurched as though praise for Caitlin was criticism for me. Deep down I knew Nico was just raw with frustration that he couldn't help his daughter. But when I'd imagined our lives together, I'd seen myself as the friend, the one Francesca would confide in, the bridge between her and her dad, helping Nico understand the mind of a teenage girl. Instead, I was an enemy to barge out of the way so that Francesca could claw her way back to the status quo, trapping her and Nico in a constant homage to Caitlin.

Nico disappeared upstairs. I imagined him lurking outside Francesca's bedroom, waiting to see if Mum could work her magic.

I was stopped from plunging into even murkier misery by the arrival of the other Farinellis.

Massimo was first into the kitchen, rubbing his hands. He came bundling up to me, threw his arm around my shoulder and in an undertone asked, "Francesca all right?"

I grimaced. "Mum and Nico are upstairs with her now."

He nodded. "It will get better, you know."

I bloody hoped he was right.

He sniffed the air. "Smells good in here. Vegetable soup? Brilliant. We're ready for something hot. It was freezing at the cemetery."

I was so grateful to Massimo for acknowledging I had something to bring to the party. "It won't be long. Have a seat and I'll make some tea," I said, feeling embarrassed, as though I had no right to be welcoming people into Nico's house.

"I tell you what—I'll pop next door and fetch some wine. I think everyone could do with a little pick-me-up," he said.

I hovered in front of the kettle, not wanting to ignore his offer but afraid of being too enthusiastic and coming across as graspy or inhospitable. The wine rack in the sitting room was full but I wouldn't know if I was uncorking a valuable vintage or insulting him with a bottle of plonk destined for a beef stew. "If you just hang on a mo, Nico has got plenty of wine; he'll sort you out when he comes down."

Massimo smiled, a glittering grin, so like his brother's but without the hint of reserve that tempered Nico's. "No worries, you save that for another day. I've got plenty. Do you like Picpoul?"

I wasn't sure whether we were still on wine or had switched to a discussion about a new form of snooker. I was trying to decide between "I like any white wine" and "I'm a dab hand at bar billiards," when I was saved from answering by Anna sweeping in with Lara and Sandro. As I stepped forward to welcome them, Anna was already handing me her trench coat without even bothering to say hello. I half-expected her to wait for a cloakroom ticket.

I reminded myself Nico had enough to deal with without a second wife showdown, so I muttered some juicy rude words to myself and did a curtsy in the coat cupboard while flicking the finger in the direction of where I imagined she was standing.

When I emerged from my secret swearfest, Nico and Mum were coming down with Francesca. The desolation on her face made me call into question the wisdom of marking anniversaries with miserable pilgrimages to gravesides. No wonder the poor girl had had a meltdown. Since I'd read that David Bowie didn't have a funeral, I'd resolved to instruct Sam to donate my body to medical science and to celebrate random memories of me as they popped up without the stress of a big gloomy date rolling around every year.

I dithered between racing over to her to see if she was all right and not wanting to look as though I thought I could replace her mother in any way. Very softly, I said, "Hot chocolate, Francesca?"

She nodded.

Nico mouthed, "Thank you."

I delegated the task to Mum then called Sam to fetch

Sandro. He wasn't as keen on Sandro coming around to us, as the real pull for him was Sandro's Scalextric. And watching Sandro make his way up the stairs, sliding shyly along the wall, I understood. It was astonishing how little of his dad's exuberance he'd inherited, a pastel watercolor of the bold and bright outline of Massimo.

As I busied about making tea for Anna and Lara, Massimo swept back in with a whole crate of wine, plonking it down on the table with a flourish. "Thought we'd have a little drink in Caitlin's memory."

Nico started to protest. "I've got loads of wine; you didn't need to bring that."

"Ah, but this is really good stuff. A grateful client slipped it my way after I managed to find a little tax loophole."

Nico shrugged. Massimo clapped his hands. "Who wants a little drink? Maggie, darling sister-in-law of mine, would you be so kind as to find me some glasses?" Today didn't feel like a day to be shouting the sister-in-law label far and wide. But given that Lara and Anna seemed happy for me to wait on them but could barely bring themselves to acknowledge my presence, it was wonderful to have at least one person in the room who considered me part of the family. I dug out some wineglasses. He pulled a face and whispered, "Thank God you've arrived on the scene, Maggie. You're going to have to sort my brother out with some decent glasses. Sacrilege to serve Picpoul in these."

I was glad he had never witnessed Mum and me pouring lemonade into the disgusting red wine we got free with our Chinese takeaways and slugging it out of mugs.

Nico called everyone to the table. I served up the soup, asking Lara, "Will Sandro eat this? Do you want me to make him some little sandwiches?"

Before she could reply, Massimo waved me away,

"You've got enough to do, Maggie; you don't need to go to that trouble."

Sandro took one look at the soup ladle, jumped off his chair and buried his face in Lara's lap. "I don't like soup. I want ham sandwiches."

Massimo tickled the back of Sandro's neck then peeled him off Lara and sat him back onto his chair. "Come on, buddy. Sit down now." Sandro sat with his arms folded, looking as though he was going to have to plow his way through a bowl of liver and onions.

I tried to make light of it. "Honestly, Massimo, it's fine. I can easily make a few sandwiches." I bent down to Sandro's eye level. "Soup's a bit of a grown-up thing when you're seven, isn't it, darling?"

Before Sandro could answer, Massimo said, "You're such a sweetheart, but Italian children don't get a separate menu. There's no such thing as children's food. They eat what we eat."

Sandro looked as though he was about to cry. Christ. I'd opened a right can of worms. Part of me admired Massimo's energy. On the other hand, would it matter in two weeks' time that Sandro had had a sandwich instead of minestrone? My rules for Sam had petered out after "Don't steal" and "Don't swear." I'd never been one to get excited over eating your peas—or soup.

Nico rescued me. "Come and sit next to me."

He called across the table to Sandro. "Here, have some bread and dip it in. You'll grow muscles on your muscles." But Sandro refused to look up, putting his head down low over his bowl, where I'd ladled in the tiniest amount possible.

As Sandro slugged down great gulps of water after every mouthful of soup, I wished I'd served everyone fish fingers, jelly and ice cream and had done with it.

The rest of lunch slunk on in an uneasy clattering of spoons on bowls, caught between Lara quietly encouraging Sandro to eat, Francesca punishing Nico with monosyllabic answers and my mother chattering on about the price of fresh flowers "considering they only lasted a few days." I tried to block out the image of Francesca's roses in front of the cemetery gates, the white petals ground into the pavement, the stems bruised and broken.

For a brief moment when Anna clacked her nails on the side of her glass, I hoped she was going to find a topic of conversation to move us on from funereal thoughts.

"As it's the anniversary of my dear daughter-in-law's death, I thought we should take it in turns to share our favorite memory of Caitlin."

It took me all my restraint not to squeal with laughter. I'd seen it all now. The disapproved-of second wife expected to sit through family homage to the fabulous first wife. I hopped up. "I'll leave you to it," I said, my words falling into an uncomfortable silence. "Mum, give me a hand clearing away." My mother, who'd been feeding little bits of bread to Sandro and tricking him into eating the soup, got to her feet, quickly slipping Sandro's bowl under hers.

Nico said something to his mother in Italian I couldn't understand, but there was a definite rebuke in his words.

I started gathering things up. "Go ahead. It's nice to remember the good times. Mum and I will go into the kitchen." Instead of crashing the crockery together, I gently piled up the plates, refusing to give Anna the satisfaction of knowing that actually, I'd like to be Frisbeeing them against the wall, bellowing, "It's not my bloody fault Caitlin died!"

As Massimo got to his feet to speak, the agony of indecision was marbling Nico's cheeks. I had a little sieve through my feelings. Part of me felt sorry for him, pulled every which way by Francesca and Anna. Part of me wanted to shout, "Just grow a pair. Tell your mother to get stuffed. That whether she likes it or not, I am here to stay. Or at least I will be if she doesn't completely bugger it up for both of us."

Which was not a good thought to be having just over a month into my marriage.

CHAPTER SIX

LARA

It was classic Anna—elevating Caitlin to a saint's status now that she wasn't here to clash swords with her about everything from how she ironed Nico's shirts to whether she'd put enough salt in the pasta. Massimo was the first to join in the charade. Though of course, he hedged his bets.

"First of all, I'd like us to raise a glass to Maggie and her mum for cooking for us today. Delicious, thank you." He caught Sandro's eye. Thank goodness Beryl had managed a sleight of hand with his soup bowl.

I was desperate to follow Maggie and Beryl. The mere thought of dredging up a lovely memory of Caitlin made me all hot. I couldn't think of anything that would satisfy everyone left at the table.

Massimo chose to focus on her vitality and energy, directing his entire speech to Francesca. "Your mother was amazing. Every morning when Lara and I were barely out of bed, we'd see her jogging back from her run, all fresh-faced and looking like she was ready for the day."

I loosened my top over my stomach with a fresh wave of self-loathing for every piece of pasta picked off Sandro's plate, every biscuit sneaked out of the pack, every leftover fish finger I'd hoovered up.

Massimo hadn't finished yet. "I still can't believe that someone who ate so well, exercised and took such good care of herself could die so young." He took a slug of his wine. "But, in you, darling Francesca, she has left behind such a delightful daughter. I know she would be thrilled about how beautiful and how sporty you are. I wish she'd seen you win the county swimming championship."

Massimo would—of course—choose sport to praise. That superior Farinelli athletic gene that had them all hurdling their way through life with their mega backhand, their bloody butterfly, their ability to pick up any racket, bat or club and have everyone applaud in awe.

All of them except Sandro.

Francesca sat ripping at little bits of napkin as Massimo spoke. She probably didn't need reminding of all the events her mother had missed out on. I could hear her sucking air through her nostrils in uneven bursts. Rosettes of emotion studded her cheeks, as though she was talking herself down from telling us all to go to hell. But then she had every right to be angry at losing her mother so young. Every birthday I still felt a mixture of sadness and fury that my mum had died before I was five. No amount of being called "beautiful" and "fantastic" would make up for being "left behind." Throughout my childhood, I'd forever been "that poor girl whose mum died." The weird kid with the dad who was much older than the other parents, a bearded oddity squashed in among the handbags and heels at school events.

I pushed away the thoughts of my own loss as Massimo called our attention, demanding a toast to "the wonderful Caitlin, gone but not forgotten."

Anna was next up. I could see Maggie and her mum moving about in the kitchen. They must have been able to hear what was being said. I couldn't blame Maggie for wondering what kind of madhouse she'd married into. But if what Anna said was true, it had been a calculated move: Maggie'd had an affair with Nico before Caitlin was even dead.

I'd overheard Anna imitating Maggie: " 'No one believes us but we didn't get together for ages afterward.' Absolute rubbish! And that mother of hers was just as bad. 'Poor Caitlin, let me plump up your pillows for you, ducky.' " Anna had rattled on, scathing about Beryl. "And all the while she had her eye on the main chance—masterminding a meal ticket for her daughter and grandson. Not a bad result for someone who sews on buttons for a living."

I wondered if Beryl had the measure of Anna. She wasn't stupid. She'd clocked Anna practically reaching for the smelling salts when Beryl didn't know the difference between *penne* and *fusilli*—"It's all pasta, isn't it?"

But unlike me, Beryl didn't resolve to do better, to read more, to think faster, to learn the steps to dance to the Farinellis' tune. She found their idiosyncrasies and criticism *funny*. Little flashes of irreverence versus Anna's pomposity. God only knew what face she was pulling over the washing-up as Anna pontificated about what a fabulous homemaker Caitlin was, reminiscing about the "most magnificent" Victorian grape scissors she'd unearthed at an antiques fair. If Anna deemed me worthy of this sort of morbid memorial, I hoped that she'd remember me for something more noteworthy than my ability to spot a pair of fruit scissors in a tray of tat. Then Anna turned to Francesca.

"Your turn, *amore*."

I wanted to leap up and call a halt to this macabre theater. I was desperate to tell Francesca she didn't have to participate. She needed to be able to accept her feelings, take comfort in her memories without the rest of the bloody family assessing her ability to perform. But she looked at the table, then got to her feet as though what she was about to share had more of a purpose than voicing a random recollection.

Briefly, her face softened, taking on the rounder, more relaxed features of a child rather than the prickly teenager she'd become. Then, glaring at Nico, her eyes red-rimmed, her features pinched and hard, she said, "The thing I remember most about Mum is that she was there for me one hundred percent. No one was more important to her than me. And I miss that." Her voice tapered away, crumbling into misery.

Nico flinched. He stretched out his hand to her. "I'm here for you, Cessie. I hope you know that."

He tried to pull her around for a cuddle but she shook him off. "I have to share you with Maggie now."

Nico sagged into his chair. Despite being just forty, five years younger than Massimo, he could easily be mistaken for the eldest son, with his air of the worn and weary, the flecks of gray in his dark hair, the sense that something vital had seeped out, sucked away in battles with Francesca, wars he could never win.

I couldn't help feeling sorry for him; I related so completely to that feeling of never quite getting it right, however hard you tried. I'd thought parenthood would be such a breeze, especially with Massimo by my side. His enthusiasm for starting a family had silenced my reservations about putting my fledgling career in accountancy on hold for motherhood, conscious that his first marriage had failed because Dawn hadn't wanted children. And there'd never seemed a "right" time to go back to work since. At least not in Massimo's eyes and certainly not in Anna's, who'd been horrified I might leave Sandro in nursery with "silly young girls who've never even had babies of their own!"

I pushed away the stab of sorrow at how optimistically I'd embraced motherhood and the grind it had become.

Right on cue, Sandro whispered he didn't feel very well, that his stomach hurt. I didn't want to get into a discussion at the table about which end he thought might be the trouble—the Farinellis for all their scorn for other people's weaknesses were ridiculously prudish when it came to bodily functions. So I got up to take Sandro out, but Massimo put his hand over mine.

"He can wait for a minute. Don't miss out on sharing your memory of Caitlin. It's important for you, Francesca, isn't it, to hear how much your mum meant to us all?"

Francesca had captured—and perfected—Caitlin's ability to look at her audience as though they were honored to be in her company, as though she pitied the trees that produced the oxygen wasted on my words.

I sat down, muttering to Sandro to go to the loo, that I'd pop out in a minute. But he shook his head and tugged at my hand. My shoulders tensed, my mind racing. I needed to nip this in the bud right now before it escalated, before we set off down that well-trodden path of Massimo versus Sandro, with me dancing between them like a demented puppet. The dull weight of inevitability competed with my sense of urgency.

Massimo patted Sandro's shoulder. Only I could see the hard fingers of the other hand digging into his arm, prying him off me. "Come on, son. Let Mummy talk about Auntie Caitlin." His tone was light but Sandro's practiced ear would be able to discern the thin thread of threat.

Sandro leaned into me, holding his breath, his stomach puffing out in a concave circle. I prayed that we weren't about to see a splatter painting of soup.

I tapped Massimo's arm. "I don't think he feels very well. Could you take him out then?"

Massimo's nostrils flared with impatience but his words

played to the gallery. "Where does it hurt, son? Come here and let me have a look."

I didn't need to see Anna to know she'd have that expression, that face semaphoring to the world that "Poor Lara does her best, but Massimo has to step in so often. That boy's so sickly, I don't think she can be feeding him right."

Sandro squiggled away from Massimo, leaning toward me, his back rigid, his bony shoulders digging into my ribs. I sat on my hands to stop myself from scooping him up, lifting him onto my knee, rubbing his stomach and cuddling all his knots of angst away.

I could have leaped up and kissed Beryl when she came bustling in with a Cornetto—"Sandro—come into the kitchen and have this while the grown-ups do their talking."

She'd swept him out before Massimo could react, before he could insist on Sandro standing in front of him to be prodded and poked, before the inevitable announcement: "There's nothing wrong with you."

The surge of apprehension loosened inside me as Sandro ran off holding Beryl's hand, snuggled in close to her ample hips as if leaning into a windbreak in a storm, safe for the moment.

Irritation flashed across Massimo's face but he settled back into his chair, arms folded, expectation chiseled onto his features. "The floor's yours then, Lara. I know how much you miss Caitlin."

I groped around for something, anything other than the thought that was burning in my head, blotting out everything else. The scar on the back of my hand from an old dog bite tightened and itched as it always did when I was nervous. I glanced around wildly, feeling Massimo shift beside me. I spotted the little vase of snowdrops on the side. "Gardening," I said, as though I'd just come out with the answer for a million-pound prize. "She was brilliant at gardening." I prepared myself to start naming spring bulbs, gearing up for a eulogy about her daffodils, hyacinths and crocuses.

Anything to stop myself from saying, "The thing I remember most about Caitlin is how much I hated her and her perfect life."

CHAPTER SEVEN

MAGGIE

Now that I wasn't spending the mornings in my shop working out how many dresses I needed to alter to pay for new football boots for Sam, my old love for sewing returned. And by mid-March, when Francesca had ramped up her hostilities—flouncing out of the room whenever I walked in, barging me out of the way to sit next to Nico on the couch, encouraging Sam to be cheeky to me—it had also become my haven. I loved opening the door into my own private space where I wasn't constantly on the back foot, feeling as though I had to make excuses for still sucking in air. At work I knew the answers. People looked to me for help and didn't go all out to contradict me once I'd found a solution. In the long hours I spent bent over buttons, hems and hooks, the nagging feeling of not being good enough subsided only to claw its way to the forefront again as I drew closer to the place I still didn't think of as home.

So that March evening when the landlord of my shop shuffled about on the spot before blurting out—"Ever so sorry"—he'd sold the whole building and was giving me four weeks' notice to leave, big fat tears blobbed onto the silk skirt I'd been mending. I'd rented this little place for next-to-nothing for so long, there was no way I'd find another shop I could afford. And if I didn't sew, I couldn't earn and I really would fulfill everyone's gold-digging expectations. The sneering about "It didn't take her long to become a lady of leisure" would be ricocheting around certain houses on Siena Avenue before I'd even packed up my pin cushions.

I was tempted to give my mates on the estate a ring, disappear down The Hat and Feather and drink enough vodka until I saw the funny side. Or skip the alcohol and head over to Mum's where Sam stayed after football practice every Wednesday. I allowed myself to consider how comforting it would be to burst through my old front door and slump down on Mum's knackered couch while she bustled about with tea and crumpets. All the seats in Nico's house were designed to encourage you to get up and do something else. And for once, I wanted to eat takeaway curry out of a foil dish, mopping up the sauce with a chunk of naan bread, not fiddle about with garlic, herbs and proper chicken stock.

But I was a wife now, so I had to go home. Nico was already back from the garden center when I got in. He looked up from the risotto he was stirring and rushed over. "Maggie! Are you okay? What's the matter?" And despite feeling that with Francesca so unhappy, it was up to me to keep the faith that everyone would come around eventually, my brave face crumpled there and then. Nico held out his arms to me. Francesca, who'd been doing her homework at the kitchen table, slammed out of the room.

And once I'd started, Nico must have wished he'd done a bulk buy of Kleenex and paper towels. Out it all poured, spewing into the atmosphere. Me losing the sewing shop. Caitlin's clothes in the wardrobe of the spare room, beige, black and navy, hanging there like a reproach. Francesca waging—and winning—a war that meant we never got any time together. I wished I could fix her, wished I could make it better, stop her from hurting and being so angry.

But I couldn't.

Which meant we could never relax in case Francesca needed Nico. Even when we went to bed, there was often a nightly drama: "Dad, there's an earwig in my room/I can hear a noise downstairs/I can't sleep/I've got a headache." Despite growing up on the housing estate where the walls were so thin you could hear the neighbors fart and fornicate, fear of Francesca's footsteps along the landing was the most effective antidote to newlywed libido known to man—or woman.

Nico looked almost relieved. "I thought you'd discovered you didn't fancy me." He stroked my hair. "I'm sorry being married to me hasn't been a bit better."

"Don't be silly. I love being married to you. I just feel that I'm letting you down all the time. I knew I'd never replace Caitlin, but no one has ever hated me as much as Francesca."

"She doesn't hate you. How could she? You're lovely. It's what she's lost and what you represent. So do you know what I suggest, Mrs. Farinelli?" he asked, pulling out a chair for me.

Even though he sounded cheery and positive, fear must have flashed across my face. Two months into our marriage and I was still waiting for him to realize it was all a big mistake.

He leaned over and kissed me. "We're going to set up a workshop for you in the attic. It's quite nice up there. Before she got ill, Caitlin was going to make it into a yoga studio, so we've already done the electrics and whitewashed the walls. There's a big Velux window so it's light and we can commission some built-in worktables, shelves and cupboards—whatever you need—to make the most of the space."

Commission. God, that was a word I'd never needed to use. Make do. Barter. Cobble together. A little thread of hope curled around my heart. My own special space. I might be able to offer proper dressmaking services rather than just alterations and repairs.

"And the big plus is that it's rent-free."

"Are you sure? You won't feel taken advantage of?"

"Don't be silly! I'm your husband, not your landlord. That's what couples do. They share each other's problems and work out solutions."

That set me off blubbering again. After so many years on my own, battling for a way out of trouble that wouldn't lead to me relying on Mum for money or Sam going short, Nico's words were like fairy dust floating about, magicking sparkly little solutions out of thin air.

"We'll have to clear out the attic though." He pulled a face. "We might have to get Francesca to help with that. There's a lot of Caitlin's stuff up there. God knows what. Her books from university, walking and diving gear, her riding stuff, scrapbooks—she was a great one for hanging onto concert programs, plane tickets, all that sort of thing. But there might be some bits and pieces Francesca will want to keep."

I closed my mind to how many memories sorting out Caitlin's belongings would stir up for Nico. Given how sporty she'd been, it was astonishing he'd ended up with a pudding like me. I'd never sat on a horse in my life. I didn't like the idea of being on anything without a reliable brake. I wasn't sure I wanted to be there while he talked Francesca through the places they'd visited, the bands they'd seen, the beaches where they'd watched the sun go down. I didn't want to spoil anything we did together by wondering if he'd had a better time with Caitlin. Or find there was a whole list of places in the world where he'd already had sex with his first wife.

I was keen to sound suitably grateful so I tried a diplomatic approach: "I'm happy to help, but do you think it's something you might want to do on your own together? I shouldn't have a say in what stays and what goes. If it's a big space, you could keep some of it to one side and I'll use the rest."

"If you don't mind, it's probably better if you do it with us, otherwise we'll just keep putting it off. And I can't expect you to coexist with Caitlin's stuff sitting in the corner. I wouldn't want to keep your ex-boyfriend's knickknacks under my desk. It's time. Francesca can put the things she wants in her room."

I hugged him. Now we just had to pitch the idea to Francesca.

CHAPTER EIGHT

LARA

Toward the end of March, with Easter just around the corner, I could no longer kid myself about how long it was since I'd seen Dad. New Year's Day. The last time Massimo had been free to drive me to the nursing home deep in the Sussex countryside.

I didn't want to think about that afternoon and how badly Dad had behaved toward Massimo. Shouting unintelligible nonsense about "purple windows" and threatening to hit him with his walking stick. I'd sat shaken and sobbing in the car on the way home while Massimo railed about the "ungrateful sod," detailing how much he spent on the nursing home. "Do you know how much getting him a haircut sets me back even though he's only got five strands left? Seventeen pounds!"

Massimo had always been too busy to take me again— too stressed, too away, too tied up. And ironically, because Dad had always discouraged me from learning to drive because he didn't want me to die in a car crash like my mother, I couldn't get there under my own steam. Of course, in the beginning, I'd had a few friends left to give me a lift. But Massimo had eventually made them so unwelcome, or caused such a scene when I wanted to see them, that over time they'd fallen by the wayside, finding our friendship too much like hard work. And I still couldn't allow myself to think about what Massimo had done the last time I'd spent a fortune on a taxi.

So now I couldn't see Dad at all.

But recently, Massimo seemed more amenable to everything. Perhaps he was just less stressed at work, but cups of tea in bed were becoming the norm, shoulder massages, even rational conversations about exploring possible jobs at his firm for me—"Let's look into it after the summer when Sandro's back at school." It was a change from his usual "The firm's become so much more cutthroat than when you were there. I don't think you'll cope."

Tonight, too, he was in a good mood. He'd read a story to Sandro at bedtime, opened a lovely bottle of Sancerre and I'd roasted some monkfish with garlic, just as he liked it. The perfect evening for broaching the subject of Dad.

"I know it won't be your favorite day out, but I really need to go and see Dad over Easter. I hate the thought of everyone else spending time with their families and him sitting there on his own with a nursing home Easter egg."

Massimo forked in a piece of fish, dabbing at the corner of his mouth with a napkin. "I don't want you getting upset over Easter. You know how depressing you find going to visit him. I've only got the four days off and I thought we could have a little trip to London, take Sandro to the London Dungeons or the Tower of London? Get a hotel up there?"

I stared at him, being careful not to sound dismissive. The London Dungeons? Sandro would have the screaming abdabs for months afterward. "That sounds great. I'll have a look and see what's on. Perhaps we could go to a show if you fancy it. Is there any chance we could perhaps pop over to

Dad's on the evening before Good Friday if you finish work early enough?"

"I'm going to be right up against it on the Thursday, just to get everything done so I don't have to work over Easter. Your dad won't know it's Easter, will he? You could go any time. The week after or the one after that."

Massimo was pleating his napkin. Swigging at his wine. His knife was tapping a little tune on the edge of his plate.

It was three months since I'd seen Dad. I had to go. I tried to keep my voice calm, to stop it veering into begging or demanding. "Would you be okay if I got a bus to Worthing and then a cab from there, one day next week?"

"That's a pretty expensive cab journey. I've just had notice the fees are going up in the home. I think we should try and rein in unnecessary expenditure where we can."

I took a deep breath. "You've been incredibly generous paying for his care until now, but it might be time to get some proper legal advice and get permission to use the money from the sale of his house to fund his care. That way the whole burden wouldn't fall on you." I stopped myself from adding, "And we might be able to free up fifty pounds so I can actually visit him."

Massimo sighed as though he was talking to someone with limited intellectual capacity. "I don't think you have any idea how much it costs for him to be in that home." He patted my hand. "He could live to be ninety-five. If I don't bankroll him, he'll run out of money in no time. And I'd hate for him to end up in some shitty place that stinks of cabbage, where they all sit around in nappies."

My stomach clenched. I couldn't let that happen to my dad with his cufflinks and his "little spritz of aftershave." He still insisted on struggling to his feet whenever a female nurse walked into the room. I should have worked out how to make proper provisions for Dad when we sold his house, instead of relying on the knife edge of Massimo's goodwill. But then, as now, my husband had been so hard to refuse: "You've got enough to worry about. I'll deal with the money side of things. It's what your dad would want. After all, people pay me a fortune to look after their affairs. Let me share some of the stress, otherwise you'll end up on antidepressants again."

And because Massimo always fluttered his fingers at me when I asked to see the paperwork—"I'll take care of all that, it's my pleasure"—I had no idea how long Dad would be able to pay for himself even if I did manage to wrest financial control from Massimo and get access to Dad's money.

Massimo was mashing his fish hard against the side of the plate. I was in danger of spoiling the evening. I'd try again tomorrow.

He looked up. "Anyway, if you've got so much free time, why don't you get yourself off to the doctor's and get to the bottom of why you can't get pregnant again? You seem to have found plenty of time to send out search parties for the bloody cat but haven't quite got around to finding out why there's no brother or sister for Sandro."

I should have known better than to push it. Typical Massimo to tolerate, even embrace, something that was important to me until he got bored, until there was no glory left in it for him, no one to say, "You should see the way he tried to cheer up that little boy when their cat went missing."

"I'll try and get an appointment but the doctor who specializes in family planning and fertility issues has been off for a while." I stood up to fetch a glass of water so that he wouldn't see me blushing at the lie. "As soon as she gets back, I'll see what she says. She'll probably want to examine both of us at some point."

Massimo banged his knife down. "There's never been a problem with fertility in the Farinelli family. Nico only had the one daughter because Caitlin didn't want any more. You do the tests and see what they come up with."

I nodded as though I'd be booking my appointment just as soon as I could.

But Massimo couldn't control everything.

Yet.

CHAPTER NINE

MAGGIE

For the first time since I'd moved in, I had a sense of claiming my place in the home instead of hovering apologetically in the wings. I was going to have my own workshop, make an area of the house mine, rather than squat in a space belonging to another woman. I was just about to trot downstairs for breakfast, light of step, when I heard a strange noise on the landing. It reminded me of a fox I'd once seen get hit by joyriders on our housing estate writhing in the gutter in agony.

I rushed to the end of the landing. Francesca's room. I hesitated, afraid that she might scream at me to get out. Then I decided there might be a real emergency on the other side and dashed in, shouting for Nico as I went. Her curtains were still drawn and it took me a moment to locate her, upside down on the bed, half in, half out of the duvet, crying as though the world had ended.

"Francesca!" I ran over to her and put my hand on her hot little back. "What's the matter?" I tried to turn her over but she buried further into the duvet.

Then I saw the big blotches of blood all over her sheets.

"You poor thing. Is this your first period?"

She nodded into the duvet.

"Have you got anything?"

She sobbed out a "No."

Nico appeared at the door, "What's going on?"

I put my finger to my lips and waved him away, mouthing, "It's okay." Nico's ability to turn green at the discussion of "women's things" was not what was called for right now. He looked puzzled but backed out of the room. I loved him for trusting me.

I fetched Francesca's dressing gown from the hook on the back of her door. "Right, lovey. You go and have a shower; you'll feel so much better. I'll find some pads for you."

To my surprise, she flung her arms around me, her face hot and damp on my shoulder. "I want my mum. I really want my mum. I wish she was here."

I forced myself not to think about how Sam would cope if I dropped dead tomorrow. Even now, at thirty-five, I couldn't imagine my mum not being around—how alone would I have felt walking down the aisle to marry Nico if she hadn't been in the front row, smelling of the rip-off Coco Chanel she bought on the market? I'd had over three decades of Mum telling me how amazing I was, when in reality, I was so ordinary. But to her, I was extraordinary, in a way no one else could ever be. Even now, she sometimes called me her "baby girl" as a joke. But I loved being someone's baby, even at my age. A safety barrier between me and the outside world, someone who would do her best to make life come good for me, without any agenda or expectation of payback.

Francesca had had such a short time to absorb that "biggest fan in the world" feeling from Caitlin. And now here she was on the cusp of womanhood battling with all those child-versus-adult feelings, plus a bag of nutty hormones bouncing around, without the one person who could help her make sense of it all.

It made me want to cry myself.

I'd never felt more useless, more unable to provide for the needs of another human being. While her tears poured out, all the usual anger and spikiness washed away in a raw explosion of grief, I held her, stroking her back, whispering, "There, there," as Mum used to when I was upset. I lifted her hair off her neck, trying to cool down the turmoil of emotion that was consuming her.

Slowly, Francesca's sobs lost their intensity. She sat back, not meeting my eye. I tried to hang onto this moment of connection, suspended between us, fragile as a soap bubble. I touched her hand.

"I understand. Really I do. If I was you, I would want my mum too. Not someone my dad had married."

Francesca bit her lip. She didn't move, just sat there with tears regrouping along the line of her lower lashes, waiting to splash down. I wondered how many evenings she'd been crying into her pillow when Nico and I had been sitting downstairs, sipping our wine after she'd flounced off in a huff. While we'd been talking about how to "deal with her behavior," had she been pressing her face into her mother's blouses, desperate for a trace of her familiar scent? Sifting through her jewelry box, untangling necklaces, trying on rings, attempting to conjure up the essence of her? And all the time I'd been thinking about myself, feeling thwarted by a thirteen-year-old and wondering how I could ask Nico to put a lock on our bedroom door?

Finally, I was understanding what it meant to be the grown-up.

And to be a stepmum to a daughter whose own mother had died.

If ever there was a time to stop wallowing in self-pity that my fabulous new world had a couple of minor imperfections, this was it. "I'm going to go and get those pads for you now. Why don't you use the en suite in the guest room so you can have a bit of privacy? I'll change your sheets for you. Just pop your pajamas in the wash basket and I'll sort them."

Francesca nodded. "Thank you." And she gave me another hug.

It was only Francesca's sad little face that stopped me bouncing on the bed, dirty sheets and all.

CHAPTER TEN

LARA

On Good Friday, when Massimo hopped out of bed at seven o'clock, kissing me on the cheek and saying, "You stay in bed, beautiful. I'm just off to collect your Easter present," I had to stop myself from saying, "We could have been with Dad by eight-thirty." However, on the upside, I'd managed to sidestep torturing Sandro with a weekend at some of London's most macabre attractions by reminding Massimo we needed to "rein in" our spending.

I snuggled back down into my pillow, my mind churning around the contradictions of my husband. So many thoughtful gestures to balance his hurtful outbursts. But I'd known that from the beginning, when he'd first made a play for me at work. He'd brightened my day by noticing a new blouse. Then crushed my confidence by wrinkling his nose at my latest haircut. Brought me coffee when I worked through my lunch hour. Then driven off without me if I was five minutes late leaving the office. But whenever I was with him, I was part of the action, absorbing his energy—good or bad—rather than a passive bystander. And without the Farinellis, with all their collective faults, I'd now be alone in my world, except for my dad who was slowly losing the grip on his. I consoled myself that even if I'd rather have gone to visit Dad, Massimo making a special effort with an Easter present was another little crumb on the right side of the "He loves me, he loves me not" scales.

But by ten o'clock, I was starting to wonder where Massimo had gotten to. Like my dad, I hated people being out in the car and taking longer than I expected. So my first reaction when Massimo came bursting through the door with a big ginger puppy in his arms was one of relief. Followed by bemusement, then fear.

Massimo's face, that beautiful, haughty face, was alive with excitement. "Look what I found!"

I backed away, imagining he must have found the dog wandering outside and had brought it in to stop it from getting run over. I wished he'd tied it up outside.

He came right up to me with it struggling and flailing to get out of his arms. I stood on the second step of the stairs. He thrust the dog toward me, nearly making me scream.

"A little something to make up for losing Misty. A Rhodesian Ridgeback. Last one in the litter. Nearly six months. They were going to breed from him but he turned out to have a kink in his tail so they wanted to find a new home for him. I persuaded them he'd have an amazing life with us."

I tried to smile but I wanted to stampede up the stairs and lock myself in the bedroom until he'd shut the animal away. He couldn't be serious. He knew I was terrified of dogs since I'd been bitten by a collie as a child, knew I'd stopped taking Sandro to the park because I couldn't relax if there were any dogs running around. Even if they were on a lead, I couldn't take my eyes off them in case they suddenly slipped their collar and attacked us.

To my horror, Massimo shouted up the stairs for Sandro, who shot out of his bedroom immediately, his expression a mixture of eagerness and trepidation.

"Ta-da! Say hello to your new pet, Lupo. It means wolf in Italian."

Sandro's face dropped, then he glanced at me and wrenched his mouth into a smile. He hovered on the landing, while Massimo beckoned enthusiastically.

"Look how cute he is. Man's best friend. You're going to love him, Sandro. Perhaps even more than Misty. Dogs are such good companions."

Massimo's excitement was clouding over as neither of us responded. I couldn't let him down, couldn't throw back in his face what he'd done to cheer us up. He'd probably thought I'd be okay with a dog of our own. And rationally, I knew most of them were fine. Plus we'd had lots of conversations about how I didn't want Sandro to go through life freezing on the spot every time a dog was coming the other way. So I swallowed down my fear and walked over to Lupo, forcing myself to stroke its head.

"He's gorgeous, Sandro; look how friendly he is," I said, pressing myself against the hall wall as Lupo strained toward me, his big tongue flapping in my direction. I could feel the fear circulating at the back of my knees, making my legs tremble.

I summoned up the voice I'd heard dog owners using, with the little endearments that always ended in a "y."

"There's a lovely doggy."

"These dogs are native to Africa, Sandro. I drove all the way to Whitstable to fetch him," Massimo said, impatience gathering in his voice.

But among all the other rubbish traits Sandro had inherited from me—an overlong second toe, a wonky canine tooth, a tendency to chapped lips—a paralyzing fear of dogs was on the list. I couldn't let Massimo notice Sandro was reversing up the stairs rather than motoring down. I clapped my hands with delight like a nursery teacher about to burst into a rendition of "Wheels on the Bus."

"Come on, let's see if he likes our garden. He might want to do a wee if he's had a long journey, and we don't want him making a mess in the house." I beckoned him down the stairs.

Massimo put down the dog on the hallway floor, where it started to jump up and scrabble at my thighs. I wanted to burst into tears.

Massimo eyed me closely. "So what do you think of your present?"

I forced a big smile. "A complete surprise! I didn't even know you wanted a dog."

"I bought it for Sandro. It will do him good. And he'll be a brilliant guard dog for you when I'm away."

It was a measure of how bonkers my life had become that I was prepared to put up with a dog that frightened me rather than risk my husband's wrath at my ingratitude.

CHAPTER ELEVEN

MAGGIE

Even if Francesca saw me only as a source of sanitary napkins she didn't have to ask her dad to buy, her attitude toward me had definitely softened during the last fortnight.

As a result, I dithered over broaching the attic clearing with her, torn between needing a proper workspace and the fear of smashing the delicate truce that had sprung from such an unlikely source. However, with the middle of April, my deadline for moving out of the shop, fast approaching, Nico was adamant. "You need a place to work and we need the house to be a home, not a shrine."

Contrarily, as soon as he showed any signs of being able to sweep Caitlin into a corner, I took it not as a sign he loved me so deeply he was now able to move on, but as an indication that he didn't let himself get too attached to anyone. I hoped if I dropped dead tomorrow, I wouldn't be brushed out of his life into a few bin bags and a couple of wicker baskets and carted off to Oxfam.

I sat downstairs in the kitchen while Nico discussed it with Francesca, bracing myself for raised voices. But when Francesca came down, she leaned shyly against the doorjamb.

"When you've got your sewing room finished, I was

wondering if you could make me a dress for the end-of-year party? If you want, that is."

I wanted to leap off my chair and promise to make fifty-five dresses, each in a different color. The opportunity to do something we could discuss together, that wasn't Nico manufacturing a "And now you will get to know Maggie" occasion, filled me with hope for the future that I couldn't have predicted even two weeks ago.

When Saturday rolled around, Massimo and Sandro invited Sam to the park with them. He'd settled in very well to having an extended family. In fact, for two pins, he'd probably move into Massimo's house, with the double lure of football and Lupo. I wasn't sure how keen he'd be on living with Lara though. She was what my mum would call "dour," endlessly looking like she was waiting for rain to come bucketing down despite a cloudless sky. Massimo seemed to adore her though, always putting his arm around her and saying, "I do love you" if she even brought him a cup of tea.

As I watched Sandro scuffing along behind, trailing his hand along the top of walls, stopping to pick up a feather, I had a sneaking suspicion Massimo was enjoying having my football-mad Sam to indulge. Every time I saw them together, they were discussing players in the Premier League I'd never heard of. Nico wasn't very blokey in that way, far more interested in *Gardeners' World* than Sky Sports, so it was brilliant that Massimo was genuinely interested, rather than just pretending like me. I tried not to think about how much Sam had missed out on by having Dean as a father who, apart from the occasional postcard, had never troubled us with his presence. To be fair though, Dean had never made any pretense about who he was: a jack of all trades, working on building sites just long enough to make enough money to take off to a straw hut on some exotic island for months at a time. He was always telling me, "Mags, you're too serious. Live for today. As long as I've got a beer and a bit of sunshine, I'm king of the world." But it had still hurt when he'd walked out.

I consoled myself that although I'd picked a dud for his father, at least I'd found a great stepdad for Sam in the end.

And today—the day we'd set aside for "sorting the attic"— Nico astonished me again with his kindness, less worried about how traumatic he'd find it and more concerned about how difficult it might be for me picking through his dead wife's things. I hugged him. "We'll get through it."

For my part, I was more nervous about how Francesca would react. I hovered awkwardly on the landing when he went to fetch her from her bedroom. But any embarrassment dissipated as I struggled to hook the ladder down, an exercise akin to fishing for a plastic duckling at the fairground, only twice as frustrating. I hoped I'd get the knack of it, otherwise getting to work every day was going to be a pain in the arse. I was grateful, however, that we'd found something to laugh about and solve together before we delved into the real task of the day.

I loved the attic. I felt a buzz of excitement as I imagined a sewing table under the window, shelves in the alcove to hold all my cottons, pins and paraphernalia. And unlike Mum's meter cupboard in the flat, where I was too scared to move anything in case a rat was dislodged from an ancient football boot, there was nothing "glory hole" about this space, with its bright lighting and array of boxes, neatly lined up and marked in red pen: "Jodhpurs/riding hats," "Small weights/ resistance bands," "Cassettes—A-J." I felt a bit queasy seeing Caitlin's writing there, big and bold. The confident form captain writing I associated with someone who'd been goal attack in netball and center on the hockey team. I wondered if these boxes were already up here or whether she'd started packing up things when she knew she was dying, tidying up to save everyone else the trouble.

I hoped if my days were on countdown, I'd find more pressing things to do than put my CDs in alphabetical order. Or maybe when she had so little control over her health, ensuring Abba was next to Aerosmith provided a grain of comfort, of certainty, in the face of the great unknown.

I couldn't imagine knowing I had a finite time to live. But if I did, would I want to spend my last months parachuting out of planes, walking the Great Wall of China and diving on the Great Barrier Reef, when those activities had never appealed to me while I thought I had another fifty years? Depressingly, I had a sneaking suspicion I'd spend my last few weeks getting rid of manky old T-shirts, graying under-wear and holey socks so I didn't go down in history as the woman with the baggy knickers and saggy bras.

Plus I'd definitely have to prune through my photo albums and weed out any dodgy photos that might change the way people saw me when I wasn't there to defend myself and explain that it really wasn't "as bad as it looks." Sam probably didn't need to stumble across posthumous pictures of me slumped over a tequila bottle with the worm balanced on my cheek, dancing with a life-sized inflatable penis or snogging one of the long line of ne'er-do-wells, any one of whom would probably have done a better job than his lesser-spotted father.

Nico stood with his hands on his hips while Francesca looked to him for guidance. I hung back by the attic hatch, afraid to encroach on the emotions swooping between the boxes.

Nico turned to Francesca. "What do you want to start with? Shall we have a look through your mum's cassettes?"

Francesca looked as though Nico had asked her if she was wearing a crinoline to the end-of-term party. Cassettes were pretty passé by the time I was a teenager. To Francesca, they must have seemed as antiquated as a wringer. Mum hadn't had the cash to splash out on a CD player, so I was still pulling endless chewed-up tape out of my crappy Walkman and winding it back in with a pencil long after my friends had moved on to CDs. But given that I was trying to become Francesca's friend, I didn't want to underline that I was old enough to remember life without iTunes. I let Nico reach his own conclusion that the cassettes could be the first thing shuffled toward the hatch.

I examined the other boxes, looking for one with the least amount of emotional baggage. I definitely didn't want to come across the photos of Nico and Caitlin cutting their wedding cake, gazing lovingly at baby Francesca or raising glasses of champagne to each other by the Christmas tree. I scanned the labels, looking for the deceased first wife's equivalent of drain-unblocking equipment.

Clearly not the one marked "Francesca."

I pointed to it. "Here, look, there's one with your name on it. Do you want to start with that?"

Francesca looked a bit uncertain and, to be honest, I didn't blame her. Christ knows what a box with "Maggie" on it would hold—probably twenty bottles of half-used anti-frizz serum in my endless quest to have smooth, shiny hair, abandoned when nature's superior curling power defeated my optimism.

I shot Nico a meaningful look, which seemed to shake him out of his stupor.

He reached for the box and started picking at the tape. "Come on, love, shall we have a look?"

As their dark heads pressed together to peer inside, I inspected the other labels.

"Outdoor wear"? I wondered if Caitlin had been so organized that every April, scarves, macs and bobble hats were folded away so she wouldn't spend the summer fighting her way through various wooly garments before the flip-flops could be unearthed.

Nope. The whole clothes thing was too personal, too real. I didn't want to start looking at every little trace of mud on Caitlin's boots and wonder whether she'd worn them walking hand-in-hand with Nico, sheltering under a tree in a summer shower, kissing and cuddling until the downpour passed.

I marched over to a box marked "Textbooks." That didn't sound like it would be home to too many lovey-dovey memories. I slit it open and scanned the titles—Caitlin's books on nutrition and exercise. I lifted out a few from the top layer just to check that I wasn't about to jettison a first edition of *Fit or Fat?* or a must-have volume about "mastering your metabolism," "strengthening your core" or any number of un-fun things I'd existed for thirty-five years without worrying about.

I called over to Francesca, "You're not thinking of studying nutrition and sport science, are you?"

She snorted. "No chance. I'm not spending my life trying to lick a load of old fatties into shape."

I sucked in my stomach.

I picked out an enormous illustrated tome about the place of exercise in psychotherapy. It looked like the huge French dictionaries Mum had staggered home with after a clearout from the local library in case she could flog them. We never did find any takers but we stacked them up and used them as a stand for the hamster cage. Nico must find me very limited if Caitlin had a brain big enough to understand how skipping on the spot could make you less of a loony.

I looked over at Nico on the other side of the attic, hoping I'd be enough for him in the long term. He was sitting side-by-side with Francesca, delving into a white wicker chest, exclaiming quietly over tiny pairs of toddler shoes, a little tulip-print baby bodysuit, a blue bunny with one ear. I wasn't sure Sam's dad would even be able to pick him out of a lineup of ten-year-olds with sandy hair and freckles, let alone remember his baby toys. Francesca was stroking things, pressing them to her face. My heart ached as I watched her straining for a memory of Caitlin, a remnant of a scent, a whisper of a touch contained within random objects that probably smelled more of dust and damp.

She pulled out some school exercise books. "Look, Dad, creative writing in Miss Roland's class!" Nico started reading her story about her new dog, "Polly-Dolly," out loud, while Francesca squealed with embarrassment. "And it wasn't even true! Mum never did let me have a dog." She tapped the page. "Look how fat I've drawn Mum. I don't remember her like that."

I tried not to listen to their conversation, rummaging noisily into the box, the private emotions between father and daughter making me feel like a cuckoo in a nest for two.

"The dust is making my throat dry. I'm going to pop down and fetch us some tea."

"I'll go," Nico said, jumping up as though he was grateful to have an excuse to escape for a minute.

I wanted to bound down the ladder, to get away from all the grief and regret and someone else's love spreading like ivy out of everything we opened but I knelt down again to carry on sorting.

I came across a gold jewelry box tucked away underneath

another layer of books. Good job I hadn't just glanced in, seen a few dusty old books on how to stop wetting yourself on the trampoline and dumped the lot. I picked it up, running my fingers over the heart shape studded in what looked like rubies on the top. I opened the lid. It was empty, just a padded cushion at the bottom, but a blast of classical music filled the attic, making me jump. Francesca craned over to see what I'd found. I stood up and squeezed around Caitlin's exercise bike, stepping over yoga mats and a half-deflated Pilates ball to show her.

She stroked the blue velvet inside and said, "I don't remember Mum having this. It's really pretty." She shut the box then opened it again. "What's that music?"

"I don't know. You'll have to ask your dad. I don't know anything about classical music." Straight out of my "How to be a Fab Stepmum" manual, I grabbed my opportunity to engage. "Do you like this sort of music?" I asked, dreading that she'd launch into some comparison of composers I'd never heard of. All the Farinellis seemed to scoff up the arts and culture section of newspapers with their breakfast.

Francesca wrinkled her nose. "Not really. Mum used to listen to opera all the time but I'm not that keen."

"You might be later on. Shall I put this to one side for you? It's real gold, judging by the hallmark on the bottom, so it's definitely worth hanging onto," I said.

Francesca nodded. "Yes please. I could use it for my earrings."

My moment of usefulness faded away and she started looking at her old schoolbooks again. I rotated my shoulders, picking my way back to the other side of the attic. As I stood deciding between tackling the bag labeled "bed linen" or opening up an old-fashioned chest that contained God knows what to make me doubt myself a little bit more, I sneezed and the gold box flew out of my grasp.

It landed lid open on a pile of rucksacks, the sound of violins and flutes blaring out.

"Sorry, sorry, must be all the dust." I scrabbled to retrieve it, praying that I hadn't dented something that would turn out to be a priceless heirloom.

As I picked it up, tipping it upside down to inspect for damage, the padded velvet bottom fell out. A shower of papers fluttered down: tickets, a postcard, a couple of hand-written notes, a folded-up menu from the National Portrait Gallery. I gathered them together to stuff them back in, noticing an engraving inside on the bottom.

> *My darling Caity-Cat,*
>
> *Whenever I hear this music, I will think of you and wish we'd made different choices.*
>
> *Yours always, P*

I frowned and peered closer. Yes, definitely "P." I really didn't want to know what pet name Caitlin had for Nico. "Petal?" "Pumpkin?" "Precious?" Ugh. Thank God Nico hadn't thought up a Caity-Cat equivalent for me. Maggie-Moo. Or if I didn't get on top of my weight soon, Maggie Muffin-top. I'd once had a boyfriend who called me "Shnoo-dle Bum." It had put me off nicknames for life.

"Wish we'd made different choices." What did that mean? What choices? I peered down at the pieces of paper in my hand, the souvenirs of Caitlin's life. She'd missed out on so much. Would she have enjoyed all of these concerts, these places, these dinners just that little bit more, sought to wring a fraction more fun out of every minute, if she'd known that her minutes were in limited supply? Decided to have another drink, another iced bun, sod tomorrow?

I glanced over at Francesca, who was still flicking through her books, biting her lip in concentration. Despite knowing that discovering any more details about Nico's relationship with the woman who preceded me would just be extra torture, I flipped through the tickets. Opera tickets. *Pelléas and Mélisande* at the Royal Opera House in Covent Garden. *La Traviata* at the London Coliseum, *Così Fan Tutte* at the Theatre Royal in Bath. I shoved the tickets back in the box, along with a flyer for "Late Turner: Painting Set Free at Tate Britain."

Nico had never mentioned opera to me. He'd clearly dismissed me as a complete numbskull and decided to stick to safe topics like *I'm A Celebrity...Get Me Out of Here*, the latest James Bond films, and Natural Calico or Orchid White paint for the dining room. I felt a stab of hurt. If I'd grown up in an Italian family where weekends were about museums, concerts and cooking, I'd probably have known about opera and art too. Mum, for all her warm and wonderful qualities, was far more interested in *Coronation Street* and a bucket of KFC than culture and "foreign" cuisine. I hoped Nico wouldn't expect me to go to anything more sophisticated than Adele. I didn't think I could bear an evening with the whole Farinelli family summarizing the main plot of *Turandot* for me, while singing along in Italian themselves.

I sneaked a glance at the other pieces of paper. A dinner menu from the Ritz. Christ, I'd be grateful for breakfast at a Premier Inn. I'd always had the impression that Nico liked rustic, spit and sawdust type restaurants rather than uber-posh places. Or maybe he just thought I'd feel more comfortable there. Perhaps he thought I'd let him down by sloshing wine into my water glass or tipping the free mints into my handbag for later. To be fair, I might do that, indoctrinated as I was with Mum's scooping up of sugar sachets and serviettes. She couldn't walk past a plastic spoon in a café without thinking it might somehow come in handy.

Next was a birthday card with a filthy joke on the front about how much sex would keep him happy. That was a side to Nico I hadn't seen. More in keeping with the sort of thing Sam's dad would find funny. The thought of Caitlin and Nico having sex made me feel queasy.

Tickets for Andrea Bocelli in Leeds, November 2013. Il Divo concert, Rotterdam, April 2012. I'd better not admit I'd only been to one live concert and that was One Direction with Sam.

I picked up a postcard of Bath Abbey. I'd always fancied a weekend in Bath. Sam's dad had pushed the boat out and taken me for a night at a pub in Dudley once, where he'd proceeded to drink himself to a standstill on snakebite. I should have realized he wasn't in it for the long term.

I turned the postcard over.

> *June 2012*
> *My darling Caitlin,*
> *Whenever I go to Bath I will think of that wonderful*
> *weekend. I'm still trying to work out a way for us to be*
> *together forever!*
> *All my love, always, P.*

I looked at the date. Four years ago. What did he mean about "a way to be together"? Surely he didn't mean for him to die as well? Had he contemplated a suicide pact? Did he know she was ill then? I remembered my mum telling me that she'd been absolutely fine, developed stomach pains over Easter 2013 and died the following year in February. Anyway, none of my business, whatever he'd meant.

I heard Nico call from the bottom of the ladder. I jammed

everything back into the box and bunged the padded cushion on top, my heart skipping guiltily at poking into his private love notes, the little snippets of his life before me.

Before cancer had chosen his door to knock on.

I leaned out of the hatch and took the mugs of tea from him as he climbed up.

The little break had done him good. His face was less pinched. He made his way over to Francesca. "How are you getting on?"

"Okay. I should chuck all these old schoolbooks away. But, I don't know, I just feel that I won't ever get the chance to write about Mum or draw her again. I sort of like the idea of having pictures of her that I drew before she was ill."

"Darling, you keep whatever you want."

"Maggie found a lovely jewelry box for me, didn't you? The one that plays opera music when you open it."

Nico looked puzzled. I lifted it up, bracing myself for "Oh yes, I bought that when we had an amazing weekend in Vienna/Verona/Paris."

He frowned. "I don't remember that."

I opened the lid.

He rolled his eyes. "I didn't know you could even get jewelry boxes that played opera."

"Which opera is it?" Francesca asked.

Nico laughed. "No idea. Opera's such a racket. I used to send her with your grandmother whenever I got the chance. God knows where that box came from."

A shared passion for opera was not going to be my route to bonding with Anna. I tried not to feel uncomfortable about all the little insights I was absorbing about Caitlin. I didn't want to find fifty-five thousand more areas where I could consider myself inferior. Thankfully Francesca pulling out a pair of tiny ladybird wellies distracted Nico.

"I remember you wearing those! You went in a puddle so deep that all the water came over the top and I had to carry you home on my shoulders with bare feet."

Grateful as I was that I didn't have to hand over the box and watch his face take on the bittersweet glow of forgotten memories, I still couldn't understand how any man could possibly engrave a present for his wife then totally forget about it. Was he protecting my feelings?

But I didn't feel I could march over there, rip out the velvet padding and start jabbing my finger at the writing inside, "Look, look, you had it engraved for her!" without appearing completely unhinged. Which, if the sick feeling in my stomach was anything to go by, I might become.

Francesca stood up, stretching her back. "Right. Which one shall we do next, Dad?"

"Take your pick," Nico said, swiveling around toward me. "How are you getting on, Maggie?"

Tempting as it was to say, "Feeling more inadequate by the minute," I managed a relatively cheery "Fine, I don't think there's much here you're going to want to keep. Just university course books. Perhaps we could donate them to the library?"

Nico shrugged. "Or there's a book bank down at Morrisons' car park."

We sorted through a couple more crates, putting all the photo albums to one side. I promised myself I would never be tempted to open them, concentrating instead on the idea that if we tied up Caitlin's loose ends as soon as possible, I'd feel less like an impostor bluffing my way in through the door with a stick-on mustache. But despite my best intentions, my mind kept drifting back to the postcard. The depth of devotion Nico had for Caitlin had floored me. Maybe I was just a housekeeper with benefits, rather than a second chance at love.

Eventually, Francesca looked up and said, "Can that be enough for one day?"

I was knackered myself but given that we were doing this for my benefit I didn't feel I could start moaning. "I don't mind. Nico?"

"We've broken the back of it. Let's have a rest and pick it up again tomorrow."

I pointed to an old-fashioned box file. "Do you want to take this down and see if you still need any of the paperwork?"

Nico laughed. "God, that's from before Francesca was born." He prodded her. "Look, before we had you, I even had time to write little labels and file all my documents. Not quite as organized now."

Halfway through wondering who would ever sit down in the evening and think, what I have time to do right now is write Car MOT/appliance guarantees/health insurance on neon pink labels, I realized, with a jolt to my stomach, why none of the keepsakes that fell out of the box resonated with the image I had of Nico. Nico's handwriting had curly capital "I"s and funny tails on the "g"s and "y"s, like little handlebar mustaches.

It wasn't Nico's handwriting.

And if it wasn't his writing, who was engraving little messages on jewelry boxes crammed full with love notes to his wife?

CHAPTER TWELVE

LARA

A month on, as we moved into May, Lupo was becoming huge. A much bigger, bitier, boisterous version that scared us half to death. When Massimo wasn't around, I wouldn't leave him alone with Sandro, who—to Massimo's fury—flapped about and squealed whenever Lupo went near him. I wasn't much better myself, shutting the dog in the utility room whenever I could, throwing in a disgusting bit of dried fish skin so I didn't have to get too near. Massimo's interest in Lupo was confined to parading him about in the park, like an expensive toy, with all the yummy mummies falling over themselves to chat about how to stop dogs jumping up/messing in the house/barking in the garden. And all the while, Massimo would be giving them the spiel about whistle-training and indestructible dog beds, while swapping "it was so mortifying when…" stories.

He omitted to mention he'd never opened a single tin of dog food, picked up a poo or wiped up a puddle when Lupo got overexcited at Massimo's return home.

What he did show a great interest in though, was that I now had something to keep me "occupied." Effectively, he'd used the arrival of the dog as the death knell to any discussion about me returning to work, saying, "It wouldn't be fair to leave Lupo shut up all day."

On bad days, I wished I'd never given up my job to stay at home with Sandro, convinced that if I'd delegated his upbringing to a nanny or nursery, he'd be more confident. And perhaps I would be too. Accountancy suited me. I'd taken such pride in being "the one to watch." The one they'd all teased Massimo about, saying I'd be snapping at his heels before long. There'd been more than one joke about "marrying the competition" at our wedding. But after Sandro was born, Massimo stopped talking to me about work, encouraging me to stay at home and take it easy for a while.

When so many women in my postnatal group were frantically working out how they could have one day a week at home with their babies, fretting about nursery fees and drawing up complicated schedules involving in-laws and childminders, it seemed churlish to insist on going back to work. But it didn't stop me from hankering after it—the prospect of a couple of days a week, taking refuge in orderly columns of figures, the predictability of a rational outcome, the sense of a job well done. Rather than the illogical world that became my prison, trapped with a baby who wouldn't sleep, so angry with the world he would refuse to feed, his fists balled with rage, while I walked, jiggled, sang, soothed—and failed.

Every time I broached the subject, Massimo had put his arm around me and said, "You've only just started getting more than five hours' sleep. I don't want you getting run-down because you're stretched too thinly. And Sandro is still a bit underweight. Why don't you wait until he's a year old?" And then, "He's still getting lots of chest infections; there's no point in going back when you'd have to have so much time off." And so it carried on, right up until Sandro went to school. And by that time, I wasn't sure I could load a dishwasher to Massimo's satisfaction, let alone explain to senior executives why a company had failed its audit.

And now, because of Massimo's "generous and thoughtful" present, not only was it unlikely I'd ever make it back into the workplace, but I had more ground to cover to prevent the days from disintegrating into tense recriminations.

Today I had failed to plug the gaps. Lupo had done a puddle on the floor just as I put the eggs in. While I was cleaning up under Massimo's hawkeye supervision to his exact specification: paper towels, shopping bag, bleach on the floor, outside garbage bin, nailbrush on my hands, Lupo darted about, trying to lick my face. I imagined him turning nasty, hanging off my cheek, biting my nose, disfiguring me forever. It made my hands shake, causing me to be clumsy and slow, forgetful of the damned eggs and the precise three and a half minutes Massimo required for his soft to medium yolks.

I stared into the pan, wondering what would set a worse tone for the day: to serve solid yolks or to tip them into the bin and risk a delay while I made some more with runny centers. I lost precious seconds dithering. And then it was too late. Massimo looked up from his newspaper. "Are my eggs ready?"

"Just coming. More coffee?"

Massimo nodded and went back to *The Times,* idly scratching the dog behind its ears. I willed the kettle to boil quickly.

Fortunately he was distracted by a column in the paper about workplace equality. "What a load of old rubbish. Encouraging women to think they can do the same jobs as men for the same money. The women in my office are always having to leave early because their kid's got earache or a bloody concert."

I nodded along, as though I agreed with his antiquated

views, suppressing my smile at the big fat cross I'd put next to the Green candidate in the local elections. Little rebellions saved me from total insanity.

I managed to get perfectly poached eggs onto the spinach, with a splash of cream and grating of garlic, just as he liked them, before he noticed how long it had taken me.

At that moment, Sandro sidled in, glancing first at Lupo, who was now lying under the table, then at Massimo to check he was absorbed in his paper. He showed me the pictures he'd made with his Spirograph. I nodded, smiling and kissing him on the head before saying loudly, "Right, you'd better put your homework away and come and have some breakfast."

"But I don't want any breakfast. I want to draw."

Massimo looked up. "You'd better get a move on. You're trying out the judo class at the leisure center this morning."

Sandro's face fell. He looked down at the floor. "I didn't know it was this week."

I turned away and started wiping down the work surfaces, little starbursts of anxiety building. Without looking around, I went for a cheery "I'm sure you'll enjoy it once you're there. What about some scrambled eggs to give you a bit of energy?"

Sandro moved into my line of vision, his shoulders slumping, his eyes beseeching me to make it better.

"Perhaps this afternoon we can get out the paints that you got for your birthday?"

That wasn't the making it better he wanted but it was the best I was allowed to do.

He shuffled out to the playroom.

Massimo slammed his knife and fork down. "So he's happy to prat about on his own with his paints but doesn't want to get stuck in and have some fun with boys his age? Let me go and talk to him."

My heart leaped at Massimo's chair scraping back, the predictable roar. "Sandro!" The sound of little feet in slippery socks skidding across the parquet floor in the playroom. He'd be gathering up his precious pencils, the gorgeous Caran D'Ache crayons Nico had bought him as a surprise. A rattling of the door into the hallway. But no frantic thumping up the stairs. He wasn't quick enough. I closed my eyes.

Massimo's bellow reached me in the kitchen. "When are you going to get it into your head that the only way to do well in life is to learn lots of different skills? It's no good sitting in the playroom messing about with your pens. You need to get out there and start joining in. Now go and put your tracksuit on."

Sandro scuffed upstairs to his bedroom. The familiar feeling of having my heart pinned in one place when it was straining to be in another swept over me. My poor boy, the loser—again—in the dynamics of the Farinelli family.

I dried my hands and went to find Massimo in the playroom. He had that energy about him, that switch waiting to flick. I could still turn this around. I could.

I presented a neutral face. "I've just remembered I washed his tracksuit. It's in the airing cupboard. You eat your eggs and I'll pop up and find it so you're not late." I hesitated a fraction of a second, weighing up whether I'd got away with my excuse to go to Sandro or whether I'd just unleash a rage about my "bloody mollycoddling."

I took Massimo's grunt as assent and ran upstairs, wondering how I'd become this person. I tried to recall whether my mother had been mild-mannered and gentle, but my memories of her refused to be pinned down. I remembered feeling safe, as though she would take care of things so I didn't have to worry. Yet again, I felt a rush of guilt that Sandro would never be able to say the same about me.

I crept into Sandro's room. He was sitting with his head on his desk, felt-tip in hand, drawing a house. I didn't even want to see what fucked-up family he would depict living in it. I cuddled him and he leaned into me, as though I could protect him. How could a seven-year-old possibly understand that every time I fought his corner, every time I stood up to his father, drew my line in the sand, the whole landscape shifted, bringing with it a raft of new ways for Massimo to enforce his will on me? I couldn't bear to think about the time I'd told Massimo I didn't want Sandro to do football training anymore. Explained that I couldn't stand to see his skinny legs blue with cold, the fear on his face when a crowd of boys steamed toward him, the humiliation when—yet again—he tried to kick the ball and fluffed it, with all his little teammates jeering in frustration. I'd actually thought Massimo would applaud me for realizing that he was unhappy, discuss constructive options about which other sports might be good to encourage.

Not sign him up for rugby coaching to "help him stop being such a wuss."

I kissed Sandro's cheek and told him Daddy didn't mean to get cross, he just felt very strongly that he wanted him to make friends to play with because he was an only child. And it was a long time since Daddy had been seven years old, so sometimes he didn't understand that although Sandro was on his own, he wasn't lonely. Sandro nodded but didn't speak.

"Do you understand what I'm saying?"

He nodded again, looking up at me, dry-eyed and defeated, without lifting his head from the desk.

I couldn't decipher what was going on in his mind. Whatever it was, it was far too complicated for a seven-year-old boy, who should have been thinking about Disney films, Lego and Meccano sets, not trying to grasp the rudiments of power politics before he'd even stopped believing in Father Christmas.

But how could he make sense of a world where one person dictated and the other acquiesced? Where was the "We listen to what each other has to say" in that? The "We look after each other" that Massimo was so keen on ramming home—when it suited him? How would he ever understand why I hadn't stepped in—right in the middle of one of Massimo's diatribes about Sandro poncing about with his paints and pencils—and put my face right up to his father's, stuck my hand in his chest and said, "Enough. I'm leaving you and taking him with me"?

Maybe he'd understand when he was older. That if I left, I'd have to leave without him. Massimo had made it clear he'd fight me, follow me. We'd never be rid of him. I'd seen enough of the Farinellis to know Anna and Massimo would never accept defeat; that their idea of winning was not just getting what they wanted but making sure their opponents lay gasping their last. And if, by some miracle, I managed to share custody, *half* the time Sandro would be alone with Massimo without me to anticipate, to calm, to sacrifice myself if necessary. Half the time left on his own to second-guess whether the nine out of ten in spellings that was acceptable last week would be a cause for an eruption this week. To sit in front of a fish dinner he hated and wonder whether it was worse to refuse to eat it or throw up trying. To lie in bed in a pool of urine rather than wake his father.

And that was without considering what would happen to my poor befuddled dad, currently safe in his private nursing home specializing in Alzheimer patients. Paid for by my generous husband who "only wanted the best for us all."

So instead of standing there cuddling that sweet little boy, his face clouded with bemusement at why his mother couldn't make things better by talking to Daddy, I got his tracksuit out of the drawer and watched him put it on with agonizing slowness.

I patted him on the shoulder. "I'll go and get your snack ready. Don't be long because Daddy's waiting."

As I walked downstairs, I peered through the banister into the playroom where I could see Massimo moving about. A hundred little pieces of paper with snippets of circles on them were scattered across the room like the aftermath of a demented wedding. Then the unmistakable snap of wood, the sound of Sandro's treasured pencils falling to the floor in a rainbow of insanity.

A punishment for Sandro for being quiet and arty, not sporty, not man enough for Massimo.

And a punishment for me.

CHAPTER THIRTEEN

MAGGIE

Nico bought me the most wonderful worktable with built-in lights and tiny drawers. He commissioned—I didn't think I'd ever tire of that word—a fabulous cupboard with a hanging rail high enough for the most elaborate long dress. We got rid of most of the boxes, stacking the ones Francesca thought she might want when she was older in a corner. I'd hidden the gold jewelry box under a pile of fabric at the back of one of my cupboards. Every other day I'd pull it out, wondering if I'd somehow gotten the wrong end of the stick. Between Francesca and Anna, they'd planted a picture in my head of this slender saint of a woman, her house, her belongings, her *whole* life neatly shuffled into tidy categories, with no room for a jam doughnut, let alone furtive conversations and sneaky sex sessions. Nowhere in my imaginings did a wild hussy feature, jaunting off to Bath for an illicit rendezvous, lies laid out, alibis aligned. Could anyone who was uptight enough to buy sock dividers for her drawers really be getting her baps out for someone other than her own husband? I didn't associate a woman who had owned a special brush for dusting behind the radiators with rash and reckless sex.

I traced my fingers over the engraving in the bottom of the box, squinting at the postcards and notes, studying that unfamiliar writing and comparing it with Nico's. I dithered. Whichever way I looked at it—and I was pretty sure there was only one way—Caitlin's halo was hovering around her ankles, along with her pants.

It was madness to hang onto something that could only cause my husband pain. Surely the kindest thing would be to throw it out, pack it off to a landfill site, to keep its secrets forever among the rotting nappies, holey trainers and VHS tapes? Perhaps someone would get lucky in a hundred years' time and come up trumps with a metal detector, but for now, knowing the truth could only bring up a whole load of questions to hurt Nico, with no possibility of answers. As well as adding yet another thing onto the bonfire of conflicting feelings Francesca was already trying to tame.

But still I kept it, unable or unwilling to part with it without being able to pinpoint why. As some kind of weird protection against Anna when she made me feel Nico would never be as happy with me as he was with Caitlin? To prove that I hadn't dreamed it up, that it wasn't the warped and bitter mind of "she who came next," looking for treachery and betrayal where there wasn't any?

I considered showing Nico. Maybe there was a simple explanation, though I couldn't think what. But I didn't want to humiliate him or hurt him by proxy. I couldn't quite get my head around comforting him through the discovery that Caitlin had had an affair. It was easier to accept his grief that she'd died than his devastation that she'd betrayed him.

The irony of it falling to Nico's second wife to protect him from the betrayal of the first wasn't lost on me. It wasn't so much keeping it from Nico that worried me. The real challenge was resisting the temptation to see the look on

Anna's face if I blurted out the fabulous first wife had been bonking her dodgy lover in Bath.

As May rolled into June, I thought about it less and less. Since I'd made Francesca a couple of dresses, she'd been a walking advert for my business. The first time she'd worn one to a party, she looked so stunning I wanted to send Sam with her to fight off the boys. Choosing "my" dress to wear from the hundreds of outfits discarded on her bedroom floor was such a mark of acceptance that I had to work hard at not ruining the moment with my over-the-top enthusiasm. Word was spreading that "Francesca's stepmum makes really cool clothes." A few parents had contacted me about prom dresses for the end of July and I was becoming really busy. I'd even had a commission to make an evening dress with a peacock-feather bodice "for a milestone birthday." Every time I worked on it, I felt like a seamstress to a Hollywood star.

One of the things I loved about my little attic workshop were the two dormer windows where I could see out over the neighborhood. When I'd been squinting over hooks and eyes or—truly evil—sewing on sequins as I was today, I'd readjust my vision by looking out into the distance, letting my eyes focus on the tops of trees. I could see right into Lara and Massimo's garden, which looked like an upmarket park with a wooden tree house, tire swings and a trampoline. Sam pretended to be too old for all that, but when he was next door, I'd spy him racing out to the trampoline to do somersaults and back flips I was better off not seeing.

Today I could see Sandro lying on his side on the trampoline, playing with something. He sat up as their Rhodesian Ridgeback wandered out from the French windows at the back of the house. Such a majestic creature. Massimo told me they were bred to hunt lions in Africa, which made me wonder whether poor old Lupo felt a bit short-changed at finding himself confined to a suburban garden in Sussex.

There was something about the way Sandro moved that caught my eye. He was crawling tentatively across the trampoline, as though he was avoiding sniper fire. Then he suddenly jumped down and hared across the garden, clambering up the rope ladder to the tree house with panicky gestures, missing his footing and dangling precariously. I realized why when Lupo raced after him, his deep bark reverberating around the neighborhood. Sandro shrank back into the top of the tree house, while Lupo launched himself onto his back legs, front paws scrabbling at the ladder.

I threw open the window and yelled as loud as I could. "Lupo! Lupo!" But the dog was fixated on getting up that ladder as though an injured gazelle lay just within chomping distance. I could hear Sandro screaming. Where the hell was Lara? I scuttled down the attic steps as fast as I could without becoming a casualty myself. I'd have to worry about the embarrassment of admitting to spying on them later. I flew out of the house and ran around to Lara's, hammering on the front door. Then hammered some more when no one arrived.

Eventually she came to the door with a feather duster in her hand. If I hadn't been in such a panic, I might have made some off-color joke.

"Maggie?" She didn't stand aside or beckon me in, looking at me as though unexpected visitors were somehow confusing.

"Lupo's got Sandro trapped in the tree house. He's really frightened. I don't think the dog can get up there but he's definitely not acting friendly."

"Oh my god! I was vacuuming upstairs, I didn't hear him. I locked the dog in the utility room. He must have jumped over the stable door."

She charged down the hallway and out through the French windows in the kitchen. I followed her, even though she still hadn't invited me in. We belted down the garden to where the dog was dancing on its hind legs in frustration. Sandro was pinned to the back of the tree house, crying.

Lara rushed over to grab the dog, but it snarled at her and she jumped back. My heart was thumping, wondering whether we were about to be prairie prey. Lara was shouting at Lupo but I could hear the fear reducing her voice to a thread. I reminded myself that the Parkers weren't scared of anything, let alone some ginger hound on the wrong continent.

I dashed back into the house, braced against the sudden screeching of four paws behind me, trying not to imagine exactly what percentage of a buttock Lupo could fit in his mouth if he decided to attack. I ran to the fridge, grabbed the first thing I saw, which was a chicken breast wrapped in prosciutto—so Lara—and shot back outside.

"Lupo, what's this? Look what I've got for you."

The dog paused in its barking, dropping down onto all fours while it sniffed the air. Then it charged toward me in a way that made me want to lie on the floor covered in gravy just to get "the kill" over with. Instead, he started wagging his tail, smiling a great big toothy grin. I put out my palm flat in a stop sign and hoped I'd still have five fingers when I'd finished.

"Sit. Sit!" I pulled myself up to my full height in the vain hope I'd look big and dominant.

Incredibly the hound stuck its backside on the floor. I ripped off a piece of ham and gestured to Lara to get Sandro. After a few moments, Lara managed to coax Sandro onto the top of the rope ladder. She lifted him down and rushed toward the house, his thin arms wrapped around her neck.

I tore off a chunk of chicken and the dog was almost singing with delight, happy little yowling sounds coming from his throat.

When I heard Lara close the French windows, I shredded the rest of the meat, threw it down the garden and scuttled off myself.

Lara opened the door to me and collapsed down onto a stool.

"Maggie, thank you. Thank you. Bloody bastard dog. Fucking hate it."

The after-adrenaline shock and hearing Lara swear like that when she looked like she'd think twice about saying "Bother" if she dropped a brick on her foot, made me burst out laughing as though I had half a bottle of vodka and a spliff under my belt.

Sandro was sitting on the worktop, his feet drawn up under his chin.

"Has Lupo ever done that before?"

Lara sighed. "Massimo wanted a proper guard dog. He wants us to be safe when he's not here, but Lupo needs a firm hand and I don't think we've quite trained him properly. I might have preferred a budgerigar." She started to laugh, then didn't quite find the humor and a sob came bubbling out instead, causing Sandro to start crying again.

"Well, maybe it's time to think about rehoming him? Massimo's not going to want Lupo terrorizing you all."

Lara shook her head, her voice rising. "No. No. We couldn't do that. Massimo adores that dog. He'd be devastated if we had to get rid of him."

"He'd be more devastated if Sandro had a chunk of flesh missing out of his cheek."

Sandro looked into the garden then lowered himself down from the worktop. His little voice rang out in the kitchen.

"When Lupo bit Mum, Dad said it was her fault for not training him properly."

"He's bitten you?"

"It was nothing, just puppy playfulness; you know how sharp their teeth are when they're little. And I had let him get away with murder, Massimo was right."

"He made you bleed, Mum." Sandro stood there, his dark eyes worried and watchful.

Lara laughed. "They were just little surface scratches, darling; their teeth are like tiny needles when they are young. Anyway, why don't you go and draw a picture for Auntie Maggie?"

Sandro disappeared into the playroom.

"Did Lupo really bite you?" I asked.

"No, not really, he was just doing that funny mouthing thing puppies do. It went a bit far."

"What does Massimo say? Is he worried about how Lupo behaves?"

Lara smiled. "Lupo's always as good as gold for Massimo. The dog's fine really, just gets a bit overexcited sometimes when Sandro winds him up."

"Lara, I was watching out of the window." I paused, realizing how weirdy stalker/nosy neighbor that sounded. "Only because I heard the barking. Anyway, Sandro wasn't teasing Lupo. He was just minding his own business. You saw the dog; he wasn't playing, he was being really aggressive. Even you were frightened of him."

"That's because I'm not very good with dogs. I was bitten as a child," she said, showing me a jagged scar on her right hand. "I prefer cats, but when Misty went missing, we decided a dog would be more of a family pet. Lupo will be fine if we just show him who's boss."

I stared at her. This was the woman who spent half her life

faffing about with exact tomato/cucumber/red pepper ratios for her son, serving up mackerel for the omega-3 "essential for your brain, Sandro" and brazil nuts for selenium, whatever that did, but seemed far less concerned about the possibility of the dog making off down the garden with a juicy selection of her son's limbs.

Lara started bustling about, wiping down an already immaculate table and work surfaces. "Anyway, sorry for interrupting your afternoon with our nonsense. I know how busy you are with all your sewing."

There was definite dismissal in her tone. She'd reverted to her old self, a bit frosty and reserved. I wondered if she thought I was judging her for being upstairs cleaning instead of supervising her son in the garden.

I tried again. "As you say, no harm done. You can't be watching Sandro every minute of the day, can you? Would you like me to teach him how to become a bit more confident with the dog? My mother had a right nightmare of a Jack Russell when I was in my teens. We just had to show it where it was in the pecking order and it soon toed the line."

Lara looked around from her polishing of the cupboard door handles in a manner that suggested there were multiple carriers of E. coli in the house. Everything about her seemed dazed, as though I'd asked her to multiply a few fractions and give me the answer as a percentage of 319. I liked her better when she was F-ing and blinding rather than showcasing her talent for exterminating kitchen bacteria. She nodded slowly but didn't say anything.

I plowed on. "Lupo needs to learn that he's not as important in the hierarchy as Sandro." I started to outline how Sandro needed to feed him, walk through the door before him, train him to the whistle and establish himself as the superior "dog" in the pack.

"Would you really do that?" Lara always sounded as though her expectations of life were only visible with the help of a microscope, when as far as I could see, apart from a son who needed a bit of a confidence boost, there wasn't a lot wrong. I had to work hard not to wish Nico paid me as much attention as Massimo did Lara. A kiss on her head, a stroke of her hand, "Coffee/tea/a drink, darling?" They were more like newlyweds than we were.

"Of course. In fact, I'll get Sam to come around with me tonight when he gets home from football training and we can make a bit of a game of it. Probably a good idea to start as soon as possible before Sandro has time to dwell on what happened today."

"No! You can't come tonight."

I must have looked pretty pissed off at the force of her answer—after all, if it had been left to her to ride to the rescue, Sandro would still be shaking in his shoes at the top of the tree house.

"Sorry, it's just that Massimo is coming home early today and he likes to spend a bit of time on his own with Sandro. He's very good like that, puts a lot of store by quality time."

I resisted the temptation to say, "I'll let you get back to your vacuuming then." Instead, I did a "That's fine, no worries at all. Just let me know when it's convenient and I'll pop around. Anyway, you go and check on Sandro and I'll see myself out." None of my other friends gave me time slots like Lara. In fact, whenever I had a girls' night out, there was always an outcry if I tried to leave before midnight.

I was just stomping home along the street, muttering "Ungrateful cow," as Massimo drew up in his car.

He jumped out and swept me into a hug. "How's my gorgeous sister-in-law? Come in for a coffee. We're popping around to yours later to discuss our summer holiday but I want to hear how you're getting on without that brother of mine monopolizing you."

I hesitated, not wanting to appear rude but pretty sure Lara wouldn't want to see me again quite so soon. I tried to tell him that I'd just come from his house but he was having none of it. Lara must have been watching out the window because she suddenly appeared at the door. Massimo ran up the steps and gave her a kiss on the lips, so lingering that I found myself pulling the face Sam did when we watched romantic comedies on telly. Nico was much less flamboyant than Massimo in that way, thank God. Though I had a twinge of envy that they were still so passionate about each other ten years on. From what Nico had told me, everyone had thought Massimo's relationship with Lara wouldn't last, a cliché of a senior partner at work taking advantage of an inexperienced junior. To me, he still seemed besotted with her.

Massimo waved his arm in my direction. "Maggie's just coming in for a coffee."

"I don't want to intrude, I've already taken up enough of Lara's time this afternoon," I began, waiting for Lara to step in with the drama of the afternoon, and if I was absolutely honest, a little smidge of gratitude.

"Nonsense. We're delighted to see you. You can catch me up on what you've been talking about," Massimo said, beckoning me up the steps.

Lara hovered on the threshold, a bit like automatic doors on the blink that can't decide whether to move back and allow you entry or to seize up altogether and block you out. I wondered how someone as buttoned-up and chilly as her had ever attracted someone warm and generous-spirited like Massimo. According to Nico, his first wife had been much more outgoing. Maybe he'd gone to the other extreme and had developed a penchant for enigmatic women. Or maybe there was a simple explanation—for all his apparent intelligence, the thing that motivated him most was that old chestnut of a much younger body. Then I had the very mean thought that if Lara's main charm had been her size ten bottom when they met, she was living on borrowed time now. Massimo swept me through the door, saying, "I'm just going to change out of my suit. La, would you make us a pot of coffee?"

I followed Lara back into the kitchen. Everything about her was tense, her movements tight and stiff. I'd have felt more welcome taking a turn on the karaoke machine at a silent order of nuns. Maybe Lara liked "quality time" on her own with Massimo as well.

I didn't want to be a middle-aged gooseberry. "I won't stay long. Sam will be home from football training soon."

Lara glanced toward the hallway, then whispered, "Could you not mention the whole dog thing to Massimo? He's so stressed at work at the moment, I don't want him to feel I can't cope with everything at home when he's working so hard."

I didn't subscribe to all this bollocky "Mustn't bother the big man with domestic detail" especially when the "domestic detail" had big snarling, snapping teeth. And Massimo didn't look anywhere near as knackered strolling in from his accountant's office at six-fifteen, as Nico did, bent and buckled from shifting stone statues in the garden center at eight. But Lara looked so strung out that I nodded. "Okay, but you really ought to let him know how hard you're finding it to cope with the dog. He'd be horrified if he knew."

Lara didn't respond for a second. Then she brightened. "I'm sure Lupo will grow out of this naughty phase. I never leave him with Sandro on his own. He only got into the garden today because he jumped over the stable door. And as

Sandro matures a bit, he won't get so frightened by every-thing. The last thing I need is Anna hearing what happened. She'll inevitably find a way to make Lupo having a go at Sandro some terrible failing on my part."

Then she looked startled, as though an opinion had swooped out of her mouth before she'd had a chance to bleach it into a bland statement of nothingness.

I wanted to cheer. It was one of the few occasions since I'd known her that she'd articulated something real and true. I'd only had a couple of years of bracing myself every time Anna whirled in with her opinions. They began innocently enough, little crumbs of observation, which then puffed up like carrier bags caught in the wind, whirling around the room, carrying clouds of criticism. Lara had had the bene-fit of her morale-crushing observations for nearly a decade and from a much younger, more vulnerable age. I was about to dig a little deeper—not least to find out if Anna had a key to their house as well—when Massimo trotted back in, bringing a waft of aftershave with him. In a pale green open-necked shirt, he looked as though he'd just stepped off a yacht moored in Sardinia. Then the moment was lost as Lara turned away, busying herself with arranging biscuits on a pretty plate, while Massimo opened the French windows and called in the dog.

As Lupo dashed in to greet him, Lara positioned herself behind the bar stools. Christ, if a dog frightened me that much, I'd have it down at the rescue center before you could say "Get in your basket." Massimo barked a quick "lie" at Lupo and he immediately dropped to the floor, head down, as though he spent the days meekly waiting for someone to remember he needed feeding.

"So what have you been up to today?" Massimo asked, as Lupo rolled onto his back.

Lara darted a look at me and rushed in with, "This and that. Sandro's been playing on the trampoline. Gave me a little bit of time to get shipshape upstairs."

Watching Lara was like looking at Sudoku without any numbers in the grid. I knew there was a puzzle to solve but I was damned if I could see where to start. Massimo was so open and friendly, whereas Lara always gave the impression she was trying not to deplete her daily word count. I'd hate to be so riddled with insecurities that I couldn't even be honest with my own husband. Though it was unlikely Sam was going to meet a sticky end because I was too absorbed in housework. Sewing maybe, but dusting and vacuuming, definitely not.

They were a funny lot, these Farinellis.

CHAPTER FOURTEEN

MAGGIE

Even without the prospect of Anna and Massimo coming over to discuss holiday plans for the "Farinelli fortnight," the evening had gotten off to a bad start. Francesca had made some jewelry in her design class at school and wanted the gold box to display it in.

I hesitated. "Not quite sure where I put it. I think it's too valuable to take to school anyway."

She stood there, hands on her hips, with that teenage expectation that I'd immediately rush to look for it. To be fair, whenever Francesca showed any signs of wanting anything from me, I did hop to it. She probably couldn't understand why I carried on peeling potatoes, when normally I'd fling down the knife and run around like a wind-up toy, so grateful for the little promise of connection.

I couldn't think how to put her off. "Just let me finish making dinner and then I'll see if I can find it." With every slice of the knife, my mind darted about, wondering what to do for the best. Tell her I'd accidentally thrown it away? Mislaid it? Chuck out all the keepsakes and mementos and press the padded cushion tight into the box and hope she'd never find the inscription?

We'd had a couple of months of relative peace. Francesca wasn't yet rushing to hug me good night but sometimes she sat on a stool in the kitchen even when Nico was still at work and told me about something that had happened at school or showed me a YouTube video she found funny. But at least the stomping about slamming doors seemed to be a thing of the past and I was determined that the disappearance of a bloody box wasn't going to screw that up for me.

I was still scrabbling around for a solution when Anna and Massimo rang the bell. Long before we got married, when I was still waiting for Nico to discover that although I made him laugh, I wasn't a "keeper," he'd spoken about the family tradition of taking over the same castle in the Tuscan countryside for the first two weeks of August every year. I'd envied him. That closeness, the lively dinners under the stars, the banter bouncing between the sun loungers, the raucous races in the swimming pool. I'd felt ashamed of my fleeting comparison with the four days Mum, Sam and I had managed two years ago, in a caravan on the Isle of Sheppey, sleeping in beds barely wider than a shelf, turning on the gas hob to keep warm.

Now though, the prospect of being cooped up under Anna's microscope for fourteen whole days filled me with dread. She sat on the settee, queen buzzy bee holding court about how we'd take turns cooking, shopping, supervising the kids in the pool. "And *someone* is going to have to mop that kitchen floor every day. Last year it was disgusting with everyone paddling in and out with wet feet."

"Nico, you'll have to go shopping with Maggie. It's a shame she doesn't speak Italian like Caitlin did. Lara can manage; she's picked up the basics fairly well over the years."

Nico put out his hand to squeeze mine. "Give Maggie a

chance, Mum. She's never been to Italy before. Everyone else has been going for years." He sighed. "Anyway, I'm looking forward to sharing all the chores with Maggie."

He turned to me. "Food shopping in Italy is great fun, all that fresh basil and tomatoes you can smell the sun on. We always buy a big wheel of Parmesan to hack our way through. Can't wait to show you around."

I loved Nico for defending me. I tried to offset my dead-wood status by offering to get busy with the mop on a daily basis. Perhaps I could balance out my lack of linguistic ability with my mopping skills. And at least I wouldn't have to make small talk with my mother-in-law around the pool while I was Cinderella-ing inside.

A flash of frustration passed over Anna's face as though her little dig at me had missed its bull's-eye.

Nico smiled and went off to fetch some wine.

Massimo winked at me. "You'll have a brilliant time, Maggie. All the surrounding villages have little fiestas and open-air concerts in the evenings. We'll have to take you up on the castle ramparts. You can see for miles across the vineyards and fields of sunflowers. Sandro will love having Sam to play with in the pool. We'll organize some swimming competitions."

As he filled me in on all the things we'd be able to do, I could have hugged him for making me feel just a tiny bit welcome rather than a cumbersome suitcase they'd have to shell out extra for to put in the hold. "It will be great for Sam to have some company. He finds Mum and me a bit dull on holiday."

Nico reappeared with a tray of drinks. "Be careful what you wish for. Massimo is the mastermind of holiday activities. We won't just have a bit of a splash-about in the pool, we'll have the Olympics of swimming competitions. You know Massimo used to swim for the county, right? We'll have to give him a handicap, otherwise he'll have done five lengths in the time it takes me to do one."

"Meant to say, I gather Francesca's been doing pretty well in the county trials recently," Massimo said.

"Yeah, she's got your killer competitive streak."

Massimo pulled a face. "Doesn't seem to have rubbed off on Sandro yet."

Nico took a sip of wine. "Mate, you might just have to face the fact that he's inherited my arty genes, not your Superman ones."

Massimo frowned. "Nothing to do with genes, it's about wanting it enough and being prepared to put the hours in." He turned to me. "I'll get you all in training this holiday. You didn't realize you were coming to the Farinelli boot camp, did you, Maggie?"

Although he was joking, my stomach tightened at the thought of being the fatty at the back. Nico slapped Massimo on the shoulder. "I'm not having you bullying my young bride." He squeezed my knee. "If Massimo suggests any-thing, say no. You'll think you're just going for a little walk, but Massimo will have you hiking up and down the near-est mountains in double quick time. And don't even think about getting out a pack of playing cards. Never has a game of Snap been so fiercely contested."

Massimo raised his eyebrows at Nico. "No point in par-ticipating if you don't intend to win. Why be mediocre when you can be the best?"

"I can't get excited about a game of Snap," Nico said. He shook his head at me. "Massimo can't even stand losing to Sandro, can't bear to be beaten by a seven-year-old."

"Too right. Winning's a state of mind, dear brother. That's why you're driving a Volvo and I've got a BMW."

Nico laughed. "No point in ruining a posh car with all the muck from the garden center. At least I'm not so tight that I won't stump up for driving lessons for my wife."

Massimo threw his hands up in the air in mock despair. "Maggie, help me out here. Is it really my fault that my wife is so environmentally conscious that she refuses to learn to drive? I'd *love* her to have a car but she won't."

I felt a rush of admiration for Lara and her right-on attitudes, though I wasn't sure how she squared her conscience with the patio heaters and Aga. Mainly though, I was envious she actually had time to walk everywhere, rather than squealing about town rushing here, there and everywhere like I seemed to do.

Massimo winked at me. "And talking of tightwads, isn't it time Nico got you a little upgrade?"

I glanced over at Nico to see if any of these little barbs—which appeared to pass for humor in the Farinelli family—were bothering him, but they seemed to be rolling off him, good-natured man that he was.

I jumped in. "I don't want a new car. I love my old Fiesta because I don't have to worry about it—no one is ever going to bother stealing that, when they could pinch a decent car instead."

Nico said, "Save your breath, my darling wife. Massimo doesn't understand being satisfied with what you've got; he wants to be the best and have the best."

I wanted Nico to know I was on his side. "It was a good job you weren't in my sports team at school, Massimo. I was the one who would start waving at my mum on sports day and forget that I was supposed to be sprinting."

He laughed. "But you're a girl, Maggie. You can get away with it."

Jesus. The Farinellis did like their handsome prince,

distressed princess up the tower shit. A fortnight of "my willy's bigger than yours" might get pretty wearing. I hoped I'd have a little bit of time on my own with Nico. I wondered if it would be sacrilege to suggest slipping off for a meal one evening just the two of us. I tested the water. "If you and Lara want to go out for dinner one night on your own, I'd be more than happy to babysit Sandro."

Massimo grinned. "That would be great, Maggie. I'll see if I can get Lara to agree; she doesn't really like leaving him."

Anna butted in. "Sandro doesn't know you very well yet, though, does he?"

"No, but if it was toward the end of the holiday, hopefully we'll have built up a bit more of a bond. And anyway, he's very comfortable with Nico, isn't he?"

I don't think that woman had been contradicted enough in her life. She sat back in her chair with a surprised sigh that someone other than her had an opinion. She paused for a moment, as though she was formulating a strategy to keep me in my place, then picked up her handbag. "Right, Massimo, let's make a move."

I'd tread carefully for the moment, but however much she pontificated on the fact that the Farinellis did this, that or the other, she was forgetting one thing: in my head, I was still a Parker and Parkers hadn't made much of a career out of toeing the line.

After they'd left, with Anna practically looking over her right shoulder as I pecked her on the cheek, Nico pulled me into his arms. "It will be fun, I promise. Mum will calm down when she gets there."

I flopped into an armchair, deliberately hanging my legs over the arm in a childish rebellion against Anna always telling Sandro to sit up straight or Sam to take his shoes off or even nagging Nico not to leave his coat on the back of the chair in his own bloody house, aged forty.

Nico poured me a glass of wine and massaged my shoulders. "You're all tense."

"Sorry. I don't want to be ungrateful. I'm not used to all these family dynamics as an only child myself and just having Sam. I always wanted a sibling—I didn't realize there would be so much rivalry."

"Massimo's all right, just likes to be the top dog. He was a nightmare when we were kids. Whatever I had, he always wanted it—my bike, my Action Man, even my friends. Even if we had exactly the same thing, he'd want mine."

"Do you mind?"

"I'm used to it. He's all bluster anyway. We look out for each other now. It really rocked him when Dawn left him because they couldn't agree on having kids. I don't think anyone had ever refused him anything before. He was a bit of a lost soul, so we used to invite him around a lot."

He winced at his use of "we."

I smiled, trying to be a grown-up. "It's okay. I do know you were married before."

He hugged me to him. "I know, I just feel awkward. I don't want you to think I don't love you, well, as much..."

"I don't think that at all; I know it's just different," I said, blushing slightly at his accurate reading of my mind.

He paused. "Anyway, Massimo's been great for Francesca, really encouraged her with her swimming. Of course, I'm interested in how she's getting on but I don't understand the whole training program the way he does."

I couldn't help myself, even though I knew it sounded mean. "It's brilliant that he can help Francesca but it wouldn't do him any harm to pay a bit more attention to Sandro. They've got a right nightmare going on next door."

I filled in Nico on the whole dog saga and how Lara wouldn't tell Massimo what had happened, plus my dog training plan.

"Just be careful. Lara shouldn't be risking anyone getting bitten. I don't know why she acts as though we're judging her. It's so difficult to tell what's she thinking half the time. Dawn was much more open. Lara's so prickly about everything."

He ruffled my hair.

"You wouldn't struggle on your own, would you? I'd hate it if you felt you had to bottle things up because of what I might think of you."

I didn't meet his eye. My thoughts strayed to that box in the attic. It wasn't what he would think of *me* that was the problem.

Now, thanks to Caitlin, I had to make a call on which wife was going to be the bad guy.

CHAPTER FIFTEEN

LARA

Maggie was as good as her word. Armed with dog-whispering manuals, the smelliest sausage and a shrill whistle that made me jump every time someone blew it, the training of Lupo—and Sandro—began in earnest. Straight after school, every day. I concentrated on not feeling threatened she could get Sandro to step out of his comfort zone with such ease, doing things that if I had asked him he would have run off and hidden with his pens and paper. Or become entrenched in a stalemate with Massimo that would have had me dancing about, cooking Massimo's favorite *spaghetti alle vongole*, taking all his suits to the dry cleaners, changing the beds every two days, anything to keep his mood cheery and his attention away from Sandro.

Maggie had the Midas touch. Her calm, no-nonsense approach, her expectation that Sandro was capable, that "everyone has to learn," that he would—of course—get it wrong a few times but then get it right, seemed to rub off on him. After a series of shrieks and dashes behind Maggie and Sam when Lupo started to run toward him, Maggie persuaded him to whistle the dog and feed him a treat from his open palm. After two months of making sure the dog couldn't get anywhere near Sandro when I wasn't around, I had to force myself not to rush out and shout, "Careful!"

I was my father's daughter.

From there, Sandro graduated to feeding the dog his dinner. Instead of me preparing it in the utility room and then diving out while Lupo charged in, Maggie decreed that Lupo would learn to eat to a whistle command.

Whistle, sit, stay, wait, eat was the new routine. Maggie would allow Sandro to throw the ball ten times, then put it away when Lupo still wanted to play. "You're in charge, Sandro. You decide when and how long the dog can play for." And then she came up with some funny rule about not letting the dog walk through the door in front of any human.

But, weirdly, it seemed to work. Encouraged by Sam, who had designs on making Lupo the star of *Britain's Got Talent*, over the next month, the training regimen slowly turned from survival into a hobby.

And all the while, Maggie's bemusement that I hadn't made Massimo get rid of the damn dog if my son was in danger hung over us like an organza canopy. A couple of times while she'd been standing watching Sam and Sandro teach Lupo to lie down, she asked leading questions like, "Has Massimo ever seen Lupo get aggressive with Sandro?" "Did you tell Massimo that Lupo trapped Sandro in the tree house?"

There was something so honest about her, so down-to-earth that I nearly told her the truth: that if I dared to question any decision Massimo had made, the stakes would rocket from just about manageable to unbearable. The disrespect he would feel if I dared to put forward an opinion different from his would deliver a consequence.

And never a pleasant one.

It wouldn't be beyond him to decide Sandro needed more

exposure to a variety of dogs. I had visions of him turning up with a posse of mongrels from the local rescue center. The staff would forever talk about him as the kindhearted, generous Massimo, "offering a home to some of our most challenging dogs," while, in reality, he'd be berating both of us for our fear, screaming about how pathetic we were, how we just needed to get a grip.

She wouldn't believe me. Who would? The man who anticipated everyone's needs, pulling out chairs, opening doors, noticing new hairstyles, successful dieting, remembering children's names, holiday destinations, elderly parents? The loving son-in-law who paid a fortune for my father to receive the best care? The man who modestly brushed away any praise with "It's the least I can do. Anything that makes things easier for Lara..."

They'd think I was deranged, their faces screwing up in disbelief: "I can't imagine him acting like that, can you? She must be making it up."

If I hadn't experienced every sorry little minute of the sham that I was living, I would have been the first to pull that face. Any intelligent woman knew *no* intelligent woman would stay with a man like that.

Or so I thought, before I had my life.

Once, when Maggie asked me whether we should have just bought another cat instead of a dog, I nearly blurted out what had really happened to Misty. Just for the satisfaction of testing whether what was merely pretty shocking for me was outrageous and demented to everyone else. I'd been living this way for so long, the point on my life barometer for normal was probably everyone else's emergency appointment with a psychoanalyst.

I fantasized about watching her face change from puzzlement to horror as I told her what I'd discovered when I was washing Massimo's car because he was running late to visit a client. "I can't turn up looking like bloody Farmer Giles."

As I stood on the drive, hosing down the wheels, I noticed something tucked behind the hubcap. Soft and gray. I pulled it out, rolling it between my thumb and forefinger. Fur. I craned my head closer. Dry rust-colored blood on the inside edge of the chrome metal.

I sank back onto the tarmac, not caring that my jeans were soaking up mud and water. Massimo had known all along that Misty wasn't coming home. He'd let me believe he was worried, sorry for me.

The expression on Massimo's face as Misty scratched and snarled at him flashed into my mind.

I burst into the house, racing up the stairs to where Massimo was packing his shirts, smoothing the sleeves with precision.

My tongue felt thick, unable to form the words, as though they were forcing themselves out through a layer of loft insulation, my mind refusing to let my mouth articulate something that should never even have become a coherent idea in my brain.

"You ran Misty over, didn't you? I've found her fur on your wheel."

I expected Massimo to laugh, to deny it outright. But he looked straight at me. "Stupid cat ran in front of me just up the road from the house."

"You bastard. You absolute bastard. You did it on purpose! Because she hated you and loved us? And you, you couldn't stand it."

I'd never sworn at Massimo. In any confrontation, I'd learned the quickest route to calm was silence.

In the space of a few seconds, his face went from mild amusement at me, his meek, approval-seeking wife throwing a tantrum, to a twisted, sneering caricature of the handsome demeanor he took care to present to the world. But today I didn't care. I was leaving him and taking Sandro with me.

He took a step toward me. "What did you call me?"

"A bastard, a complete and total bastard." But I could hear the bravery seeping out of my words, terror falling into the space where my anger had boiled moments before.

He took a step toward me. I forced myself to stare him out, lifting my chin. My knees were going but I couldn't let this moment pass. I thought of my dad, the way he'd always walked on the outside of the pavement as though a horse-drawn carriage was about to blunder through a muddy puddle and soak me. His hand in the small of my back, guiding me to the inside, a world of caring wrapped up in that little sidestep, that tiny gesture. That man who left the outside light on for me and waited up to see I was safely home even when I was in my twenties, hovering at the window if I was a few minutes late. Even now, in his muddled state, he'd pat my hand and say, "You're taking care of yourself, aren't you?"

He would be horrified if he knew the truth.

This was my moment. The time I needed to harness my rage and accept that Massimo would never be who I needed him to be. I conjured up a picture of Misty, bloodied and smashed, twitching at the edge of the road, and fury surged through me again. "You've let us search for Misty all this time when you knew she was dead? Where is she? What did you do with her? Did she die immediately?"

"Yes, the wheel went right over her head. I chucked her in the dumpster at the end of the road." He said it in a matter-of-fact way as though he was just mentioning in passing he'd knocked over a box of cornflakes and made a bit of a mess.

I started to shake, tears for my poor cat clogging my

throat. I got the words out, the ones I'd thought about so often, dreamed about making contact with the air. So much so I wasn't sure whether I'd actually spoken them out loud.

"I'm leaving you."

Massimo laughed, a bitter noise rasping around the room, a sound that needed oiling to stop it rusting away.

He grabbed me, pushed me onto the bed, pinning my arms behind my head. I was wriggling, kicking, while his face hovered above me, smug with his superior strength, relishing my frustration.

"You won't leave me. You love me too much." He grabbed my right hand and clamped it to his crotch. Shock snuffed out the fight in me for a second. He started to undo my jeans with one hand, twirling a little piece of my hair around his finger—tenderly—with the other.

Gathering as much moisture into my mouth as possible, I spat, hitting his cheek, managing to jerk my head up and bite his chin, sinking my teeth into the fleshy curve. With a roar of rage he shot off me. I dived for the door, but I wasn't quick enough. He slammed it shut, leaning against it.

He wiped his face with his hand, pressing his fingertips against his chin, where a little crescent of teeth marks sat. "You bitch. You're not leaving me. Don't even try it. I'll follow you and find you. And if you try anything, anything at all, I'll take Sandro to Italy. My company is bursting for me to move out and run our Italian branch. One word from me and I'll be set up with a very nice life out there. I've got Sandro's passport somewhere you'll never find it."

I stared at him, trying to recall whether I'd seen it in the safe the last time I'd put my diamond and platinum necklace away, the one Massimo insisted I wore to any company do: "You don't want to look like you're the caretaker's wife, do you?"

"He won't go with you. I'll fight you. I'll take you to court. I'll go to a solicitor," I said, already feeling as though I was scrabbling at a smooth concrete wall devoid of footholds.

He rubbed his chin again. "You know how quickly Italian bureaucracy works? 'Oops, sorry, judge, I made a mistake about the court dates, sorry, I need more time to file my paperwork.' A quick backhand to the solicitor, a chat to my friend who works at the tribunal, a delay, a strike in the judiciary system. 'Sorry, the mother's unstable, on antidepressants for years after the boy was born; she attacked me, I'd be worried for the child's safety.' Sandro will be leaving home by the time you even get to state your pathetic little case for custody."

For a moment I was stunned that he'd be such a bastard as to use the antidepressants against me: he'd been the one to insist I went on them in the first place, coming with me to the doctor and telling him I couldn't cope. At the time, I was prepared to agree to anything that would stop Massimo being so angry with me for finding motherhood so hard. With hindsight, I probably just needed a few nights of unbroken sleep.

Then I flew at him, desperate to run to the safe and see whether it was true, that we were now reduced to warfare over Sandro's passport to define the shape of the next few years of our lives.

Massimo held me off, keeping me at arm's length. But I saw something I hadn't seen before. Shock. Shock that I still had enough spirit to go against him, that even now he hadn't worn me down completely. I tried to channel the sharp edges of my energy into a barb I could dig in deep and gouge at his heart.

"What would your family think if they knew what you were really like? Anna's always boasting about you to the woman at Waitrose: 'Such a family man. Absolute rock to me when my husband died. And such a good father to that little boy. Not afraid to roll up his sleeves and help out.' What would she say if she knew what a bully you were? Do you think Nico would want you hanging around Francesca, giving her tips on her swimming if he knew that you were such a headcase you ran over cats that didn't like you?"

He screwed his face into a sneer, a rush of defiance clenching his jaw before a little flash of fear, a glimmer of uncertainty replaced it.

"You wouldn't dare. They wouldn't believe you. Blood's thicker than water, remember."

And then he opened the door with a flourish. "After you. I'm off to take some selfies of my chin in case I need them in court."

Yep, I wondered what the hell Maggie would make of a man who ran over the pet cat and decided to buy a dog because he knew it would terrify his wife.

CHAPTER SIXTEEN

LARA

I couldn't believe how quickly Thursdays came around, carrying the great gloom cloud of dread for Sandro and me. I bet Maggie never counted down the days, wincing on a Tuesday at the inevitability of Thursday and the dreaded swimming lessons. I wished I was more like her. Resourceful. Optimistic. Confident. Able to brush any obstacles out of the way with minimum drama.

Maggie had made great strides in sorting out Lupo. She was still coming around several times a week, helping Sandro to rein Lupo back in whenever he started to slip back into his boisterous behavior. I couldn't run to her again. She had enough on her plate adjusting to Anna sticking her nose in, getting used to having a stepdaughter and a husband, let alone keeping on top of her own son and running a business.

And even if I could rely on her for advice, it was hard to imagine anyone in the world had the solution to Sandro and his fear of water.

It didn't help that the spare bedroom was lined with swimming cups, medals and photos of Massimo, hands raised in triumph, his dark hair hanging in wet curls.

Sandro, on the other hand, had a full-blown tantrum

every time I got his face wet in the bath as a baby. Massimo accused me of transmitting my own anxieties to him. "You make him like that; you're always so stressed about everything," convinced that without my negative vibes, Sandro would have been an Olympic swimming gold medalist in the making.

By the time Sandro was three, Massimo decided to take control of my stop-start attempts to teach him to swim.

"He needs to learn before he loses his nerve altogether." And as always Massimo was the man to "make it happen." With a wave of his hand, all "experienced swimmer heading to the pool to show off family-man credentials," Massimo arranged lessons for Sandro every Saturday morning. The first time, I'd made the mistake of going to watch. Initially I'd felt a little burst of pride when I'd seen Massimo stroll out with our son, looking so handsome in his swim shorts, tanned and muscly, nothing like the other men splashing about in the adult pool with their paunches and tattoos. I'd watched the women in the toddler class adjust their swimsuits and suck in their stomachs, brightening up at this novelty, a modern man joining their ranks. No doubt they were wondering which lucky wife was sipping lattes with her friends while her husband took charge of Freddy frog floats.

My pride turned to distress when Sandro started to scream as soon as he touched the water. Massimo did all the right things, tried to make a game of it, peek-a-booing and "Here comes the shipping" for all he was worth. But as the other two- and three-year-olds kicked their feet, some of the braver ones even jumping off the side, the rigidity of Massimo's smile increased in line with Sandro's wailing.

Massimo kept scowling at me as though I was sending Sandro "squawk louder" vibes. Eventually, to my relief, the swimming teacher suggested they try again next week and

Massimo carried Sandro out, waving a laughing good-bye to all the mothers whose faces suffered the loss of animation I'd seen so many times before: Massimo frowning off back to the footbath deprived them of a focal point, leaving them bumbling about like earwigs plunged into the light after months under a flowerpot.

Massimo refused to concede defeat even though the mere suggestion of a towel being rolled into a bag was enough to have Sandro cling to my leg with, "No swim, Mummy, no swim, stay home, stay home." Nonetheless, Massimo remained relentless in his optimism that Sandro would soon be clutching a raft of Duckling Award certificates.

Three months in and an excruciating floating poo incident later, Massimo's swimming pool bonhomie disappeared down the drain with all the verruca plasters and hair. In its place was blame that I'd spoiled the boy and it was up to me to sort him out. For the next few years, I mollified Massimo by Googling articles about Olympic swimmers who didn't begin swimming until they started school. I'd made a huge deal about the British gold medal winner at the Rio Olympics who had been so scared of water he used to stand up in the bath. But as Massimo was so fond of telling me, the Farinellis weren't lily-livered. They had grit, determination and probably world dominance in their genes. When Francesca showed Massimo her latest trophy, he couldn't quite manage a "well done" without making some reference to how he thought Sandro was going to have a swimmer's build, that when he was a bit older they'd make a formidable team.

Now that Sandro was seven, Massimo's patience had run out.

However, I still wasn't ready for the traumatic palaver that defined every Thursday afternoon's swimming lessons. I cajoled and dragged Sandro along, dread rising on his face the nearer we got to the leisure center. If he managed to get into the water at all, he'd cling rigidly to the side, little rumbles of terror leaching out of his throat while the teacher shouted at him to "Kick, kick, kick." More often than not, he wouldn't get into the pool at all, just stand on the side, silent tears slipping down his face, while I watched helplessly from the balcony above. So many times I'd nearly raced down and called a halt to the whole bloody charade but I knew the relief would be short-lived if I did it without Massimo's agreement.

So the next time Massimo was talking about our annual trip to Italy, I took the opportunity to suggest that we should perhaps abandon swimming lessons for the time being and try again in August, when we'd be on holiday in the sunshine and he might be motivated to learn so he could join in with Sam and Francesca.

The chatty "Maybe this year we could try and get tickets to the Palio?" husband vanished instantly. He slammed his hand on the table. "Do you know how I learned to swim? My dad pushed me in the deep end a few times. I soon learned to keep my head above water so I didn't drink half of the pool. And trust me, if Sandro doesn't pull his finger out and start putting some effort in, I'll be doing the same in Italy this summer."

As always I'd made things worse by trying to help. Now, I not only had the insurmountable problem of persuading Sandro to continue his lessons but a deadline for success as well.

As a result, that Thursday when Maggie came walking up the road, Sandro was sitting on the curb, his face buried in the swimming bag on his knee. "Please don't make me go, please don't make me go, please don't make me go."

I was kneeling next to him, drilling into every last resource to find the magic sentence to make Sandro summon up the courage to get into that hated pool. If I didn't insist he go, Massimo would think up a horrendous reprisal that would make an afternoon at the leisure center look like an outing to the funfair: "That boy's got to learn to do as he's told!"

Maggie wandered over. "Lara? Is everything okay?"

I dredged up a smile. "We're fine; Sandro's not very keen on going to the pool today. I think he's a bit tired." I felt him waver between leaning into me for comfort and resisting in case I tricked him and hauled him to his feet.

Maggie crouched down to Sandro. "Hey you. Can you ride a bike?"

Sandro nodded.

"Swimming is a bit like that. Before you get the hang of it, it feels like you'll never ever get it. And then suddenly, wham! You just click and you're off."

Sandro's head had gone down again. Something slumped inside me. Maggie was trying to be kind but my whole parenting life had been a long round of people who thought they had the answer, the wave of the wand to make Sandro into what we wanted. What Massimo wanted. Everyone had a simple solution to get him to toughen up, to be brave, to join in, to enjoy sport, to not be afraid of insects, of speaking up, of life. But what if that's who he was? What if he never managed to be any of those things that society demanded he must be to gain approval?

I forced myself to smile at Maggie. I tried to push away the nagging doubt that *I* had made him like this, always seeing the pitfalls, the result of years of living with my dad's well-intentioned warnings. I'd even lived at home while I'd studied for my accountancy degree, commuting to London, heeding my dad's advice there was no point in running up a lifetime of debt to live in a hovel of a flat. "Besides, London's not safe at night." Yet again I'd been the odd one out, leaving for my evening train just as the fun was starting.

As I started to haul Sandro to his feet, my mobile went off. No doubt Massimo checking up to see that we'd gone to the leisure center.

But it was the number for Dad's nursing home. I jumped to my feet, my heart hammering. No Dad-related phone calls ever brought good news.

"Mrs. Farinelli? I'm calling because your dad's had a fall and hurt his ankle. We've got the doctor in with him now. We're not sure if he's broken it, but he's not very compliant and keeps asking for you."

"Oh God, oh God." I felt everything go loose in me, as though my second chances were running out. There was so much I needed to say to Dad, to articulate, before the ghost of what was left disappeared completely. I kept trying to pin down Massimo to a time to take me to see him, but he was always so busy. But I had to go now. My mind flitted between the practicalities and possibilities of only having ten pounds in my purse. I glanced at Maggie, who was still huddled up with Sandro. I'd have to ask her to lend me some money.

She looked up. "Is there a problem?"

I filled her in. "I'm going to have to get a bus over to Dad. Is there any chance you could look after Sandro for me for a couple of hours?"

"A bus? Isn't he in the middle of nowhere though, near Worthing? That'll take you ages."

"Yes, but Massimo's in London today so he can't take me. The bus will be fine." I didn't even know when they ran in the afternoons or how far ten pounds would get me. I tried to come up with an excuse for not having a cash card to get any money out. I couldn't tell her the truth: that the last time I'd taken a taxi to see Dad, Massimo had cut up all my bank cards, then scratched "Bitch" with one of the sharp edges into my lower back until it bled. I'd resolved to leave him, but then Sandro got a chest infection and Massimo had been so concerned, helping me steam his chest every day, buying vaporizers for the room, ringing the doctors, that I'd missed the moment. I was so wrung out by the time Sandro was better, I didn't have the energy to fight Massimo's decision to dole out a daily allowance, left in cash on the table after breakfast every day, much less to pack my bags and go.

My mind was whirling. I'd have to pretend I'd lost my purse. I could hear the panic in my voice, the fear that Dad's distress would be growing, spiraling down into confusion, thinking his daughter couldn't be bothered with him, not even when he was in pain.

But before I could launch into an explanation about my lack of money, Maggie said, "Let me take you, if you don't mind a trip in the boneshaker. We can drop Sandro at Mum's and she can fetch Sam from training and bring them back here."

"No, no, that's too much trouble."

Maggie grabbed hold of my arm. "It's fine, come on, let's go."

Sandro looked as though my dad breaking an ankle was the best Christmas present he could have.

Sugar. Swimming.

I knew what Massimo would say. I could feel his hands on my upper arm, his forefingers digging into the muscle to leave identical dotty bruises on either side. He'd be so close, I'd be able to smell what he had for lunch on his breath. "You thought seeing your father who won't even fucking remember you've been there was more important than teaching our son not to drown?"

I'd be silent. And so would Sandro.

And tomorrow morning, I'd rush to get Sandro's sheets before Massimo discovered them. And another little flake of varnish from the dull patina of Sandro's self-esteem would peel away.

"Lara?" Maggie's voice was gentle, but puzzled. "Shall we go?"

I hesitated. "I don't want to put you to a lot of trouble. Perhaps I'll take Sandro swimming as planned and wait for Massimo to come home. He'll take me later. The doctors are with Dad; he's in good hands."

She sounded exasperated. "It's no trouble. You'd do it for me." She turned to Sandro. "And you're not looking too unhappy about eating biscuits with Beryl instead of practicing your doggy-paddle, are you?"

My thoughts were jumbling around. Everyone wanting a piece of me. Sandro perking up and making doe eyes at me. Maggie expecting me to be capable of rational decisions when my entire life was about as far from logical as it was possible to get. The horrible image of Dad wrestling with his carers, the confused tentacles of his mind wriggling to grasp onto the memory of his daughter and wondering where she was.

And none of them with a pull as powerful as my fear of Massimo and what he would say when he found out that we hadn't been to a *swimming lesson*.

Maggie ran her hands through her curly hair, making it stand out even more as though she'd just emerged from a couple of nights sleeping rough under a bridge. Her eyes flicked from me to Sandro and back again. I nodded and stepped toward the car. She helped Sandro to his feet. "Let's go and find a Kit-Kat, shall we?"

The tension dropped in Sandro's shoulders.

I could see why Nico loved her.

CHAPTER SEVENTEEN

MAGGIE

Discovering Lara in a right tizzy outside the house was just the distraction I needed. Over the last few weeks, Francesca had been asking about the bloody gold box as though she had a sixth sense that I was holding something back. Her sulky attitude with me was starting to creep back in, the nasty gibes resurfacing. And last night she'd snapped at me, "I don't know why you haven't bothered to find it yet. Just tell me where you think it might be and I'll go and look myself. I don't know what your problem is."

My problem was that I wished I'd never found the sodding thing. I'd sat for ages that afternoon, weighing up what would be worse: to change her memory of her mum forever, to allow her to discover that her parents' relationship wasn't what it seemed and to let her question Nico about the inscription and watch the certainties of his first marriage shrivel and shrink, rewriting a happy history into a flawed and buckled mess. Or to ditch the box and hope Francesca would eventually forget about it and get over her fury at its disappearance. In the end, I went with my heart. They'd both suffered enough and I'd just have to put up with Francesca being a bit pissed off with me.

So that afternoon, I'd waited until the house was empty, then peered out of the upstairs window to double-check that Anna's car wasn't there. I couldn't have her popping up like an all-seeing jack-in-the-box. The last thing I needed was her catching me in the act of what was effectively stealing.

But for very good reasons.

I shoved the box and all its contents into a plastic bag and strode off to the dumpster that seemed to have taken up permanent residence at the end of the road. As I got closer, my heart felt like it was going to squeeze through the gaps in my ribs and start ricocheting around the street. I didn't know how burglars ever got up the courage to break into someone's house.

I paused for a moment, looking up and down like some shifty lowlife about to leave a bag of cocaine in a hiding place. I had no idea how much the box was worth but it had to be approaching six or seven hundred quid. God. I could buy Mum a new fridge with that. And replace her telly with something that didn't have high definition as a futuristic concept. I'd never owned anything that expensive in my life and now I was going to chuck it into a dumpster. I might as well take a wodge of twenties and scatter them into the sea. I'd even thought about taking it to one of the charity shops in town but decided against it in case Francesca spotted it in there on one of her shopping marathons.

I hesitated, peering over the metal lip into the junk below. No money in the world would buy back the comfort of good memories. The happy family fug that Francesca was clinging onto had to be worth more than a few hundred quid. In the end, I convinced myself that several years paying for therapy if she found out what her mother was really like would cost much more than the fricking jewelry box.

So, with a quick glance around, I poked the bag between

an old sofa and a broken rocking horse, hearing a last gasp of flutes and violins as it slid, then crashed, into a space at the bottom. As soon as I'd done it, worry and guilt engulfed me, leading me into a thousand what ifs. Plus Beryl-like thoughts of what I could have spent the money on if I'd flogged it on eBay.

But Lara greeted me with such a level of nuttiness on the pavement outside my house that I barely had time to dwell on whether I'd made a great decision or a fatal one. I was capable of weird and wonderful behavior myself—Nico was always teasing me about how he could hear me talking to myself as I sewed: "Perhaps a silver sequin next to the red one?" "What that needs is a nice bit of black lace"—but Lara took it to another level.

Apart from the weirdo "we're really rich but I've never bothered learning to drive" bullshit, she seemed so dithery about getting to her dad, driveling on about Sandro's bloody swimming, which he didn't seem to give the slightest hoot about missing. Christ, Mum's rage if I put Sam perfecting his crawl above making sure she wouldn't be in a wheelchair for the rest of her life would be enough to keep the whole of Scotland warm in winter.

When I finally persuaded Lara to let me take her to her dad via Mum's, her reaction to seeing the estate reminded me of Nico the first time he'd come with me. Their middle-classness stood out like a vegan sausage in a greasy spoon café. Lara's navy scarf, draped around her neck in a decorative rather than keep-the-cold-out loop, her light green cardigan with heart-shaped buttons, her hair shiny with expensive shampoo—she was missing that sharp edge of on-guard that defined the majority of the people who lived here.

But I had to love her for the way she was struggling not to look horrified at the puddles of piss, the remains of bicycles chained to the railings, the doors with their peeling paint. Such a contrast to the Victorian terraces we lived in now, painted pale pastel colors, with their dawn-to-dusk sensor lights creating a welcoming glow.

"Did you live here for very long?" Lara said as we ran up the stairs to Mum's flat.

"All my life until I had Sam. I was back here for three years before I met Nico because I just couldn't afford to rent my own place anymore."

As I spoke, I realized I sounded as though I'd married Nico for his money. I hoped Lara knew me well enough by now to know it wasn't true. Though she probably wouldn't blame me for wanting to get Sam off the estate—her grip tightened on Sandro's hand as we passed a couple of teenagers on the stairwell, the unmistakable smell of cannabis surrounding them.

Lara couldn't have looked more twinset and pearls if she'd been carrying Margaret Thatcher's handbag. She had the air of someone setting off on an adventure from which she wasn't certain to return.

I propelled her toward Mum's door before the threshold of her adventurous spirit was exceeded. On the other hand, the promise of a chocolate biscuit seemed to work wonders for Sandro's courage, or maybe it was just the euphoria of his unexpected escape from armbands.

Mum threw open the door with her hair in a towel turban, even though I'd texted her to say we were on our way.

Lara looked as though she wanted to snatch up Sandro and hightail it back to the Boden areas of Brighton, where guest-greeting was more likely to involve a tray of home-made beetroot brownies or a gluten-free flapjack.

Mum swept Sandro in, not giving Lara a chance to whittle or worry or issue any instructions. If Mum had her way,

Sandro would be bouncing on the settee and eating chips out of newspaper by the time we got back. "Poor little bugger. So many rules I wonder his head don't blow off. And all that talk of when he goes to university and how many pages he's got to read every day. Lord, it's enough to make him turn into a druggy dropout."

I hurried Lara out of there before she could change her mind. But by the time we were halfway to the nursing home, Lara was so tense, she looked as though she was suspended on a coat hanger. She kept checking for messages on her mobile. I wasn't sure what was worrying her more: Sandro left with Mum in a den of iniquity or her dad confused and in pain. I tried to reassure her. "Not too long to go. Your dad will probably have settled down a bit now."

"God, I hope so. The nurse that was dealing with him said he was getting a bit aggressive. He's always been such a gentle person. Maybe he's just in a lot of pain." She lapsed back into silence.

I never noticed the creaks, rattles and squeaks that were all part of my Fiesta's ancient appeal, but with no conversation to distract us, they were impossible to ignore. Lara hadn't ever shown any signs of wanting to discuss anything more personal than what she had for breakfast, so I didn't feel I could blunder in with loads of questions but a desire to talk over the squeaking outweighed my tact.

"How long has your dad been ill for?"

"I'm not really sure." She looked out of the window. "He was forty-three when I was born so he was much older than other dads. My mum was twelve years younger. After she was killed in the car accident, he was always terrified of something happening to me. So he always had lots of funny little quirks, double-checking tire pressure before we went anywhere, a fire extinguisher in every room, carbon monoxide monitors everywhere, ridiculously big locks on the doors. Sort of health and safety gone mad."

I wondered what he would have made of Mum lighting her cigarettes off the gas burner and sealing up the air vents to keep the heat in.

She shuffled in her seat. I waited, thinking that unless I'd missed something, she hadn't really answered my question. My back wheel started to make a new whirring sound. Lara glanced around.

I tried to talk over the noise. "So did he just get more extreme?"

Lara grabbed the seat as a truck rattled past. It was a good job she didn't know how to drive, otherwise her right foot would have been aching by the time we passed Worthing.

"He started barricading the doors, and every time I went to see him, there was another padlock or bolt and he couldn't open the door properly. And then one day Massimo took me to visit and we had to get the fire brigade to let us in. After that, we concluded he wasn't safe to live on his own anymore and he went into a home."

I couldn't imagine putting Mum into a home. I hoped if it came to it, Nico would let her come and live with us.

"How often do you go and visit?"

"Not as often as I'd like. Dad was such a worrywart about me going in a car at all that he never wanted me to learn to drive. So now I have to rely on Massimo to take me and he's away such a lot and so busy when he's here. I wish I had learned now."

I glanced at her. "Massimo said you wouldn't learn because you were so environmentally conscious that you didn't want to pollute the atmosphere?"

She frowned, then burst out laughing. "He's probably embarrassed that at the grand old age of thirty-five, I couldn't even drive a go-kart. Do you see me as an eco-warrior? Come on! I don't even use a food-waste caddy in case it gets maggots in it."

I loved it when Lara had an outburst of spontaneity. Most of the time she looked so fearful of letting out any opinion that hadn't been Farinelli-approved, it thrilled me to know she wasn't quite the pushover she seemed.

"It's never too late to learn. Then you could come and see your dad whenever you wanted to without involving Massimo."

The shutters crashed back down. "I probably wouldn't be very good at it. Anyway, walking everywhere keeps me fit, stops me putting on too much weight."

That glimpse of the funny Lara disappeared. I couldn't understand intelligent women like her, women with degrees, who could add up a column of numbers and work out tax-efficient this, that and the other, allowing themselves to be so dependent on a man, thinking that their role in life was to be slim and pretty to please their husbands. It was so 1950s. I'd seen Massimo popping home for lunch, Lara coming to the door in an apron as though she'd spent the morning making a shepherd's pie. I wondered if she produced his slippers and a cardigan as soon as he got through the door. Maybe Nico was secretly disappointed with his ham roll and a handful of cherry tomatoes when he worked from home.

After an eternity on winding country roads, we finally drew into the nursing home.

"Shall I wait in the car?" I asked.

Her face clouded over. "Could you bear to come in with me if he's not badly injured? I think it's stimulating for Dad to see new faces. And it would be nice to have someone chat to him while I deal with any admin stuff."

"Of course."

One of the nursing home staff who introduced herself as

Pam took us through the entrance hall, reassuring Lara that the doctor thought her father had only sprained his ankle, not broken it, but they would monitor it. Lara reeled through an impressive list of things she wanted to know, with Pam nodding and giving the distinct impression that she would be hopping to it right away. I wouldn't even have thought to ask about blood pressure, special shoes to support the ankle or vitamin supplements to speed recovery.

Despite Nico telling me how bright Lara was, I'd never been able to imagine her as a career woman flying about the world with her folders, taking for granted airport lounges, hotel restaurants, valet parking. This clipped briskness and quiet authority was a different side to her, completely at odds with the flaky "But what about Sandro's swimming lesson?" of earlier.

The home itself was a surprise to me. I'd been braced for brown carpets, tubes and trollies, with patients wandering about in gowns that barely covered their modesty. But in fact it was more like the reception of a fancy hotel, with vases of those lilies that dropped pollen on your clothes and posh magazines with ads about heirloom watches. There was still a repellent air of human decay though, however much air freshener they'd squirted. I had renewed respect for Mum and her complete lack of squeamishness, her ability to combine a practical "let's sort those pillows out" approach with a gentle word.

Pam showed us into a room where a little old man sat in an armchair, a strapped-up foot resting on a stool. Lara's dad's reaction to seeing his daughter was the stuff of You-Tube vines. He looked up, peered at her, his eyes sweeping up and down, then he stretched out his arm, his face beaming into a smile. The whole scenario reminded me of the videos Sam loved watching, owners reunited with their dogs who'd walked half of Australia to find them or a baby creasing into laughter when his mother came into view.

I hung back, not wanting to intrude.

Lara flew over to her dad. "Dad, what did you do? How's your foot?" She leaned down and hugged him.

He clung onto her as though he was sucking her energy into his tired old body. He grabbed her hand and shouted to me, "My daughter! My daughter! Beautiful! Beautiful! L—, L—" His fingers were drumming on the arm of the chair with frustration.

"Lara, Dad."

Lara kept twitching her lips as though there was so much to say and so little certainty of being able to express it in a way that her dad would be able to process. Her face was mottled with emotions; sadness, love and tenderness all shifting like shadows across her features.

Lara beckoned me over. "This is Maggie. She's married to Nico."

His brow furrowed. "Nico, Nico, Nico…"

Lara paused. Her dad looked as though he was going through the mental process of sieving a muddy puddle, anxiously trying to find a shiny coin in its murky depths.

"You know, my husband's brother."

He shook his head. "Your husband. Are you married? When did you get married? Why didn't you tell me?"

"I did tell you. You came to the wedding, Dad. Remember? We got married in the Majestic, you know, that big hotel in the center of Brighton?"

I would have liked to slink away. I didn't want this lovely old man with the smile so like Sandro's to be humiliated in front of a stranger, to have the holes in the honeycomb of his memory laid bare. Or for Lara's private anguish to be played out in front of me.

"You remember Massimo, don't you, Dad?" Lara asked, her voice getting more and more distressed.

He started ripping a tissue into tiny pieces. "Massimo, Massimo, Massimo…" It was like watching one of those grab machines in an amusement arcade, swinging wildly, flexing its claws but just failing to snatch the iPod. Then suddenly, he tried to get up, grappling for the stick at the side of his chair. "Massimo! Massimo!" He was yelling, with Lara trying to calm him. A nurse came running.

"Mr. Dalton, careful, come on now, sit down, remember you've hurt your foot."

Eventually, they got him back into his chair. He was so agitated it was uncomfortable to watch.

Lara sat next to him and patted his hand. "I'll bring Massimo with me next time. He's a very good man. He looks after us all."

Her dad worried at the cuffs of his shirt.

The nurse mouthed, "Not too long now; he needs to rest."

I leaned toward Lara. "I'll let you have a chat. I'll wait outside. No rush at all." I did a small wave and said, "Mr. Dalton, I'm going now, but I hope I'll see you again. Look after your foot."

He looked at me as though I'd just appeared. Then with a great big grin, he said, "Ta-tah. Come again with Shirley. It's good for my wife to have some company till I get home."

Lara's head slumped toward her chest. She started to pick her way through an explanation of who she was.

I went out to sit in the car.

Lara appeared about twenty minutes later, red-eyed and subdued.

I left her alone with her thoughts as the Fiesta rattled along.

Halfway home she said, "I've got to go and visit Dad

more often. He's gone downhill so quickly. I wish Massimo could find more time to take me."

There was an obvious solution. I organized my words to leave "duh" off the end of my question.

"Shall I teach you to drive?"

CHAPTER EIGHTEEN

LARA

As we left the nursing home I felt as though little bits of my heart were snapping off until I'd be left with a shriveled walnut capable of only the most basic emotions. Dad, the man who'd made me the center of his universe after my mother died, probably wouldn't know who I was in a few years' time.

Massimo's promise to take me straight after Easter never materialized. To my shame, I'd let six months pass since I'd seen him at New Year. Six months that I hadn't felt that craggy hand on mine, hadn't seen the fog clouding his brain slowly disperse as my face became familiar again.

I slumped into the seat, puzzling over what had triggered Dad's agitation when I'd mentioned Massimo. Maybe it was simple frustration. God knows how awful it must be to peer into the dark chambers of your mind in the hope of walking into the one holding the illuminating answer to something as simple as remembering who your children were.

I still wanted to believe Massimo had chosen that particular nursing home for the right reasons. He'd brushed away my concerns about the expense. "If it was my mother, I'd expect her to get the best treatment. Your dad is no different and, luckily, we can afford it." At the time, I was so grateful when he insisted on the top neurologists and the best residential care: "It is a bit far away, but you don't want him vegetating in some state-run dump where they'll just stick him in front of the telly."

I'd squashed my reservations about how far away it was under his promises that we'd work it out, that he'd make sure I saw him as often as I wanted to. But, in reality, "a bit far away" meant that yet another person had disappeared from my life. I didn't even want to tally up how seldom we'd visited overall in the last twelve months. Part of the nursing staff's training must be presenting a smooth and neutral face for relatives who only turn up when there's a crisis to be solved, leaving them to make excuses to the residents about why their sons and daughters don't visit. It was better Dad's memory would fail without ever knowing the truth.

As Maggie drove along, kind enough not to talk while I gathered myself, a scene played on a continuous loop in my head. Massimo, ten years ago, driving me from Brighton to Oxford at the crack of dawn every Monday for my client meetings. Me telling him that I wanted to learn to drive, that it was ridiculous him slogging around the M25 then hanging around working on his laptop in a hotel bar waiting to take me home again. And, in the meantime, I'd take the train.

But he wouldn't hear of it. "I'm not having you risking your life on these busy motorways. I'd be so worried about you with all the trucks thundering past. The roads are different now—when I learned to drive, there was so much less traffic. It's not safe."

How flattered I was that this charming man—who could have had his pick of the girls in the office—would get up at 5:30 a.m. to chauffeur me about. "You're just like my dad, wanting to keep me wrapped up in cotton wool."

He sounded hurt. "What's wrong with wanting to keep the woman I love safe? Besides, we get time together to chat, just you and me. There's no one I'd rather be with. Of course, if you'd prefer to hang around train stations on your own in the dark, I'll get my secretary to book some tickets."

Then a huffy silence descended, making me feel guilty for not appreciating him. And I couldn't cope with that. Dad's catchphrase when I was growing up whenever I went to someone's house, was "Make sure you're grateful; don't forget to say thank you." He was terrified in case other people's parents found me rude, the odd little girl without a mother whose father hadn't taken care of all that "please and thank you" business.

So instead of insisting on being independent, I'd convinced myself I was lucky to have someone to run me around, someone prepared to put themselves out for me. Half the women I worked with spent their lives stressing up and down the motorways or shivering on train platforms. I imagined that, sooner or later, the novelty of carting me about would wear off and I'd eventually get some learner plates.

But then Sandro was born and Massimo was convinced his screaming would distract me and cause an accident. Then he was concerned about my health. "You're not doing as much exercise as you once were. Walking everywhere keeps you fit and I need you to live a long time." And he'd squeeze my hand, assure me that whenever I needed to go somewhere, he was at my beck and call.

Somehow, the years slipped by and the right time to bring up driving lessons again never materialized, tinged as it was with underlying tension, that wanting my own driving license somehow insulted Massimo's ability to take care of me.

But that was then. Now, my dad was disappearing into darkness and I was stranded, miles away, reliant on the stars, moon and Massimo's moods aligning to give me a lift to see him.

With the unwelcome knowledge that all that ferrying about, all that concern for my safety was just control by another name.

Massimo would block me if I told him I was going to learn to drive. He'd be far too clever to announce to the world that he was forbidding me to do it. But there'd be a financial crisis of some sort that led to spending less on "nonessentials," a drama that required me to cancel my lessons and, crucially, a drip feed of how I didn't have the coordination, the anticipation, the reactions necessary to pass a test, topped off with "we know what happened to your mother," until I barely felt safe using a vegetable peeler.

But Dad needed me.

So when Maggie offered to teach me to drive, I grabbed onto it, refusing to fall into the usual trap of talking myself out of it. My thoughts flitted about, trying to find a tightrope strung between the obstacles to overcome. I couldn't tell Massimo I was learning because he'd dream up a way to stop me. And I couldn't ask Maggie to lie to Massimo.

"Would you really do that for me?"

Maggie laughed in the way that people who expect good things from the world find people who don't funny. "I'd love it. It would give me huge satisfaction. Mum never learned to drive because we were too poor and it really limits what she can do. And anyway, you don't want to be dependent on Massimo to trolley you about when he's away so much. You'd be able to nip over and see your dad whenever you wanted."

I tried not to sound as desperate as I felt, aiming for a

"Yep, great idea, I'll have a bash at this driving lark" rather than like someone who'd fallen overboard on a cross-channel ferry and was clinging to a lifebelt. But, to my horror, I got all choked up. It was so long since anyone had offered to resolve any of my problems rather than just adding to them. But around Maggie, I always got a giddy feeling. Her down-to-earth optimism was infectious, the sense that yes, things might get a bit troublesome but putting the kettle on and calming down would be a good starting point. That even if I was myself—rather than the me that Massimo poured into a mold ten years ago—she'd still like me.

She stopped in a rest stop.

"Oh bless you, you poor thing."

As naturally as anything, she undid our seat belts and pulled me into a big hug. I never had any spontaneous physical interaction with anyone anymore and it was as though my brain had to be told my body didn't need to be on standby. I was permanently braced for Massimo to turn on me, ready to dart out of his way, or primed to anticipate that any affection was a prelude to a demanding sexual marathon.

I drew back for a second before deliberately relaxing.

Maggie smoothed my hair while all my confusion, my fury for allowing myself to become this person, bubbled out of me. She was so capable, even though she was always saying things like, "What do I know? I just sew on zips. You're the brainbox, Lara. I'd love to be able to tell people I had a degree in accountancy and have them all look at me thinking, wow, she must be bright."

Yes, so bright that I'd allowed Massimo to stop me seeing my own dad.

I pulled back, away from the warmth and comfort Maggie offered. If I told her the truth, she'd expect me to rush home, pack my bags and do something about it. But what could I do? What could a woman like me, with no money of her own, no family and, thanks to Massimo, no friends, *do*? Where could I take Sandro, where could I go, that wouldn't traumatize him more than Massimo's irrational behavior?

I did what I always did. Forced the emotion back inside me and sieved through the stock of reasons I usually used when I had reacted badly to Massimo or, God forbid, stood up for myself: "I'm tired." "I've had a difficult day with Sandro." "Sorry, I know you didn't mean anything by what you said, I'm just a bit oversensitive today." Anything to keep the peace and stop a heated discussion escalating to such an intensity that Sandro would run up to his bedroom with his hands over his ears or the dog would start barking, dancing around, growling, while Massimo goaded him into snapping at me.

I cleared my throat. "Sorry, Maggie. I'm overreacting. It's such a shock seeing Dad like that. He thought I was my mother."

She put her head on one side and held me by the shoulders. "You're not overreacting. Your dad is confused and hurt and you're upset. There's nothing weird about that. God, Lara, give yourself a break. You're not some bloody block of concrete." She paused. "Do you want me to give Massimo a ring and let him know what's happened?"

I had no plans to tell him that Dad was getting worse. "No thanks. I'd hate him to worry and rush home. He's got enough on his plate at work."

And she pulled *the face*, the expression I'd seen on my friends' faces—when I still had some—the one that said, "Don't be such a doormat." And like them, a sigh of exasperation.

But I needed this friendship, this shred of normality in my insane world. "I would love you to teach me to drive, though. Do you think we could do it without telling anyone? I'd love to surprise Massimo and just turn up one day behind the steering wheel."

I held my breath, wondering whether I'd gotten away with it, whether that seemingly innocent suggestion would be enough to get Maggie on board.

She nodded. "Always good to surprise husbands just when they think they know you! We'll have to meet around the corner, because I swear Anna has CCTV cameras trained on me to check I'm not flogging the family silver."

I felt a thrill of excitement, a starburst of rebellion, sing to me, like the bars of an anthemic song drifting in from a distant party where everyone was stamping their feet, thumping their fists in the air as though the lyrics were written for them alone. I'd work out a way to squirrel enough money from the food shopping to apply for a provisional license before I talked myself out of it. If I showed Massimo I was determined to take back control of my life, to stand up to him, he'd respect me more.

I was sure he would.

CHAPTER NINETEEN

MAGGIE

Over the next week, I dithered about telling Nico I was going to teach Lara to drive as soon as her provisional license came through. I didn't want him to blurt it out to Massimo and spoil her surprise, but in the end I felt I'd already deceived him enough over that bloody box.

He laughed. "God help us. She'll think that riding two inches from the bumper in front is normal."

I swatted him with the newspaper. "You Farinellis are a bunch of bloody chauvinists. It will do Lara good to do something for herself, instead of just running around after Massimo and Sandro. And she'll be able to see her dad more often."

He reached for my hand. "I think it's great and you're very kind to do it. And don't worry, mum's the word. Massimo will be delighted—poor man won't have to take her to the supermarket every Saturday."

"Yeah, that is a bit weird. So old-fashioned." I did peer into my heart and double-check that I wasn't just a tiny bit jealous that Massimo loved doing mundane things with her. And was actually *available* to do mundane things with her, rather than being absent every Saturday, driving Francesca to yet another swimming competition.

I shooed away conflicting thoughts: that I didn't want Nico hanging around me and that I'd like him to *want* to hang around me. Marriage was obviously turning me a bit soft in the head.

Nico stuck out his bottom lip. "Wouldn't you like me coming to pick out my blueberries and raspberries with you?"

"Sorry, but no. Maybe I've been on my own for too long, but I don't need a bloke to help me choose what sort of lettuce to buy. Massimo and Lara do take that couply-couply doing everything together to a bit of an extreme."

Nico shot to Massimo's defense. "You've got to remember that Dawn walked out on him. It really shocked him. He's just trying not to make the same mistakes again. He puts in much more effort with Lara. And I think she finds Sandro hard-going, so she needs a lot of support."

I crossed my arms. "I know your mother likes to make out Lara can't sort anything out by herself, but is that really true? I saw her take charge at the nursing home and I think she's more capable than you all give her credit for."

Nico frowned. "What's this, a Farinelli-bashing session? Are you going off us already?"

"Sorry, I didn't mean it like that, but motherhood is hard. Everyone is so quick to point the finger and have a go if your kid doesn't eat peas, can't spell onomatopoeia or, like Sandro, can't swim. I think she needs a break. No one is tut-tutting at Massimo and saying he's done a crap job. Somehow it's Lara's fault that Sandro isn't a county swimmer like Francesca or doesn't really like dogs."

Nico started clearing the table. I felt an unexpected desire to start a row with him. It just seemed so unfair Lara was always putting herself through hoops to please everyone and no one could see what a lot she had on her plate.

But Nico, lovely man that he was, actually listened to what I was saying.

"You're probably right. Lara does put a lot of pressure on herself to be the perfect mother. Anyway, I'm sure they'll sort it out. We've got our own kids to worry about."

I did love it when he talked about the children as "ours." He'd come to Sam's parents' evening with me the week before and I'd barely been able to concentrate on whether Sam had gotten the hang of metaphors and similes because I was ridiculously proud to have Nico with me, sporting him like the winning rosette. For the first time, I felt as though his teachers wouldn't be seeing any failings on Sam's part through the filter of single motherhood: no dad around, lives on that crappy estate, what can you expect? Even though deep down I knew he had more love from me and Mum than half the kids whose dads never looked up from their iPhones and still thought ironing was an activity defined by gender. But just for once, it was lovely to have someone else's ears on whether Sam could get into the grammar school, someone who didn't think education was an optional extra, who— unlike my mum—thought books weren't just for propping up the broken leg on the sofa.

Thoughts of Lara continued to gnaw away at me. I wondered about having a quiet word with Massimo, to let him know how upset she was about her dad. She seemed to have some old shite going on about not bothering him. Personally, I hoped Nico would want to know if I was distraught about something. I'd take Lara over to see her father as often as I could, but once his foot was better, maybe she could have him over to visit for the day if I got Mum around to help. I was sure Mum would love to be involved.

But all these thoughts were wiped out when I went up to bed and saw the ladder to my workshop pulled down. I always put it back up when I'd finished. The light was on up there. I hesitated at the bottom of the steps, my imagination conjuring up burglars in balaclavas popping through the hatch waving machine guns. I shouted to Nico, "Someone's up in my workshop." I heard a crash, the sound of something scattering across the floor. "Nico!" He came charging out of the bathroom, my white knight in a stripy bathrobe, and hurried up the ladder.

I don't think I'd ever heard him raise his voice before. "Francesca! What on earth's happened up here?"

I couldn't hear the response, just a low growl, followed by some sharp, then softer words from Nico. I started to climb up, but Nico appeared above me. "Don't come up for the moment. I'm just sorting Francesca out. I think there's been a bit of a miscommunication. Francesca thinks you've thrown out her mother's jewelry box. She says she's been asking for it and you keep fobbing her off, and it's the design display tomorrow so she's come up here to find it."

My heart lurched. The image of me glancing around to see if anyone was watching before flinging the box into the dumpster rushed into my mind. How could I admit what I'd done without connecting a gigantic tin opener to a writhing can of worms?

Maybe I could brazen it out with "I've looked everywhere for it and think it must have found its way into one of the bags I took to the charity shop. I'm so sorry. Let me buy you a new one." My heart sank at how much work I'd have to do to pay for that.

But I'd gone back on my word and now it was up to me to fix it. I'd sat there, that morning we'd cleared out the attic, and promised I'd never throw anything away without her permission. I'd insisted that she shouldn't feel embarrassed about having her mother's things around. Apart from Lara, none of us had any experience of losing a mother at a young age and she was entitled to handle it any way she wanted. Though of course, I hadn't expected to discover an unexploded bomb among Caitlin's belongings with the power to blast Francesca's memories of her mother to smithereens.

I heard their feet crunching across the floorboards I'd painted white and sealed with ship's varnish. My mind was puzzling over the unfamiliar noise. Then I realized. She'd overturned the printer's letterpress tray with all the little compartments that held my beads, sequins and gems, the ones I browsed for at flea markets, bid for on eBay, scoured charity shops for. My own little haven of pearls, diamante and jewels, scattered everywhere and crushed underfoot. In that moment, I hated her. I was sick of being the grown-up, of accepting bad behavior, of biting my tongue and letting Nico deal. Yes, of course, I was sorry her mother had died, sorry I couldn't replace her, right now sorry I'd ever laid eyes on the Farinelli family. But even I would have to draw the line at a thirteen-year-old wrecking my business when all I'd been trying to do was protect her from the truth about her mother and her loose knicker elastic.

I wanted to clatter up those steps, bellow at Nico for being so bloody blind he hadn't even noticed that every time his wife was trotting off clutching her flipping opera glasses, she was carrying on with some fancy man, crooking her little finger over her Earl Grey and cucumber sandwiches while Nico was disappearing off to the garden center with no more on his mind than reducing the price of the geraniums before they were past their best.

But even as rage swept through me, I knew I'd never wield Caitlin's shit behavior as a weapon. However much Sam's dad had let me down, I'd known who and what he was right from the start—a player, a shirker and an irresponsible flirt. He probably thought the word "faithful" was a quirky oddity to be trotted out once a year in a Christmas carol. And still I'd cried into my pillow, heartbroken and bereft, clutching my newborn baby and wondering what the future would look like.

God knows how painful it would be to superimpose those feelings on the perfect image of a woman, who had a drawer containing a clothes brush, a shoehorn and paper clips. But that thought wasn't quite enough to calm me down. Especially when Nico appeared out of the attic with something close to a look of satisfaction on his face.

He dropped his voice. "She's really sorry about the mess but we are making progress. She feels ready—finally—to go to the graveyard. She thinks it would help her."

I stared at him as though he'd grown two heads and finished the look with a couple of deerstalkers. My bloody workshop, the place where I earned my money, was completely trashed and Nico was presenting it to me as though some frigging triumph had taken place. In that moment, I had to cling onto every fiber of maturity and resist turning into a toddler myself. I wanted to march along the corridor to Francesca's room, rip all the bloody posters off the wall, fling every bottle of nail varnish about until her bedroom resembled a giant splatter painting and burst a few feather pillows for good measure.

When I'd tried out the word "stepmother" before I got married, rolling it around my tongue to see how it sounded, I'd imagined being laid-back and chummy. I'd hoped Francesca would be telling her friends: "My stepmother's really cool, I'm so lucky." I wanted to be the type that planned picnics, days to the beach where we all held hands and jumped over waves, flew kites at the Seven Sisters, our laughter swept away on the wind. Although she'd never forget Caitlin,

I longed for her to think her life was richer for having me in it.

Instead here I was, swallowing down the big burning ball of anger into my stomach—probably gumming up an artery or two with something toxic that would kill me off at a young age—gritting my teeth as though I'd trapped a tadpole in my mouth and saying, "Great. Let's clear up tomorrow."

Clearly I'd been far too Disney and nowhere near enough Jeremy Kyle.

CHAPTER TWENTY

MAGGIE

The next morning, the only person with any bounce at breakfast was Sam, who wanted to know whether he could have a party for his eleventh birthday.

"Massimo offered to help, Mum. He said he knew loads of ball games and he'd do it all if you didn't want to."

I didn't know whether to give in to irritation that Massimo had raised Sam's expectations or be grateful that with all the shit going on with Francesca, at least someone was taking notice of Sam. He never complained, but it seemed a long time since I'd sat down with him and he'd had my full attention. When we lived at Mum's we seemed to have so much more time to chat, watch telly together, just be. Now, I was so busy trying to make headway with Francesca, it felt as though I just patted Sam on the head now and again, saying, "All right, love?" as I ran past, rather than standing still long enough to hear the answer. But maybe it was good for him to separate from me a little, forge relationships with other people who could show him another world beyond my narrow horizons.

But if Sam even noticed that I wasn't as focused on him as I used to be, it hadn't dented his confidence. He was nothing if not tenacious. "So can I have a football party? Can I, Mum?"

Given the general atmosphere in the house that morning, it didn't seem quite the right moment to discuss plans for a birthday party involving football games among the precious plants Nico deadheaded and doctored with such care.

"Can we talk about this another time, darling? I've got a lot to think about today."

Like how I was going to cope in a family that felt like those unpredictable fountains spurting up in a random sequence, sometimes a dribble, sometimes a full-blown water jet, knocking me off my feet just when I thought I was beginning to fit in.

Francesca hadn't apologized and Nico hadn't made her. I'd been so upset the night before, we'd just gone to bed, Nico cuddling me and telling me we'd sort it out, there'd be a solution and perhaps now that she was ready to go to the cemetery, she might find it easier to accept that he'd married again. But this morning, with perfect bloke timing as I was struggling to do up the zip on my jeans, he'd asked me what had "really" happened to the jewelry box with something a bit dodgy in his tone, as though I'd slipped it out of the cloakroom window to a waiting hoodlum. Even though I had taken it, I still felt insulted that *he* considered the possibility. He'd furrowed his brows and said, "I remember it being on your worktable, then I don't think I saw it after that. Has anyone else been up there who might have moved it?"

I couldn't work out whether he was insinuating Sam or Mum had snaffled it, thought I'd pinched it myself or was simply trying to eliminate potential scenarios. Giving him the benefit of the doubt didn't rush to the top of my tick list. Resentment that bloody Caitlin had caused all this trouble and it had fallen to me to cover for her did.

"For Christ's sake, I don't know where it is. I put it to one side and it must have got swept up in another bag that we dumped. Why does everything that doesn't go quite right for Francesca have to be my fault?"

There was a little pause while we both adjusted to the fact that, whatever the provocation, I'd never been openly hostile to Francesca before, always taken the grown-up line of "She's had so much to cope with," even when her behavior was so bratty and spoiled it was hard to focus on anything beyond it. But suddenly it seemed that if I wasn't running along in front of the Farinellis, smoothing the ice like the sweeper in a game of curling, it wouldn't be long before we all ended up in a huge tangle of bubbling resentment, individual agendas erupting out of their hiding places and into the daylight.

Nico stood there doing up his tie, looking knackered and done in.

I'd stomped downstairs, too livid to give a shit what Nico thought. I was tempted to run down the road and start burrowing into the dumpster. I entertained the idea of producing the box and all those little opera ticket stubs, love notes and menus, the evidence of Caitlin's secret life, shoving it at him with "Here, look, not such a bloody perfect wife and mother after all."

But I wanted to think I was better than that.

I hoped I was.

Francesca slammed off to school, plunging straight out into a summer downpour without a coat. Sam hugged me and skipped out of the door, oblivious to anything other than the fact that Massimo had promised him an England football shirt for his birthday. Thank God someone in the family liked us. Nico was definitely a bit off me, going to work with a subdued, "Back around six tonight. I'll help you tidy up the attic."

I put my head on the table, trying to fathom what would be the right thing. The only thought running around my brain was "rock, hard place." Just as I was steeling myself to go up to the attic to see if the mess was really as bad as the chaos I'd glimpsed from the fifth rung of the ladder, the doorbell went off. Through the frosted glass, I saw the outline of a raincoat that looked like a little turquoise marquee.

I threw the door open. "Mum! Are you okay?"

"Thought I'd pop in on my way home. Just finished doing the early shift with Daphne."

I frowned. "Daphne?"

"Yes, the old lady who's losing it, the batty one who thinks the Germans are coming."

"Of course. Come on in. You've missed Sam. He's already gone to school."

"I see plenty of him; it's you that I need a photo of to remind me what you look like."

Guilt rushed through me. "Sorry. It's been a bit..." I stopped. I couldn't tell her how bad it really was, though sometimes I ached for the days when all three of us squashed on the couch in her flat in front of *Deal or No Deal*, Sam's legs across our knees, taking it in turns to imagine what we'd do if we won the top prize.

Mum always said the same. "I don't want anything, but I'd like to see you and Sam set up somewhere of your own. Just enough to know when I peg out you'll be all right. And maybe a nice bloke for you, Mags."

And then we'd tease her about having one foot in the grave before she was even sixty. She'd tickle Sam and although we could hear Mr. Emerson shuffling across the floor upstairs and the louts kicking the bins downstairs, I was happy. I belonged.

So I couldn't tell her now I'd achieved her dream, even

without Noel Edmonds's help, it wasn't all that. I was finding it hard to meet her eye. Mum had perfected the "nowhere to hide" stare.

"Any chance of a cup of tea?" She didn't take off her coat or march in and bung on the kettle like she normally would.

"Are you keeping your coat on?"

"Didn't dare take it off in case I made the place look untidy," she said.

"Don't be silly. Give it here."

I grabbed her coat and bustled her through to the kitchen. She looked around, her gaze settling on the new coffee machine in the corner. Nico had bought it, an all-singing, all-dancing, grind your own beans chrome monster: "Sold a couple of those deluxe summer houses this week and a couple of ride-on lawnmowers, so I'm having a little celebration." I knew it had cost nearly as much as the rent on Mum's flat for a month. And while she wouldn't know the prices of gadgets designed to "make coffee just like the Italians do," she wasn't stupid either.

I forced a laugh. "Yep, that's Nico's new toy. You know what a fusspot he is about his coffee. Do you want to try some?"

"If you've got time."

My shoulders sagged. "I've always got time for you, Mum."

My eyes started to prickle. Mum usually breezed in, full of stories about the people she looked after, but today she seemed out of sorts. With hook and eye carnage upstairs, Nico barely speaking, never mind Francesca, Mum huffing and puffing might just about finish me off.

"I'm sorry I haven't been around. It's been a bit full-on here, sorting out the workshop and getting the business up and running again."

Mum brightened. "Is it finished? Can I see it?"

I switched on the coffee grinder to give me a second to think. "It's nearly there. I'll invite you around for the great unveiling."

Mum would have known how to get Francesca onside, even in the face of the disappearing keepsake saga. She always had the right word for everyone. Even the hard-nut hoodies on the estate stepped back to let her pass, elbowed each other out of the way and curbed the worst of their language when Mum went striding by with her cheery "Hello, my lovelies" as though they were all dolled up in Scout uniforms, offering to pick up litter and wash cars.

But as her only daughter, the single receptacle of all her modest dreams and ambitions, I couldn't make myself utter the words, "This marriage lark is not all it's cracked up to be." I didn't even want to admit to myself that Francesca hated me so much she'd deliberately ruined something really precious to me.

I finished making the coffee, watching her resist the temptation to look at the bottom of the mug to see what make it was. I smiled. "Have you had a car boot sale lately?"

Mum clapped her hands. "You know that funny little stool that was in the corner of the lounge with the plant on it? Some old boy bought it for fifteen quid last Saturday. Gave half of it to Sam toward a new pair of goalie gloves."

"You didn't need to do that. You should be treating yourself."

Mum looked at me over her coffee cup. "I *want* to treat him. He's still my grandson, you know."

I'd never known Mum prickly like this. "Mum, no one's saying otherwise. Have I done something to upset you?"

With that, her face, which even when she was miserable still had an air of waiting to catch a thread of fun, crumpled into tears. I hadn't seen Mum cry since our snappy old Jack

Russell was put down about ten years earlier. I hated to think Sam and I were the cause of it. She fumbled in her sleeve for a tissue, which I recognized as one of her haul of the serviettes she snaffled every time she took Sam to McDonald's.

"Sorry, sorry, Mags. I don't want to come here and blub. I'm happy for you, really I am. I suppose I miss you and Sam. I'm a bit lonely without you." I'd expected her to be pleased to have her flat back, with room to move again. But now, an image of Mum sitting on her couch with no one to discuss the disastrous meringues on the *Great British Bake Off* came into my head. Guilt at my selfishness, dancing off to my new home with barely a backward glance, made me want to cry myself.

Mum rubbed the little patches of dry skin on her knuckles, as if weighing up whether our relationship could withstand what was coming next. She sniffed. "I think you're ashamed of me now you've married into the Farinellis and 'bettered' yourself. That's why you don't want me to come around."

"I've never stopped you coming around!" I braced myself for Mum's next comment, wondering what other bloody thing I'd done wrong, what other flaming shortcoming I had, what other little gap I'd failed to fill.

"So when was the last time you phoned me and invited me for anything?"

"You're family. I don't need to invite you. You can come anytime."

There was a pattern developing here. Last time I'd gone out with the girls for a drink, they'd teased me about whether I'd deleted their numbers from my mobile. And I'd felt a bit offended though I knew I didn't go out as much as I used to. But wasn't that the same for everyone who got married? Otherwise I might as well have stayed single.

My stomach knotted as Mum shook her head. We did rub each other up the wrong way sometimes, but we never really fell out properly. And I didn't want to start now that life was supposed to be getting better.

"You might say I'm always welcome, but if I do pop in, you're always like, just hang your coat up, just put your mug on a coaster, just wash your hands before you help me with dinner, just be careful not to knock over that glass, like I'm a five-year-old who can't be trusted to have a drink without spilling it everywhere."

I sighed, feeling my annoyance subside. Where to start? How could I even begin to explain the burden I felt of looking after everything that belonged to Caitlin, so Francesca could never say, "I loved that table/glass/bowl/tea bloody spoon but Maggie's family ruined it"? How could I tell her that I dreaded Anna coming in, taking in the avalanche of Sam's shoes and boots, the carrier bags I didn't quite finish emptying of groceries, the pens without lids scattered on the kitchen table, the shabby, slovenly second wife? That I spent my whole life sweeping up after myself and Sam, but never quite managed to tidy us away enough to feel that we weren't somehow a tickling hair of irritation caught in the collar of the Farinelli glamor?

It wasn't that Mum didn't belong.

It was that I didn't.

I took her hand. "I'm sorry that I've made you feel like that. It's a bit of an adjustment period for all of us, isn't it? We'd been a little unit of three for so long that I feel a bit caught in the middle, trying to please everyone."

A more accurate description would have been stretched like a frayed elastic bungee cord that was about to snap and hook someone's eye out.

Mum's face relaxed. "You know Daphne that I'm looking

after? Her son is taking her on holiday for the first two weeks of August, so I can have some time off. I've been saving up my car boot money. I've got enough for a caravan in Cornwall. Do you think Nico would let you and Sam come away?"

"Of course he will. He'll be pleased for us to spend time with you. It's not really a case of him 'letting' us anyway... we're a bit more equal than that."

Even Mum had fallen into the trap of thinking that I needed to throw myself on the floor, grateful for a husband. I wondered if *anyone* thought Nico was lucky to have me. But Mum was so thrilled about our Cornwall adventure she didn't notice my sharp words.

"We can go to the Eden project—I think I can swap my Tesco vouchers for tickets—and I saw on telly that there's surfing down there, perhaps Sam can try it, there are some lovely beaches, with a bit of sun, it'll be as good as going abroad."

The word "abroad" woke me up. God. Tuscany. First two weeks of August.

Mum was still extolling the virtues of Cornish cream teas and planning to hire a windbreak if it was a bit blowy. I couldn't tell her we couldn't go. Not now. Not when she was already feeling as though we were looking down our noses at her.

But I couldn't allow her to make plans then let her down at a later date. I sat there, my face, my heart burning. I needed to get the words out.

"Actually, Mum, I'm really sorry but I've just realized Sam and I are flying to Tuscany then."

She looked at me as though I'd said we were off to America on a private jet. "Tuscany?"

I nodded, hoping today wouldn't be the day that I would have to articulate the words, "We're staying in a castle."

Something shifted on her face, as though Sam and I were drifting further and further out of her reach. I wanted to row back toward her and scoop her into the boat with us, not leave her stranded, an unwilling spectator of a life she couldn't share.

Which is probably why the next sentence flew out of my mouth, a crazy idea formulated by an unbalanced mind, a suggestion with "disaster" written all over it, flashing about the kitchen in strobe lighting.

"Why don't you come to Italy with us?"

CHAPTER TWENTY-ONE

LARA

My provisional license arrived after five days. I stared at my haunted face on the little photocard, feeling terrified. I'd somehow imagined it wouldn't turn up for a month or two. I'd managed to get the cash out of Massimo by telling him Sandro was going on a school trip. Riddled with guilt, I'd schooled Sandro in the lie. It couldn't be helped. Dad had to come first for the moment.

Before I lost my nerve, I walked into town and bought some magnetic learner plates, shoving them into my bag as though I'd bought a leopard-skin thong I didn't want anyone to see. I went straight around to Maggie's, feeling nervous in case she'd gone off the idea. She came to the door looking as though she hadn't been to bed for a week.

"Are you okay?"

And this time, it was her turn to burst into tears.

"What's the matter?" I wanted to hug her, but instead I shuffled about in the hallway, embarrassed. I was so out of practice at the warts and all of friendship. When I was at work, boyfriend bust-ups, being bawled out by the boss and IVF failures had me shouting through loo doors on a regular basis. Now I was so busy keeping a lid on my own life, I'd gotten lulled into thinking everyone else was so happy they did a little disco dance in front of the mirror every morning.

She started to fill me in on what had happened the night before.

"Oh my god. What did Nico say? Was he furious?" I asked.

"I don't think he realized how important it is to me to keep working. I don't earn anything like he does, so I think everyone assumes I'm just titting about sewing on a few buttons. But I want to pay my way. Everyone already thinks I just married Nico for his money." She gave a little sob.

I felt a rush of shame for getting sucked into Anna's little power-play. "No one thinks that."

Maggie broke away. "I love you for saying that, Lara, but I could name at least one person who does. You and Massimo have made me really welcome though."

Thank God she hadn't overheard Massimo when Sandro had let slip that he'd been to Beryl's last week instead of going swimming. He'd ranted on about "fat-arsed Fanny next door coming up with the brilliant idea of leaving our son in a bloody drugs den while you two go gallivanting off to see a bloke who doesn't know what day of the week it is."

"Can I help you tidy up?"

"I'm not sure how bad it is yet. I couldn't face looking at it properly last night. I was just about to go up."

"Come on, let's do it now. The sooner you're shipshape again, the less angry you'll feel."

Maggie gave me a little ghost of a smile. "Thank you. And as soon as we've finished, let's head out of town and find somewhere quiet to turn you into Lewis Hamilton."

God knows how Maggie felt, because I nearly screamed when I saw the state of her workshop. But, unlike me, Maggie was made of tough stuff. She closed her eyes, took a big breath and handed me one of the printers' trays.

"Could you pick up the blue and green beads, and anything diamante?"

We worked in silence for a bit, until I couldn't bear it anymore.

"Was there a particular trigger for this? When I saw you with Francesca a few weeks ago, I thought you were getting on really well?"

I remembered watching Maggie's curly head next to Francesca's smooth dark one as they pored over a pattern for a summer top Francesca wanted. I'd felt a little stab of envy about Maggie's natural affinity with children. I found it hard to be spontaneous and relaxed with Sandro, my maternal instinct straitjacketed by what Massimo would find acceptable, my affection diluted by fear.

A mix of emotions dappled Maggie's face, like leaves against summer sunlight. "We had a bit of an issue over a box belonging to her mum. She thought I'd thrown it out and got really upset."

"Was it a special box?"

"It was quite pretty. Gold, studded with red stones in the shape of a heart. Probably worth a bob or two."

My skin started to prickle, sick dread chiseling another slither of ballast from my already fragile universe. The insidious voices of suspicion I'd smothered over the years were clamoring to be heard.

"So what did happen to it?"

She hesitated. I could see that, unlike me, lies weren't the oil that smoothed her path through life. They were the things that tripped her up, stopped her in her tracks because of the infrequent need to tell them. Her answer when it came was thin and high.

"I'm not sure. We can't find it anywhere, so I think I might have thrown it out—accidentally, obviously—when I was clearing out some other stuff." She tried to make a joke. "It was a funny old thing, played some sort of opera when you opened it up, right old racket."

"Opera?"

"Yeah. Apparently Caitlin loved all that stuff, though I don't think Nico is very keen. Or if he is, he's not telling me. Probably doesn't want to make me feel a thicko."

Red stones in the shape of a heart. Opera music when you opened it. The box I found tucked at the back of the drawer under some of Massimo's jumpers.

The present I waited for him to give me on Christmas Day five years ago.

CHAPTER TWENTY-TWO

MAGGIE

After we'd finished sorting out the workshop, Lara couldn't escape me quickly enough, coming up with the excuse that she "needed to walk Lupo." Maybe she'd lost her nerve about driving, but all of a sudden, the dog she hated became a much greater pull than learning the difference between a clutch and an accelerator.

Once, I was a person that everyone liked. Customers at the shop used to chat to me long after they'd spelled out their requirements for hems, zips and necklines. I'd get thank-you cards for saving the day from women who needed a dress letting out for a special event, flowers from men who'd split their one decent suit.

And now, everyone I knew ran from me as though an extra fifteen minutes in my company would bring them out in purple boils.

Nico had phoned me a couple of times to check that I was okay, begging me to forgive Francesca, telling me "if we could just get through this rough patch, we'll laugh about it in a few years' time." Right now, it seemed highly unlikely I'd be ha-ha hee-heeing about having to spend a whole afternoon repairing a seam on a dress that Francesca had wrenched apart in her frenzy.

I wanted to find a way back to how we were before the jewelry box saga, when she sometimes laughed at my jokes, or even took my side against Nico when he teased me about my untidiness. When I no longer had to steel myself to go into a room she was sitting in. And I needed to do it before I didn't care anymore, before that little bit of self-preservation kicked in and guillotined off the "giving a shit about trying to make someone who hates me like me" gene. Of course she was still a child. Maybe I was immature myself. And poor Nico was caught in the middle. But my conversations with him ended with me feeling slightly more irritated than before.

I went to school to meet Sam, just to get out of the house, even though he preferred walking home on his own. As I stood waiting at the school gate, one of the mothers came up to me, the sort that wore 1950s-style dresses with ballerina pumps and little cardigans. "You're Francesca's stepmum, aren't you?"

I managed a suspicious-sounding yes, as though I'd just picked up the phone and the other person had said, "Are you the homeowner?"

"I just wanted to say what an incredible swimmer she is. I saw her in the trials at the weekend. Amazing butterfly. And such a lovely girl, so polite whenever I see her."

I made my brain override the "You are actually kidding, aren't you?" that was sitting so far forward on the tip of my tongue that I must have looked like a snake trying to make sense of my surroundings.

"Thank you" wheezed out of me. Obviously, I didn't sound interested enough, as a whisper of offense passed over the woman's face. I got a grip and said, "Yes, I'm really looking forward to seeing her swim."

"She's qualified for the regionals, so perhaps we'll see

you there," the woman said, before giving me a little wave good-bye as Sam scuffed up and thrust a huge rucksack at me. Honestly, it wouldn't surprise me if the next generation turned out to be shorter than their parents, the sheer weight of books on their back stunting their growth. But I knew better than to mention the word "locker" and send laughter reverberating around the playground.

We walked home with Sam nattering on about Massimo and how cool he was. "Did you know he did the accounts for one of the big football clubs in the north? He can't say which one, but he knows all the players. Anyway...can we go around tonight and sort out my birthday party with him?"

"For God's sake! Stop banging on about your party. There's so much going on at the moment, and I'm sorry to say, your birthday isn't the flaming priority."

Sam marched off ahead of me, hurt and disappointment in the slump of his shoulders.

I ran after him, guilt surging through me. "Sam! Sam!" But he stomped off.

When I finally caught up to him, he was brushing tears off his face with the sleeve of his blazer. "Sam, I'm sorry. I've had a horrible day and I've taken it out on you. Of course we can sort out your party. I'll talk to Nico about it tonight."

Sam gave me a look that ripped deep into my heart. "It's the first time we've ever had a garden for a party. I've been telling everyone. I've invited the whole class. You said it was okay this morning."

A perfect example of everyone in the house hearing what they wanted to hear. "The whole class? How many's that?"

"About thirty-five?"

I didn't say anything in case I started shouting again.

"That's okay, isn't it? I can't not invite them. No one believes I've got a nice house now. Matt Reynolds said I was lying, that I still lived on the estate with all the druggies. And then he started pretending to inject himself with heroin and falling on the floor."

I didn't know who Matt Reynolds was, but if he ever came to my house, I was going to rub his hamburger bun around the rim of the toilet before serving it to him with a smile.

"You leave it with me, love. I'll see what I can do."

In between Googling soft footballs that don't smash the heads off plants, I spent the few hours before Nico got home debating how to broach the subject of thirty-plus kids taking over his garden in two weeks' time. Just when Nico's beloved echinaceas would be at their best. Could we risk peony and lupin apocalypse, after all the hours Nico spent out there digging in mushroom compost and scattering his grim concoctions of fish, bone and blood? Maybe we could put screens up. Perhaps we could invite a load of parents to stand like sentinels in front of the hollyhocks.

I was wandering around the garden, trying to work out whether there was any way at all that a whole army of kids could have two hours of football games without causing floral heartbreak to Nico, when Massimo appeared at the French windows, followed by Sam wearing a satisfied "I've brought in the big guns" expression.

Massimo sauntered over, one hand in the pocket of his suit trousers.

"You should be very proud of your son. He's going to go far in life. He's already learned that very important lesson of how to get what he wants." He ruffled Sam's hair and leaned forward to kiss me on both cheeks, Italian-style. That was one area where I would get an A* for improvement. With a bit of concentration, it had been a while since I'd gotten in a tangle, swooping in for the wrong cheek and looking like a right old pleb who'd never been out of England.

I looked at Sam. "Don't tell me you've been bothering Massimo about the party."

Sam didn't look the slightest bit abashed.

With a theatrical wave of his hand, Massimo said, "Let's just say he is a man with a plan and he knows how to execute it."

I was hoping Massimo was going to help me let Sam down gently but instead he seemed to be fanning his hopes.

"We can't have Sam here disappointed, especially not after those vile creatures that masquerade as his classmates *dared* to poke fun at him. Little toerags. So what we are going to do is put on the party to end all parties and show them what the Farinelli family is capable of."

Sam was hopping up and down with excitement. I was eyeing Nico's roses and imagining the fat pink heads plunging to their deaths, scattering their petals into a scented carpet.

"I'm a bit worried about how much damage there'll be in the garden."

Massimo patted my shoulder. "That, my darling Maggie, is where you will be truly grateful to have married into the Farinelli family. We cannot have my dear brother shortening his life because a hydrangea has taken a hit. So, we invite you to hold your party next door, where child and dog have already taken their toll."

Sam burst out, "And Massimo's thought up some really good ideas for games on the trampoline."

"That's really kind of you but what does Lara say? She's not going to want a load of kids rampaging around the house. Do you know what you're letting yourself in for? Has Sandro ever had a party?"

A flicker of exasperation passed across Massimo's face. "Sandro has never wanted a party."

There was a little moment of silence when I felt like I'd

said something rude without meaning to. Massimo steam-rollered on. "Lara won't mind: we're a lot less worried about our garden than Nico is about his. Lupo has seen to that." He rolled his eyes. "When Caitlin was alive, we barely dared walk on the grass. Part of the reason she wouldn't get a dog was because she was worried about the yellow patches on the lawn."

I could have hugged him. Someone finding one tiny fault in Saint Caitlin. It was like finding a twenty-pound note on the pavement. Not life-changing but ridiculously uplifting on a temporary basis.

"If you're sure? And Lara won't mind?" I was still smarting from her sudden exit this morning. I didn't want to add "party for rowdy kids" to my wrongdoings.

"She'll be fine with it."

Lara had many qualities but I didn't feel relaxed and ready to entertain were among them. But Massimo was doing that thing of being so ridiculously generous and enthusiastic that any argument would make me look like I was the most ungrateful person breathing in Brighton air.

"Shall we do it on Sunday in two weeks' time? Then that'll give me the Saturday to get it all set up. Shall we say three till five? The parents can have a drink when they come to pick up. I'll sort out all of the games . . . I've got loads of ideas."

If Sandro had never had a party, I was afraid Massimo was falling into that typical bloke trap of assuming he could turn up for the main event without worrying about any of the details leading up to it. Lara would get lumbered with cleaning the house to her exacting standards so all the kids' parents could scoff their vol-au-vents directly off the floor if necessary, while he trollied in twirling a football on one finger.

I couldn't let him present Lara with a fait accompli. I didn't want her to feel taken advantage of. I tried again. "Why don't we pop around there now and run it past Lara before we get too far down the line and I claim my spot in family history as the most unpopular relative ever?"

Massimo surprised me. He threw his arms around me and whirled me around. "You, darling Maggie, are the best thing that ever happened to my brother, a wonderful breath of fresh air breezing through his uptight life. You deal with him and I'll talk to Lara." He turned to Sam. "It'll be the best party you've ever had, mate; they'll all be talking about it for a week afterward."

Sam looked delighted. But in among the worry about imposing ourselves on next door, I felt a little pang it wasn't Nico making a massive effort for Sam. My hopes of being one big happy family, where our kids just saw us as "the parents" regardless of origin, were looking increasingly unlikely.

Thank God I would be able to repay their generosity by teaching Lara to drive, assuming I did actually manage to get her to plant her backside in the car sometime soon. I couldn't wait to surprise Massimo when she came roaring around the corner waving her driving license. It would definitely take a load off him when he no longer had to taxi them everywhere. Finally I'd have my own little part in the family history, smiling modestly as Massimo regaled everyone with the story of when "Maggie, that little minx of my sister-in-law, helped Lara pass her test without me knowing a thing about it."

CHAPTER TWENTY-THREE

LARA

Since I'd come home from Maggie's at lunchtime, my stomach was so hollow I felt as though a big echo would reverberate inside me if I ate a peanut. What did Massimo giving Caitlin that box mean? That they'd had an affair? Or that he'd just given her a present he hadn't told me about? Had I really been blind to something going on under my nose or was Massimo just doing his usual trick of presenting himself as a thoughtful man, finding the perfect gift for his sister-in-law?

I sieved through my memory for any standout moments of "Aha!" but could only find a jumble of possibilities that could easily be a product of what Massimo would describe as my penchant for "blowing everything out of proportion." Was Massimo reading out loud to her when she was ill, suspicious or an act of kindness? Going to the opera with her because Nico hated it and he loved it, a subterfuge or a practicality? Guiding her hand while she added truffles to the mushroom risotto he'd taught her to cook on our last Italian holiday together, blatant betrayal or his usual tactile nature?

I made myself a cup of tea and tried to think straight. Five years ago, when I'd discovered the gold box in the drawer just before Christmas, Sandro had been two and a half. And it was fair to say Massimo and I weren't quite seeing eye-to-eye, though I'd never envisaged it might lead to him hopping over the garden fence for a bit of "my wife doesn't understand me" therapy with Caitlin.

That Christmas had coincided with a period when bedtime—or Sandro's rebellion against it—had become the subject of all Farinelli gatherings. Anna led the "bedtime by seven or great calamity will ensue" campaign, shrugging off my counterargument that kids in Italy seemed to be up till all hours. She simply sniffed and said, "But Sandro lives in England, Lara."

Caitlin would then launch into her own "Research shows…" diatribe and I'd be left isolated in the useless parent corner, with Massimo placing the blame firmly on my shoulders for the fact that Sandro would only fall asleep if I sat with him until he dropped off.

But in the lead-up to Christmas, Massimo had decided that, as he was on holiday for a couple of weeks, he was "going to get on top of all this nighttime nonsense."

I sipped my drink, raking up memories of that particular "festive season," then regretting it and trying to blank them out. I didn't want to remember Massimo's footsteps on the landing, his fingers closing around my wrist as I stroked Sandro's forehead, my ears alert for the regular deep breathing that would signify he'd finally given into sleep.

"You're not sitting here all night."

"Ssshhhh. He'll be off in a minute." And then it would start. Sandro disturbed by Massimo's harsh tones, flinging open his eyes: "Mummy, Mummy, stay me, stay me."

Massimo wrenched me away. "It's bedtime, Sandro."

His chin would lift. "No bedtime, Daddy." And Sandro

would wriggle out of the little dinosaur duvet, ready to clamber out of bed and into my arms.

And I'd try: "Let me just settle him down and then I'll come downstairs."

But Massimo would wrestle him back in, Sandro becoming more and more hysterical, with Massimo bellowing over him, trying to silence him with the sheer volume of his voice. Massimo would hustle me out of the room to a growing crescendo of screaming, slam the door shut and stand in front of it. "Go downstairs."

If I tried to argue, pleading to go back in and calm Sandro down, Massimo would threaten to go in and smack him. "I'll shut that boy up. I'll show him who's in charge."

I'd watch the door handle rattling up and down from the inside while Massimo held it closed, every tiny piece of me yearning to rush in and tell him he was safe, that he didn't need to be afraid, that Mummy was just outside the door. Eventually I'd stand in the kitchen humming to myself to mask the screaming, but not so loud that I wouldn't hear Massimo going into Sandro's bedroom. Massimo had never smacked Sandro but there was always that tenseness about him, as though he was holding himself back, a looming threat that might one day break loose.

Every night was the same. I'd start getting stressed about bedtime just after breakfast. But after two weeks, Massimo declared himself triumphant, cock-a-hoop about fuss-free bedtimes, crowing about Sandro just needing "a firm hand."

I didn't tell him that Sandro had started wetting the bed at night again after a good two months' dry. That, I would handle myself. Quietly.

But just because Massimo had had an authoritarian take on bedtimes, it didn't mean that he was a philanderer. I couldn't remember him going missing for long periods.

Instead I recalled how the house seemed to breathe around us when he wasn't there, when I didn't have to worry if I was being too soft or "not showing Sandro who's boss," when I could just enjoy a bit of time with my two-year-old son and follow my instincts instead of filtering them through the great avalanche of Massimo's expectations.

But surely I would have noticed him having an affair. Wouldn't I? Maybe I was so relieved to have a break from monitoring Sandro's behavior for Massimo's approval that he never seemed gone long enough.

I put my teacup in the sink and got out my window cleaning stuff. Some women sang and danced to cheer themselves up, I cleaned windows. I found solace in removing dirt, fingerprints, everything that went before, leaving a sparkling view onto the world outside and the crisp smell of the recently polished.

I started in the guest bedroom. It was amazing that the windows got dirty in here, given that the last time anyone had stayed in it was Dad a few years ago, before he moved into the home. As I sprayed the window, busy with my duster, I stared over to Nico and Maggie's house, admiring the clematis around their bedroom window. Nico really did have green fingers.

I scrubbed away at the corners of the window, my mind picking away at the possibility of Massimo having an affair with Caitlin. Massimo wouldn't do that to his brother. He always looked out for Nico. A far more likely explanation was that Massimo had mentioned the present to me at the time and I hadn't remembered. Back then, he was always telling me that it was high time I got over my "pregnancy brain" and stopped forgetting things.

I tutted at my own stupidity. No wonder Massimo got frustrated with me: I was probably doing what I always did, getting overanxious about everything, too quick to believe the worst. But after years of Dad saying, "Fear keeps you safe, darling, because, as we know, the worst can happen," it was a hard habit to break.

I'd have to take a lesson from Maggie. She always expected the best of everyone and laughed at people who let her down.

Today, at the age of thirty-five and a half I was going to make my own joy. I'd start with inviting Dad over for a day, maybe even to stay the night once we'd seen how he coped. I'd love to have him sleep in this bedroom again. It would take a bit of organization, but with Beryl's help, I was sure we could look after him. If I planned it when Massimo was away for work, then he couldn't really object. In his own way, Massimo did want the best for Dad, he just found the reality of the nose blowing and toileting accidents a bit distasteful. Still, there weren't many men who'd be prepared to shell out a fortune for someone they'd inherited through marriage. When the right moment presented itself though, I'd explore other options for Dad's care. Somewhere closer, that maybe didn't cost as much. Dad didn't need fresh lilies in the hallway, he needed his family around him.

I finished off with a jaunty sweep of the windowsill, delighted to have a plan in place. Window cleaning, Dad to visit, nursing homes to investigate, driving lessons, banishing the ridiculous notion that my husband had had an affair with my sister-in-law . . . Lara "seize the day" Farinelli.

I trotted off downstairs just as Massimo was coming in through the door. On a wave of newfound confidence, I threw my arms around him and kissed him.

"To what do I owe this pleasure?" He pulled me close, his hands caressing my back. "Where's Sandro?" he whispered.

"He's gone over to your mother's for dinner."

"Upstairs with you then, Mrs. Farinelli."

Proof that he still loved me, right there. I needed to stop doubting him. Whatever his faults, Massimo had always fancied me. Even in our worst times, we'd never stopped having sex.

He wouldn't have allowed me to.

CHAPTER TWENTY-FOUR

MAGGIE

Before I could get a chance to okay the party with Lara, she came around, full of ideas for "finger food." I think she meant "ham and cheese sandwiches." I was only slightly tempted to tease her by suggesting the fish paste and sandwich spread sarnies Mum swore by.

"Massimo's got all sorts lined up—water football—so it might get a bit messy and muddy, dodge football with a couple of kids on the trampoline, and some assault courses. He's bought some basketball nets as well and some hula hoops... not quite sure what he's going to do with those but no doubt he'll have a plan."

I bit my lip. "Are you sure you're all right with this? It's so generous of you both."

"It's fine. Honestly, Massimo is brilliant with kids; he's like the Pied Piper. We can just worry about the food."

I scrabbled about for a pen and paper to make a list. "Obviously I'll go and buy it all."

"Not necessary. Massimo's already ordered everything from the Cash and Carry." Lara was glowing, triumphant her husband was such a pillar of efficiency.

It was a mark of my mingy mean spirit that I felt a little

dart of disappointment. Sam had never had a proper party before—we'd never had room—and I'd looked forward to choosing the food with him, standing there while he made the excruciating decision between Monster Munch and Pringles, margherita or pepperoni pizza.

Lara's face fell. "Is that okay?"

"Yes, yes, of course, thank you. I'm just a bit embarrassed about how much trouble you're both going to and how little I'm doing." I fidgeted self-consciously, wondering whether to start pressing tenners into her hand, or whether talking about something as vulgar as money would contravene some other family rule that I hadn't yet grasped. I decided to let Nico deal with that one.

On the day of the party, Sam was up at the crack of dawn begging to go next door. Although Francesca was still showing me all the warmth of a barely flickering candle, she did at least have moments when she couldn't resist Sam's enthusiasm. Thankfully he managed to coerce her into playing a complicated ball game on the bit of patio Nico had kept plant-free for that specific purpose. Despite their banter being utterly un-PC, it kept him out from under my feet. "I could do better than you with one leg tied behind my back." "You're a girl, you're only good for a bit of splashing about in the pool."

By two o'clock I couldn't keep him at home any longer and we went around to help Lara get the food ready. Mum couldn't have echoed my thoughts more accurately. "Cor! Didn't realize we were having a tea party for the queen!"

Sam started gesticulating and mouthing "Where are the crisps?" at me while Lara was looking in the fridge. I shooed him out into the garden to throw the ball for Lupo before the whispering became any louder.

I shut Mum up with, "This looks fantastic, Lara," thinking that all the fiddly little vol-au-vents and little crispbreads with dobs of—what the hell was that?—Olive tapenade? Anchovy paste?—wouldn't keep a bunch of marauding ten-year-olds going for long. I wasn't sure the sundried tomatoes and goat's cheese tartlets were going to be all the rage either. In my experience, the more doorsteppy the sandwiches, the better.

Unfortunately, Mum wasn't reading my signals. "I reckon we get some cheese and pineapple on cocktail sticks and a few proper buns going too—they're bound to build up a bit of an appetite running around."

Massimo came in on the tail end of the conversation, looking all sporty and tanned, like a youthful football manager. He glanced at the spread and said, "I'm with you, Beryl; this will be a wonderful starting point, but ten-year-olds are like locusts."

Lara's color rose. She stuttered, "I thought you said not to do the rolls, burgers and sausages?"

Massimo took a theatrical step back. "No, I said we *should* do them. All these fancy bits will be great for the grown-ups though." He ruffled her hair. "Honestly, my darling wife, I think you get more and more absentminded every day. It's a good job I love you."

Lara scuttled off to the freezer and started defrosting sausages in the microwave. She was smoothing her hands on her jeans, looking so hassled I wanted to cancel the whole thing and just take them down the park for a kickabout as I'd done in other years.

Massimo seemed oblivious to Lara's stress, immediately raising mine by asking where Nico was.

"He's taken Francesca to another swimming competition. He should be back just after the party starts."

Massimo frowned. "On a Sunday? Wasn't he out with her yesterday as well? It wouldn't have killed him to let one of the other parents give her a lift today."

I wanted to say, "Hear, bloody hear!" and tell Massimo that we'd had words that morning because, yet again, even though I now had a husband, I was still relying on my mum to help me. But I was obviously more 1950s housewife than I gave myself credit for, perhaps without the apron, but certainly with the loyalty that must not let a single word be said against the man of the house. "I know, but Francesca is still very unsettled and he has to put her first." I did feel that a huge cavernous cauldron of bubbling oil might open up beneath my bum to boil the hypocrisy out of me.

I half-expected Massimo to burst into a song from *The Sound of Music* in honor of my saint-like status but he just harrumphed and started issuing instructions.

He sent Mum off to the garage to fetch paper cups, motioned to Lara to put the oven on, then steered me out to the garden to show me all the games he'd set up. I was itching to rush back in and help Lara, but I forgot all about her for a second when I took in what a huge effort Massimo had made. I had to work hard not to burst into tears and fling myself on him. He'd nailed hoops onto the side of the house, filled a dustbin full of footballs, set up an obstacle course with jumps and beams and buckets, with a couple of brand-new goal nets at the end. I'd pegged my expectations at a couple of cheapo footballs and a few cones to dribble around.

"This must have cost a fortune, Massimo. You must let me know what I owe you," I said, trying not to look shocked at the huge outlay for one day. He must have spent hundreds of pounds. I started doing quick calculations about how much money I had coming in from sewing in the next few weeks, forcing myself to focus on what a great party Sam would have rather than how long it would take to pay it off.

Massimo laughed. "Wouldn't dream of it. He's a great lad and I just want him to have a brilliant birthday."

"Thank you. I don't know what to say."

He took both of my wrists and stared straight into my eyes, head on one side. "You don't need to say anything. Sam's a lucky boy and that brother of mine is a very lucky man."

It had to be an Italian thing, this whole need to turn up the heat on emotions all the time, to dissect, comment and microscope on the detail of everyone's relationships. I was beginning to see the appeal of Mum and her horror of public displays of affection. On our estate, men might take off a top of a beer bottle for you, but they wouldn't get all touchy-feely unless they were planning on relieving you of a different sort of top later on.

We didn't go without cuddles in our family but neither did we hang off each other like rucksacks. Touching any man who wasn't my husband made me feel as though I was doing something I shouldn't.

I waited a second before wriggling free, clocking Lara staring out of the window straight at us as I did so.

CHAPTER TWENTY-FIVE

LARA

It was my own stupid fault. Of course I should have known a few silly little vol-au-vents weren't going to be enough. Maybe I was losing it like my dad. No wonder Massimo preferred to stand in the garden with Maggie, staring into her eyes rather than preparing burgers with me.

I tried not to let a seed of resentment take root. Maggie hadn't sought this. Massimo had done his usual trick of showering all his charm on everyone else, with none left over for me. I wished I could turn the clock back to the blissful fourteen months before we got engaged, when he couldn't bear a cross word between us. When he was working so hard to win my trust, to convince me a man ten years my senior, with money, authority and charisma, really couldn't live without mousy old me. When the slightest disagreement would provoke a flurry of texts all day, bouquets arriving at my desk to the envy of all the other girls, double-checking that we were "all good," that I hadn't gone off him. Once I'd agreed to marry him the following year, I noticed little flashes of temper, episodes of rage, which he put down to the stress of organizing the wedding: "I just want to make everything perfect for you." I convinced myself he'd be calmer once I was his wife. But now I knew that "calm" when applied to Massimo only came in the context of "before the storm."

Fortunately, this morning Beryl was distracting everyone with a monologue about some woman who'd tripped into a basket of melons by the door in Aldi, and sent the whole lot rolling off down the hill outside. "It was like melon bowling, people dodging out of the way." And off she cackled, infecting me with her laughter and even Sandro, who'd crept in and was sitting listening on a bar stool. He didn't seem as shy with Beryl as he did with Anna. And then just as I'd had that thought, like some Medici queen, Anna let herself in. It did irritate me that she used her key even when I was at home. She'd barely put down her handbag before she started complaining.

"I don't know why Massimo decided to cause all this extra work. It wasn't up to you to do a party for Sam. We've got enough with the birthdays in our own family."

I wondered if she could actually see Beryl—Sam's *grandmother*—standing there or whether her self-importance blinded her to the presence of other human beings.

I was just about to leap to Sam's defense when Beryl took on the expression of a cow in a field that had happily been minding its own business before suddenly stalking in the direction of something that's caught its attention.

She started jabbing a buttery knife in Anna's direction. "Do you know what, love? I've got news for you. Sam is *your* family now, poor kid. So get used to it, get over it and stop floating about like your shit doesn't stink. You should be encouraging your sons to support each other's families, not do your best to set them at loggerheads."

Anna looked as though she had a crisp stuck in her throat, her mouth open, her eyes bulging, but no words coming out. I'd never seen anyone stand up to her before—not properly—and I had to close my own mouth to stop a cheer from escaping. I expected her to shout back, but she channeled her inner Maggie Smith, readjusted her gold bangles and said, "Beryl, no one champions my sons and their families more than me, but it simply isn't fair to let outsiders divert energy from their own children. Nico has to concentrate on Francesca and Massimo has quite enough with Sandro."

I flinched at Anna's insinuation Sandro was so problematic as to be a full-time job for Massimo, whereas clearly my contribution to parenthood was almost a hindrance. I stood, bread roll in hand, waiting to see which blow would land next. Beryl probably had a bit more practice at slanging matches with people who didn't have to overcome their natural middle-classness, prefacing everything with "I don't mean to be rude" and "Don't take this the wrong way but…" though I had absolutely no doubt Anna would be nastier.

Beryl slammed down her knife with a clatter, wiped her hands on her jumper and wobbled her way up to Anna, who was doing an excellent impression of a poplar tree.

"Look, I get it that Nico and Massimo have responsibilities to their own kids, no one's saying otherwise. But I won't have my Sam talked about like he's just an old shoe to be chucked in a cupboard until he's eighteen and they can get rid of him. You're all the same, you posh people. It ain't a limited pot of love and kindness, you know. If you're nice to Sam, it doesn't mean that there won't be nothing left over for the others."

Anna took a step back as though Beryl was a pesky baby rhino butting her with a horn. But she didn't get to reply because Massimo and Maggie came in the door.

Maggie clocked the standoff immediately. "Mum? Everything okay?"

I loved Beryl's fearlessness. She put her hands on her hips and stared directly at Anna and said, "Anna seems to think that Lara and Massimo shouldn't make so much effort because Sam is not really part of the family. I was just helping her out with my opinion."

Maggie's face dropped, but Massimo stepped in before she could speak. "Whoaaa, ladies, ladies. We're all on the same side here." He put his arm around Beryl. "You're my favorite mother-in-law by proxy. And we do consider Sam— and Maggie—family. I think Mum is just worried about Lara, because she gets so stressed about everything. Her concern comes from a place of love, doesn't it, Mum?"

Anna looked like a cobra geared up to strike but which, at the last minute, decided to coil up in the sun instead. "Of course. Perhaps Beryl misunderstood my concern. Perhaps now that dear Caitlin has gone and everyone has *moved on*, I feel someone has to remember what she would have wanted."

I watched Massimo closely. I hadn't dared even mention Caitlin in case I blurted out—or confirmed—my suspicions.

He moved away from Beryl and took his mother's arm. "I know you miss her, Mum, but no one has forgotten about her. She was very special, but so is Maggie. And Beryl."

I couldn't read him, this man of many faces. Was he saying "special" as in "I loved her and am bereft without her," or was he making the point that she was a big part of the family?

Anna burst into noisy tears, falling against Massimo's chest, sobbing in between gasps of grief, "I still can't believe she's gone, a lovely wife and mother like her, it's just so unfair."

I'd only ever seen Anna cry in a queenly manner, delicate tears dabbed away on a dainty handkerchief. I glanced at Maggie and Beryl.

Beryl was muttering, "Christ, I only came here to butter a few buns. Didn't realize I was coming to a bloody performance of the *Wailings of Winifred*."

Maggie's lips twitched but she still managed to hiss at Beryl to shut up.

Massimo steered Anna out into the garden and then we all looked at each other in silence for a minute until Beryl, wonderful, disrespectful, say-it-how-you-see-it Beryl, blurted out, "That's such a lot of bollocks. Anna didn't even like Caitlin. It was your lovely Massimo who sat with her most of the time when she was ill. Now he's a man who understands family. Proper gent he is."

The knife went loose in my hand. Either I was mad, suspicious and interpreted everything Massimo did wrongly or he was so clever no one else could see the truth.

After all these years, I wasn't sure I knew the answer.

CHAPTER TWENTY-SIX

MAGGIE

By the time Nico arrived, twenty minutes into the party, I was frazzled. Being anywhere around the Farinellis en masse, especially when Mum was there with her own special brand of problem-solving, did my bloody head in. And Anna doggedly clinging to the sainted deceased cliché about Caitlin made me want to sit her down, pull the pin on what I'd found in the attic and pop that particular grenade under her skinny little arse.

Even if I did give in to temptation one day, with a herd of kids marauding about sticking up the proverbial two fingers at my "three at a time" rule on the trampoline, today was definitely not the right moment.

Every time I turned my back the springs were groaning under a bunch of lively frogs somersaulting away, which made the idea of a neck brace look like a "when" and not "if" scenario. That was if the whole bloody tarpaulin didn't suddenly shear down the middle and dump them in a bone-busting heap. Another group were driving footballs into the shed door with relentless regularity, while one kid had fallen into the dustbin full of water, tipping it over and turning the lawn into a mudslide, much to the boys' delight. A couple of the girls who'd ignored the "come dressed in old clothes" on the invitation were now in tears by the privet hedge, having slipped over in the sludge. Sandro hovered close to them, looking as though he wished he was sitting in the local library with a book about fossils.

Nico raced in with a big hug and a "What can I do to help?" Just being able to direct him to trampoline supervision and know he wouldn't wander off after two minutes because it was too boring, compared to, say, getting pissed with his mates, improved my mood. I reminded myself to ask how Francesca had gotten on. He beamed with pride as he told me she'd come first in junior crawl. My heart softened. I was glad he'd been there to cheer her on. I'd have hated it if Sam had scored a hat-trick at a football match and I'd had to hear about it secondhand.

I congratulated her as she raced past. "Well done, Francesca! Dad tells me you beat them all by several strokes?"

"Yeah," she said, without bothering to pause as she ran down to Sam. I watched him throw a football at her head, which she ducked, then grabbed his ankles, pulling him to the grass and forcing him into a wheelbarrow. If she'd been in primary school, she'd have probably drawn her, Nico and Sam holding hands in front of a house with me standing alone by a tree. But I was so bloody delighted Sam had made a connection with a sibling, I'd have been happy to stand under a green lollipop on my own all day long.

Just as all the other boys joined in the wheelbarrowing—a chaotic tangle of shrieks and skinny limbs—the mayhem came to a halt. Massimo strode down the garden, dressed in a proper goalkeeping outfit, clapping his hands and barking out an authoritative, "Right, gather around."

I'd been trying to get their attention for the last half hour. It was still a man's world. But right now, I was glad this particular man with his child-taming abilities was here.

He ran through the rules of the splash and score game involving transferring water from one dustbin to another before shooting at the goal. "Two teams, you're the goalie for that one, Nico; I'll be the other."

Not for Massimo the "Ready, Steady, Go, let's all enjoy ourselves" approach. Oh no. He blew a whistle and launched into a stream of team encouragement that made me feel as though he was trying to cheer an Olympic marathon runner to the finish line rather than a gaggle of ten-year-olds carrying a bucket of water. "Line it up, stand back, take a run, NOT your left foot, aim past his head, try for the corner of the net..."

And there was no way he was letting a single goal past him. It was less like a bit of fun in the garden and more like he was on trial for a place in the World Cup squad. Nico, on the other hand, was falling over, deliberately missing the feeble balls rolling toward him, trickling off the toes of the girls in party dresses and sparkly sandals. "Good shot, Chloe! You had me there." "Josh! You're going to be playing for Man U at this rate!"

At the end of the game, Massimo did a quick tally. "Nico's team—three. My team—twenty-seven! What shall Nico's punishment be, guys and girls?"

There was a flurry of suggestions including "Kill him!" by some little charmer. But before Nico could move, Massimo upended the water dustbin over his head, leaving a drenched Nico spluttering. The ten-year-olds loved it, but I wasn't sure that Nico was so keen. Massimo started to wolf-whistle, and all the boys joined in, competing to see who could manage the shrillest sound, turning this posh terrace in Brighton into a jeering builders' yard.

I waited until the commotion had died down then sidled up to Nico. "Shall I nip next door and get you some dry clothes?"

He nodded. "Typical Massimo, always has to take it one step further."

Even though I would have hated to get soaked, I wanted to be married to someone who saw it as a bit of a laugh, a devil-may-care counterbalance to make up for my sourpuss. So although I was annoyed with Massimo, I was still irritated Nico didn't see the funny side.

I popped home for some clothes, resisting the temptation to sit in our lounge for ten minutes' peace and quiet, and hurried back to the party. While Nico got changed, I stood with Mum and Anna, who were managing to blow an arctic wind through the kitchen on this sunny July day. Lara was doing her best to jolly Mum along, asking her about her work with the lady who had dementia, trying to get tips for managing her dad. Mum, however, was taking the opportunity to have a dig at Anna. "I love looking after people who just need a bit of comfort at the end of their lives. You'd be amazed at how hard-hearted families can be, especially when it comes to the business end of mopping up and washing down."

Anna's nostrils were flaring, like a horse bothered by a particularly persistent wasp. The holiday in Tuscany and my glittering brainwave of inviting Mum to join us was looking nothing short of lunatic.

I caught Lara's eye and was relieved she could see the humor in the Italo-Anglo war of words. I got the sense Lara was doing a silent cheer for Beryl.

As Massimo blew his whistle again, I went out to take some photos of the obstacle course. Massimo ran through the rules: before either team could score, they had to knock either Massimo or Nico off the beam with a foam hand. Which was when I discovered that Nico possessed a secret skill—wonderful balance. In contrast, a little poke with a big foam hand was enough to send Massimo wibble-wobbling off his perch despite his tongue stuck out in concentration and his eyes trained on a point in the distance.

Nico teased him: "Need to get down to the gym, big man, work on your core muscles, gone to pot now that you've hit forty-five. You won't be able to touch your toes soon…" He followed this by standing on one leg and still resisting the onslaught of ten-year-olds who were bouncing up and down on the beam, trying to shake him off. He egged them on, doing funny little pirouettes, rotating one foot in front of him without toppling over, simultaneously punching footballs out of the way with his fist.

When Nico's team were celebrating their twentieth goal, with Massimo clambering back on for the umpteenth time, the winning kids set up a chant of "Losers, losers, losers."

I was watching Sam, laughing and thumping the air. I was torn between delight that he was having a brilliant time and a slight unease at the football hooligan thuggery of it all. I wasn't sure Sam's primary school with their "everyone's a winner on sports day" ethos would be impressed with the "learning objectives" of this particular birthday party.

Then out of the corner of my eye, I saw Massimo slip off the beam, barreling into Nico, which sent him flying backward with a dull thud. Nico cracked his head on the edge of the rockery as he fell, groaning as he landed like a pair of bellows forcing out the last gasp of air.

I shot over to him, my feet slipping on the mud in my panic.

Massimo leaped up, offering his hand to Nico. "Sorry, mate. Are you all right? I missed my footing."

Nico lay on his back, grunting, without reaching up for Massimo's hand.

The children went quiet. One of the girls giggled. Nico touched the back of his head, and looked at his fingers, which were covered in blood.

I knelt down next to him as Lara came rushing up with a tea towel and some water. Anna soon came witching out, screaming at the children to move back in a way they'd probably be recounting to their psychotherapists in later years to explain their fear of footballs.

Massimo hurried out an explanation. "I overbalanced and fell into him. He went toppling over and cracked his head. So unlucky."

Despite Anna shouting at them, the kids edged closer in horrified fascination, with variations of "Ugh!" "Yuk!" "Gross!" plus one little sod who shouted out a delighted "Wicked!"

I dabbed at Nico's cut. He'd gone pale. I stared into his eyes, which thankfully weren't rotating backward in their sockets. "Are you okay? Do you think you're concussed? Do we need to take you to hospital?"

Nico shook his head, then winced. "No, I think I'll be all right. Just need to take it easy for a minute."

I was torn between fear that he might have done himself serious damage and frantically trying to work out how we could take him to A & E when there was the small matter of thirty-five kids to keep under control for another hour.

Francesca was hovering next to him, looking as though she was holding back tears. I forced out a smile to reassure her. "Your dad's going to be fine. Just nip and get Beryl for me—I think she's in the garage wrapping up an extra pass-the-parcel."

Within moments, Mum came thumping down the garden, her flip-flops clattering. We helped Nico into a sitting position, while Lara called in the kids for food. I loved the fact that a sausage sandwich held far more interest for ninety-five percent of the people present than ascertaining whether Nico was going to live through the next half hour.

Massimo sat beside Nico, saying the same thing over and over again, "You're all right, mate. Sorry. Lost my footing. When you've recovered you can crack me one."

Anna was patting Massimo on the shoulder, "*Amore*, it was just an accident." She turned to me. "Poor Massimo, he's going to feel so awful about this. Nico always makes such a fuss about things."

I looked up at her, then back to Nico, who was gritting his teeth in pain.

Before I could answer, Mum turned to Anna. "Give the poor lad a break. He's got a nasty gash there. I've seen you make more fuss about burning your tongue on a cup of coffee. I don't think he's busted anything though. Let me take him home and see what the wound looks like once we've given it a bit of wash. Mags, you stay here with Sam."

I could have wept with gratitude that she was making things easy for me.

I squeezed Nico's hand. "Will you be all right with Mum? Or do you want me to come back with you?"

Before Nico could respond, Massimo said, "You'll be fine, won't you, Nico mate? Don't spoil the party for Sam and Maggie. You get home and I'll look after them both for you."

Deep down in my stomach was a thread of discomfort, a feeling something wasn't quite right, a vague sensation that I struggled to define. But like a five-pound note snatched out of my hand by a gust of wind, it danced and whirled just out of reach, until I had to admit defeat.

CHAPTER TWENTY-SEVEN

LARA

Beryl went off with Nico, and Maggie stayed to supervise Sam. I could see she was torn between dashing next door to check on Nico and not dumping us with the responsibility of all the kids, so I tried to persuade her to go home. But Massimo stepped in. "Nico wouldn't want you to miss out. A bit of rest and he'll be as right as rain." She was too polite to disagree but as soon as most of the parents had picked up, Maggie disappeared.

"Sorry to leave you with all the tidying up. I'll pop back when I know Nico is okay. Thank you so much though."

Massimo waved her away. "You really don't need to come back. My fault for being so clumsy; it's the least I can do."

"It was just a mistake. I'm sure he'll be fine."

"Will you ring me and let me know? Make sure you take him to the hospital if he starts being sick."

Maggie nodded and rushed off, shouting her thanks over her shoulder.

A few parents lingered, sipping the wine Massimo pressed on them despite the "just a drop, I've got to drive" protests. A handful of mothers remained, giggling at his stories, openly envious that I had a husband who got involved in children's parties, let alone one who did all the shopping and preparing of games. "You'll have to rent yourself out as a children's entertainer." "When you see Tony, you tell him that he's in charge of Louis's eleventh birthday party. You won't see him for dust!"

One mother bent down to Sandro. "Aren't you lucky to have such an amazing dad?"

Sandro shrank away from the gaze of the little crowd in the kitchen and didn't answer. After a few moments, he sidled out of the kitchen unnoticed. My heart sank. There'd be a price to pay for being too shy to speak and "making everyone think you've got the worst dad in the world!"

I busied myself sweeping up, while Massimo stood in the kitchen like a ringmaster, saying, "Excuse Lara tidying up, she's a bit OCD. She can't bear it when everywhere's a mess. Come and sit down and have a glass of champers, darling. You've worked so hard today, done a fantastic job. I'll help you clear up later." He patted the bar stool next to him.

There was a collective gasp of admiration as Massimo made a fuss about opening some more bubbles, rambling on about vintages and only the best for "my wonderful wife." Massimo was holding court, calling the women by their names, singling out their children for "brilliant ball control."

I looked at the faces turned rapt toward him. Which of these women with their diamond stud earrings and waxed eyebrows would believe he'd deliberately set out to injure his own brother?

I'd been washing my hands at the sink, tension tightening in my stomach when the chant of "loser" started up. Massimo was the competitive firstborn. He wouldn't lose to Sandro at a game of Snakes and Ladders, let alone to Nico in a football game. And certainly not with a crowd to witness the less sporty brother trouncing the mighty Massimo. I'd watched his face growing tighter, the pursing of the lips, the vigor with which he'd punched away the footballs, the fury every time he wobbled off the beam. When I saw him spring off and barge into Nico, I didn't even register shock. Just resignation that events had unfolded as I'd expected. And as soon as Nico had staggered next door and the kids were all hero-worshipping Massimo, he was his jovial self in the spotlight again.

The giggling women finally simpered out with their offspring. My relief was tempered with the knowledge that the real drama was about to begin. The moment Massimo had stopped waving from the front door, he said, "Stop sulking."

I tried to head him off. "I'm not sulking, I'm just tired. It's been a long day."

"I can see it in your face. You blame me for what happened to Nico. It was an accident. So typical of you to think I did it on purpose; you always look for the worst in everyone."

I knew not to contradict him directly. I carried on throwing paper plates and napkins into the bin. "We should probably pop next door and check that he's all right."

"Off you go then. I'll stay here and get Sandro ready for bed. I feel bad enough about what happened without all of you crowding around to point the finger."

Yes, so absolutely gutted that he'd been laughing and joking for the last two hours with the little harem from school. He was waiting for me to do what I always did and spend the evening trying to defrost him. "Cup of tea?" "Here's the paper," "You choose what you want to watch," until he'd reward me with a comment that wasn't barked out or grunted.

But, for today, I'd run out of placating. And tomorrow, I'd not only go out with Maggie driving, I'd book my test.

CHAPTER TWENTY-EIGHT

MAGGIE

The morning after the party, just swinging my legs out of bed when the alarm went off felt like I'd exhausted my energy reserves for the day. It was incredible that before I'd married Nico, I never worried a jot about how late I went to bed, more afraid of missing out on an extra laugh with my mates or an outrageous antic that would be recounted for weeks than feeling a bit knackered the next day. Now though, I'd fallen into Nico's rhythm of going to bed by ten-thirty. But the night before, we'd snuggled up watching films until late to make sure Nico wasn't concussed. It was hard to believe that a post-midnight bedtime had left me quite so done in. I could only put it down to the exertion of dealing with the Farinellis en masse, with all their outright trickiness, not to mention their hidden undercurrents.

So once I'd sent the kids off to school and tried and failed to persuade Nico to stay at home to rest, I was hoping to have a quiet morning in the attic to finish off the final garments before we left for holiday.

But Anna had other ideas. She let herself in, then stood shouting in the hallway, "Helloooo? Anyone home?"

I'd been tempted to pull up the hatch to the workshop and

hide up there with the suit jacket I was struggling to get right but in the end, I made my way down the steps. I wished I hadn't bothered. Anna launched into telling me off for "letting Nico go to work."

"But Anna, how am I going to stop a forty-year-old man driving off in his car if that's what he decides to do? He probably should have had a day at home but you know what he's like about work. He was a bit sore, but he did seem all right."

She sniffed and pursed her lips. "Massimo was so worried about Nico. He had a sleepless night over it."

I didn't know whether Anna said stuff like that to wind me up, but when I'd seen Massimo saunter out to his car that morning, he was whistling as though he'd had a fat eight-hour sleep then woken up to fresh coffee and croissants. And apart from a "You stopped seeing double yet?" text, he hadn't exactly been rushing around with the grapes and chocolates. I had a sneaking suspicion that Massimo, alpha male and sporting superstar, thought Nico had made a right old drama over nothing.

I'd just managed to shoo Anna out of the door and got my needle out again, when the doorbell rang. I considered ignoring it but I thought I'd better check it wasn't Nico on his last legs, crawling up to the front door on his hands and knees. As I peered out of the upstairs window, I could just see a glimpse of Lara's beige sundress.

I sighed. No doubt she wanted to see how Nico was. She was a worrier at the best of times: I couldn't leave her fretting away so I ran downstairs and invited her in.

She sat down for a coffee, and although she looked tired, there was a vigor, a determined energy about her that I didn't often see, a brisk "things to get on with" manner.

First on her checklist was Nico. "Has he been all right?

His color didn't look great yesterday evening. I kept getting up in the night and looking out of the window to see if both of your cars were there. I was so worried you'd have to take him to hospital." She paused. "Massimo wanted to pop around first thing, but he thought you'd be too busy getting everyone ready for school."

Personally, I thought Massimo hadn't covered himself in repentant glory but Lara's concern made up for him. To make her laugh, I told her about Anna's disapproval that I hadn't locked Nico in the bedroom.

Despite not working, Lara always seemed to have something urgent to do, things that would never make it onto my list such as trying to re-create some fancy dish Massimo had eaten on one of his trips away. So I fully expected her to dash off after fifteen minutes on some ridiculous chore such as hunting down wild Alaskan salmon, organic grass-fed beef or some other delicacy you couldn't buy down the road at the supermarket. But instead she fished about in her handbag and pulled out a piece of paper.

She looked at the floor. "I wondered if you were still happy to teach me to drive? I know I haven't seemed very enthusiastic." She paused, then waved the paper at me. "But I've booked my theory for next month and I'm hoping to be driving by October."

"Oh my god! That's brilliant! We'd better get you behind the wheel straightaway." Even if I had to sew every evening until holiday, I needed to get her in that car before she got cold feet.

Lara was grinning like a kid on Christmas Eve, as though it was something she'd been planning and plotting for ages, just when I'd decided she'd lost interest. She really was a woman of surprises. I'd always yearned to be like that, dark and mysterious, a woman who men tried to read, to get a handle on. Instead I was the straightforward backdrop to everyone else's complex and cunning ways. Maybe I just wasn't bright enough to pull off that "now you see me, now you don't," second-guess me stuff.

Whenever I told Nico my worries that he would find me boring once he'd heard all my stories, he just laughed and said, "I don't want to play games, Maggie. I *love* the fact that what you see is what you get. Stop doubting yourself. And me." And I'd feel a big buzz of contentment and resolve to stop expecting everything to go tits up. That usually lasted for a glorious half hour before Anna came bowling in with a mention of Caitlin's brilliant intellect or Francesca rushed to play on her phone when I was trying to empathize, telling her a story about when I was a teenager myself.

So the idea of taking Lara on secret little sorties in the car gave me a ridiculous amount of satisfaction as though somehow I wasn't quite the predictable "good egg" they all thought I was.

And that was the start of our cunning plan. For the last two weeks of July, we got into a routine of Lara slipping out of her back gate every morning after school dropoff. I'd pick her up from the corner of the alley and like two runaways on a road trip, we'd drive out into the countryside with the radio blaring. As soon as we reached a bit of quiet open space, we'd swap seats. And yet again, Lara surprised me. I'd expected her to be easily discouraged, to display her defeatist attitude of "I knew I'd be rubbish, I told you I wouldn't be any good." But in fact, she was a powerhouse of determination. Even when she hit the wrong pedal and almost shot into a ditch while I did my best not to scream, she didn't panic. She simply switched off the ignition and worked through every step in a logical manner before having another go. Other people's beeping and rude gestures didn't even worry her. She just laughed and sometimes said the odd "sod off" herself. It was a revelation to me that she wasn't as straitlaced as she seemed. Her occasional bad language opened the floodgates on my own swearing, which I would then sweat and fret about later on, wondering how many times I had stuck my middle finger up at the various people who tooted at us. Lara didn't seem to mind though. There was something carefree about her, as though our joint secret liberated her from something I couldn't quite pinpoint.

CHAPTER TWENTY-NINE

LARA

We were flying to Italy on the first day of August. I'd left it to the last afternoon to pack, sitting on the carpet, scratching at the pile, willing myself to open the door to our walk-in attic and find the suitcases. A single click of a buckle would release a cloud of memories from previous holidays, a rush of naïve expectations transformed into toxic accusations.

What would definitely get the holiday off to a bad start would be Massimo coming home and discovering that I was nowhere near ready, leading to one of his "Have you any idea how hard I work to keep your lazy arse in luxury?" rants. He'd already flung down Sandro's passport and said, "Don't get any ideas."

But now, with my mind scattering like a pack of rabbits hearing gunfire, it was difficult not to. So hard not to wonder what life could be like without Massimo and his moods, as variable as an unreliable thermostat. Instead, just like hundreds of times before, I squashed that train of thought and focused on anticipating every holiday need. I knew any oversight, any forgotten sunblock, hat or adapter would simply be further evidence of my "inherent stupidity."

With a sigh, I forced myself to go into our dusty attic.

As soon as I put my hands on those innocuous blue wheelie cases, a film of past holiday horrors flickered through my mind. Mosquitoes feasting on Sandro, which turned out to be my fault for contaminating the Farinelli Italian genes with my English skin. Making excuses to keep my clothes on after Massimo sneered at me in a swimsuit. Anna doing a complete about-turn on the seven o'clock bedtime, insisting on Sandro staying up till midnight—"We're in Italy now"— then leaving me to deal with the fallout the following day. Massimo losing his temper because Sandro was too shy to ask for a strawberry ice cream in Italian. Caitlin playing Scrabble, her wet hair swept up in a glamorous clasp, her skin a golden brown, while my nose peeled and my hair frizzed. Francesca butterflying up and down the pool as Sandro screamed to get out of the shallow end. Massimo refusing to eat a single forkful of pasta when it was my turn to cook, telling everyone he was feeling off color, then hissing at me afterward for my "disgusting English slop with no salt."

Scattered through the memories were little crumbs of affection, tiny grains of approval that I'd clung onto. Massimo lifting my chin, staring into my eyes and pronouncing me, "Bellissima." Pointing out the stars to me under the Tuscan sky. Gently rubbing sun cream into my shoulders, finishing with a flourish and a kiss. Picking some bougainvillea and tucking it behind my ear. But these little pinpricks of happiness were swallowed up, washed away by the unpredictable tides of Massimo's temper.

I'd just heaved everything out of the attic when Maggie knocked on the door. She wasn't as smiley as usual, definitely stressed around the edges. I felt a stab of surprise she wasn't sashaying up to the holiday with nothing more pressing to think about than choosing a tie-dye wrap.

"Can I come in for a minute?"

I stood back and waved her in, though really I wanted to block her path and crack on with packing before Massimo got home.

Her hair was even wilder than usual and her cotton smock top looked as though she'd fished it out of the bottom of the washing basket. She was twisting one of her curls around her finger, as though she was working up to saying something I might not want to hear. I scanned my mind for occasions when I might have let my guard down. Little truths she'd pieced together while I was chugging along, wondering whether to change into fourth gear. It was so hard not to confide in Maggie; she had a natural warmth, a way of making you feel she understood exactly, without any underlying arrogance that, in my position, she'd have handled it better. Her opinions didn't drill into every crevice of my insecurities in the hope of finding rich compost to take root in. Unlike the Farinellis, who assumed anyone with a different point of view just hadn't listened to their compelling arguments closely enough.

Maggie's eyes were flitting over my face, her tongue flicking to the corner of her mouth. I wanted to stop her before she could ask *that* question. If someone, anyone, asked out loud why I put up with Massimo, why I didn't leave him, even hinted that they knew he was steadily eroding who I was until all that was left was a bucket of Pavlovian yes/no/sorry responses, I didn't know whether I could continue to put on a performance of marital harmony and happiness. And if I couldn't pretend anymore, what then? The fallout from that was too horrible to contemplate.

My heart twisted at the thought of us wrestling over Sandro. Massimo would try everything to win. What if I actually had to leave Sandro behind, watching me walk—or

drive—away, the only person who could protect him, holding his breath to stop himself crying. I couldn't let that
happen.

I started to pave the way for getting rid of Maggie quickly,
before her words came out and forced me to face up to the
insanity of my life. "I'm still packing; you know how it is,
keep thinking of things to put in 'just in case,' but if I don't
concentrate and do it in the peace and quiet when the others
aren't here, then I'll end up forgetting something."

She nodded. "I won't be a moment; I just wondered if I
could ask you something."

Every bit of me wanted to put my hands over my ears and
seal out what she was about to say. But I couldn't be rude to
her, not when she'd been so kind to me. Reluctantly, I let her
into the kitchen, acutely aware of how unwelcoming the bare
walls and empty surfaces were. Since she'd been married to
Nico, she'd transformed Caitlin's kitchen into somewhere
you wanted to linger. Plants, furry cushions and bright
ceramic bowls bought by Beryl in junk shops encouraged
hidden thoughts to make their way out into the world, a comforting cave where conversation was in danger of bubbling
along, unfiltered and unjudged.

Maggie perched on one of our bar stools, twisting the
bottom of her smock. "Can I say something to you, something you won't repeat, not to anyone?"

I didn't respond, just felt myself gearing up to answer a
question that hadn't yet been asked. I prepared one of my
lines, my laughing dismissals, my casual "nothing to see
here" shrugs fermented to perfection over the years. I could
go for "That's just his sense of humor; he doesn't mean
anything by it." Or perhaps "It's his Italian blood, all that
Mediterranean passion. The Farinellis all have a bit of fire
in them. He gets over it quickly though." Or a simple blank

look and an "I didn't really notice. I'm not sure I know what you're talking about."

Maggie rubbed her eyes. "I'm sorry to dump this on you, Lara, but I'm so stressed about this holiday. Francesca has been so rude to me over the last month or so. It's bad enough when we're at home, but I just want to bawl my eyes out every time I think about her speaking to me like a piece of shit in front of Anna. And Mum won't put up with Francesca being mardy and horrible, so then she'll get involved and I'll be caught in the middle. I don't even want to go." And with that, she started crying, not the restrained hiccupping I did, but full-on sobbing.

All that adrenaline I'd been storing up to release as bemused indignation directed itself into making my legs tremble. I sat down on a stool, struggling to comprehend that Maggie with her joyful heart was even giving a second thought to what Anna might think.

I was so used to containing my own emotions, repackaging them into acceptable shapes to present to the world that it took me a moment to realize someone like Maggie might have her own demons. I must have looked absolutely astonished because Maggie stumbled on.

"Sorry, I probably shouldn't be telling you this, but I can't say anything to Nico because he's already worried out of his mind about Francesca. I know how hard it's been for her—but she just hates me."

Finally, the bit of my brain that operated without weighing up "what Massimo would say if he knew" cranked into action.

"Oh my god. I had no idea you felt like that. I've been so full of admiration for you. You've been so lovely to Sandro—he adores you—and you seemed to be handling everyone so well. Honestly, it's so hard to come into a family as close-knit as this one—it took me ages to feel comfortable with them all. But Nico adores you, and Massimo thinks you're wonderful." I concentrated on keeping the edge out of my voice. I forced a laugh. "Anna, well, we'd be a little deluded if we thought anyone could be good enough for her boys."

Maggie's shoulders relaxed slightly. "Really? I don't want to sound ungrateful, really I don't, I know how lucky I am, but I feel like I'm permanently on trial. In the beginning, I was doing okay with Francesca, but then there was all that to-do with the jewelry box."

I felt as though I had a balloon full of water that I was squashing between my hands, seeing which little pocket of rubber burst first. "She's not still going on about that, is she? It's not like you know what happened to it. It might not even have been you who threw it away."

Maggie bit her lip. "It was me."

"Really? Why?" As soon as the words were out, I wanted to run away. I couldn't find out that the only person I trusted to be on my side was a thief.

"I can't tell you why. It was for a good reason, though."

I wanted to be the judge of that, wanted to be sure my judgment wasn't so flawed, so damaged after ten years with Massimo that I could no longer spot a decent person in a slimy, putrid barrel of rotten apples. The see-saw of upper hand shifted slightly. I'd always been looking up to Maggie, in awe of her joie de vivre, her resilience, her cheeriness. But now she was turning to me for reassurance. I owed her. Her generosity—taking me out driving, finding things to love about Sandro, sorting out Lupo—had, little by little, made my life a less lonely place.

"Why can't you tell me?"

I winced as she wrapped one of her curls around her

finger so tightly I saw her skin lift up from her hairline. "It would hurt Nico. I did it to protect him. And Francesca."

Bile burned in the pit of my stomach. Maggie had obviously worked out that the box was some sort of love token that hadn't come from Nico. I felt as though I was staggering along on the deck of a ferry during a particularly nasty crossing, careering between finally obtaining proof that Massimo had had an affair with Caitlin and a desire to bury my head in the sand.

I stared at her, searching her face for any indication that she knew Massimo was involved. It was no good. I couldn't let her off the hook without finding out what she knew. "What do you mean?"

Maggie fiddled with her wedding ring. "I shouldn't have said anything. I just came across something in the box that—well, that Nico might not like." She got down from the stool. "Sorry, Lara, I shouldn't have dragged you into this. Forget it, it's not important."

I had to stop myself from grabbing her arm and screaming, "Do you know if my husband had an affair with Caitlin?" I couldn't let her disappear next door while I spent the evening wondering, staring at Massimo for clues until he snapped at me.

With a searing sense of shame, I stood up to let Maggie leave, saying, "I'm sorry you don't feel you can confide in me. I thought we were friends."

Maggie's face colored. "Lara, we are. It's not that. I don't want to burden you with a secret you're going to have to keep. You simply can't *not* keep it. It would be so devastating if it got out. I've nearly driven myself mad with it, wondering what to do."

I took a deep breath, hating myself for goading her with, "I thought you trusted me."

She was wavering, though whether it was because she didn't want to upset me or because she was desperate to unburden herself I couldn't tell. I wanted to shake her and shout, "Tell me! Tell me!"

She shook her head.

I tried again. "You don't have to worry about me telling Massimo. I never discuss anything to do with his family. None of them take kindly to outsiders sticking their oar in."

I could see in the way her face sagged that I'd pushed her over the line, that by presenting the two of us as a team, she'd given in.

In a small voice, as though she didn't quite believe what she'd seen, she said, "I think Caitlin was having an affair."

Even though I knew what was coming, I still felt a jolt of shock reverberate through my body. I mustered up as much surprise as I could, but my voice sounded tinny to my ears. "Caitlin? Who with?"

"I don't know. There was an engraving inside the box, 'All my love, P.' And lots of little notes and tickets."

"P? Who's P?" I said. Not the *M* I was expecting. I realized too late that I sounded more surprised about the initial than the revelation itself.

A glimmer of hope flickered then died, as Maggie told me what was in the box. Every comment about an opera in London, lunch at posh hotels, a concert at the O2 made me feel stupid and naïve, like the thick girl standing holding her boyfriend's drink at the party while he's kissing another girl in the car park. I'd worked alongside Massimo. I knew that he went away a lot for business, although it had ramped up after Sandro was born. But I'd never made the correlation between his stays away and Caitlin's yoga retreats or Pilates workshops. And apparently neither had Nico. But what warped mind would imagine his wife and my husband getting it together?

Weaving through my own pain was my absolute horror at what Massimo had done to his brother. Surely even Massimo couldn't dress that up as someone else's fault, couldn't slip-slide his way around the facts until we all felt sorry for him or began to think he was justified.

"Are you going to tell Nico?" I tried to sound caring and neutral. Instead my voice sounded eager, as though I was about to burst out with "Go on! Spit it out!"

Maggie chewed at her thumbnail and looked at the floor. Tears gathered along her bottom lids. "No. We can't even talk about the box without falling out. Now he just tells me to 'move on' whenever I bring the subject up. I get the impression he thinks I got rid of it in a fit of jealousy because I thought he'd given it to Caitlin. But of course I was just trying to protect them both. Or maybe he thinks I've flogged it to make a fast buck. I haven't got any proof of the affair now, anyway."

I passed her a tissue and loved her for the fact that she blew her nose so noisily, completely at odds with Anna, who thought any involuntary body function such as a sneeze or a cough signified a lack of personal discipline. Sandro had probably taken five years off her life with the sniffing he did when he was nervous.

I felt as though I was standing on the edge of a mountain, looking at the craggy mass below and resisting the irrational urge to throw myself over the edge. I wanted to encourage her to tell Nico. Grab hold of her hand and insist it was only fair, knowing it would only be a matter of time until Massimo's part in the whole sordid proceeding came to light without me having to drop him in it myself. And then they'd know what Massimo was like. No one would blame me for leaving him. I could be free.

Briefly, I entertained an image of Sandro and me in a

little flat with a view of the sea in the distance. My choice of pictures on the walls. Not having to double-check every tiny Lego block was tidied away before Massimo came home. Sandro drawing as much and for as long as he wanted, without being shipped off to judo or rugby. Never walking into a room again with my skin prickling, groping about for clues, assessing the temperature of Massimo's mood.

Instead, as always, my flirtation with the idea I could live a different life, that rush of energy, withered away. The sheer force of Massimo's denial, the relentlessness of it, would eat away at my conviction I was right. He'd sidestep any accusation, heaping grievances upon me—"Even if I did have an affair, with a wife as fat/slovenly/charmless as you, who could blame me?"—until some infected, gangrenous part of my soul believed I was lucky to have him. And then the sun would come out and once again, he'd make me feel as though I was the sexiest, most interesting woman he'd ever had the luck to meet.

Until the next time.

Maggie did a final snuffle into her tissue. "Sorry. I didn't come around to vomit up all my worries. I actually came around to ask if you would mind if Mum and I took Sandro out with Sam on the odd day while we're in Italy, to have a bit of a break from everyone. I don't want Anna to think we're ungrateful, but Mum is pretty outspoken at the best of times, and I just wanted to find an excuse for some time apart if it gets too hairy."

I nodded, seeing the relief wash over her face.

"Massimo would be okay with it, wouldn't he?"

"Yes, I'm sure he would. He's very fond of you." I was ashamed of the little stab of jealousy I'd felt when I saw Massimo put his hands on Maggie's arms at the party.

She smiled. "Thanks, Lara. I don't want to step on his

toes—he was just telling me the other day how much he was looking forward to spending time with Sandro. You can see he just wants the best for you both. The whole family actually. He's been so welcoming to me."

Maggie was right. Without proof, who would ever believe her?

Or me?

CHAPTER THIRTY

MAGGIE

As we traveled to Italy the next day, every now and again I'd feel a rush of worry. It had been bad enough holding the "Caitlin's not the perfect wife we all thought she was" secret to myself, without the additional fear that Lara might blurt it out. God knows what possessed me to tell her, though to be fair, if anyone ever walked this earth who personified zipped up and locked with a combination padlock, it was probably Lara.

As we reached the end of a long drive and drew into the castle grounds, Nico waved his arm theatrically and said, "Welcome to Castello della Limonaia!" I squeezed his hand, glad of a change of scene, away from the house in Brighton where every room felt as though it was whispering conflicting secrets to me. He kissed me on the cheek and as I leaned into him, I caught sight of Mum studying us from the backseat. I did sometimes feel like a science experiment—join together two people from different backgrounds and see whether the marriage turns into a mutant.

During the journey, I wanted to take in all of the scenery, lose myself in my dreams and the fields of sunflowers, soak up Nico's little nuggets of information: "Sunflowers in

Italian are called *girasoli*—*girare* means to turn, and *sole* is sun—because they turn their faces to the sun."

But every time he said something, I felt as though I needed to repeat it to myself, over and over again, to cement it in my brain so I'd be able to nod knowledgeably along with the rest of the family, without Anna chiming up, "But Nico has already explained that to you."

With Francesca sitting behind me, teen-ready with "You don't say it like that," I didn't even dare attempt to repeat the word out loud. I was dreading having to choose in restaurants in front of them all, the orders rolling off their tongues until it was my turn. I'd probably order a pizza fungus by mistake and have the whole restaurant in stitches. When I'd tried to discuss my worries with Nico, he'd kissed me on the nose and said, "It's a holiday, not an episode of *Mastermind*. We'll love showing the three of you around."

As soon as the car ground to a halt, Sam shot out, so excited to be abroad for the first time, that I pushed the previous day's weird scenario with Lara out of mind. She'd seemed almost nosy about what had happened with the box, full of questions, which was so unlike her. Half the time she seemed so uninterested in me—or anyone else—that I wondered if she even liked people. Maybe, like me, she was relieved Caitlin had fallen down a rather large crack. In short, she was human like the rest of us. Even Massimo had been known to feed into the "Caitlin dropped glitter wherever she glided" mythology. I made a mental note never to elevate Nico to hero status if he pegged it and I married again, though the odds of two husbands in one lifetime were slim. It really was so bloody tedious for the one that came next.

I gazed at the castle. Yet again, I was trapped between what I *should* be feeling and what I *really* felt. I'd never been to Italy before, never seen sunflowers in great golden swaths, just the puny little things Sam grew during primary school, withering at the window of Mum's dark flat. Yet part of me was still wishing that Mum, Sam and I were bouncing off to a crappy caravan, car piled high with everything from duvets to dishcloths, singing "We're All Going on a Summer Holiday" at the top of our voices.

But I managed to loosen up and crack a smile as I watched Sam shout to Sandro, "Wow! A real castle! Come on, let's explore!" He disappeared off into the gardens, Sandro trotting lightly in his wake, dodging in and out of huge terracotta urns filled with geraniums. Francesca was far too cool to look excited and slowly lowered her legs out of the car, checking her hair in the rearview mirror as she went.

Mum, on the other hand, was in the Sam camp of enthusiasm. "Didn't realize it would be a proper castle. Gawd, it's got turrets and everything. Do you think we can get up there? You'd be able to see for miles. Look, Mags, a drawbridge. You can just imagine them knights charging over that on their horses."

Nico put his arm around my shoulder. "So, Mrs. Farinelli, what do you think?"

"I think 'Wow'!" I hoped this holiday would put us back on track. In the month since Francesca trashed my workshop, Nico had steered a neutral line, condemning her behavior but stopping short of a one hundred percent conviction that I was entirely innocent of the box disappearing—"It is strange how it's just vanished though. Perhaps it'll turn up."

If there'd been a moment for telling the truth, I'd missed it. I couldn't think of a version of events that would keep Caitlin's affair covered up and provide a suitable excuse for the box's disappearance. I hoped over time we'd all just forget about it and it would pass into the realms of unexplained family mysteries, a bit similar to where missing socks ended up—mildly irritating but not interesting enough to waste any time on.

But just as I was relaxing into that tiny moment of connection with Nico, a little papering over the frightening amount of cracks that had crackle-glazed our marriage within a short space of time, we were interrupted. This time it was Massimo.

"So Maggie, how's the Italian experience so far? Living up to expectations? Let me show you the view from the ramparts; bring your mum."

I looked at Nico, who nodded and said, "Go on. I'll get Francesca to help me unload the car."

I hesitated. "Are you sure?" I wasn't used to someone else doing all the donkey work. He waved me off, laughing.

Mum was busy deadheading the geraniums in one of the urns.

Massimo put his hand on her shoulder. "Now, now, Beryl, this is a holiday for you. They have gardeners to do that, so I want to see you with your feet up and enjoying the sunshine. Come on, let's go and see the views."

I felt a rush of gratitude that Massimo was including her. Anna had sat at the airport making barbed comments such as "Of course, we've all been backward and forward on planes forever. I simply can't understand people who have no interest in travel. So parochial."

I hated her for banging on about how "parochial" we were. I tried to get my own back on her, adopting an evangelical concern for the environment, pointing out that air miles weren't something to boast about, that plane exhaust fumes kill more than ten thousand people a year.

But Mum handled her brilliantly. She laughed and sucked noisily at the straw in her milkshake. "You can be interested all you like, but if you haven't got the cash for it, then it's not going to happen. We'd all like to be swanning about, hopping on this and that plane, and I wouldn't say no to a bit of a cruise around the Mediterranean, but the reality is, I wouldn't be here now if Nico hadn't been so lovely and taken pity on his old mother-in-law."

Anna had folded her face in but I'd be keeping an eye on her in case she hadn't made the switch in her mind from Beryl, the carer/cleaner/general dogsbody, to Beryl, part of her extended family and holiday guest.

Other than Anna, all the other Farinellis had been very generous about the addition to their holiday. I'd gotten myself in such a state about telling Nico I'd invited Mum to Italy, fully prepared for a hands-up-in-horror scenario, leading to an awkward withdrawal of the ill-advised invitation. Instead he'd just hugged me and said, "Maggie, of course she's welcome. I hope she won't mind sharing with Sam." I'd blathered on about paying for her flight and cost of accommodation and probably her share of the loo paper and hand soap as well. He'd just put a finger on my lips and said, "Sshh. It's fine. Sam loves her and it will be nice for Sandro as well."

I had to stop worrying so much. I'd never had a relationship longer than a year before I met Nico. My tough times with a bloke had tended to be less "We'll work through this" and more "Suit yourself, you know where the door is." I turned my attention back to Massimo, who was still instructing Mum on how to have a proper holiday.

Mum wiped the sweat off her top lip. "Hot, isn't it? Shan't know what to do with myself. Not very good at putting my feet up, but I'll give it a go."

"Where's Lara? Will she want to see the view?" I didn't want to put up any black marks by taking over her husband at the wrong time.

Massimo waved the suggestion away, leading us through into a sunny courtyard, with faded frescoes and elaborate arches. "She's seen it all before. She likes to unpack and get settled in. We'll all come up later, but I just wanted to give my favorite new guests a little preview."

Mum nudged him. "Right old smooth talker you are, Massimo."

"I do my best, Beryl, I do my best."

Massimo called Sam over with a proper fingers-in-the-mouth, builder-up-a-scaffold wolf-whistle. I hoped some of Massimo's exuberance would rub off on Nico this holiday. I wanted to recapture that sweet spot from about a year ago when Nico's grief had dissipated enough to stop feeling guilty about falling in love with me but he wasn't yet worn down by the realities of blending two different families.

Massimo stood back to let us go ahead up a narrow set of stairs.

Sam scampered up with the boundless energy of an eleven-year-old. Mum hauled herself up by the banister. "Jeepers. These steps aren't made for old fatties like me with buggered knees."

"Would you like a push, Beryl?" Massimo asked, managing to sound both cheeky and helpful.

"Get away with you!" Mum was giggling in between wheezes.

My worries about the holiday began to dissolve. I never used to be so pessimistic but I hadn't had so much to lose before. A few steps up, I turned around to smile at Massimo, who was standing silhouetted at the bottom in the sunlight, so stereotypically Italian handsome, with his linen jacket slung over his shoulder. Yet again I wondered how Lara— who never seemed to relax completely—coexisted with a man who breezed through life, always looking for the fun and adventure. I told myself off. Better than anyone, I knew outsiders only saw a fraction of what a marriage was really like.

Massimo squeezed past us, pulling back a wrought-iron bolt and turning a key so huge it looked as though it should be hanging from the belt of a town crier. We burst out into bright sunshine, the sort that scorched your hair and made you want to shield your eyes in an exaggerated film star fashion. Down below us, fields shimmering with sunflowers, a frothy yellow sea, stretched for miles.

Massimo stood back, his arms folded, enjoying our pleasure. He put his hand on my back. "Look, if you lean out to the right slightly, you can see all the castle vineyards."

I nodded and moved away, conscious of my sweaty back under his hand. I didn't want to turn around and see him surreptitiously wiping his palms on his trousers. I started to tell Sam about how grapes grown on the vines were pressed and made into wine but he was more interested in whether they used to shoot arrows from the ramparts and blow up the neighbors with cannonballs.

"So Beryl, are you going to come down into the cellars with me later and check out some of the wines? They do a fantastic fizz."

Mum let out a big roar of laughter. "That's an offer I can't refuse!"

I glanced at Massimo, ready to be embarrassed that Mum read innuendo into everything, but he was laughing along. I was ashamed of wishing that she'd chosen something other than a vest T-shirt, which left the tops of her arms completely exposed, wobbling away with merriment. No doubt Anna would be a vision of maxi dresses and flowing shirts.

"We probably ought to go down and help Nico. I feel a bit guilty about leaving him to heave all the luggage about."

Massimo looked at me, his dark eyes teasing. "For you, Maggie, I'm sure it will be his pleasure."

I was old enough to recognize a load of flannel when I heard it. But I was still flattered.

I stepped away from him and hauled open the heavy door leading back downstairs. I beckoned Sam. "Come on. Let's go and find our rooms."

Massimo scooted in front of Mum. "Let me go first; the steps are a bit steep."

She lumbered down the stairs behind him, her feet spilling off the edges of her sandals. When we unpacked, I'd paint her toenails for her. Massimo offered his hand to help her down the last few steps.

"Aren't you just the gent? Anna's done a good job with you boys."

At that moment, Anna came clacking into the courtyard in an immaculate white T-shirt and knee-length shorts that would have made me look like I'd escaped from a bowling tournament.

"Massimo, you need to go and give Lara a hand. Sandro's seen a lizard and won't go into his room now."

Anna managed to put a slight sneer on "Sandro" and "Lara." It was no wonder the poor buggers were gibbering wrecks of underconfidence.

Massimo shrugged in a "What can you do?" sort of way.

"I'd better go and be the lizard slayer. See you later, ladies."

CHAPTER THIRTY-ONE

LARA

I watched Maggie shrugging off Anna's advice on the journey over. "Thanks, Anna, but Sam doesn't need his jumper. He gets hot really easily"; "I'm quite happy for him to play on the iPad for the whole flight"; "I know Coke is bad for his teeth but it's only now and again. Think of it as a service to keeping dentists in business."

Maggie's conviction that her way might not be perfect but it was good enough filled me with awe and envy. Anna only had to say "scarf" to me and I bundled up Sandro like an Egyptian mummy. Unlike Maggie I didn't have a mother to counterbalance Anna's certainty that I couldn't cope without her input. As soon as Sandro was born, Anna told anyone who listened, "Of course, he's a demanding baby, very fussy. And Lara's prone to worrying. It was a difficult pregnancy and I think she's passed her apprehension onto the little one. Thank goodness Massimo is so hands-on, otherwise I don't know what she would do."

I'd felt as though without one of them watching me I'd scald his throat with milk, burn his bottom at bath time, under- or overfeed him. And now, the habit had become ingrained. I could barely make a decision about whether Sandro needed a coat without asking someone else's opinion.

So when Sandro spotted the lizard, I started to explain he could have the bed furthest from the door, that we'd keep the windows shut, that lizards were friendly, a smaller version of the little creature in *How to Train Your Dragon*. But of course, Anna, next door, with her laser antennae for "Lara not coping," poked her head out, heard Sandro gathering all his tiny might for full-scale reptilian uproar and, with my words, "He'll be fine in a minute" bleating uselessly around the courtyard, she charged off to find Massimo.

Which would be the end of cajoling Sandro to do anything.

Massimo came barging in, squatting down in front of Sandro and hissing in his face, careful to keep his voice low so the others couldn't hear. "Don't you dare start making a fuss about a lizard! A bloody lizard! Have you seen how big they are compared to you? You'll be making a fuss about an ant next! You need to grow a pair, son. You will not be ruining this holiday by blubbing and whining about every little thing. Will you?"

Sandro shook his head.

"I can't hear you. Will you or will you not ruin my holiday by making a fuss about every last thing?"

I pushed down the torrent of fury that had been whirlpooling inside me since Maggie had come around and confirmed my suspicions the night before.

What Massimo did to me wasn't important anymore. But Sandro was another matter. I had to stay strong for him.

I willed him to answer as Massimo pushed his face right up close. Briefly, I eyed the wrought-iron lamp on the bedside table and imagined smashing it down on the back of Massimo's head, seeing fright in his eyes for a change. For a moment, my hand twitched by my side.

"No." Sandro's bare little twig of a response seemed to satisfy Massimo. He stood up, that pointing, stabbing forefinger relaxing back into his palm. Then, as though someone else had walked into the room, Massimo swept Sandro off his feet, swung him around and planted a big kiss on his head. "Good lad."

A dart of fear washed across Sandro's face, subsiding into relief as Massimo put him down again, sending him on his way with a pat on the back. "Off you go then. See if you can find where Sam's gotten to."

"He'll be all right once he settles in," I said, deliberately busying myself with unpacking so I wouldn't have to look at Massimo, wouldn't have to monitor the "insolence" on my face. I could feel him moving behind me. My shoulders tensed, my body braced for a jab in the kidneys or a shove into the wall.

He put his chin on my shoulder from behind, kissing my ear. "Of course he'll be fine."

For a split second, I relaxed, a brief flicker of hope flaring in me. But then he grabbed my wrist, digging in his thumb so hard my fingers went weak. I'd trained myself not to struggle. I let my body go loose; the inside of my wrists didn't usually bruise easily. I kept my eyes open but unseeing, blanking him out.

"He'll be fine because *I'm* going to take that boy in hand this holiday. I'm not having you mollycoddling him until he's scared of his own bloody shadow."

As always, I rebelled silently, clenching my free hand to my side and spilling out a furious argument in my head, congratulating him on bullying Sandro to get the result he wanted, that fantastic tried-and-tested parenting approach. But I couldn't let that retort come swashbuckling out into the air. Massimo had discovered my Achilles' heel all right. If I stood up to him, Sandro would get the brunt of it. It wasn't hard for a forty-five-year-old to get the better of a seven-year-old boy. Or apparently, a thirty-five-year-old woman.

How many times had I been sucked in? No doubt tonight, when we were in bed, he'd stroke my face, work his way slowly on top of me, murmuring some weasely excuse that I had once fallen for, some pathetic version of "I'm only like this with Sandro because it would break my heart if people thought you were a bad mother."

It would just be one among so many other excuses, those impostor sentences posing as love, but in reality nothing but hollow worms of words: "I only tell you what to wear because I want everyone to see what a beautiful wife I've got." "What you want matters to me more than anything; it's just that sometimes I make mistakes about what you want."

It would only be a short hop from there to trying to convince me he had had sex with Caitlin so he wouldn't have to bother me when I was so tired all the time.

"Or some old bollocks," as Maggie would say.

On the journey over, I'd deliberately avoided getting into conversation about what she'd told me. How could I admit—ever—what I knew and still stay with Massimo? She'd just think I was the most pathetic person who walked this planet. And maybe I was, allowing myself to be taken in, Massimo's will encroaching on me over the years, eroding my sense of self like a winter sea hammering against chalky cliffs.

But I'd wanted to be taken in. I was the one who allowed him to behave like that, smiling for the public photo then smashing the scenery when the lens cap was back on.

I'd been so proud of the surprise that flashed onto people's faces when first, I introduced my handsome Italian fiancé, and later, my gregarious husband, smug at the "She's done well for herself" marbling people's faces. How I'd loved leaving work, enjoyed the envious looks as I climbed into Massimo's waiting BMW, swept along by the man who knew which wine to order, how to get the best room in hotels, how to make an ordinary girl feel extraordinary.

And how abruptly that honeymoon had ended. The birth of Sandro snapping us out of an intensity I'd mistaken for love, his all-consuming interest in me. Fascinated by who I'd spoken to, what I said, what I was thinking, how much I loved him. Within days of Sandro's birth, it was as though a party in full swing had been shut down, the plug pulled on the electricity, leaving us paddling about on a sticky floor, knee-deep in punctured balloons and beer-soaked streamers.

I carried on unpacking, trying to banish the memories swooping out of the suitcase with everything I picked up. The T-shirt I'd been wearing when Sandro had accidentally knocked Massimo's iPhone off the table and smashed it. The maxi dress I'd sobbed into in the back of the cab coming home from his company's summer party. The flip-flops I'd been wearing as slippers when he'd locked me outside in the snow, Sandro's little palms pressed on the window.

I put the silver locket that belonged to my mother onto my bedside table, fingering the little bump where I'd had the chain soldered back together. The other furious rows blurred into each other, but I'd had to work hard to bury that particular one.

I looked out of the window onto the terra-cotta tiles of the courtyard, forcing myself to imagine the hustle and bustle of sixteenth-century castle life. But despite studying the frescoes, the lovely curves of the arches, the memory I had suffocated, depriving it of air until I could tell myself it had never happened, rose to the surface. I put the locket in the drawer. But it was too late to stop the feelings of that day reemerging.

Sandro was about four months old. I'd been up all night,

my nipples sore and cracked from the relentless routine of feed, scream, feed. Every suck of milk sent a jag of pain through me. Sandro had finally fallen asleep in the Moses basket next to the bed and I collapsed into the pillow, my head fuddled with fatigue, too terrified to drop off in case he woke up again and I'd have to drag myself from a deep dark place of utter exhaustion.

Massimo tiptoed in. Not with a cup of tea, piece of toast or even some bloody cabbage leaves. But with a complaint that we hadn't had sex for over a week, he "had his needs" and my poor leaking aching body was going to oblige. I'd barely had enough energy to turn over and pull up the duvet, muttering, "Not today, I can't."

But Massimo had had other ideas.

It astonished me now that I'd had the drive and will to resist him. As I'd struggled against him, he'd ripped off my precious locket, with the picture of my mum, the last one before she died.

My neck twinged as I recalled the chain biting into my neck. I closed my mind to the memory of Sandro waking, as Massimo tried to force himself on me. But even Massimo couldn't focus on sex against the backdrop of Sandro's screaming, the shrillness reverberating around the bedroom. He'd rolled off me. "Shut that baby up!"

He'd been sorry.

Then.

And hundreds of times since.

I'd believed him. I'd been sure deep down that Massimo loved me; that my lot in life was to support, to anchor this flawed man, to save him from himself, that without me, he'd be rudderless, alone with the demons that made him lash out at the people he loved.

But I couldn't pretend anymore. He didn't love me.

He loved himself.

And maybe he'd loved Caitlin.

The thought made me nauseous. How had I ended up telling myself some bullshit about where the box had finished up? Convincing myself that he'd decided not to give it to me because the gravy had lumps in it, there'd been a stray sock under the sofa, Sandro had refused to use the potty? Any of a million and one ridiculous reasons why the present he chose for me might not have materialized. But that was the trouble with living with someone like Massimo. Mad bad behavior became normal, until you lost sight of how people like Maggie and Nico resolved things. The idea of sitting down with Massimo and saying something honest like, "You really upset me when you . . ." just felt like a line that existed in romantic comedies, not in the unloving, unfunny tale of my life.

I hadn't asked him what happened to the gold box—or indeed any of the hundreds of other things I didn't quite grasp—because I was a coward. Far easier to absorb his unpleasantness than to challenge it.

As I walked out into the castle garden, remembering the last holiday we were all together before Caitlin died, little details came back to me, swept in on a tide of self-loathing. Caitlin and Massimo splashing about in the pool, ducking each other like flirtatious teenagers. Caitlin in her bikini showing Massimo some Pilates moves, her long fingers pressing on his stomach. "Inner core, Massimo, tuck it in." And sitting on the sun loungers side by side, their conversation low and intense, Massimo bathing Caitlin in the full beam of his attention. Not for her the refracted rays of someone else's spotlight. She was always center stage, adored by Nico and Francesca and—so it would seem—Massimo.

Had I known? Was it something else I'd forced to the

back of my mind, choosing not to see? As soon as Maggie
mentioned the contents of the box, it was as though someone had pressed down fifty switches in my head, illuminating my world and shining beams into the cobwebby recesses
where memories were smothered and stored.

I tried to imagine tackling him. Sitting at a family dinner
under the arches. Rattling my teaspoon on a glass. "Anna,
Nico, Massimo...I've got a little question to ask that hopefully one of you will be able to shed some light on..."

Maggie walked by with Nico. Everything about her was
relaxed, her movements fluid and uncensored. No makeup,
her hair flowing, frayed denim shorts. She looked every bit
as though she was off to Glastonbury. Such a contrast to
Caitlin with her crisp nautical T-shirts, her white jeans, her
sun visor perched above her ponytail. I'd never have sought
Maggie out before I met Massimo. Too scruffy, too unpol-
ished, too straightforward. Even when I had friends, I didn't
have any who didn't wear lipstick, who often used a carrier
bag instead of a handbag. And now, the very things I loved
about her meant that we could never be close friends.

I couldn't risk being tempted to tell the truth.

CHAPTER THIRTY-TWO

MAGGIE

Within a few days, I found myself getting used to the good life. I even felt the beginnings of belonging, as though I was quietly taking root, a bit like one of Nico's "easy ground-cover plants" ivying over the sharper, more resistant edges of the family boundaries. Sam seemed to be having a great time, never out of the water. Massimo was the undisputed pool games ringmaster, never running out of energy, shooting Sam up into the air like a rocket, holding a hoop for him to dive through, tipping him off the pool floats. I loved the fact that Sam finally had some decent male role models, the best of both worlds with Nico's quiet thoughtfulness and Massimo's rough-and-tumble energy. Thank God what made me happy hadn't made Sam miserable.

And I had high hopes Lara and I would cement our unlikely friendship, especially now that I'd trusted her with my big secret. That aside, since we'd been driving together, I figured that suffering the shame of sitting through several sets of traffic lights while horns blared behind entitled me to a bit of good-humored teasing. I got the sense that of all the qualities her dad had instilled in her, learning to laugh at herself wasn't in the top twenty. I'd nearly wet myself at breakfast when she'd asked me in all seriousness: "Do you think I'm letting Sandro down if I don't get him a Mandarin tutor?"

I'd just managed to rein in a "coffee out of my nose" moment. Most of my friends were more concerned about whether their kids would manage a GCSE in English. "Jesus. Sam's only just nailed saying, 'We were' instead of 'We was,' and that's only because Francesca points it out on a regular basis. We're just going to have to stick with prawn crackers and sweet and sour as far as our Chinese goes."

Lara got halfway through saying, "But Massimo thinks we need to get ahead of the game" before her face moved from offended to seeing the funny side.

"I can think of a million ways I've let Sam down—crap birth control and a feckless eejit of a father just for starters—but depriving him of learning Chinese would be a new low, even for me."

For her part, she couldn't disguise her delight at having an ally against Anna on holiday with her. I made her look amazing: I wasn't monitoring how long Sam played on the iPad to the last millisecond, I didn't ration out sweets with wartime alacrity and I didn't 'fall on the floor if Sam wore the same T-shirt complete with ice cream splodge two days in a row. Presumably not being anywhere near "as bad as Maggie" had eased the pain of not being as bloody marvelous as Caitlin.

And that was before anyone drew a physical comparison between Caitlin and me—I had no doubt she'd have been wafting about in an itsy-bitsy barely there bikini while I flubbered about in my one-piece swimsuit. The revulsion on Francesca's face every time Nico rubbed suntan lotion into my back didn't do a lot for my confidence. My fear of getting swimsuit sag and looking down to see half a squirrel of pubes hanging out was leading to a ridiculous amount of undercarriage monitoring and rearrangement.

But today, I was feeling good. I'd caught enough sun to take the blue tinge off my white limbs and the warm weather had acted like Miracle-Gro on my optimism. I took off my sarong without looking at Anna sitting there with her stomach suspended like a smooth hammock between jutting hip bones. Too much watercress and not enough Mars Bars. Next time I saw an article in the paper about why chocolate/vats of wine/sugar-covered doughnuts were good for you, I'd bring it out with a flourish. Plus one on how being thin can suck the joy out of your life and make people hate you.

However, within moments of getting into the pool, I stopped worrying about that "big bum coming through" stuff and found a childish pleasure in joining in volleyball, keepy-uppy, dodgeball. The swimming pool turned out to be a place for bonding and bridge-building. I'd often had to ride a bike when I'd run out of money for petrol, so despite being a little short-arse, my legs were perfect powerhouses for leaping up in volleyball. My school had only had a scrubby patch of waste ground masquerading as playing fields, so apart from a "sports day" once a year where there was more emphasis on sack races than sprinting, I'd never had much opportunity to find out if I was competitive. But aged thirty-five, I had a definite killer instinct for battering a ball over the net. Even Sandro joined in with "Maggie, Maggie, Maggie, Go, Go, Go" from the edge of the pool.

The unexpected spin-off was that although Francesca was still talking to me in monosyllables, her desire to win meant she wanted me on her team. When she picked me above Nico, I didn't immediately move to her side of the net in case I'd heard wrong. But as she beckoned me over, I felt all that hard-done-by feeling loosen, as though I'd taken everything far too personally.

When we beat Massimo and Nico, we high-fived and a

tiny shoot of belief that we might move forward uncurled. Even though I was still secretly replaying my spectacular winning smash in my mind, I said, "You deserve a medal! You were brilliant!"

Her face creased into a big grin, then, almost as though she'd reminded herself I was the enemy, her smile faded.

"Shame I haven't got a jewelry box to keep it in," she said, plunging into the water and disappearing off down the other end of the pool doing butterfly. So bloody Farinelli. Nothing so common for them as a bit of breaststroke or nondescript doggy-paddle.

I repeated, "Baby steps, one at a time" to myself.

Nico gave me one of those smiles I was beginning to dread, the one full of sympathy that said, "Be patient, we'll get there." I did sometimes have an overwhelming desire to sing, "There Are Worse Things I Could Do," accompanied by some chicken-wing movements and Olivia Newton-John jiving not strictly in keeping with the song.

Just occasionally I'd like him to pull her up on her bloody rudeness.

So, with this thought clouding my original hopes for a guilt-free sunny day, I didn't offer to go with Nico and Anna to the market to do the food shopping. Even though it was my turn, as marked in pink highlighter on Anna's inflexible little chores rota, I was going to rebel: sit on my sun lounger and read "one of those dreadful celebrity gossip magazines" instead of pontificating about whether tonight's dinner required a porcino mushroom, an asparagus tip or a bloody snuffle of truffle. Nor was I in the mood to appease Anna's endless fishing for compliments with arse-licky answers: "Yes, the castle is fantastic. Yes, it is a real privilege to be here. No, Sam hasn't ever traveled anywhere as lovely before."

Instead I wrapped myself in a towel, waving a cheery

good-bye, watching to see if there was a furtive dip of the
head as Anna whispered a little dig about me out of earshot.
I wasn't disappointed. I wanted to chase after them down the
cobblestones, wobble my fat thighs at her, grab my belly and
squidge it into a speaking mouth that said in a high-pitched
voice, "Go screw yourself." The temptation to thunder over
to her and tell her that even though I could do with stepping
through the doors of Slimming World, at least I was faithful
and true to her son, unlike Caitlin. I might even share the
tongue-twister I'd invented to distract myself when Anna's
Caitlin hyperbole got too much. "The pin-thin paragon of all
things Pilates with a penchant for penises."

Massimo appeared carrying a tray of beer. "Pre-lunch
tipple?"

Thank God for Massimo and his free-flowing booze. I
swore Anna had put little marks on the gin bottle in case I
had an unauthorized slurp.

Just as I was thinking the day was improving, Massimo said, "I've booked us all tickets to the open-air opera
tonight." He looked like one of the excited emojis on Francesca's phone.

I stared at him, hoping he was joking.

But no. He was serious. "What's the matter?"

"I've never been to the opera. I'm worried I won't understand it." I felt hot just thinking about sitting through two
hours with everyone else nodding along, following the story
whereas I'd probably feel like Sandro, forced to go to Mandarin lessons, unable to distinguish between the word for a
marshmallow or a mop bucket.

Massimo threw his hands up in mock horror. "Never
been to an opera! You'll love it . . . words and wisdom joined
together in perfect musical harmony. You sit next to me, I'll
help you out."

I wished I'd gone with Nico now. I was pretty sure he wouldn't be thrilled to hear the news.

I pretended I needed to cool down to escape the conversation and swam over to Mum. Massimo had managed to persuade her into the pool despite the fact that she'd never learned to swim. She sat on the steps in the shallow end, a little Buddha in blue, holding her head out of the water like a nosy ostrich. I'd let Massimo break the news of this evening's entertainment to her.

Mum kept trying to encourage Sandro in. "Aren't you hot? Why don't you put your armbands on and come and sit in here with me? I can't swim either but it's lovely here on the steps. You'll be quite safe because I'll murder anyone who gets my hair wet."

God bless Mum passing her pacifist tendencies onto the next generation. Thank God Anna wasn't there to rev up her scissors for snipping a piece out of the paper about the effect of aggressive language on children.

Sandro shook his head. He was arranging pebbles into a shape on the paving stones, sitting by Lara's sun lounger. I wondered if he minded his dad spending all of his time with Sam and Francesca.

I got out of the pool and dried myself off, intending to redress the balance a bit and see if Sandro wanted to come up onto the ramparts with me to do some drawing, while I took a few photos. The colors of the countryside, the sunflowers and poppies, had given me an idea for a floral patchwork design.

But before I could walk over there, a little altercation broke out, with Lara and Massimo talking to each other in hissy voices, the sort I used on Sam when I didn't want everyone to know I was telling him off for picking his nose. Massimo had his hands on his hips, jerking his head to the pool, then to Sandro. Not for the first time I was grateful I'd been able to bring up Sam on my own during those crucial first years. The pitying looks that I was "doing it all myself" were nothing compared to the freedom of not having to take into account someone else's views on what was good for Sam.

Lara and Sandro had exactly the same "waiting for this to be over" expressions on their faces. For someone who was so open, so out there with his thoughts and ideas, I could see why Massimo got frustrated with Lara. As much as I enjoyed her company, trying to resolve problems with her must be like shouting over a six-foot-high garden wall when you couldn't see whether the person was still listening on the other side or long gone, sipping coffee at their kitchen table while you bellowed your suggestions and solutions into oblivion. Sandro had inherited the same trait of stonewalling. I only knew he was taking in my suggestions for his art when I saw his drawings.

Sandro pushed himself slowly to his feet. Lara fussed about, putting extra air into his armbands, wetting them in the pool and forcing them up over Sandro's skinny little arms. He flinched as Sam splashed him when he was trying to tip Francesca off her float. I went over to ask them to calm it down.

Sam looked up. "Sandro's such a loser. Why does he make such a fuss about everything?"

Mum's foghorn had passed down the Parker genes to Sam.

I tried to *sshh* him but it was too late. Massimo suddenly became much more assertive, a little edge creeping into his voice.

"Right, Sandro, what we're going to do is walk down the steps in the shallow end and see if you can put your face underwater."

Lara's face was a mask of worry. I couldn't help feeling that having someone sitting on the side looking as though you were off to the electric chair wasn't quite the boost of confidence you needed when you were shitting yourself in the first place. Especially when it was a little dip in a warm pool on a sunny Tuscan day rather than an open-water swim in alligator country.

Sandro started to balk the closer to the steps he got. He hated being center stage at the best of times, but with Lara sitting there chewing on a thumbnail, Mum making well-intentioned but completely unhelpful "You don't want to be my age and still wear a rubber ring" comments, Sam and Francesca whispering and laughing together, I could see the circumstances for attempting doggy-paddle weren't aligning.

Then suddenly Massimo swept Sandro up into his arms, ran to the side and jumped in with him. Lara leaped to her feet. My brain hovered between "That's one way of doing it" and "Christ, he'll never even get in a bath again."

Sandro bobbed to the surface, with Massimo booming, "Right, now kick to the side!" But panic had overwhelmed him. He flailed about, gulping in water, sinking and surfacing, choking and coughing, until I thought Lara was going to leap in, sunglasses, sun hat and all.

I waited for Massimo to scoop him up and comfort him. I'd never known Lara to raise her voice before but in a tone that was somewhere between a scream and a bellow she was shouting: "Get him out now!"

But Massimo stood back, watching Sandro flounder about, oblivious to Lara's distress. "Go on! Kick your feet!"

It was like watching a scene from a 1960s orphanage where there was no warmth, no empathy, just a method—and a madness—applied to all children regardless of needs or personality. I kept waiting for Lara to shout at Massimo

again or failing that, chuck her sun hat on the floor, dive in
and intervene. Instead she seemed to go into a panic, flapping her hands about and looking like she was going to burst
into tears.

In the end, I couldn't bear the squelching, rasping sounds
anymore. In a minute, Sandro was going to throw up. I
jumped in. I didn't look at Massimo, didn't ask his permission. I grabbed Sandro, who flung his arms around my neck,
coughing water and crying.

I was about to apologize to Massimo for butting in when
he said, "Maggie? What do you think you're doing?" No
smile, no gentle embarrassment of "That particular teaching
technique went well."

I could barely speak through the stranglehold Sandro had
around my neck. "Sorry, but he was half-choking to death."

Massimo frowned. "I had it under control. You women
get so hysterical about nothing. That's half his problem. He's
got no backbone."

Sandro's little chest was shuddering against my shoulder.
For all Massimo's intelligence, he was pretty thick about
how to get the best out of his son. And I wasn't bowled over
by his view of women either: if there was one word guaranteed to make me search for a scythe with a particularly sharp
blade and get hacking, "hysterical" was it.

Instead of bursting in with my own insults, I tapped
into my newfound maturity. If nothing else, married life
had taught me to bite my tongue so often it was a wonder it
wasn't frilly. I tried to take the heat out of the situation. Not,
however, without a desire to look over my shoulder and wonder where the hot-headed mamma of my twenties had disappeared to. "You're brilliant with all kids, just not Sandro, but
I don't think this is doing his confidence any good. Would
you let me try with him?"

I bent my head to whisper in Sandro's ear. "Would you have a little go at swimming with me?"

Sandro nodded, his sobs slowing down to a shallow rattle.

But Massimo wasn't having any of it. "I don't want to fall out with you, Maggie, but I do know what's best for my own son."

I was just about to try another tack but hadn't bargained on Mum.

"What's the matter with you both? That poor little mite needs to get out and get over his fright. Mags, bring him over here now and me and him will go and have a walk down the village for an ice cream. That's enough of this swimming nonsense for one day. He can have another go tomorrow. I've managed to get to nearly sixty without learning and it hasn't done me any harm."

Mum got to her feet, heaving her bulk out of the water. I glanced over at Lara, who was standing on the side, her eyes darting about, rooted to the spot like a mother duck whose weakest duckling was in danger of being sucked down a weir. I felt a flash of irritation that Mum and I were doing her dirty work. There was no bloody way I'd let Nico half-drown Francesca without stepping in, let alone my own flesh and blood. Sure, not everyone had the gobby Parker attitude to life, but I couldn't ever imagine Minnie Mousing about when it came to keeping Sam safe.

Massimo stood firm and held his arms out for Sandro, who was squashing into me so hard, it would be like ripping off a plaster when I finally put him down. Just as I was debating whether I really had the guts to tell Massimo that no, I wouldn't be handing his own son over to him, Lara finally jumped in.

She swam over to us, grabbed Sandro from me with a "Come on, come to Mummy."

But Massimo wasn't going down without a fight. "No wonder women never make it to the top in business. The slightest difficulty or setback and you're running down the corridor screaming."

And then Lara really did surprise me.

"At least I don't need to bully a seven-year-old to feel good about myself."

CHAPTER THIRTY-THREE

MAGGIE

I hadn't seen Lara since the swimming pool "incident" that morning. I'd walked past her bedroom but hadn't wanted to knock in case she was having a nap with Sandro. I'd heard Massimo screech off across the gravel before lunch and had been ridiculously pleased to have an hour alone on my sun bed, dozing in the sun while the kids dived for pebbles in the pool.

With the opera starting at nine, we were having an early dinner, which delighted Mum, who thought anything later than five was eating "just before bedtime." Nico and I were at the table as instructed on the dot of six. I'd filled him in on Massimo's foray into swimming coaching and was gratified to hear him pronounce Massimo "a knob." I didn't launch into agreeing too heartily as I knew from experience the Farinellis drew up the drawbridge the second an outsider breathed a criticism.

"Honestly, I don't know what gets into him sometimes. But I also don't get why Lara doesn't put her foot down more often. I can't imagine you letting me get away with behaving like that."

I flicked him with my hand. "Too bloody right. I hope

he's not upset with me though. It was a bit tricky refusing to hand back his own son."

Nico pulled a face. "I think Massimo's got enough ego to see him through it. Anyway, let's have a drink and leave them to sort themselves out."

I sat myself down at the dining table in the castle court-yard. Nico nipped down to the wine cellar and reappeared with some sparkling Prosecco "made from the grapes in the vineyards you saw from the ramparts."

He handed me a glass and clinked his against mine.

"Where are the others? I thought we were all meeting at six?" I said.

"Relax, bride of mine. We're on Italian time."

I reached for his hand. "I'm not complaining. I'm very happy to have you to myself." I didn't add, "And hoping to be too late for the opera."

He kissed my head and sat down next to me. "And I am very happy to have you here." I listened for any reservation in his voice, any leftover residue of suspicion that I was run-ning a sideline in melting down precious metals. I could only hear tenderness. Thank God.

Lara appeared from her room with Sandro in tow. "Evening." There was something brittle in her voice, as though she'd had to steel herself to face us all. She did have a knack for approaching life as though it was a crossword of fiendish difficulty.

Nico handed her a glass of Prosecco.

I watched her take a huge gulp. I'd barely seen her take a sip of a shandy before. My Parker genes associated good times with wine, and less reliably, vodka. Or wince-makingly, Pernod. But I'd love to do a run of the optics with Lara. See what lay beneath that restrained exterior once the shot glasses were on the table.

Massimo had come back a couple of hours ago. Secretly,

I'd hoped the big row might linger on long enough for us to somehow have to stay at the castle that evening. If it was my husband, I'd be thinking up all sorts of revenge involving gardening shears and delicate anatomy for daring to call me hysterical. I wondered if Lara usually stood up to Massimo in private. It was certainly the first time I'd seen her have a go at him in public. However, if we still had to go to the blooming opera, I hoped they'd ironed it all out so we didn't have to deal with the double hell of a load of people squawking onstage as well as trying to look oblivious to the Massimo and Lara drama offstage.

Massimo had been a right dickhead but Lara could help herself by not taking motherhood quite so seriously. Sandro was a bit shy and awkward but her hovering over him every second of the day must make him feel the whole world was one giant buzzer just waiting to deliver an electric shock. Lara really did obsess over what she "should be doing." We all knew kids needed the odd grape and a few apples to stay healthy, but I was far too lazy for the "just three more peas" shenanigans. And that whole cooking from scratch thing—"Massimo wants Sandro to see preparing meals as part of his Italian heritage." All very well for him but I didn't see much evidence of Massimo farting about chopping onions and garlic and slow-simmering sauces. By the time Lara got dinner on the table, Sandro would probably have been happy to share a few dry biscuits with Lupo.

Thank God I didn't have all that cultural stuff weighing me down. I didn't rush to announce at the school gates that sometimes Sam just had chips for dinner, but that was mainly to save myself the "quinoa or die" lecture from all the mums who were competing to see which disgusting lentil/chickpea/avocado ice cream concoction they could force down their children.

I topped up her glass. "Have you been asleep this afternoon? It's been so hot, hasn't it?"

"Too hot."

Pause.

"Are you okay?" I said in an undertone, just to let her know I was on her side.

She bit her lip and looked away. "Yes, fine."

Clearly I was more like Mum than I thought, failing to see the cue to shut the fuck up even though Lara was busy putting up "Don't go there" signs as big as billboards. "Don't worry about this morning. You should see some of the dingdongs Nico and I have, right, Nico?"

He tried to make a joke. "Well, you shout and I listen and absorb your wisdom."

Lara did something funny with her mouth as though she didn't quite have the muscle tone to form a smile.

I felt a pang of disappointment. Just when I thought Lara was beginning to relax with me, she was back to her closed-off self, tightened like a jar of jam against mold-carrying spores. Couldn't even admit that she was a bit pissed off. I'd really hoped we'd built a bit of a friendship, two outsiders mounting their own little rebellion, bonding over shared secrets and the dubious joys of integrating into the Farinelli family. But I was beginning to feel duped.

Right now, rather than a newfound warmth between us, she was looking as though she'd penciled in dates on the calendar to have emotions. Wednesday three-thirty p.m.: small burst of joy when Sandro comes out of school. Thursday ten a.m.: surge of frustration at having to pick up Lego yet again. Saturday eleven p.m.: allow excitement at prospect of intercourse with gorgeous Italian husband. I wondered if she was ever spontaneous with Massimo. I couldn't imagine her banging the bedroom door shut and jumping on him out of sheer lust and love.

The air in the courtyard became more and more oppressive. She sat at the end of the table, saying things like "Let's hope the weather cools down slightly," and "The bougainvillea is quite something." The sort of "take your mind off it" stuff you might say if you were waiting to go in for a hospital scan, rather than sitting around a table hoovering up olives and wine, with a whole stretch of sunny days ahead. Sandro was drawing, occasionally whispering something to Lara. She'd become animated for a moment then slump back into silence.

Nico stepped in. "So Lara, before the dreaded opera, where should we take Maggie in San Gimignano?"

"The squares."

Nico waited for her to elaborate after she'd taken another slug of Prosecco but silence gathered around us again. I pushed back the disloyal thought that I wondered if I'd have had a bit more fun at family gatherings if Massimo was still married to Dawn. From the way Anna snorted if anyone was brave enough to mention her name, I'd gathered she was pretty feisty and more than a challenge for Anna's dictatorship. We could have formed a great little expats' army, sniper sisters covering each other's arses and gunning down Anna's pomposity.

I tried to help out Nico's valiant efforts at "the loosening up of Lara" by asking loads of questions about San Gimignano but had to stop before I got the giggles at her monosyllabic answers.

Thankfully, Mum came wheezing down the stairs looking like a tie-dye target, with a red central circle blurring out into turquoise, bright pink and yellow. We could take up holiday archery.

Nico caught my eye. "Glass of bubbles, Beryl?"

"Oh lovely, don't mind if I do, thanks."

She leaned over to Lara.

"You all right, lovey? What's with Massimo this morning? I haven't ever seen him like that," Mum said, tiptoeing around tricky subjects as usual.

"He's fine now."

I watched Lara with admiration. Before I died, I *would* master the technique of not expanding on my thoughts just because the other person had their eyebrows raised in expectation.

Mum squinted at Lara through sunglasses that made her look like a podgy John Lennon. "There's a reason I never bothered with a husband. Didn't want anyone telling me what I thought and what was right for me and Mags. To my mind, it can't be right to get a child half-frightened out of his wits, practically drowned, then call it teaching him to swim."

Nico rolled his eyes and reached for my hand. "Bloody hell, Beryl, not all husbands are the devil's spawn. Don't put Maggie off me with your scaremongering."

Mum batted him away. "Get off with you. You're not so bad as a son-in-law."

Nico laughed. "Thank God for that. Massimo's all right as well. He just gets frustrated because he's sporty himself and he finds it hard to accept that the rest of us mere mortals struggle. But we'll get you swimming like a dolphin by the end of the holiday, won't we, Sandro?"

Mum harrumphed. "Leave the poor kid alone. You'll do it when you're good and ready, won't you, lovey? But can you imagine your dad's face if you learn and surprise him at the end of the holiday? Then you could duck him under until he's spluttering and get your own back."

God knows what un-PC view on life Sandro would have after a fortnight with Mum.

Just then Massimo swept in, an expansive whirl of kisses, handshakes and hugs. He dropped a kiss onto Lara's head with a "Hello, gorgeous one. This is where you disappeared to. I was worried you'd run off with the gardener, leaving me lonely and brokenhearted."

I guessed that was Massimo's way of apologizing publicly. I admired his ability to articulate his feelings in front of everyone, even if he covered them in a veneer of humor. Yet again I found myself making a comparison between the two brothers. I wished Nico was a bit more out there. A bit of broadcasting about how the only way we'd split up would be when one of us was carried out in a wooden box might help Anna stop seeing me as an optional extra, like, say, a sunroof or satellite navigation.

Lara almost ignored him. In fact, her fingers squeezed the stem of her wineglass and she became engrossed in Sandro's drawing. She'd obviously decided she wasn't going to let him off that easily. I wanted her to forgive him. Say her piece, have a blow-up and then move on. That whole mooching about with a long face, an undercurrent of unresolved anger tightening the tension around the table, just spoiled the evening for everyone else.

But Massimo barely seemed to notice, turning his attention to us.

"See you've gotten started on the Prosecco, *salute*. Mum's making enough pasta to keep the whole of Tuscany going for a month."

He leaned over to see what Sandro was drawing. Sandro flicked his sketchbook shut.

Massimo said, "Let me have a look, buddy."

Sandro glanced at Lara, who nodded and said, "He's been drawing the castle."

Massimo lifted up the book and started leafing through

the pages. Sandro tensed, as though an invisible drawstring was pulling his features taut. He was biting his lip, desire for approval blaring out of his eyes. He was his mother's son, all right, approaching life as though it was something to endure rather than embrace.

Massimo was doing that logical bloke thing of assessing the drawing rather looking down at Sandro's eager little face and realizing that he had a chance to even the stakes a bit, shift the glittering halo of glory away from Francesca with her county freestyle medals and make up for his misjudged "swimming lesson" this morning. I wanted to thump the table until the olives jumped out of the ceramic bowls. Never mind Anna running around to their house with "research" she'd cut out of the newspaper about how bicycles harbor more bacteria than a toilet seat and giving Lara yet another thing to worry about, they could all benefit from the *Dorky Guide to Establishing a Tiny Smidge of Self-Esteem*.

I couldn't bear it. "Isn't he a great artist, Massimo? I'm always so impressed by his drawings."

A shy smile crept onto Sandro's face.

Massimo looked surprised as though he wasn't quite sure how I would know. I wanted to say, "Look, mate, if you asked anyone at all the three things they know about your son, what a brilliant artist he is would be one of them."

"Yes, he certainly is." Massimo's face flickered, as though he was preparing to move on to a far more interesting subject. I felt a stab of injustice that Massimo often went along with Nico to watch his niece compete, could talk you through every bloody detail of Francesca's winning strokes but couldn't linger on his own son's achievements for more than two seconds.

Maybe I understood Sandro more because most people dismissed my tailoring business as a jolly little hobby rather than the job I earned my living from. Just the day before, Anna had asked me how I was getting on with my "sewing project" as though I was dicking about making a summer scarf. Of course, if I had been making a summer scarf, I would have had an immediate and alternative use for it. I wasn't going to let Massimo dismiss Sandro that easily.

"Does he get his drawing talent from you?"

Massimo threw back his head and laughed. "No! I can't draw a stickman. Always been a numbers man, eye-on-the-bottom-line sort of bloke. Nico was the one faffing about with pencils, picking up leaves, smelling the flowers. I was far more interested in maths. And winning swimming competitions."

I took a slurp of Prosecco, frustration inflating inside me like a balloon. Sandro had his head down, his eyes focused on his page but his crayon wasn't moving.

Just before I gave in to my desire to let my eyes roll into the back of my head until I looked like a zombie, Massimo tapped on the pages of Sandro's sketch pad.

"If you put as much effort into learning to swim as you do into drawing castles, you could be on Team GB in a few years!"

Lara and Sandro exchanged glances. Instead of Lara giving him a little wink and reassuring smile like I would have done, she started picking at her cuticles. No wonder Sandro sidled through life, soaking up the message he was a failure. Poor kid.

Watching Sandro churn himself inside out with the weight of expectation was more than I could bear. Massimo and Lara's push-pull parenting made Mum and me look as though, with the addition of a bit more broccoli and spinach, we could star in a super-parent reality show.

It was pretty rare I was grateful for Anna's arrival but her

bustling out of the kitchen bearing a huge bowl of pasta carbonara was a welcome diversion. The enticing smell wafting
across the courtyard was enough to magic up Sam and Francesca from the depths of the garden.

Anna sat at the head of the table—where else?—and
served up trailing plates of spaghetti, while Massimo sorted
the wine, telling Mum he'd like to introduce her to a "cheeky
little number." I hated myself for even looking at Anna when
Mum cracked back, "I need all the cheeky little numbers I
can get at my age, last chance saloon before it all starts to
go south." But she reserved her real sneer for when Mum
chopped her spaghetti into little bits while Sam slurped his,
great creamy strands trailing across his chin.

Anna put her hand to her neck as though she'd swallowed
a fish bone. "*Dio mio!* That is not how you eat spaghetti.
Sam, Beryl, let me show you." She brandished her fork and,
with a dramatic flourish, dug into the pile of spaghetti and
wound it into a bite-sized bundle.

I waited to see whether Mum would rebel, but for once,
she seemed prepared to accept advice and merrily twirled
and whirled, laughing as the spaghetti dolloped off her fork
and splatted back onto her plate. Sam found it hilarious and
soon everyone was showing off their twirling abilities.

Mum leaned into Sandro. "Here, you talk me through it;
I'm not much good at this spaghetti lark."

And bless him, tongue poking out of the side of his
mouth, eyes narrowed in concentration, he showed Mum
exactly what to do, a confidence settling on him under
Mum's cheerleading.

"You're very smart to do that at your age. Look at me, I'm
fifty-nine and can't do that. Clever boy."

For the first time that evening, Lara engaged with the conversation, asking Mum, "Have you been to the opera before?"

Mum shook her head and said, "My ticket will probably be a waste of money, but Massimo tells me I'll love it, so I'm trying to keep an open mind. I can fall asleep if it's too bad."

Massimo threw his hands up. "Sacrilege, Beryl! Wash your mouth out with wine!" And took another big gulp himself.

In an undertone I said to Nico, "Isn't he supposed to be driving?"

Massimo obviously had bionic hearing and butted in before Nico could answer. "Don't be so English, Maggie! We're in Italy, the land of wine. We don't worry too much about that, as long as we're not seeing double. I've only had a glass anyway, but I'll stick with water now since you're being the wine monitor."

I was getting a bit bored with being talked down to. "There is a reason we have drink-driving laws. I think it's something to do with not killing people."

Massimo laughed as though I had the sophistication of someone who'd been born in a hamlet on a hillside. "I didn't have you down for being so law-abiding, Maggie."

I knew he was joking but I still felt like the killjoy at the party, the person going around putting the bottles in the recycling instead of opening all the cupboards to see if there was a secret stash of booze.

Thankfully Mum and Sam bulldozed through any tension by comparing how many Italian words they'd learned so far. Mum made us laugh, adamant as she was that the word for swimming pool—*piscina*—had its origins in the fact that so many people had a wee in it.

I hoped that today's clashes would be forgotten as we headed out to the cars after dinner, but Massimo made a point of telling me to go in the one Anna was driving "as she hasn't had anything to drink," trapping me between wishing

I'd never commented and treating him to a salute with my middle finger.

As soon as we arrived in San Gimignano, though, I forgot about Massimo. It was like walking onto a movie set. Fourteen towers rose up into the starry sky. I fully expected to see Spider-Man swinging from the crenelated tops.

Mum grasped my arm. "Lordy, it's like being in Hollywood. It don't look real."

Just behind us, I heard Francesca say, "Doesn't" under her breath.

I hoped Mum hadn't heard but she turned around and said, "My grammar's a shocker, isn't it? You are so lucky to speak lovely. It's too late for me, but you make sure you get Sam speaking nice like you."

Francesca had the good grace to mumble, "Sorry," and yet again, I felt a rush of affection toward Mum. I saw Anna roll her eyes when Mum said, "Pacific" when she meant "specific," but as far as I was concerned, her generous heart trumped all of Anna's pontificating about grammar as though she needed to prove her intellect was so dazzling that her grasp of English was better than any native speaker. Even though a missing "s," dropped "h" or swallowed "t" was clearly on Anna's list of top ten first-world worries, it would only ever make number twelve thousand and seventy-two on mine, way below my fear of a moth flying into my ear and dying there.

The squares thronged with kids dashing about, splashing in the fountain, grandfathers sitting on the benches in their smart trousers and white shirts, portly grandmothers waving their arms about in animated conversations that looked for all the world as though the topic in hand was a life-or-death scenario.

I walked down the cobbled street with Nico, his hand in

mine, and allowed myself to think our funny little family would be okay in the end.

We stopped at an ice cream parlor with about a hundred different flavors. Francesca explained to Mum and Sam what all the names were.

"That one, *bacio,* that means 'kiss,' it's sort of hazelnut, then that one *zuppa inglese* is 'English soup,' a bit like custard..."

As we wandered through the square, Nico and I swapping ice creams—licorice—yuk—tiramisu—yum—I felt a surge of happiness I hadn't felt since before "Boxgate." Sam and Francesca kept scooting off to look in clothes shops, trying to give Anna, who thought she was the last word on style, the slip. Mum was walking on ahead with Sandro, arm-in-arm. Every now and then he'd stop to look in a window of a ceramic shop with all the mini reproductions of San Gimignano. I looked forward to seeing his drawings later on in the week.

I'd deliberately walked off ahead of Massimo so that he couldn't spoil my evening. He was following behind with Lara, though judging by the way they were scuffing along in silence, she hadn't yet decided to forgive him. But Massimo wasn't going to let anything blight our opera experience, trotting up and chivvying us along, determined to make sure we didn't miss the start. "Honestly, nothing beats sitting under the stars with fabulous singing, surrounded by the towers. It's just magical."

I decided to offer an olive branch by showing some enthusiasm, despite wishing we could just sit and have a drink in one of the little squares.

"Remind me which one we're seeing again?"

"Debussy's *Pelléas and Mélisande.* It's about a woman married to the wrong brother." He nudged me. "You never know, you might realize that you made a duff choice."

"Oy! Cheeky sod," Nico said, pretending to throw a punch at Massimo.

Massimo ran his fingers through his hair and turned up the collar on his jacket. "Who would turn me down, suave, sporty, sophisticated?"

Nico countered with, "Yes, but I'm much kinder than you, more sensitive, more in tune with what women want."

"I'm much more manly." Massimo did a Popeye pose. "Aren't I, Lara?"

She didn't reply. I looked at her, struck by the expression on her face, as though she was about to cry or perhaps throw a tantrum. I barely heard the rest of Nico and Massimo's silly banter. I tried to work out if she was jealous: I didn't have her down as one of those women who thought everyone was after her husband. Although, to be fair, lots of women probably were floating about with their fishing rods hoping to reel Massimo in.

Nico carried on, oblivious. "But I listen; that's what a girl wants."

"I'm a sex-god though. When it comes down to it, a woman will choose a good time between the sheets over you and your cup of tea and biscuit any day. Isn't that right, Maggie?"

I tried and failed to find a way to steer the conversation in a different direction and did a noncommittal grunt.

Massimo threw his arm around Lara's shoulder, which looked about as welcoming as a strip of barbed wire. "Come on, La-La. Tell them how important it is for a man to be good at sex."

Silence.

He peered around at her. "So, what's the answer? Perhaps I've been doing it wrong all these years. We don't seem to be able to make another baby. Perhaps you need me to listen more. Maybe I'll sit opposite you while you tell me all the exciting things you've done in your day. Maybe that's the secret to getting pregnant, because nothing else has worked."

And with that, the temperature of the evening changed, catapulting us from lighthearted teasing into one of the tangled issues that creep like knotweed through the heart of any relationship, as likely to divide as bind.

Lara turned to face us, her eyes darting about, as though we'd all been whispering about her failure to provide baby number two. I'd assumed that they hadn't wanted any more children and Nico had never suggested otherwise.

Lara shrugged. "Who knows what the problem is? Just the way things are." Her voice was trembling, as though an earthquake was sending out an advance warning. She probably didn't like their personal problems being aired which, added to her fury about Massimo throwing Sandro in the pool, had combined into a cocktail of unfortunate ingredients that could only result in a bust-up.

But interesting as it would be to see what Lara was like when she lost it, I knew she'd hate a public fracas.

So I walked along wondering whether to keep quiet rather than risk making it worse. In the end, the Parker horror of silence won the day. The awkward pause while we adjusted to something private being broadcast in the middle of a bit of fun was killing me. I gave it a go. "Who wants to go back to nappies and sleepless nights and all that making up bloody bottles anyway?"

Massimo responded straightaway. "Lara breastfed for ages and loved it," which just made me feel as though somehow I'd not only insulted her, but had yet another judgment go against me for daring to suggest a baby might be bottle-fed—and survive.

Lara's face closed down. She wriggled out from under

Massimo's arm and wandered over to where Mum and Sandro were peering at a large-scale model of San Gimignano
in a nearby shop window. "Look at that. Can you see the
gates in the town walls? They used to be closed when the
people went to bed to keep the baddies out."

I bit my lip and looked at Nico, who did a "How could we
possibly have known that?" face.

Massimo didn't seem at all bothered that Lara was upset,
ushering us along and saying, "Right. Shall we go in then
and see which brother triumphs?"

CHAPTER THIRTY-FOUR

LARA

Massimo speaking so glibly about the opera, even daring to tease Nico about the fact that Maggie might fancy him summed up how smart he thought he was. Or how gormless he considered the rest of us. I'd never felt rage like it. It reminded me of a friendship cake that I'd been given, a pot of sourdough sitting on the side in the kitchen, fermenting and bubbling away, fed with sugar, flour and milk at regular intervals. Except it was injustice, jealousy and resentment stoking my anger. Usually I was so adept at disguising my feelings, putting on a face to keep the peace. But as Massimo filled in Maggie on what was happening onstage, my stomach was churning as though the sourness inside me might burrow out and gush forth in a spectacular explosion of truths, lighting up that starry sky with a firework display of expletives.

Anna was singing along, her fingers bending and stretching as she conducted an invisible orchestra. Every now and then, she'd hiss at Sam and Francesca, who were flicking little bits of torn-off program into the audience, then killing themselves laughing when people started peering around to see where the spit-covered missile had come from. Beryl kept looking at her watch and slipping toffees to Sandro. I loved her for being so totally on his side. Nico looked as though he'd fallen into a sea of memories, sitting back, his eyes flickering about the stage, as though each note, each gesture was taking him back in time. Opera had to remind him of Caitlin, the hundreds of evenings when it seeped out into the garden, filling the neighborhood with rousing notes of thwarted love, broken dreams and untimely deaths.

I hoped Nico would never have to find out what she'd done.

What Massimo had done.

I couldn't wait for the opera to be over. I wasn't alone: over half of our party displayed more animation at the final encore than at any other moment during the whole show. I tried not to feel betrayed by Maggie's enthusiasm as we walked back to the car.

"Oh my god, that was amazing! I'm not going to lie, I thought I'd be half-dead with boredom. But you were right, Massimo, the way they act almost tells you what the story is, even if you don't understand. And that lead woman's costume was incredible. I'd love to know what stones they'd used to make them sparkle like that. The music seemed a bit familiar to me, though God knows when I've ever listened to any opera."

On and on with questions and observations, like the swotty girl in the class. And Massimo at his best, the teacher, the holder of the knowledge, patiently explaining. I wanted to shake Maggie, tell her not to get sucked in, not to fall for that veneer, that layer so fine that the slightest irritation, obstacle or differing opinion would rub it away to reveal the vindictive unpleasantness beneath.

When we reached the cars, Anna waved the children away. "Nico, Beryl, Maggie, you come with me. I cannot stand their screeching anymore."

Sam and Francesca bundled into Massimo's car, with Sam demanding that Massimo put down the roof. "We'll be like James Bond!"

Sandro squeezed in next to them, pale and listless as though he should have been in bed several hours ago.

Massimo always drove hard on the accelerator and brakes, but this evening, he was testosterone in overdrive, revving through the outskirts of the town before shooting off into the countryside, swinging around the corners with Sam and Francesca egging him on. Sandro's face kept flashing up, wide-eyed and terrified in my wing mirror, his hair flying about all over the place like a demented puppet.

In the end I couldn't bear it any longer. "Slow down! Just stop it!"

Massimo shouted through to the back. "Who thinks Lara's a scaredy-cat?" Sam was shouting at Massimo to go faster, with Francesca joining in, though I thought I detected a note of fear in her voice. But Massimo was always telling her how brave she was, "tough as old boots, determined like your mother," usually followed by "unlike my great big wuss of a son." She was never going to be my ally.

I thought about my mother driving along, sticking to the speed limits, leaning forward over the steering wheel, close to the windscreen, the perfect example of "mirror, signal, maneuver." Yet she hadn't stood a chance when the truck had veered over the central reservation on the dual carriageway. Now, Massimo was breaking every rule in the book—probably over the limit, showing off, speeding—if we hit anything, we'd be thrown out of the car, smashed onto the verges like boiled eggs cracked on the top by a spoon. I begged. "Stop! Stop!" but Massimo just stepped harder on the accelerator, laughing as the tires squealed around the corners. I clung onto the door with my right hand and slipped my other one between the seats to find Sandro. His fingers grabbed mine and we hung onto each other in silent fear.

By the time we screeched up to the castle, I had wet patches under the arms of my T-shirt and cramps searing through my stomach. Anna's car wasn't home, of course. As fast as my trembling legs would move, I scooped up a tearful Sandro, running up the stone staircase to our bedroom. I tucked Sandro into his bed, smoothing his hair back from his face and feeling the pull of that dream vision of us in a little flat, where he'd never be frightened again.

Where *I'd* never be frightened again.

I got into bed quickly, hoping I might get away with pretending to be asleep. By the time Massimo decided to follow, he'd obviously had another couple of drinks. Outside in the corridor, he was full of bonhomie, doing his big-man "You need anything, anything at all, just ask" to Beryl and high-fiving Sam: "My plucky little copilot."

Once he was inside with those thick medieval walls sound-proofing his anger, he steamed about our bedroom, thumping the poles of the four-poster bed. "You made me look like a complete dick tonight. No resounding endorsement from my wife on the sex front, was there? I bet they think I can't even get it up. God, I've been so unlucky with my wives. One stupid cow who didn't want children and another who produces a kid afraid of anything and everything and then can't get pregnant again."

If I'd drawn a template of our holidays, I was sure Massimo's graph would look the same, year on year. Initial excitement at having a break from work. Rumbling irritations at having to be with everyone twenty-four/seven. Other people in the party daring to have their own needs, wants and opinions that didn't slot directly into his template for the perfect world. Renewed criticism of the traits in Sandro that he found "pathetic/spineless/whining." Frustration that Sandro wasn't more "gutsy, like Francesca." Temperature rise over trivial incident. Apologies, calm for a few days. Final blow-up, followed by charm personified and a discussion on the way home about how he considered that holiday up there among the best ones ever.

I lay rigid in the bed, ready to spring up or fight him off me if necessary. The conversations Massimo and I had were like a scene from a quiz show, where someone was trying to sing one song while a different tune was playing through the headphones. The effect was the same—a jumble of mixed messages—but with no hope of the jackpot at the end. I gathered the energy for a rebuttal. "I didn't say anything about sex. I've never discussed our sex life with anyone. You were the one who decided to broadcast the fact we couldn't have any more children."

I realized too late I'd made a mistake. One of the many. I'd dared to flop an accusatory "You were the one..." out into the airspace.

"You made me feel this big," Massimo said, shoving his thumb and forefinger together in front of my nose.

Sometimes I got away without answering and just let him rant on until he ran out of steam. But tonight, he wanted an answer. No response would satisfy him. And this evening, I couldn't make myself contrite. The smug, satisfied look on his face as he explained the plot to *Pelléas and Mélisande* was playing on a slow-moving loop in my head, against a backdrop of "You might find you're in love with the wrong brother." The words I usually used to take the heat out of the situation deserted me. I couldn't suck in my anger that it was pure luck that we'd gotten home alive. That when I'd begged him to stop, he'd taken pleasure in playing on my fear. That he'd put our son in danger, not to mention the rest of the kids.

I sat up in bed. "You bastard. You complete arsehole. My mother *died* in a car accident. My life was changed *forever* because of it. But because your stupid little ego had taken umbrage because I hadn't stood up in the streets of San Gimignano and told the whole world at the top of my voice what a great big Italian stallion you were in bed, you decided to drive like a total dickhead." Even I flinched at my language, as though someone standing behind me was shouting it on my behalf.

Massimo would probably have looked less surprised if the woman with the frilly nightie in the portrait by our bed had suddenly popped out of the picture and taken him to task.

He opened his mouth to respond, a big blue vein throbbing on the side of his head, like an earthworm slithering along below the soil surface.

Surprise at me fighting back stalled him for a moment, but his chest was rising, air was entering his lungs, ready to be expelled in an invective designed to bring me back into line. He managed to get out: "Don't you ever—"

"Ever what? Ever swear at you? Ever voice an opinion? Ever mention the small fact that you're a bloody great bully who gets off on intimidating his son until he's half-choking with fright? Look at you. The big man waving his wallet about, the jovial chap with the word for everyone."

Massimo had his hand up. "Shut up, you stupid bitch! I'd like to see where you'd be without me. Who do you think got you the promotions at work? You'd never have made it past photocopying my reports if I hadn't been pulling the strings. You'd still be living at home with your deranged dad while he drank the bathwater and ate the cat food."

A voice in my head was telling me not to make the final leap. That once it was out there, my world as I knew it would not just be shaken, but smashed to smithereens. But Massimo using my dad to taunt me acted like a battering ram against the last little stick of self-preservation.

I swung my legs out of the bed. "Don't give me that 'You'd be nowhere without me.' It's a miracle I've survived at all. Sorry if I'm not suitably grateful that the fascinating, oh so generous Massimo chose ordinary old me. But do you know what? I don't actually feel very grateful right now. I know what you did. It's taken me some time to work it out, but even 'a thick cow' like me got there in the end. And now that you've had your fun, I'm going to have mine. When I get up tomorrow morning I'm going to take your mother for a coffee. Sit her down with a nice little latte and explain to her how her precious firstborn was having an affair with her youngest son's wife."

I grounded my feet. I rubbed my lips together and swallowed, preparing to produce a scream to shatter the stained glass in the chapel below if he so much as jabbed a finger in my direction. The noise of my heart seemed to be in my ears. Energy was surging into my fingertips, all the tiny bones in my feet contracting ready for action.

He stood opposite me, chest out, fists flexing. I glanced at the door. I'd never make it. And I almost didn't care. I was suspended in that split second between release and pain, as though a boil had been lanced and relief blocked out the stinging agony that would follow. I stared at him, throwing down the challenge, trying to dam the fear already filling the void where all those feelings I'd buried had resided. I wanted to cover my head, protect my face, from those hands.

Those tender, gentle, vicious hands.

Then Massimo buckled to the floor, tears leaching down his face, dark curls clinging to his hairline in damp tendrils.

"I'm so sorry."

CHAPTER THIRTY-FIVE

LARA

I felt as though I'd been asleep for about thirty seconds when I woke up to find Sandro standing over me, hissing "Mum" and shooting frightened glances at Massimo. I hauled myself out of bed, looking at the back of Massimo's head on the pillow, the sheet obscuring his face. Would this really be the last time that I woke up next to him? All that life before, snapped off on its stalk, one random day?

I didn't have to ask what Sandro's problem was. I knew from the look on his face. Shame. Humiliation. "I'll come and help you. Let me just put some clothes on." I crept out, leaving the door ajar, my eyes watering as the early morning sunlight bounced up off the cobbles.

I wrinkled my nose as I walked into his room and started stripping the bed. "Don't worry. There's a laundry by the kitchen. I'll pop these in now and no one will know."

"Don't tell Daddy, will you? Or Sam and Francesca? They already think I'm a baby."

"Come here." I hugged him to me, closing my gritty eyes and resting my face on his head. "You'll grow out of it. It's just taking a bit longer for you. We all do things at different times—some children walk and talk long after everyone else, some stop wetting the bed late—we all get there in the end. But I wouldn't swap you for anyone in the world."

"Mum?"

"Yes?" I said, balling up the sheets.

"Why were you swearing at Daddy last night?"

"What do you mean?" I asked, my mind recoiling from the idea that Sandro had heard any of that conversation.

"I wet the bed before you'd gone to sleep but then I heard you arguing, so I didn't come in."

"Have you been sleeping in a wet bed all night?"

Sandro shrugged. "I put a towel over it."

"Were you crying?"

"Not really." His stoicism—or low expectations of life— would have finished me off if I'd had any more despair left to squeeze out.

He sat on the bed, his feet dangling over the edge. "Was it my fault you were shouting at Daddy? Because he tried to help me swim yesterday morning?"

I felt my heart leap. Sandro was already doing what I did. Rewriting history, because facing up to the truth was too brutal.

I knelt down beside him. "What Daddy did was horrible. He wasn't really trying to help you, he was trying to force you to do something you weren't ready to do. But that wasn't why I was shouting."

I hadn't rehearsed this. I hadn't even spelled it out to Massimo that I was leaving him yet, let alone worked out how to have the "Mummy's not going to live with Daddy" conversation. My thoughts were bumping about like moths in the light, blundering into so many things that would have to happen before I could consider having that talk. Number-one priority would be taking Sandro's passport out of the flight bag. Number two would be coming up with a plan for what I could do with less than twenty pounds to my name. But I—we—couldn't stay.

Sandro hugged me. "I'll be good today." He paused. I felt him take a deep breath, as though he was trying to find courage within him. "Do you think Daddy would be happy if I try to swim with Maggie?"

His shoulders grew tense under my arms.

I bent over, so he couldn't see my eyes fill. "You haven't done anything wrong; it isn't your responsibility to make us happy. Only Mummy and Daddy can make each other happy." And as I said it, I realized that neither of us appeared to have achieved that in a very long time.

My tears splashed onto the terra-cotta tiles.

Sandro fetched a towel and wiped the floor. "Don't cry, Mummy."

I tried to smile but I couldn't keep the emotions trapped inside anymore. Telling Massimo what I thought was like opening the door to an aviary. One by one, feelings that had been perched quietly pecking away, with no expectation of being released, were pouring out of the door, flapping toward freedom without being sure that they'd survive in the outside world but willing to take the risk. Anything to stop living in a cage of misery.

Sandro tapped me. "Shhh. Stop crying. It will make Daddy cross."

Yes it would. But this time I'd just have to face his anger.

I got out some clean clothes for Sandro and left him to get ready. As I walked out of his room, I looked over to the pool area. No one else was about yet. The idea of marching to the sun loungers in a couple of hours' time and clapping my hands for my little announcement seemed nowhere near as feasible as it had in the early hours of the morning.

Despite Massimo's pleading, I'd blanked his apologies,

his excuses. Of course he hadn't slept with her; it was a meeting of minds more than anything; just overfamiliarity, really; she'd listened when he'd felt despairing and alone, when I'd been unreachable, distant, wrapped up in the baby; then it had become a habit, then she'd gotten ill herself and needed him more than ever.

Bullshit.

I'd turned away from his hands reaching out for mine, reminding myself that, sooner or later, his promises would tarnish like silver candlesticks in a charity shop. He'd only cried out of fear that I'd call his bluff and show the whole family what he was really like.

I imagined calling everyone's attention. Maggie and Beryl looking up from commenting on Kate Middleton's hairstyle in *Heat* magazine. Anna scowling at the interruption to experimenting with anagrams for her cryptic crossword. Nico sitting up, slipping a bookmark into his tome about "Ideal plants for acidic soils." Everyone waiting for me to run the day's menu past them, taking into account that Francesca didn't like tomatoes, Sam didn't want any Parmesan because it smelled like sick, Nico wasn't keen on lamb unless it was very lean. Was I really going to stand there and announce that "I know this will come as a bit of a surprise to you all, but my husband, your brother, your son, has been living a lie for years. And so have the rest of us because of it…" Was I really going to watch their faces falling, like a reverse Mexican wave, dominoing around before descending into a collective pit of shock? What about Sandro?

My shoulders sagged. I hesitated before going into our bedroom. I wondered if I could get through the holiday, wait until we got home, when I could plan and prepare, without an audience.

I opened the door but remained on the threshold. Massimo

was pulling on his trousers, not a spare ounce of gut to sully his perfect physique. I tucked in my stomach out of habit, preparing myself for one of his observations, presented as general conversation but laced with hidden instructions about how I was to behave and lurking threats on what would happen if I didn't. Instead he held out his hand to me, his face drawn and anguished. I put my hands in my pockets.

"I love you, Lara. I know I can't make you stay, but please don't do anything yet."

I shook my head. "You can't love me if you behave like that. You weren't thinking about anyone except yourself."

I stepped into the room but kept my heel in the door to stop it from closing completely. Maggie and Nico were in the room over the way if he turned nasty.

"What would I have to do for you to give me a chance to make it up to you? And Sandro?"

My question, "What do you suggest?" surprised me, a distant reminder of the woman I used to be at work, negotiating, gathering information, open to other people's views rather than entrenched around my own. I'd failed to guard the last fragments of my personality before they disappeared under the onslaught of Massimo telling me who I was. I'd have to relearn independent thought.

His face cleared. "You make a list of all the things you want to change and give me till Christmas to do it."

"You've had ten years from me, Massimo. Our son wet the bed last night because you frightened him so much by throwing him in the pool, yet he's been lying in soaking sheets all night because he was too scared to wake us up because he knew you'd be angry."

Massimo ran his fingers through his hair, his curls spiraling around his face, giving him that gypsy look I'd loved so much. "I'm sorry. I've done it all wrong and now I've lost you. That age-old thing, you don't know what you've got till it's gone. Will you at least stay for the holiday?"

I wanted to say no. I wanted to pack my bag and run, run far away, where Massimo's flattery and remorse and clever words wouldn't reel me back in. I had to stop believing he would change. I stood looking at him, a million images racing through my head. Champagne glasses we'd clinked to "good health," ceramic bowls he'd thrown at the wall. Gentle kisses on the lips, harsh yanks on my arm. The way his optimism and vitality lit up a room. How his black moods wrapped themselves around us like a damp towel left outside overnight. That man who, despite everything, I'd loved. Laughed with when he hadn't made me cry. Been proud of when I wasn't ashamed. Admired when I hadn't despised him.

Before I could reach down into the swirling mud of emotions and pluck out a coherent answer, a shout disturbed the moment. "Help! Help! Someone!" I strained my ears, wondering whether it was Francesca and Sam messing about in the pool, playing one of their silly games, with one pretending to be a shark and the other the victim. But the sound grew nearer and more frantic.

I flung the door open to find Beryl puffing up from the swimming pool, her long cheesecloth skirt held high, one flip-flop missing.

"Sandro's in the pool without his armbands!"

I didn't wait to hear anything else, just started to run, the thick denim of my shorts chafing my thighs. Massimo darted out into the courtyard, sprinting toward the pool, barefoot over the gravel without pausing. I flew after him, my legs refusing to cooperate, my panic intensified by the two orange armbands side by side on the sun lounger. Massimo dived straight in, fully clothed. Sandro was underwater in the center of the pool, his sandy hair spread out like a dandelion clock, facedown but his limbs moving. Or maybe that was just the force of the water banging against his body as Massimo powered toward him. I wanted to scream but my throat was closed off. Massimo reached him, hoisted him out of the water, where Sandro flopped against his arm, his back resolutely sunburned despite my constant applying of factor fifty, a pale contrast against Massimo's dark skin.

"Massimo! Is he breathing?" My voice skidded across the surface of the pool, a wobble rather than a scream. Not hysterical as I'd imagined myself in the many disaster scenarios that haunted me in the middle of the night. Not a thrashing about, a raging, nor anything that could go under the banner of making a scene. Something worse than hysterical. A scorching fear, as though all the blood had left my body, replaced with an acid searing through the veins, closing down organs as it circulated, pooling in the final resting place of the heart, only to discover on arrival that there was nothing there, just a burned-out curl of flesh, no longer beating toward the future but grieving already for the past.

The effort of swimming with Sandro meant Massimo's voice came out as a grunt. "I don't know. Call an ambulance."

I was vaguely aware of Beryl clattering up, Maggie putting her hand on my arm. Anna bellowing instructions down the phone to the emergency services. Nico hauling Sandro out and heaving him onto the paving, leaning him on his side. Usually he seemed so light, a wisp of a boy, with barely enough substance to plow forward through life. Now, his uncooperative body was causing muscles to flex, backs to bend, the sound of physical exertion to fill the space.

Dropping to my knees, disjointed thoughts racing about—the paving stones are warm, that's good, he'll be cold—I grabbed his hand, squeezing it, trying to transmit my love, wanting him to know that I was there, desperate for him to feel the sheer force of maternal love to pull him back from wherever he'd faded away to.

Massimo began to pummel his chest. Breathing into his mouth. A strangled "Come *on*" from me. Or perhaps from Massimo. I didn't know whether the thoughts in my head were making it out into the atmosphere. Noticing the hairs on the back of Massimo's hands, the steady, strong fingers rigid against Sandro's chest, willing him back to life. Beryl's voice with nothing like its usual raucous timbre, counting the intervals, giving instructions. Registering a dragonfly skimming the surface of the water, wondering if that would be what I remembered, the rainbow of colors glittering in the sunlight as my son died.

And then, the smallest sound from Sandro. So small that I wasn't sure if it had come from him, or escaped from the bubble of terror compressing my chest. Then a violence of movement, Sandro's head jerked up and a wash of vomit spurted up Massimo's chest and trousers. He didn't flinch, didn't move. His shoulders slumped. "Thank God. Thank God."

Sandro's eyes opened. "Mummy?"

I took a breath. My lungs sucked greedily on the air as though my airways had hibernated without me noticing. "I'm here, darling. I think you fell into the pool. But Daddy saved you. You're all right now."

The distant sound of a siren, drawing closer.

Sandro blinking a few times, screwing his eyes up. His voice, hoarse as though he had tonsillitis, scraped out. "I didn't fall in, Mummy. I tried to swim to make Daddy happy."

CHAPTER THIRTY-SIX

MAGGIE

The last few days of the holiday bore no resemblance to the edgy bear-pit moments that had preceded it. Massimo displayed a tenderness with Sandro I found so moving that my eyes prickled every time I saw them together. Massimo had always been restless, a man of movement, in and out of the pool, off to the shops, poking about in the garden, finding basil and rosemary to go with lunch. Now, instead of the pool king, he was the champion of Uno tournaments, Sandro's favorite game. Both Francesca and Sam pronounced it "too silly, too young" but were soon begging to join in, drawn to the way Massimo made everything sound so much fun.

Since the near-drowning experience, Sandro had been like a flower opening under time lapse photography, a tight bud relaxing its protective layers to expose the colorful petals within.

I nudged Lara next to me on the sun bed. "Maybe some good has come out of it," I said, indicating Sandro's little face, shining with pleasure as he slapped down his last card.

She nodded. "I think it was a lesson to us all. Because he doesn't say very much, I don't think we realized how much he was absorbing. Without meaning to, we'd made him feel a failure. It's really upset Massimo because he feels responsible."

It was a testament to Lara's generosity of spirit that she hadn't felt the need to play the blame game. I hoped I wouldn't have been that person shaking my husband awake in the middle of the night to relive the horror of what nearly happened and finishing with "And it would have been all your fault!" I was still waking up myself, images of Sandro's body, lying at an unnatural angle by the pool, creeping into the nighttime hours.

God knows which emotions and pictures were on a never-ending loop in Massimo and Lara's minds. Lara kept praising Massimo's quick action—"Thank God he was there. I was just a jelly. Pathetic. I don't know whether I'd have had the strength to get him out."

"Don't underestimate yourself. Of course you would, if Massimo hadn't been there," I said.

"I'm not so sure. I would have gone to pieces completely. Thank God I never had to find out. It was partly my fault anyway. I should have been far more forceful about telling Sandro to stay away from the pool when there were no adults around. Because he was scared of the water, it never occurred to me he would go anywhere near it when I wasn't there." Her voice raised a little, emotion clouding her words.

Massimo threw down his cards and grabbed Sandro's arm, raising it above his head. "I officially proclaim you the Uno champion of Castello della Limonaia!" Sandro's face creased into a big smile.

Then Massimo knelt down by Lara and reached for her hand. "Are you all right, darling? Will you do me the honor of walking around the garden with me? Maggie, would you keep an eye on Sandro for us?"

Lara hesitated.

"Go on. I won't even blink until you come back," I said, sounding more confident than I felt. As Massimo pulled her to her feet, I felt weighed down by what seemed like a crushing responsibility of keeping three kids alive for the next half hour. I'd never been one for helicoptering around Sam as long as I knew roughly where he was, but now I felt as though I wanted to attach him to me with a pair of toddler reins. I found myself stressing about things I'd never given a hoot about before, like throwing up grapes in the air and catching them in his mouth, somersaulting off the side of the pool, swimming straight after lunch. And every time Francesca cartwheeled off the side into the pool, I had visions of her skull smashing on the concrete edge, making my heart lurch.

With a new intensity, I appreciated having a husband to share my worries with. Someone to put his hand out in the middle of the night and say, "I can feel you fidgeting. Snuggle up." Someone who didn't make me feel stupid and attention-seeking for not being able to stop crying, even when Lara and Massimo got back from the hospital with an all-clear for Sandro, Massimo barely visible behind an enormous bunch of flowers for Mum.

Despite the fact that Sandro owed his life to her raising the alarm, she'd brushed off all thanks and praise. "Get off with you! I'd have been a darned sight more useful if I'd been able to swim meself. Good job Massimo spends so much time down the gym, ran like the wind he did."

I prayed she'd be gracious about the flowers. And in deference to the seriousness of the day, the sense that our whole lives could have turned on a sixpence, she managed not to do her usual, "What a waste of money. Poor things. I prefer to see them growing in gardens rather than stuck in a vase."

But the days had definitely taken on a more mellow feel

with everyone being kind to each other. I drifted down to dinner without worrying whether Anna would pick on Mum for saying, "My most beautifullest grandson" and launch into a boring explanation about superlatives, which Mum would wave away with "Oh, who cares about superla-things. You know what I'm on about, so what does it matter?"

I called Sandro over, feeling nervous he wasn't within grabbing distance of my sun lounger. "Are you all right, lovey? What are you drawing?"

"That's the nurse who looked after me. And that's me with water coming out of my mouth."

I wondered what his teacher would make of the "show and tell" on the first day back at school: "This is a picture of me in hospital after I nearly drowned."

Time to move on. "Would you like to learn how to draw a flower? I think you'd be brilliant at it. Come on, let's go and find a good one for you."

After instructing Nico to keep his eye on the other two kids even though Francesca was a better swimmer than any of us, I took Sandro's hand and walked around the side of the castle where I'd spotted some large rosebushes. The simplicity of their flowers would be perfect. I looked up at the sky, a proper postcard blue, and thought how lucky we were that we could simply enjoy the day, fiddle about choosing a flower to draw rather than be making plans to transport a body back to England.

As we came around the corner I heard a noise, perhaps a voice. I scanned the formal gardens for any signs of life, but could only see a few stone busts and a small fountain. I pointed toward the rosebush—"Look, they're the flowers I think you could draw."

Then out of the corner of my eye, tucked inside the little summerhouse Beryl had called "that bus shelter thing" and received a proper dirty look from Anna, I saw Lara and Massimo. He was leaning toward her, holding both her hands, everything about him intense and focused, almost as though he was trying to convince her of something. That she wasn't to blame? That he wasn't? She was tucking her hair behind her ears, looking at the floor. Then Massimo pulled her into a kiss, not a little peck, but a full-on snog. I didn't wait to see any more in case Massimo had a bit of al fresco nooky planned for the afternoon.

I hurried Sandro to the other side of the garden, exclaiming that the roses looked a bit past it and perhaps a cactus would be better.

As Sandro and I inspected the plants for one with simple leaves, I wished that Nico would find little corners for us to get naughty in. Outside of the bedroom it already felt like a triumph if he held my hand. Francesca still looked as though she'd found a rancid green loaf in the bread bin if she ever caught us cuddling, which just about killed off any spontaneous touching.

And made me feel strangely envious of Lara and Massimo's little rendezvous in the summerhouse.

CHAPTER THIRTY-SEVEN

LARA

If it were possible, Sandro nearly drowning had rocked Massimo more than me. We'd clung to each other that evening, too shocked to persist in our opposing positions in our marriage, the whole Caitlin affair paling into insignificance compared with almost losing our son. My body craved the comfort of the only other person in the world who shared the same visceral love for Sandro, however imperfectly he displayed it. We fell asleep, wrung out, sandwiched against each other, unified in our relief, our rejoicing that fate hadn't chosen us to punish. Every time I moved, Massimo startled himself awake, pulling me close again.

The following morning we'd made love, passionate but gentle, a delicate exchange of emotion, a liberation from fear, a wordless preamble to a conversation we weren't yet ready for. I didn't ask myself any questions; I just gave in to channeling all that energy, that adrenaline, into a physical release without worrying about what tomorrow would look like. Massimo was tender in a way that he hadn't been in such a long time, I could no longer recall whether he ever was.

Afterward I wanted to freeze time, to keep us locked in

that moment when nothing jagged, spiteful or unexpected would hurt me again.

But far too soon the last few calm days passed and it was the roll call for Anna's traditional family photo before we drove back to the airport. Massimo's arm was tight around my shoulder as though I was a treasure to protect. In turn, the mere thought that it could all have been so different made me squeeze Sandro's hand until he squirmed free. I chased away the idea that instead of the current rabble Anna was attempting to herd into her viewfinder, we could have been gathering together a procession of devastated relatives preparing to face a painful journey home, one child short. The familiarity of Anna bossing everyone around soothed and comforted me.

"In! In! Nico, you're blocking Lara. Sam—out of the way of Sandro. Francesca, just pull your skirt down, I do want to be able to show my friends at least one photo of the whole family."

I had to smile when Maggie defended her. "Come on, Anna, she's got a lovely figure. Wouldn't look good on me, I grant you, but it is the fashion." I expected Francesca to show some sign of gratitude but her face didn't flicker. Poor Maggie really did need the patience of a saint for that particular dynamic.

When Anna was satisfied she had a photograph to rival the very best of the "Look at us with our sunset/cocktail/bikini bodies/perfect children with their violins and sporting cups" photos on Facebook, we all scattered for a last-minute sweep of the garden area for rogue sunglasses and flip-flops. Although I went through the motions, I was more worried about how close Sandro got to the pool than leaving a half-used bottle of factor fifty behind.

Massimo walked with me. "So, Mrs. Farinelli? Are you prepared to give me another chance?"

I turned to face him. I hoped this wasn't some elaborate hoax that would have me standing with my hands over Sandro's ears in two weeks' time, saying, "Shhh, Daddy's just a bit cross today." But Sandro nearly drowning had turned my grievances on their head. What if Massimo hadn't been there, the strong swimmer, the cool head to concentrate on what needed to happen instead of losing himself to panic as I had done? It was down to him that I still had a son, a family.

But maybe I was just falling back into pushover territory. I tested the water with, "I don't want to go back to how we were before. I've got to be able to express an opinion without worrying about you flying into a rage." I studied his face for a flicker, a shadow, a pursing of lips.

"I understand that," he said. "I will make it up to you, make you trust me again."

Those eyes. So sincere. He hadn't aged apart from a few flecks of gray in his fringe. Still that boyish appeal reeling me in.

"We're going to have to sit down and talk at some point, not just brush it under the carpet."

He laughed. "Can we talk and, you know…perhaps get to know each other all over again?" he said, running his hand over my breast.

I moved his hand away. "You seem so angry all the time. You always give the impression that it's us in the way of whatever would make you happy. Do you really want another chance?" If I'd flipped a coin, I wouldn't have known whether I was wishing for heads or tails—go or stay.

He pressed his lips onto mine, lingering there until I felt myself folding into him. "Does that answer your question?"

I reached into my heart where just days ago all the fragments of betrayal and bullying had resided, their sharp edges lacerating my emotions into a harsh and jagged mass around which I had no choice but to build a permanent and resilient shelter. If I pressed hard, located the exact spot, like a tooth with a hairline crack, I could feel a sore when I thought of Massimo plotting and planning with Caitlin, skipping off on weekends of opera and—whatever he said—nights of passion. But the pain was so dull in the face of the agony of nearly losing Sandro as to seem almost risible.

There'd been so many false dawns, so many times Massimo had promised to change and so many disappointments. But I'd watched him with Sandro since the pool incident. He'd been patient, encouraging, the Massimo I'd fallen in love with, not the one I'd had to endure.

It was beyond ironic that Sandro had nearly had to die before we'd woken up to what we had. It would be foolish to compound our stupidity for the sake of getting even.

"One last chance."

CHAPTER THIRTY-EIGHT

LARA

Once we were back in England, Massimo was so sunny-side up that the man who'd bent my fingers until I thought they'd snap, slept with my sister-in-law, hissed in Sandro's face until his eyes were round with fright seemed like someone I'd invented to justify my decision to leave. Since Italy, it was as though we'd both decided to appreciate the good things we shared, not fixate on the bad. For years I'd had to remind myself why we'd gotten together in the first place, questioning my judgment, my actions, my whole personality. But now, for the first time in a long time, Massimo became a source of refuge rather than a font of attack.

We were spending more time on our own, just the two of us. Beryl was always happy to babysit: "I don't want your money; it's my pleasure." But Massimo would always press a couple of twenties into her hand after we'd spent evenings reminiscing about the past and planning for the future.

"When Sandro's a bit older, let's take an extended holiday and travel around Italy." "Maybe I could look at retiring a little earlier or cutting down to four days a week, have a few long weekends, catch up on lost time."

However, after the initial euphoria that we were still

a family of three, not two, my ability to brush everything under the carpet had deserted me. I couldn't just slot back into our old lives, even if on the face of it, they looked vastly improved. Try as I might, while Massimo was waxing lyrical: "I feel like I've gotten my wife back. I hated seeing you depressed like that. I should have gotten you help sooner," I couldn't suppress the thought that he'd had an affair. And not with just anyone, with the one person guaranteed to wreak maximum damage on the whole family. Until I had a bit of clarity on that, Massimo's desire "to wipe the slate clean" was impossible.

I needed proof the person who'd frightened me wasn't real, that between us we'd fashioned an environment that had trapped him into a corner, turning him into an intimidating tyrant driven by loneliness, fear and impotence. So, buoyed by the champagne, wine and the cozy little alcove in our local Italian trattoria, I forced myself to test Massimo, to be brave enough to bring up subjects that would have sent a recent version of him into a rage.

I leaned over the table toward him. "You never did explain why you had an affair with Caitlin."

I steeled myself for a fist slamming on the table. But instead he just looked surprised, as if it was a truly odd question to be asking. He reached for my hand.

And for the first time since the holiday, I wanted to ball my hand into a fist. Fold my arms. Hear a proper explanation. The fright that had made me cling to him after Sandro's accident, the belief that everything else in life was irrelevant, was receding. A tiny seedling of rebellion and resentment was residing in the greenhouse of my marriage. My conversations with Maggie during the driving lessons I was still keeping a secret provided a cocktail of grow-faster nutrients.

Just the day before, I'd had a discussion with Maggie

about being faithful. I'd had to make a real effort not to let my jaw clang open at her honesty.

She fluttered her fingers, saying, "Don't get me wrong, I've not been an angel in my life with the men, lost count a bit, definitely run out of fingers and think Nico was probably the last toe I had left, but once you've taken that vow, that's it, isn't it? Otherwise you might as well stay single and just do your own washing."

She was right. Not about who did the washing, but that there was a contract involved. And if you didn't take your vows seriously, then what was the point?

I needed some answers. "How did it start?"

Massimo looked at the table. "It wasn't an affair like you're thinking. You were so distant after Sandro was born, like you weren't interested in me. I felt so irrelevant, and Caitlin, she was around a lot; she was the only other woman I knew really well who'd had a baby. We just overstepped the line of friendship, really."

I was relieved we were speaking more honestly than we had for years, though half of the things he told me about what had happened when Sandro was born shocked me. I'd obviously been burying it for years. It was all a blur to me now. How I'd refused to get out of bed. How Massimo rushed in from work and often found Sandro screaming in his cot. How I left him crying for hours.

I sat opposite, staring in horror. "I always thought I'd gotten up to him as soon as he made a noise. I couldn't stand for him to be distressed." I was sure we'd rowed about me being too soft, never letting him "cry it out."

"It wasn't your fault, Lara. You were probably so exhausted, you didn't hear him." Massimo squeezed my hand. "I should have asked for compassionate leave at work. I was too stuck in my ways, thinking the best thing I could do was go to work and earn money. Typical hunter-gatherer thinking. I used to dash home from work in the middle of the day to check that you were all right."

To me, the days had stretched on interminably. I didn't remember Massimo coming in at lunchtime. Maybe we'd been asleep, finally collapsed.

I did remember Anna popping in and out. She'd stay just long enough to drill it into me how many women would kill to be in my situation: "No money worries, a lovely house, a husband who adores you." She'd stand over me, readjusting Sandro's nappy, sticking her face right into my breasts to see if Sandro was latched on properly, taking off his cardigan, putting one on, never quite being happy with how I'd dressed him whatever the weather. But if I asked her to watch Sandro so that I could shower without the backdrop of screaming that made me think he'd somehow catapulted himself out of his cot, she always had an appointment at the dentist, a plumber coming, a cake in the oven.

Massimo carried on. "I wanted a family with you so much. It frightened me that you were so unhappy. I didn't know how to handle it. I was too proud to ask for help—I saw Nico and Caitlin with Francesca—the perfect huddle of three—and they made it look so easy."

I couldn't help wincing at the mention of Caitlin even though I'd asked about her. Listening to him talk about how lonely and frightened he'd felt after Sandro was born made me realize how we'd created the right circumstances for a chink in our marriage, for someone to slip in and shower him with comfort, attention and care. While I was pushing myself to the point of nervous exhaustion, pressing a glass on Sandro's limbs, seeing meningitis rashes everywhere, fretting over his refusal to eat anything that didn't come out of a jar, taking his rejection of my pureed kale and courgette personally, the proof that I was a hopeless mother, devoid of that most basic of skills—the ability to feed my baby— Massimo was helpless and isolated.

Then I thought of Maggie and what she would say if she could hear Massimo. "My heart's not bleeding for him too much! Bless him with his full night's sleep, secretary bringing him coffee and time to drink it before it's stone cold. You must be off your rocker, letting him get away with that as an excuse."

I would definitely have fallen into Maggie's "wet drip" category, the term she used for women who wouldn't walk into a pub on their own, who needed their husbands to deal with "workmen" and didn't have their own bank accounts. I'd never dared admit it was only since we'd gotten back from holiday that Massimo had given me back my bank cards instead of leaving a ten-pound note on the table for me before he went to work.

I felt a surge of rage, as though I had too much blood in my veins and it was just searching for a weak wall to burst through. Instead of relying on her own husband, Caitlin had stolen mine. Standing there in her yoga Lycra while my stomach frilled onto my knees. Giving me a lecture about the importance of making time to do pelvic floor exercises when it was all I could do to put on clean underwear. And behind my back, she was planning little trips to the opera with Massimo, dinner out, jaunts to the Ritz. The Ritz! When I was lucky to manage a piece of cold toast by two in the afternoon.

I'd looked to her for reassurance. I remembered sitting there, trying to hold in my despair that everyone thought I should be so overjoyed at having a baby. The shame that I sometimes looked into the squalling, angry mass in the Moses basket and thought longingly of Sunday morning lie-ins,

dinners in posh restaurants, dinners anywhere when I could
pick up a fork without being braced for the wail that would
signal another couple of hours of pacing and patting. I'd
looked to Caitlin, the only recent mother I knew, in my quest
for advice on how to break the pattern of feed, cry, snooze
before the whole madness-inducing cycle started again.

Caitlin simply furrowed her brow and said, "Francesca
slept through the night at eight weeks. I don't recall it being
a problem. Perhaps your milk isn't satisfying him. Maybe
better to get him on a bottle."

There was no such thing as a difficult baby, just a useless
mother. Both Caitlin and Anna wrinkled their noses in dis-
gust when I produced a dummy, scouring off another layer
of self-belief, leaving me raw, exposed and vulnerable.

Just the thought of Caitlin's hypocrisy made me want to
slam down my cutlery and stomp out of the restaurant.

"But why did it carry on for five years? I'd been okay for
a while by the time Sandro went to school. I hadn't been on
antidepressants for several years."

Massimo scraped his fork in the remains of the sauce on
his plate.

"Caitlin was ill. She needed me. It wasn't really an affair;
we just supported each other."

I wanted to stand on my chair and shout, "Anything that
took you away from me when I needed you was a bloody
affair!" But I had to hear him out. Whatever he said would
be better than the thoughts that kept crowding into my mind.

Massimo pleated and unpleated his napkin. "Nico couldn't
cope with her illness. You know what he's like. He doesn't
communicate well at the best of times. Caitlin was terrified
of dying but trying to protect Nico and Francesca. She found
it easier to talk to me. I was slightly detached."

I tried to be generous. She must have looked down the

barrel of the future with fear in her heart. God knows what it felt like to look at your child and wonder whether you'd be there, for the big events, yes, school, marriage, babies, but also the little ones—not getting invited to *the* party, the bouts of tonsillitis, the "no one loves me" days. But she was only ill for one year of a five-year affair.

I surprised myself. "I don't know whether I can forgive you."

Massimo leaned back in his chair. "I was so lonely. I missed you so much. It's not an excuse, but you'd cut yourself off from me. I know you don't believe me, but Caitlin and I didn't have sex. Yes, we held each other and comforted each other, but it wasn't physical. I needed someone to talk to, she needed someone to talk to, and we found each other." He paused. "Do you think Maggie will tell Nico?" His brow furrowed as he computed the probabilities and possibilities of disaster.

My desire to let him stew was outweighed by my respect for Maggie, bearing the burden of the knowledge, of Francesca's outrage, of the injustice of their finger-pointing, without wavering. "I'm sure she won't, and even if she did, she doesn't know it was you Caitlin was having an affair with. If she was going to say something, she'd have done it by now. Even though they're both blaming her for throwing away Caitlin's stuff, Maggie's so decent she's still protecting them from what Caitlin did." I let the "And you" hang silently, a cloud of accusation as dense as a mountain fog.

We got up to leave. Massimo paused outside the restaurant. "I've behaved terribly, let you down. I'll make it up to you for the rest of my life. But don't destroy my family."

I caught a glimpse of my expression reflected in the shop window next door: serious and determined rather than meek and passive. The woman I used to be.

I hoped I could hold onto her.

CHAPTER THIRTY-NINE

MAGGIE

Since we'd come back from Italy, Lara was like a woman possessed. I no longer had to chase her to come out driving, wondering whether she wanted to learn or whether she was doing it as a favor to me, too polite to say no. We'd fallen into a routine of driving to visit her dad two or three times a week. I'd pop in for a few minutes, he'd shake my hand and introduce himself, so solemnly and delightfully—"I'm Robert Dalton. But Margaret, you may call me Bob."

"And you, Bob, may call me Maggie."

Once, just to make conversation, I made the mistake of telling him I was teaching Lara to drive.

He stood up, shaking his head. "No. No driving. No cars," becoming more and more agitated, slapping at me with his newspaper until the nurse had to come and settle him down.

Lara was very kind about it. "Maggie, at least you come and talk to him. That's more than can be said for anyone else in the family."

He didn't seem to hold it against me though and still greeted me the next time with a handshake and gorgeous old-fashioned gentlemanly introduction. I liked to let Lara have a bit of privacy with him, so usually I'd slip off to do some sewing in the lounge. Her dad would wave me off cheerily, saying, "Who was that?" to Lara. She often tried to jog his memory with photos—sometimes I'd glance back at them, crouched over pictures of Lara as a child with her mother, Shirley. I'd see his old face soften as he peered into the photo and wonder what fog was parting in the memories in his mind. He'd start looking around: "When's Shirley coming?"

And I'd see Lara's face tighten, her expression caught between a forced smile and suppressed pain. She'd try and distract him with photos of Sandro. "Look, he likes building things, clever with his hands like you."

And then sometimes I'd see him stab at a photo. "Him. I hate him."

Lara would look puzzled. "That's Massimo, Dad. My husband. He's a good man." And then she'd get caught in explaining that yes, she had gotten married. Yes, he had been invited to the wedding.

Poor Massimo. Robert was so gentle in so many ways, it was weird that he had a downer on the one bloke who coughed up for him to live in a decent nursing home where he stood half a chance of getting his own pants back from the laundry.

As we walked out to the car, Lara always turned to wave at her dad as he stood watching her leave through the big bay window in the residents' lounge. She gave him a big grin, waving furiously as he pressed his hands against the glass. Then always crumpled into little sobs as we reached the car.

"I feel so guilty leaving him. I can't wait to pass my test so I can come whenever I want." She paused. "Not that you haven't been really generous bringing me here. I've been more times in the last few months than in the whole of the previous couple of years."

"Why don't you take him to yours one day so he can see Sandro? Mum would come and help with any nursing stuff. He's not really infirm, is he? You'd just need to keep a careful eye on him."

Her face clouded over. "I keep thinking about it, but I'm worried Massimo wouldn't be very keen. Dad can be quite difficult, though I'd love Sandro to spend some time with him. I can't really bring Sandro here because it would give him nightmares. I mean, it's all right, but there is something of the *One Flew Over the Cuckoo's Nest* about it."

Sometimes I could shake that people-pleasing "mustn't put you out" nonsense out of her. "It's your dad. If Massimo has a problem with it, perhaps you should point out he only has to see your dad a few times a year, whereas we have to put up with his old witch of a mother 365 days, 24/7."

She nodded. "You do have a point there."

Thank God my own mum was such a breeze with her retiring nature and understated opinions.

CHAPTER FORTY

LARA

I continued trying to catch Massimo out. Kept informing him of what I was doing, buying, deciding without consulting him, waiting for him to turn on me. But apart from the occasional raised eyebrow, he just hugged me and said, "Whatever makes you happy." He'd had the odd flash of temper—no one could be expected to behave perfectly all the time—but it was never aimed at me, just a rant about work, the sort of behavior I'd see from Nico, a moan about the incompetence of colleagues, a curse about the broadband going down. But for me, just praise and kindness. He'd walk up and massage my neck, bring me flowers, ladle out compliments about how I was the most attractive woman he knew. He went wild on gifts when he came back from trips—handbags, a watch, even a red and green coat, which felt a little flamboyant to me but that he thought made me look "Italian stylish."

But I couldn't relax. Couldn't quite believe the man who'd killed my cat had come back to me with all the bad parts sieved out and the gold nugget remains gathered in one place. It was as though a dandelion of distrust was lodged deep within me, scattering seeds every time I tried to tug up its insistent root.

But today I couldn't think about any of that. I needed a clear head for my driving test. I'd managed the theory, thanks to Maggie quizzing me every time we drove to see Dad, but now I had to perform for real. I'd deliberately booked for a Friday in October when I knew Massimo was away for work. I had enough trouble keeping my own self-doubt at bay without worrying about his reaction to my little surprise. As Maggie dropped me off at the test center, it was as though she could see into my brain. She had a way of staring that made me want to shrink away from her gaze, in case she could see the truths buried within me. Fear of failure, fear of change, fear of getting it wrong. Her fingers were drumming on the steering wheel.

"You're talking yourself out of it. I can see the cogs whirring. 'I won't be able to do my three-point turn.' 'Dad always told me I didn't need to learn to drive.' 'Massimo might be cross we've done it behind his back.' Come on! Do this for you, for Sandro, for your dad. It will be so good for you to have a bit of freedom. You don't want to be that person depending on other people—you're smart, you're educated, you don't have to be that little woman at home. God, if I had your brains, I'd be running for Prime Minister."

I nodded, wiping my hands on my trousers. She pulled me into a big hug. I still had to instruct myself to relax into her exuberance. I envied the way she scooped up everyone into an embrace, throwing herself on Sam, gathering up Beryl, giving Nico a cuddle when he came in from work. Just a casual "glad you're back" greeting. Not the full-on kiss Massimo favored, with its implied message of sex at its heart.

I got out of the car. "I'll give it my best shot." I clung onto my determination, forcing myself to muffle the negative voices crowding in as I stood at the desk, giving my name.

*   *   *

When I drove back into the test center, Maggie was sitting on the wall smoking, which I had only seen her do once before when she'd had too much wine. She leaped up. I tried not to look at her before I'd parked and put the handbrake on. She wanted me to pass so badly, I wouldn't have put it past her to bang on the examiner's window and press her face on the glass to see what he was writing. I leaned back in my seat while the examiner finished ticking a few boxes on his clipboard, my mind switching between potential mistakes—pulling away from a junction too slowly, not looking in the rearview mirror enough, getting too close to a cyclist. And then he said, "I'm delighted to tell you, Mrs. Farinelli, that you have passed."

If I'd been Maggie, I'd have hugged him. As it was, I put out my hand and said, "Thank you. Thank you! You've made my day!" Which for me was quite gushy.

I bounded out of the car, waving my test certificate.

Maggie chucked her cigarette on the ground, grabbed my hands and twirled me around and around in a circle like two little girls in a playground. "Get you! Bloody brilliant!"

I felt as though a door was cranking open inside me, filling a corner with pride where doubt used to reside.

"Right. First thing tomorrow morning we're going to fetch your dad and you're going to drive him back to yours so he can see Sandro."

I stopped. "We can't just turn up there and get him. They'll want some notice."

Maggie shrugged. "I rang them last week so they could prepare all his medication. I knew you'd pass."

"I thought they weren't allowed to discuss him with anyone other than family?"

Maggie laughed. "I didn't let that worry me. I just pretended to be Lara Farinelli and told them we wanted to take him out for a day," she said in a voice that was a pretty good imitation of me.

What a different life I'd have led if I'd have had half of her gall. "What if I hadn't passed?"

"I'd have fetched him for you. I've got Mum on standby to help—she'll pop around and stay as long as you need her to make sure all his meds are as they should be."

"Do you think he'll need anything special?"

"I'm quite sure seeing his grandson will be special enough."

I loved her enthusiasm, which swept me along. Massimo was away until tomorrow afternoon. I'd be able to get through the worst of settling in Dad before Massimo had to face him. By the time he got back, he'd only have to put up with Dad for a few hours.

The next morning we got up at the crack of dawn so we could fetch Dad straight after breakfast at eight o'clock before he got settled into the daily routine of the nursing home. I forgot all about Massimo when I saw Dad in the reception area, eyes bright with excitement. "Am I going home? Where's Shirley?"

I'd trained myself to block out the pain of hearing him say my mother's name with hope, with optimistic longing. Like a microscopic shard of glass lodged deep under a fingernail I'd become so used to it I hardly registered the twinge. "We're not going to your home, but we're going to see Sandro." I said his name slowly to see if that would register.

Dad frowned and started fiddling with the cuff on his jacket.

Talking to him was like trying all the switches to see which one turned the lamp on.

I tried again. "My son?"

"You have a son!"

And his old face lit up, making me indulge in a little fantasy of him sitting drawing with Sandro.

Then he noticed Maggie and we did the usual introductions, which Maggie, bless her heart, performed with aplomb as though it was the first, not the twenty-first, time she was doing them.

Maggie took hold of his arm. "You'll come with me to the car, Robert, won't you? While Lara just has a chat to the nurse?"

Dad never ceased to surprise me. "It would be my pleasure." He did a little bow.

I didn't know how Dad would react to me getting in the driving seat, but Maggie was brilliant. She sat in the back with him and started chatting about the flowers lining the driveway to the nursing home. So different from Anna. She'd last seen Dad when he was starting to get muddled, way before he didn't know who people were. Whenever he said something a little odd, she'd wave her hand and say, "I don't know what you're talking about, Robert," and my poor old dad would stand there, digging around for the right words to describe what he meant, then lapsing into silence, muttering about becoming a little forgetful these days. Yet Maggie, who'd never had the luxury of knowing my dad when he was well, instinctively knew how to steer him onto a topic of conversation he could manage.

In between reminding myself to keep my eyes on the road rather than watching them in the rearview mirror, I listened to Dad. "At my house, I've got rudbeckias like that. But best—Shirley loves them—are my hollyhocks, so dark they're almost black." So cruel he could remember the colors of flowers from my childhood but not that I had a son.

I hoped this wouldn't turn out to be a terrible mistake. Despite Maggie's bluster about how Massimo should be grateful he didn't have to put up with Dad every day of the year, my husband had never been big on surprises that weren't his own.

Maggie winked at me in the mirror as Dad started singing "Tiptoe Through the Tulips" without getting a single word wrong. Seeing him so animated, so joyful, whittled away my concerns about Massimo's reaction to Dad.

I really needed to become more like Maggie and follow her "Worry about worries when you need to worry" philosophy.

If nothing else, I'd see whether Massimo really had changed his spots.

CHAPTER FORTY-ONE

MAGGIE

There were so few moments in life when I thought, "I played that right." Mainly I looked back and thought, *What a bloody numpty. What was I thinking of?* Usually when tequila or vodka had been doing the thinking for me. Yet when Lara did a perfect bit of parallel parking and Sandro dashed over from Anna's house, skipping with pleasure at seeing Robert, I could have danced for joy.

I left Lara to settle Robert and went off to fetch Mum. By the time I got back, Sandro was teaching Lupo to give a paw to Robert, who seemed to like the feel of Lupo's coat and kept stroking him. There was a reason old people with dogs lived longer. I was delighted to see Sandro taking charge of Lupo, so far removed from that little boy who'd been cowering in the tree house. Lara was taking a video, her whole face lit with cheery anticipation as though she'd walked onto a sunny beach on the first day of a fortnight's holiday.

Mum was thrilled to be involved, fussing around Robert, singing little tunes she knew from the sixties and encouraging him to join in. I could see his mind working like a jukebox, spinning around, often failing to grab the right disc, but sometimes coming up with the goods. The atmosphere reminded me of a street party, with Mum swaying her hips and Robert croaking out "Hello, Dolly!" A bit of Union Jack bunting and some Victoria sponge and we'd be good to go.

I was just getting into the swing of it, when Nico came around, his face taut with tension.

"They've discovered a break-in at one of the storage facilities for the garden center. I need to talk to the police and give them a rundown on what's missing."

"What about Francesca's regional finals?"

"She'll be devastated if she misses them, but I'm not going to be finished with the police in time. Such a bugger that Massimo's away."

"Do you want me to take her?"

His face shifted between relief and that little giveaway flick of "How am I going to sell this to Francesca?" I was a bit tired of the do-si-do "three steps to the right!" dances we were still having to do just to keep Francesca on an even keel.

I wasn't busting to spend my Saturday driving to Portsmouth with someone pouting away next to me, so I said, "She's got two choices. Either she goes with me or she'll have to miss them."

Nico nodded. "I'll go and tell her." He kissed me. "Thank you."

I said good-bye, resentfully readjusting my expectation of a fun day with everyone else in favor of dusting down my dutiful stepmother/chauffeur cap.

Nico had obviously read the riot act because Francesca did have the good grace to thank me when I got home. It was pathetic how little watering I needed. "Shall I make you some eggs to give you a bit of energy?"

She shook her head. "No, I've had some Nutella."

I raised my eyebrows at Nico, telepathically transmitting my "That won't keep her going beyond the first five strokes," but he shrugged and said, "Take a banana with you." I knew there was no point in trying to reason with her.

I asked Sam if he wanted to come with us, in the vain hope he might fancy a two-hour round trip to Portsmouth but he laughed and said, "Why would I want to do that? I'd rather stay here with Nan."

When we got into the car, it was a bit like being on a first date with someone who'd already decided you were too fat, too ugly or too boring, but had made the mistake of signing up to a seven-course meal.

I made an effort anyway. "Do you want to tune the radio into a station you like?"

I swear she'd never listened to heavy metal in her life. But there we sat, in radio purgatory until we passed the A3 when the signal got so poor I just tuned into Radio Two. In between times, I asked her questions, questions I already knew the answers to, valiantly trying to create the illusion there was a fragment of a relationship there, she had some connection to me, something we could build on.

"Are you nervous?"

"Not really."

"Which is your favorite race?"

"Crawl."

"Isn't that the stroke Uncle Massimo won the Regional Championship with?"

"Yep. But that was in, like, 1986."

Then the radio would fill the silence and I'd remind myself not to sing. Francesca never felt any need to fill the quiet enveloping the car. I wondered if it was because she didn't think I had anything worth saying. Or because she didn't know what to ask me. Or whether I was so far down on her list of things to think about, it simply didn't occur to her to waste five seconds on making me feel comfortable.

Just before we got out of the car, I said, "Will you know many people there?"

"What do you mean?" she asked, as though I was trying to catch her out.

"Other competitors, their parents, coaches, supporters?"

"There'll probably be a few people I know from the county championships. Why?"

"I just wondered how you wanted me to introduce myself? As a friend? Your dad's wife? Your stepmother?" There was a pause. I tried to make a joke. "Perhaps stepmother sounds a bit 'Come on, dearie, have a nice bite of the apple.'"

Francesca looked at me as though she thought I might try and hold her hand or kiss her good-bye. She shrugged. "I don't know. Anyway, I've got to go and get changed." And she scooted off, leaving me trailing behind.

The trouble was, I didn't know either. Despite my best intentions, Nico and Francesca were falling onto one side of the Farinelli fence, with Sam happy in either camp and me left isolated on my own.

I followed the crowds and settled myself into the viewing gallery. Everywhere I looked there were parents with clipboards and stopwatches. Nothing about them said, "Just thought I'd pop along and see how little Johnny is getting on with his breaststroke." The heat was stifling. By the time Francesca came out, my back was prickling with sweat. But as soon as she started to line up, I couldn't take my eyes off her. Her face was so determined, filled with that same concentration I saw on Nico when he was assessing which particular element of the garden wasn't working. The same look Massimo had when he was trying to teach Sandro to throw a rugby ball.

When the whistle went, Francesca shot off the block and powered her way down the pool. Suddenly I wanted her to win so badly, my biceps were flexing in time with every stroke. For most of the length she was neck and neck with another girl. I wished excruciating cramps on her competitor. Then Francesca edged half a body length ahead. I couldn't sit still. The crowd around me was starting to cheer and rumble, various names being bandied about, "Go on, Katie!" "Come on, Olivia!" I couldn't hear anyone shouting for Francesca. I ran down to the front, leaning over the barrier. "Get a move on, Francesca! She's catching up to you. Come ONNNN!"

Francesca slipped into second place at the turn. I bloody hoped she never made it to the Olympics; I'd end up in an early grave.

I cheered and shouted her name, willing her on. God, this was more nerve-wracking than the Grand National when Mum had bet the rent on it and won.

There must have been about ten strokes left when she suddenly found another gear and touched the side first, maybe just by a nail-length but definitely first.

As she got out, she turned to look for me in the crowd. I waved wildly, screaming "well done" at the top of my lungs, oblivious to everyone around me as her name was announced. She broke into a huge smile and waved back, her fist in the air in triumph. A true Farinelli.

I sat back down, adrenaline and excitement still coursing through me, subsiding slightly into embarrassment as I became aware of the mums and dads on either side of me, doing that British "how undignified" pursing of the lips. Presumably, I should have been tapping my fingertips together without actually making any sound. I wanted to jump on my chair again and give another "FRAN-CESCAAAAA" bellow for good measure. But instead I looked at my program to see when her next race was.

One woman a few seats down was having a really good gawk at me. If I'd have been on the estate, I might have done a "What you looking at?" As it was, I fiddled with my phone, texting Nico to tell him how well Francesca had done, wishing he was there so we could talk loudly about his daughter. I felt a sense of ownership, a rush of pride that surprised me. After all, she hadn't inherited her sporting genes from me—luckily. I stole a sideways glance to see if the staring woman had put her eyes back in. But she was still looking at me. I felt a prickle of irritation.

She smiled, stood up and walked toward me. Brown curly hair framed her freckly face. "Hi there. Are you here with Francesca Farinelli?"

I nodded.

"Are you her coach?"

I laughed. "God no! I'm her stepmum. Got a bit overexcited there."

The woman frowned. I waited to see if she'd have the guts to give me a lecture on parental etiquette at swimming competitions. If she thought I was bad, she should come to one of Sam's football matches: the dads had completely lost touch with the fact they were watching the under-elevens and not a relegation match between two Premier league teams.

"*Stepmum?*"

I nodded and stopped myself launching into a rude retort. Christ, it was bad enough Francesca making me feel like an outsider without random strangers joining in.

"That was Francesca Farinelli, Caitlin and Nico's daughter, who just won that race?"

I stared at her, wondering where she was going with this. Contrarily I wanted to keep that information to myself. I'd obviously been hanging out with Lara too often. "Yes. Do you know the family?"

"Yes. I knew Francesca when she was a tiny baby. She's a few months older than my son. But we moved to Newcastle and lost touch with them. It was just the name that rang a bell."

I wanted to ask if she knew that Caitlin had died. I wasn't quite sure of the etiquette of a conversation along the lines of "I didn't break up their marriage, you know; she died."

She paused for a moment. "Are they all still living in Siena Avenue in Brighton? Anna as well?"

"Yes." I didn't know how to add in, "Well, all if you don't count Caitlin." If she carried on like this, I'd be watching my rearview mirror for a tail on the way home.

I never used to be suspicious of strangers. Once, when Nico and I had been lying in bed, messing about, doing a silly list of the ten things we loved most about each other, he'd said, "I love how you assume everyone is your friend. How you chat to everyone, the woman in the post office, the dog tied up outside the supermarket, the bloke with the toffee vodka at the checkout."

For whatever reason, I'd blundered through life for the last thirty-five years expecting a welcoming reception. But now that I'd experienced what it was like to have someone wage a campaign of indifference and sometimes out-and-out hate, I was more guarded with everyone.

Poor woman. Here I was all Secret Squirrel when she was probably just a family acquaintance, casually interested in hearing their news from the last decade or so. I couldn't help feeling slightly pissed off, though, that it fell to me rather than some other mutual acquaintance to break the news about Caitlin. But the moment passed before I managed to get the D-word onto my lips.

The woman put her head on one side. "I didn't know Nico and Caitlin had gotten divorced."

I was going to have to say it. I hoped she wouldn't start crying. That really would be the ultimate irony, me comforting some stranger over Caitlin's death.

"Um, Caitlin died nearly three years ago."

The woman gasped. "Oh my god! Poor Nico and Francesca!"

I hoped I wasn't going to witness yet another person raising their eyebrows as they looked at me and thought, "Christ, he's gone for a completely different type."

But before I had to supply any more details, a boy about Francesca's age walked up to us, his dark hair a tangle of wet curls. Francesca would have called him "fit" for sure.

"Hi, Mum. That's it. I've finished. They've canceled the last few races because the electronic timing system has broken. We can go."

The woman smiled and said, "This is my son, Ben. He swims for the Tyne and Wear under-fourteens."

I said hello and tried not to stare. I didn't feel as though I was meeting him for the first time. My brain was ferreting about, searching for where I'd seen him before. There was something so familiar about the way one eyebrow lifted higher than the other when he smiled, the front tooth that just crossed slightly over the other, those huge dark eyes.

"Does that mean the girls' under fourteen freestyle fifty meters isn't happening?" I asked.

"Nope. Everyone was packing up to leave down there."

I was torn between disappointment at not seeing Francesca race again and pleasure that I could spend a bit of time with Lara and her dad before he had to go home.

Ben's mum opened her handbag and fished out her purse. "Do you want to go and get a sandwich from the café before we drive home?" she asked, handing him a fiver.

He took the money. "All right. Do you want anything, Mum?"

"No, I'm fine. I'll wait for you outside the front." She

picked up her coat. "Nice meeting you. Have a safe journey home."

I stood up. Some desire to prove I was as classy as Caitlin made me stick out my hand. "I'm Maggie, by the way."

She hesitated, just for a second. "I'm Dawn."

CHAPTER FORTY-TWO

MAGGIE

I didn't manage to get my filter in place in time. Or even rein in my index finger. I pointed straight at her, mouth open, which of course allowed the words, "You're Massimo's first wife" to escape.

She nodded. "That's me."

There was something defensive in her reply, as though she expected me to have an opinion about her already. I recognized her shift in attitude. It was the same one I felt when someone said to me, "Ah, you're Nico's wife…" ending the statement with a little gasp of relief that they'd managed to omit "new/second/latest" from the sentence.

I stood there for a moment, my brain like a pinball zinging around the machine, triggering a raft of bonus points. I knew why I thought I recognized Ben. He was the spitting image of Massimo. I pursed my lips together to stop that particular thought blurting out into the air before I'd had time to process it properly. But not before I'd glanced over to where he was walking up the steps to the café, the very set of his shoulders, the way his arms swung at his side, a smaller, slighter version of Massimo.

A look of weary resignation passed over her face. "He told you I didn't want children, didn't he?"

I didn't want to be disloyal to Massimo with a woman I'd only met for five minutes, even if her natural warmth made me think that in other circumstances we could easily find ourselves comparing how many men we'd been to bed with over a few vodkas and lemonade.

While I stood there trying to field an answer that kept family loyalty intact without telling a fat lie, Dawn's eyes filled with tears.

She swiped at her face. "Sorry. I should never have come over. I couldn't resist it when I heard Francesca's name. I'm my own worst enemy. I keep thinking that it can't get to me anymore."

"I assume Ben is Massimo's son?"

Dawn gave a little laugh. "Yes, there's a bit of a family resemblance, isn't there? Right chip off the old block."

"Does he know he has a son?"

The woman's face twisted into something harsh. "Of course he knows. If he'd had his own way, he wouldn't have one, but he does. Not that he's ever had anything to do with him."

"I thought Massimo was desperate for children," I said, thinking back to every conversation I'd had with Lara about how quickly she'd gotten pregnant after they got married, how much Massimo wanted a second child.

"Massimo did want children. He insisted on me having a private scan early before we told anyone I was expecting."

Sam's dad had handed me a hundred quid in grubby ten-pound notes, saying, "Up to you what you do, but I'm not really father material," before he disappeared off.

I was just thinking I would have loved someone to be interested enough to pay for an early scan when Dawn said,

"The scan showed a high probability of a heart problem so he made me swear to keep my pregnancy a secret. He didn't want a 'defective' child, as he put it. I wanted to keep the baby no matter what, but he was furious, insisting that I'd have to have an abortion if the twenty-week scan confirmed the problem."

I didn't want to believe her. Massimo—the man who taught Sam new football tricks, who got up early to give Francesca extra swimming training before he went to work—forcing his wife to abort their baby? It was like she was talking about someone else entirely, not the man who waved me in for coffee, who greeted me with extravagant kisses on the cheek, who always asked about my latest tailoring commissions, one of the few people who didn't treat my sewing business as something I dabbled in when I had a spare moment or two.

"But Ben's okay, isn't he?"

Dawn's face softened. "He is now. He had several operations when he was little."

"So Massimo came around to your way of thinking?" I felt as though I was trying to jam the last piece of a puzzle into the only remaining hole yet finding that it didn't fit. I couldn't remember anyone, ever, mentioning that Dawn had been pregnant. I sieved through all those conversations, with Massimo, with Anna, with Lara. I could only recall the phrase: "She didn't want children."

A fresh tear trailed down Dawn's face. "He was so adamant I'd have to get rid of the baby that I walked out the day before the next scan. He'd have gotten his own way in the end; no one can stand up to Massimo. I just kept driving. We ended up in Newcastle. I decided he wouldn't be able to find me there until after the baby was born."

My head filled with images of Massimo sneering at any

mention of Dawn, always pointing out how selfish she was. But here she was, right in front of me, telling me how she fought to have that baby, walked away from her life out of fear that Ben might be taken from her before he was even born.

She paused, emotion clouding her face. "Massimo's not the sort of man you can have a sensible discussion with. He wouldn't accept a child who wasn't perfect. His way or the highway. Just like that mother of his."

There were so many questions crowding into my mind that I couldn't think straight. It was like attempting to find my way through a maze that didn't actually have a path to the center, no matter how many different routes I tried. I couldn't marry up my amiable brother-in-law with the person Dawn was describing.

I didn't want to think I'd been wrong about Massimo. I was examining Dawn's story, scratching away, looking for a hole to pick in it to prove she was making the whole thing up, or at least exaggerating so wildly that if there was a grain of truth, it was so distorted as to be no longer recognizable.

Dawn moved to go. "Sorry, I didn't mean to dump all this on you. You must think I'm absolutely mad. It was all so long ago anyway. It's just that Ben's turned out to be such a lovely boy, even now I feel complete panic when I think I might have given in, never had him. Massimo just wouldn't listen, wouldn't even give us a chance. Typical Farinelli."

"Has he ever met him though?" Massimo would be so proud of Ben, tall, good-looking and sporty with that same Italian appeal. Any parent would be.

"No. Never. I sent him a note with a photo to let him know when Ben was born. Told him that he'd have to have several operations and they couldn't guarantee the outcome."

It was like watching a scary film where you wanted to

know what happened next but couldn't bear the anticipation leading up to it.

"And?" I was way beyond the Nosy Parker stage, but I had to know. Was Massimo really the sort of man who'd leave his wife to deal on her own, with his son, his own child, who might die?

"Of course he didn't want to know. Hospitals aren't really Massimo's thing. Actually nothing unpleasant is Massimo's thing."

I was searching her face, raking about for clues that this was a strange tale she'd invented.

But it was as though Dawn was reading my mind. "I wouldn't believe me either if I was in your position. I've no doubt that when you talk, Massimo stands there with his head on one side, making you feel as though what you have to say is the most interesting thing he's ever heard. But believe me, the way he behaved over Ben was the final straw, not the starting point."

I didn't want to know any more. I wanted to be able to walk away and rationalize what she'd told me into something less awful, something that wouldn't have me forever watching out for clues, signs of nasty behavior, like an undercover cop at the heart of the family. I felt like I did when I was acting as goalie for Sam and he belted a football straight into my stomach, knocking all the air out of me. Every time I thought I'd gotten a handle on my new family, I'd come across another bloody skellygog in the cupboard.

And yet again, I'd have to decide whether or not to tell everyone else. I was becoming the left-luggage storage facility for family secrets, the ones with the broken zips and dodgy wheels no one wanted to reclaim.

I stood, torn between a desire to dig much deeper and to run away, kicking up a cloud of dust to blank out the new information I couldn't now unknow.

Did Nico know? Did Lara? Anna? Were they all in on some kind of weird joke? Perhaps just Massimo knew, so ashamed of himself, he had buried it deep, hoping the rest of his family would never need to find out. I still found it difficult to accept the version of Massimo Dawn was presenting to me. The man I knew was always up for a laugh, swinging Sam onto his shoulders, ready with the jump leads whenever my knackered old Fiesta gave up the ghost.

I forced a smile. "He's a lovely boy and I'm sorry you've had such a terrible time. I don't really know what to say."

Dawn surprised me by giving me a huge and heartfelt hug. "Take care in that family. Nico is lovely but the rest are a nest of vipers. Just answer me one thing: did Massimo marry again?"

I nodded, expecting her to make some catty comment. But instead she sighed. "That poor, poor woman. She's going to have an unbearable life."

Without saying anything else, we walked out to reception, where Ben was eating great chunks of a baguette in a way that would have had Anna tutting. I tried not to stare at him, tried not to put him on weirdo woman alert, but there was absolutely no mistaking who his father was.

At that moment, Francesca arrived, tossing her bag over her shoulder.

"You did really well!" I gushed.

For once she responded like a normal person and said, "Thank you. Shame I didn't get to do the other race."

Dawn congratulated Francesca on swimming so well and pride surged through me as she chatted and laughed. Then I had the horrible thought that Francesca might fancy Ben and it would all be a bit odd as he was her cousin, so I didn't prolong the good-byes and hurried her off to the car.

I hoped—unusually—she would do what she always did,

plug herself into her headphones so I could think through what I'd just heard. But Sod's law, she wanted to talk.

"That Ben, the one whose mother you were just speaking to, he's an amazing swimmer. His freestyle time was faster than the age group above. I bet he gets scouted for the national team eventually."

As she was talking, the image of Sandro unconscious on the edge of the pool kept coming into my mind. The whole fuckedupness of it all: one son petrified of water who Massimo wanted to turn into an Olympic swimmer, and one son he wouldn't acknowledge who had the potential to be just that.

And what did Dawn mean about the way Massimo behaved over Ben being the final straw, not the starting point? Granted, if what she said was true about how Massimo had treated her, it didn't show him in a good light. But that was only her side of the story. Maybe she'd been an absolute nightmare to live with; maybe the whole Ben saga had been the last unhappy chapter in an already disintegrating relationship? But somewhere in the back of my brain, there was an anxious swirling, my mind straining to brush it out of the way so I could deal with the facts, not flimsy feelings or instincts.

A sense of unease was starting to creep through me, my thoughts turning to Lara, the watchful urgency about her, as though the pasta was about to boil over or she'd left the bath running. The frenzied rush to get the mop out if anything got spilled, even when it was just on the kitchen tiles.

But was she really like that because of Massimo? He was always so affectionate toward her, embarrassingly kissy-kissy. I could see that he was pretty dominant, a man who liked things just so and had an opinion on everything. On the other hand, I reckoned a straw poll of a cross-section of married women would prove the world hadn't moved on as much as we'd all expected by now. That given a choice and enough cash, men would still rather go hunter-gathering and come back to a woman in a polka dot pinny, serving up a steak Diane and a slab of Black Forest gateau. Nico had been a revelation to me—a man who not only knew what a Hoover was used for but could change a bag in one. Massimo expecting his wife to keep his house to show-home standards wasn't a reason to start thinking he'd bullied his ex-wife and shirked his parental responsibilities.

Thankfully this was one secret I could discuss with Nico. I'd have to be very careful not to present it as a criticism of Massimo. One of the things I loved about Nico was his loyalty, but the whole lot of them were like Shire horses with their blinders on when it came to each other's faults. But maybe it wouldn't end up being a big deal.

Something in me sagged. Everything in the Farinelli family was always a big deal.

Anyway, it could wait. If no one had known about Ben for thirteen years, a couple of days wouldn't make much difference. But I knew the bit of me that was hacked right out of my mother would be nosying away, picking through conversations for clues that it was one massive conspiracy, that everyone else was whispering, "Sshh, Maggie's coming," whenever they were talking about Ben.

My mind carried on whirling around, interspersed with the occasional "How much longer till we get home?" from Francesca.

We drew up outside our house just before four-thirty. Francesca turned to me: "Can't wait to tell Uncle Massimo that I won. Thanks for taking me, Mags."

"Wouldn't have missed it. You blew the competition out of the water."

Then we both laughed and said at the same time, "Literally."

And despite the fireworks fizzing around my head until I was worried some vital gray matter would come smoking out of my ears and I'd lose the knack of doing up my bra or cleaning my teeth, I still wanted to do a little happy dance.

But that really would have spoiled the moment.

CHAPTER FORTY-THREE

LARA

When Massimo had phoned from his conference in Liverpool, I told him I had two surprises for him when he got home on Saturday afternoon.

"Does it involve you taking your clothes off and having a go at making a baby?"

As always when the topic of another baby came up I felt a rush of guilt. Despite Massimo continuing to be a great advert for marriage, I didn't yet trust him enough to feel capable of bringing another child into the world, another being to consider—and to protect—if necessary. Although I was edging toward accepting that an overdone steak, a failure to record his favorite TV program, one of Lupo's hairs in the butter might no longer be the disasters they once were, I still wasn't ready to stop having contraceptive injections. Every time he brought up the subject of going for tests to see why we were unable to conceive, I experienced a rush of nausea so overwhelming, throwing up became a real possibility. I'd come up with a whole raft of excuses to put him off getting a medical opinion. My latest stalling tactic was to keep referring to the fact that sperm quality declined after the age of forty. His desire to have another child was currently equaled by his fear of finding out the problem lay with him, not with me. A middle-aged man with substandard rather than romp-home, spear-carrying sperm would not fit Massimo's image of himself.

When I knew Massimo was on his way home, I couldn't stay still. I kept telling myself he wouldn't have a problem with Dad being here. That he'd be thrilled I'd learned to drive. But I couldn't settle. I kept walking past the hall window, watching for his car. I'd allowed myself to get dragged back into my old habits, making sure there was white wine of every possible grape variety chilled in the fridge, every hand towel in the house was freshly laundered, Sandro had secured his curtains with the tie-backs.

In between times I kept pausing at the door to watch Sandro with Dad. One of the things that had captured and held Dad's attention was Sandro's electric keyboard. Sandro was showing him how he could play "Chopsticks." And from nowhere, Dad took over and started to play "Hey Jude," singing along in his croaky voice.

Sandro called me in. "Look at Granddad. He's really good at the piano."

I loved seeing them together. Sandro didn't seem to notice Dad made odd comments about knowing the people on TV, called Lupo a cat and was just as likely to drink out of the milk jug as a cup. Given that he'd shaken with fear when there'd been an explosion on the TV news, seeing him relaxed, embracing music and enjoying Sandro's company brought so many emotions to the fore that I didn't know whether to sing along with him or burst into tears.

At half past four, I heard the growl of Massimo's BMW pull up outside. My stomach knotted as I glanced at Dad, my ears straining for the sound of him coming up the drive, the jangle of keys, the thud of the briefcase on the top step. But instead of his footsteps after the car door slammed, Francesca's voice rang out, followed by a cheer from Massimo. I caught a "Bravo!" and "That's my girl." Maggie was booming into the mix, "Just zoomed in at the last moment and left them all standing, she did. Bloody brilliant."

Hearing her outside gave me courage. I could tell him while she was there. She'd help me out. She was brilliant at picking up a thread of discord and snipping it off before it started—smoothing down Anna squaring up to Beryl, Sam having a spat with Francesca, Massimo goading Nico—Maggie was always there with a joke or a diversion to defuse the tension.

I opened the door and waved at them all.

Massimo threw his arms wide in a big theatrical gesture. "My gorgeous wife! Have you missed me?"

Nerves made me blurt out: "I've been too busy to miss you."

Of course, it was a preamble to "Dad's come to visit and I've got my hands full," but I didn't get that far before Massimo dropped his hands to his side and said, "Did you hear that, Maggie? That's charming, isn't it? She's been too busy to miss me!"

Maggie glanced at me and said, "You know what they say, when the cat's away, the mice will play. You've no idea what we get up to in your absence."

Something in her voice made me do a double-take. I normally envied the way her conversations with Massimo were teasing and full of banter. But she sounded—I couldn't put my finger on it—sullen? Sulky? As though she was trying to pick an argument?

My heart skipped a little.

Massimo raised an eyebrow but his tone was light. "Look forward to hearing all about it. I'll just get changed out of my suit, then I'm all ears."

Massimo hated secrets, unless he was the one keeping them. Something uncertain flashed across his face. He wasn't a man who liked being on the back foot.

I jumped in. "I'm only having you on, darling. I have missed you; it's just that I've had an unexpected guest today." The added line, "And he's still here" nearly made it out of my mouth but got trapped in the web of knowing I should be able to say whatever came to mind but not wanting the proof I couldn't.

Since Sandro was born, Massimo hadn't encouraged me to invite anyone over. Initially he said it was too much for me with a baby, having to clean everywhere and get food ready. But I understood, over time, that only his family were welcome unless he was in the mode of presenting himself as a super-generous "more the merrier" host as he had for Sam's party. Everything about other people in our house irritated him. The sound of them using the loo. The way they dripped water on the floor when they washed their hands. How they dipped teaspoons into the sugar, leaving little wet trails. In short, anyone who didn't know—and adhere to—the thousands of invisible rules that infiltrated our lives. For Sandro and me, they were as reflexive as the ability to breathe. So much so, that every time someone transgressed by allowing a rogue elbow on the table or not hermetically sealing their mouths while eating, Sandro would catch my eye and we'd quietly hold our breath, knowing we'd bear the brunt of their mistakes once they'd left.

Maggie, of course, was oblivious to the million scenarios that could unfold simply by shaking the notions of "unexpected guest," "secret" and "surprise" into one combustible mix. As always, I felt a little rush of self-loathing that I'd allowed myself to play along. What kind of grown woman sneaked broken crockery out of the house to dispose of in a litter bin instead of simply saying, "I dropped a plate"? Now I couldn't even recall Massimo making a fuss about me breaking anything. I just felt like he might.

Maybe it was all in my head. Perhaps the antidepressants I'd taken after Sandro was born had permanently skewed my grip on reality. Maybe this time I really did need them, to shake me out of my warped thinking, seeing problems where there weren't any.

I forced myself to believe it would all turn out okay, taking Massimo's briefcase and coat from him and smiling, or at least, managing to turn up the corners of my mouth.

Massimo threw his arm around my shoulders. Today he certainly seemed in an expansive mood: "Let's get everyone in for a cup of tea. Francesca can tell us about her fantastic win." He turned and nudged her on the arm. "Brilliant, you are. I'm so proud of you, Cessie, you little swimming star. I'd love it if Sandro took after you."

Maggie's head snapped around, as though Massimo had said something odd.

Massimo smiled at her. "What? Are you going to give me a lecture about comparing the kids again? You know us Farinellis are ridiculously competitive; it's in our genes."

Maggie seemed to shake herself. "Yes, I'm beginning to see that."

Unlike the rest of us, Maggie was hopeless at hiding her emotions. I hoped I never bought her a present she didn't like. But it wasn't like her to be snippy and difficult. Maybe she was just exhausted after a day of biting her tongue with Francesca, though actually they seemed a little more relaxed with each other.

I paused on the doorstep, waiting to warn Massimo before we went in that Dad was here, when Maggie said, "I don't want to intrude if Massimo hasn't seen your dad yet."

I wanted to back away, afraid of seeing Massimo's expression, the big cloud that preceded a rant, the invective forming on his lips.

But all that happened was that his eyes flew open wide. "Your dad?"

Maggie rushed to apologize. "Sorry, sorry, I didn't realize Massimo didn't know. I spoiled the surprise."

Massimo just laughed. "You dark horse, Lala. Kept that quiet. I didn't know he was well enough to come out for the day."

Maggie tried to make up for putting her foot in it. "It was my idea. Mum's been helping, so if you need her at all, she's just next door."

Massimo loosened his tie. "Come on in, Maggie, I'm sure he'll be fine."

Maggie turned to me. "What do you think is best, Lara? I don't want to overwhelm him with lots of people arriving at once."

Francesca piped up. "Can we just go in for a minute? I want to show Sandro my medal."

I couldn't refuse, so I smiled and ushered them through the front door. Dad was playing "Lily the Pink" in the sitting room, with Sandro looking rather bemused at the gusto with which Dad was singing the words. Given that they were rather nonsensical at the best of times, I couldn't blame him for taking the opportunity to disappear into the playroom to watch telly with Francesca.

Maggie breezed in. "Hello, Robert! Loving the singing. You're pretty nifty on the keyboard, aren't you?"

My heart constricted as I saw him force himself to his feet, the gentlemanly habit of standing for the lady in the room still there, hovering under the surface of the person he used to be. He put his head on one side, trying to understand who she was.

She immediately put her hand out. "I'm Maggie, Lara's sister-in-law."

Dad nodded. "Sister-in-law."

The words sounded uncertain in his mouth, as though he was repeating a foreign word without knowing the meaning.

Massimo strode in. "Hello there. What a lovely surprise. Haven't seen you in ages."

All the tension I'd been clinging onto dissolved. I'd been so wrong about Massimo. He did want the best for us all. Of course there were moments when we wound each other up, but I'd blown those out of proportion. Half the time I'd probably been oversensitive anyway.

Dad's face fell. He turned to me. "Who is this?"

I put my hand on Massimo's back, pushing apology out of my fingertips, trying to transmit calm to him, hoping he wouldn't take it personally. "It's Massimo, Dad. My husband."

Dad shook his head. "No, he's not your husband."

I didn't want to make Dad feel foolish, but Massimo hadn't seen him for so long, I felt as though I had to make some kind of stand, if only to show Massimo how bad things were.

"I think you're a bit confused today, Dad."

I pulled a "bear with me" face at Massimo. I picked up our wedding picture from the top of the television. "Look, that's me on my wedding day, with Massimo. You walked me down the aisle in the church, remember?"

Dad started worrying at the buttons on his cardigan. "Not him. Not him. Not him."

Massimo put out his hand. "Well, it's nice to see you anyway, Robert."

Dad frowned and put his hand in his pocket, shaking his head. "No."

Massimo shrugged. I wanted to grab Dad by his shoulders and explain that Massimo paid for his care, that he was a good man, who looked after him and it was just *rude* not to shake his hand. Dad had never been rude. I grimaced at Massimo. I felt as though he was expecting me to defend him, but I didn't want to agitate Dad any further. I hadn't seen this side to his disease, though they had warned me at the nursing home that he might become aggressive.

Maggie tried to save the day. "Robert, what were you singing then? Do you know 'Amazing Grace'?"

And with that, she burst into a really lovely version, pausing between lines to say to me, "Why don't you make some tea?"

I could have hugged her as Dad narrowed his eyes in concentration and started to mouth the odd word, with some wheezy humming in between.

I went out to the kitchen, grief for who he was rising in my chest, filling me with sorrow for all the times I could have insisted on going to visit him, times when his brain knitted together much better than it did now, before every single memory had to be jump-started like a car with faulty spark plugs. I should have stood my ground when Massimo couldn't drive me because he had "too many e-mails," "a report for Monday." Thank God I could drive now. I'd have to talk to Massimo about buying a little secondhand car so I could nip over and see Dad at least twice a week. Tears filled my eyes as I wondered how long it would be before he didn't know me either.

Massimo followed me through. "How long has he been here?"

"We picked him up first thing this morning. He's going home in a couple of hours."

I stopped myself from making excuses about why my dad

was visiting his daughter and grandson. I wanted to wring my hands and bleat, "Hope you don't mind." But maybe that was just normal consideration from a wife toward a husband. I was so conscious of not apologizing for everything all the time, of not being "so bloody drippy" as Maggie would put it, I was probably in danger of being rude myself.

Massimo wrinkled his nose. "He's gone downhill quite fast since I last saw him. Very confused."

"I know."

"We should get him to see another neurological specialist, see if we can get some answers about how quickly his dementia is going to progress."

Everything in me slumped. "I'm not sure I want to know." I put the kettle on.

Massimo came up behind me and kissed my neck. "We'll get the best care we can for him, darling."

"There is one bit of good news though." I didn't know why I had to take a deep breath before saying that.

He raised his eyebrows. "What?"

"I've passed my driving test." I didn't manage to deliver that with the vigor I'd hoped for, leaning toward apologetic rather than triumphant.

Massimo threw his arms around me. My face was buried in his shoulder with my neck at a slightly awkward angle. I waited for him to let go of me but he squeezed me even more tightly. A bubble of panic rose inside me, I wanted to shake him off, to wriggle free. Then he released me, his face bright with delight. "You really are full of surprises today, you little superstar."

I had to stop imagining the worst all the time.

I filled him in on how Maggie had taught me in secret.

"I thought you weren't interested in learning to drive?"

Was there a note of petulance in his voice?

"I wanted to see more of Dad without involving you in the logistics. Just thought it would be easier if I could get myself there without bothering you. It's not exactly a fun day out."

"You only had to say, my darling. I thought you didn't want to go very often because you found it so distressing."

Honestly, Massimo and I had the communication skills of a mobile phone out of battery. I needed to stop guessing what Massimo thought and just ask him outright.

He took the tray and walked through to the sitting room. "We'll have to find a little car for you. Nothing too small though. I want a bit of metal around you, keep you safe."

I didn't know why I'd worried about telling him.

As Massimo put the tray down, Dad stopped singing. He looked at me, then pointed at Massimo. "Who's that?"

Very gently, I said, "My husband. Sandro's dad."

Dad said, "No. He's not your husband."

Massimo gave me a little wink and whispered, "I'll settle for being your lover."

But I was determined to help Dad have a clear picture of my nearest and dearest. I tried again, this time with the photo of Sandro's christening.

"He is my husband, Dad. Look, there's you, standing next to Anna, then Nico with his wife, Caitlin, who died. And then me with Massimo."

As clear as anything, as though he'd been rehearsing the words his whole life, Dad pointed to Massimo and then to Caitlin and said, "No. He has sex with this woman."

And then, the man who had moaned about the "shocking" language before the watershed all his life, only ever managing a mild-mannered "For goodness' sake!" when he stubbed his toe, stood in our sitting room, in front of my husband and sister-in-law and did a crude movement of his hips.

CHAPTER FORTY-FOUR

MAGGIE

There was a shocked silence in the lounge. A split second when the embarrassment of poor genteel Robert standing there, bucking his hips for all his creaking joints were worth, obliterated his words. We would have been world champions at musical statues. I glanced at Lara first. Her face was all wrong. Not shocked or hurt or angry. Her eyebrows were up. Her arms folded. Her bottom lip covering her top one.

Grim satisfaction.

My mind felt like a giant road sweeper, sucking up all sorts of debris, without enough mechanical finesse to sift through the lolly sticks and crisp packets for anything of value.

Massimo was shaking his head. "Come on, Robert, I think you're getting a bit muddled. This is my wife," he said, indicating Lara. He did a little laugh and caught my eye. "Unfortunately, she wouldn't be very keen on me having sex with anyone else."

Robert drew his shrunken frame up as far as it would go, a good five or six inches shorter than Massimo. He pointed back to the photo. "You. You. I see you." He tapped his own eye with his index finger.

Massimo sighed. "I think you've got it wrong, old man. You're mistaking me for Nico, my brother."

He turned to Lara. "We'd better let him know he needs some net curtains up at the bedroom window."

Lara still didn't say anything.

And just as I was fishing about for something to rescue the situation, to save Lara and Massimo from the hideousness of Robert's wild imaginings, the doorbell rang. Whoever it was—Jehovah's Witnesses, young offenders selling ironing board covers, the bloke selling "restaurant quality fish" out of the back of his van—I was going to fall on them and keep them captive until they were tempted to dial 999 to escape.

Francesca came clattering out of the playroom with Sandro and threw the front door open. "It's Dad!"

"How did you get on?" Nico was so busy looking at her medal and hearing about the swimming, he didn't clock the funny-farm party in the lounge. As he walked through the hallway toward us, I was tempted to throw myself against his chest where bits of plant and compost were still clinging.

I raised my eyebrows at Nico, hoping he'd cop on to my wife-speak that we were in the middle of a "tricky situation." I'd only gotten as far as "We're just talking to Robert, Lara's dad," when Massimo waved a hand toward Nico and said, "There, Robert. This is the man you saw with Caitlin. My brother, Nico."

I waited, watching Robert, seeing if anything slotted into place. It was like playing Jenga in reverse, working out which bits you could slot back into the tower to stop the structure collapsing in a heap. His eyes narrowed as though a tremendous effort was required to keep hold of solid substances in the mists of his mind.

Robert walked toward Nico and stood opposite him, within millimeters of his face.

Nico, bless him, stepped back slightly but took hold of Robert's arm. "I'm Nico, do you remember me? We met at Lara and Massimo's wedding."

The mention of Massimo was like watching someone give a cutlery drawer wedged shut by a wooden spoon a good thump. After so much tugging and banging, everything suddenly glided open with ease. Robert swung around and poked his bony finger in Massimo's chest.

Lara shot out a hand. "Dad, don't poke."

But Robert was surprisingly strong for someone who looked as though he could well have pipe cleaners in the place of bones. He wrestled his arm free, leaning right into Massimo, his milky blue eyes darting about, his tongue making little movements around his lips as though he was anticipating the arrival of a precious moment of clarity.

In a triumphant tone he shouted, "You. I did see you. I saw you in the bedroom. With that woman…Cat—Cat—" He waved at the photograph. "The bedroom where there's purple around the window. Purple, purple…" His hands were moving, as though he was trying to hook a word out of the ether. Then he forgot about it and said, "You were having sex. Sex! Sex!"

Before I could order my thoughts, Massimo's voice started to rise. "Shut up! You've just come here to make trouble. Of course I wasn't having sex with my brother's wife, you demented old fool."

Nico stepped toward them and stretched out a hand. "Massimo! Calm down! He's confused; he doesn't know what he's saying."

But there was something about the way Massimo recoiled from Nico as though he was expecting a blow that made me do a double take. Caitlin had been having sex with someone; that much I knew. But with "P." Not Massimo. Surely she wouldn't sleep with Nico's brother?

While my mind was gathering evidence, sifting through what I knew for certain and scraping about for other moments and memories I'd overlooked, Massimo and Robert were squaring up to each other, oblivious to everyone else. Robert stood unsteadily with his hands on his hips repeating, "I saw you. You! I saw you! Sex with that woman!"

Massimo towered over him. "Shut up!"

But Robert wasn't budging from his four-word refrain of "You, I saw you," nodding until he looked like he'd dislodge his remaining brain connections if someone didn't believe him soon.

Nico grabbed Massimo's upper arm. "Mass! That's enough! He can't help it, he's ill."

But Massimo shook Nico off and shoved Robert. "Shut up, you stupid old man!"

Robert went stumbling backward, crashing into a glass coffee table and buckling at the knees.

Lara flew to her dad, screaming to Massimo, "Get off, get off him. He's only telling the truth, you bullying bastard." She booted Massimo in the shins with such force that my own leg jolted. "Get away from us!"

Sandro started to cry. Before I could reach him, Francesca put her arm around him, but stood rooted to the spot, her eyes wide open in horror.

While Robert lay groaning on the floor, Massimo grabbed Lara under the jaw with an easy, practiced movement, bringing her face up to his. She struggled and his hand tightened. He stared down at her, pressing a knuckle into the soft tissue between her collarbone and shoulder. She stopped trying to get away from him. "Don't you dare kick me, you little cow."

From the corner of the room, I heard a broken wail of "Mum!" and saw Francesca hang onto Sandro to stop him from running to Lara.

And slowly, like the creaking of a steam engine sitting for years in the sidings, all the pistons in my brain started to fire up. It was the way Lara's body sagged in resignation that told me what I'd missed. She wasn't fighting, wasn't yelling or going nuts from the surge of adrenaline that goes with a new experience. There was no shock on Lara's face, no astonished horror, just acceptance, a "Here we go again."

This wasn't an out-of-character one-off.

But before I could react, Nico grabbed Massimo by the shoulders and flung him off her. "Massimo! What the hell do you think you're doing? You were half-strangling her!"

Lara rubbed her neck. She bent over Robert, easing him into a sitting position while I became everything I hated in a person, standing with my feet rooted to the sisal carpet, useless as a lamppost, not knowing who to help first. Lara looked as though someone had popped a champagne cork on her emotions.

She was shaking her head at Nico. "You've no idea what your brother's like, have you? To you, he's just a man who gets a bit competitive about sport now and again. But he's not. He's a bloody great bully who gets his own way by putting other people down, frightening them and—as you can see—hurting them. Ever wondered why Sandro is terrified to say 'boo' to a goose? Well, that's why."

Massimo was saying, "Come on, I had to stop you from attacking me—you nearly broke my shin." He was pulling a "Are you really going to listen to this crazy woman?" face, which I was ashamed to say, I'd seen many times before and joined in with the joke. Now I realized that air of tenseness around Lara, as though she was in a car running out of petrol and it was touch and go whether she could limp to the garage, wasn't because she was uptight and overprotective, or—as I'd often thought—she needed to "loosen up a bit."

It was because she was scared.

I ran over to her and between us we helped Robert to his feet, shaking and confused, his rheumy old eyes fearful as I tucked my hands under his armpits. I touched Lara's arm. "I'm sorry. I should have seen what was going on."

"No one could. Not even me, half the time."

I helped her walk Robert halfway down the hall to the kitchen, with him resisting all the way, as though he couldn't trust anyone anymore. As Nico and Massimo's voices got louder and louder in the lounge, she turned to me and said, "You go back in and see if you can calm them down. The kids shouldn't be in there hearing all that. I can manage Dad."

As I dashed back into the lounge, trying to process the family Armageddon I was witnessing, Dawn's words came back to me: "The way he behaved over Ben was the final straw." The words I'd dismissed as the legacy of a bitter ex-wife.

Nico was bellowing at Massimo. "What sort of pathetic excuse for a bloke hits a confused old man spouting nonsense, then turns on his wife? What's gotten into you, Mass?" Then I saw a hesitation on Nico's face, a jag of pain, as though the distant possibility that Robert's words might be true had just begun to sink in.

I looked from Nico to Francesca and Sandro, desperate to stop what I knew was coming next. But before I could bundle the children out of the room, Massimo lifted up his head, making use of the extra couple of inches he had on Nico. A slow smile spread over his face and my stomach churned. He looked like a cat batting a moth, deciding whether to go for the kill or play a bit longer.

"Let's just say there are some women who don't find me pathetic." He shrugged his shoulders in a "What could

I do?" gesture. "Caitlin included. While you were pratting about with your alliums and agapanthus, your wife was a bit neglected. So, let's say, when you weren't there for her, I filled the gap. So to speak."

I was pretty sure Nico had never punched anyone in temper in his life but his whole body was rigid with fury. I was ready to cheer if Massimo got the uppercut he deserved. And if Nico didn't lamp him one, I might just step in myself.

In a voice shaking with anger, Nico said, "You couldn't resist it, could you? The idea I might be happy, that someone might love me more than they loved you. You had to have her, didn't you?"

I winced. I liked to pretend to myself that Nico hadn't ever loved Caitlin. Practical, straight-talking me wanted to believe their love had been a blurry photocopy of our high-definition relationship. I was obviously falling into that second wife syndrome of denying anything good took place before my rescuing arrival.

Massimo laughed, a sarcastic sound that made me want to slap him so hard his ears would ring into the middle of next week. "She came after me, mate. Little bit of opera, little bit of afternoon tea, easy pickings. My own wife was just getting her tits out for the baby by then, so worked well for both of us."

I wanted to throw up out of pure rage. I heard Francesca sob. I spun around. "Francesca, come on, love. You don't want to hear this."

I caught hold of her arm, bracing myself for resistance, but she let herself be led out. I put my other arm around Sandro and rushed them next door to Mum, pushing them over the threshold and shouting, "I'll explain later, back in a mo," over my shoulder.

Sandro flew into Mum's arms. Poor little mite. At a later

date, I'd have to deal with my guilt at the occasions when I'd been rolling my eyes thinking he was a bit of a wet blanket.

I dashed back to Lara's and scooted into the lounge to see Nico take a swing at Massimo. There was something of the spaghetti arms about his punch, as though he hadn't used his limbs for that particular movement before. But he still made contact with Massimo's chin. Massimo staggered backward, taking with him a tray of crystal glasses before gathering himself and charging at Nico.

Massimo was the heavier and more powerful of the two but Nico was more nimble on his feet. As I watched them take swipes at each other, a little Lladro ornament was decapitated, a Wedgwood bowl went flinging off the sideboard. I tried to get between them but it was like trying to separate a couple of snarling dogs.

"Stop it!" My voice sounded as though it was coming from a distant hill, where the wind had removed all power and just a feeble echo remained. I stepped forward. "Nico! Don't do this. You're better than that. Better than him."

As though an alarm clock had suddenly penetrated a deep, red-wine sleep, Nico stopped dead, his chest heaving. I glanced at Massimo, who, despite his split lip, was still managing to contort his face into a sneer, his fingers clenching and unclenching. Nothing like the charming man I'd believed he was. I stood in front of Nico and stared Massimo down.

"What do you know about me, Maggie? What do you know about anything? Except how to gold-dig?"

Nico sent out a growl of anger to my left. I put out my hand to stop him from moving toward Massimo. Of course I registered that blow, the slice into a wound that was always ready to split open. But I wasn't the one who was going to feel bad. Oh no. Not at all. I could almost hear my inner steel oiling itself up for action.

The Beryl in me came out. "Here's what I know. I don't go through life getting what I want by hurting people. I also know it doesn't matter what I say, how much I love Nico, your shriveled little heart won't ever be able to believe I'm with him for anything other than money because people like you don't understand working together, looking out for each other. They only understand getting their own way." To my credit, I did pause for a second's consideration before I let my killer point out into the world. "You might be right that I'm a bit thick. It's taken me all this time to realize what you're really like. But I met someone today who put me in the picture. And I didn't want to believe her. I was hoping she just had an ax to grind, that her story wasn't the truth."

Massimo's eyes pinged up like a cartoon dog's. He was having to work harder at that sneer.

"Yes, I bumped into Dawn today. You do know that your 'other' son is a swimming champion? That the boy you abandoned because he was 'defective,' as you put it, came first in the swimming championships Francesca has just been to?"

Nico put his hand on his hips. "What other son?"

The relief that only Massimo knew about Ben gave my anger a sharper edge. "Tell him, Massimo. Tell him how Dawn had to run away because she was afraid you would make her abort your own son because he had a heart problem."

Nico was shaking his head, disbelief flooding his face. "What? I thought you said she didn't want children."

Massimo looked at the floor. Just for a second, I felt a sliver of sympathy for him. He'd behaved like an absolute arse but I couldn't bring myself to believe he'd done it without a lot of heartache.

But that little pause was just to allow Massimo time to reload. When he looked up again, he'd narrowed his eyes as though he was flicking through a mental armory of weapons he could use to wound me. "Don't come with that holier-than-thou shit, Maggie. At least I'm not a thief."

I wasn't quite sure how being a thief was worse than intimidating your wife so much that she had to flee and hide to save her baby. But today didn't seem to be about rational arguments. He'd picked the wrong insult to throw at me.

"I'm not a thief. I've never stolen a thing in my life. I couldn't give a shit about money. Nico is always wanting to buy me this, that and the other, but I've seen what trying to keep up with everyone else does to people and believe me, I am happy as I am."

"What about the gold box you 'lost'?"

I felt a rush of betrayal that Lara had told him. "I had to get rid of it. And you know why." I glanced at Nico, wishing I could save him from the truth.

"Why? Come on, we're all family here. Do share with us why you felt you had to take a box worth hundreds of pounds."

"How would you know how much it was worth?"

"Francesca told me that you'd stolen a real gold box."

I should have known Lara wouldn't give Massimo any ammunition against me. "Fuck off, Massimo. You know how much it was worth because you're the one who bought it for Caitlin."

Nico looked as though he was standing in a room where everyone was fluent in a language he'd only just started to learn. I wanted to pause, to bring him up to speed, anything to stop him from seeing the world as a place where the people he loved the most lied and kept secrets from him.

"What proof have you got that I gave it to her?"

I couldn't quite believe he'd admitted shagging his brother's wife but wanted to split hairs over whether or not he'd given Caitlin a present.

"Because of the inscription. That was you, wasn't it? Why 'P' though?"

A slight raising of the eyebrows that I'd discovered the inscription. He waited until he had our full attention. I didn't want to give him the satisfaction of us hanging onto his every word, but he was mesmerizing, a gypsy-haired villain deciding whether or not to put us out of our misery.

Finally he laughed. And started humming. The music from *Pelléas and Mélisande*. That's where I'd recognized it from. No run-of-the-mill bloke-next-door affair for Massimo. He'd cast himself in the role of the tragic sibling, in love with his brother's wife. In his warped mind, he was Pelléas—P. He must have been laughing his head off at my naïve questions when we were watching the opera in San Gimignano.

I turned to face Nico, wondering if I was up to the job of repairing the damage of the betrayal by his first wife *and* his brother, as well as convincing him I wasn't the light-fingered chancer Massimo was making me out to be.

"Nico, I didn't steal that box. I took it but I didn't sell it or anything. I chucked it away. In a dumpster. Maybe I should have just shown you what I'd found." My voice was shrinking. I couldn't have sounded more defensive if he'd caught me climbing out of a window with a bag marked "Swag." "I couldn't see the point of telling you Caitlin had been unfaithful. I knew you'd be devastated and it was all in the past. I was worried you or Francesca would find the box and read the engraving. You'd have known straightaway it was from a lover. I was trying to protect you both. But I didn't realize all the stuff was from Massimo."

Nico's face was blotchy with emotion. He was swallowing over and over again as though he was fighting the great swell of feelings whirlpooling inside him. I was longing to give him space to cry. To shout at me. To vent his anger, sadness, despair, whatever it was trapped inside, in all its rawness. But I didn't want Massimo to see him crumple. Or let him witness me dealing with how much Nico had loved Caitlin.

I took Nico's hand, running my fingers over his rough skin. He didn't pull away. A rush of emotion, a desire to protect him and to have revenge on Massimo overwhelmed me.

"I'm sorry. I made a shit choice about the whole bloody box thing. Come on, let's get out of here. I'll just check on Lara. You go next door and talk to Francesca." I couldn't bring myself to say "home."

After living there for ten months, I belonged less than ever.

Nico shook his head. "I'll wait for you."

"No, I'll be fine. Francesca needs you. She's in a terrible state. I'll be right around; just want to make sure Lara's okay." I didn't add "safe."

Nico turned to Massimo. "I looked up to you. I thought you had the world sussed. I envied you. But more than that, I loved you and would have done anything for you."

I stood by helplessly as Nico walked out, shaking his head as though he couldn't believe what had just happened. One thing I knew for sure. Gold-digging had nothing to do with my love for Nico. In that moment, I'd have taken his raw hurt and let it devour me alive rather than see him in such unbearable pain.

CHAPTER FORTY-FIVE

LARA

After ten years, the biggest change in my life had happened in half an hour.

When Maggie came into the kitchen, she put her hand on Dad's shoulder. "You all right, Robert?"

He didn't reply. My poor dad, the man I wanted to protect, was huddled on a chair, swaying backward and forward. God knows what damage we'd done to him.

Maggie put her hand in my dad's until he stopped rocking. Eventually he looked at her. "You're pretty."

She smiled at him. Not Maggie's usual ferocious grin that made her look about fifteen but a gentle smile that held a mix of kindness and sadness. "You're not so bad yourself, Robert."

He winked at her. My old dad, the man I'd totally failed to look after, still had the energy to wink. I didn't think I'd ever loved him more for that little flash of spirit, the proof that inside the jumbled mass of fading connections, a bit of his steadfastness, his strength remained.

My eyes filled. Maggie pulled me into her arms. And for once, I didn't have to hold myself in, didn't have to stand there like a shop dummy in case I relaxed and opened the door onto something I would later have difficulty explaining away.

She shushed me like a child. "I'm sorry. I'm so sorry for not realizing. I was so desperate to belong. It was all happening right in front of me and I couldn't see it." Her voice trailed away. "I wish you'd told me."

"Don't be silly." I couldn't let her blame herself for anything. I forced my words out. "You saved me. I didn't know anyone could even like me anymore. I should have told you. I thought you wouldn't believe me. And I kept thinking I'd find a solution, that if I just did a few things differently, we could be happy again. It wasn't all his fault. I wasn't a very good wife—or mother—when Sandro was born."

Maggie looked directly into my eyes. "It *was* all his fault. Lots of women go a bit nutty after they have babies but their husbands don't start hurting them, undermining them so they think they're a worthless piece of shit or having affairs with their sisters-in-law." She gave my arm a squeeze. "Let me get rid of Massimo and we'll take it from there. I'll come with you to take your dad home once he's gotten over the shock."

My heart sank. If I knew Massimo, he'd be canceling the direct debit to the nursing home right now and there'd be nowhere to take my dad back to.

CHAPTER FORTY-SIX

MAGGIE

I marched back down the hallway. Without Nico I wasn't half as brave. The sound of Massimo crunching about on the broken glass in the lounge did nothing to reassure me. I forced away the thought of whether I'd still be able to scream if he put his hands around my throat.

Pushing open the door, I stepped just inside the room. As much as I'd have liked to have gone in all guns blazing, I worked on not sounding aggressive or accusatory, focusing instead on getting him out of the house. "Is there somewhere you could go for a few hours until we can get Robert home?"

Massimo smiled. Bloody smiled at me. After everything he'd thrown at me, never mind everyone else. Fruitcake.

He spoke in that funny purring way he adopted sometimes, like some Z-list TV celeb convincing a member of the public to jump out of a plane. "Sorry about all that. No need to be dramatic about it and start pushing me out of the door. It just got a little out of hand."

Jesus. I hoped I was in Australia when it got fully out of hand.

"I'm worried we won't get Robert into the car if he sees you and gets agitated again."

The smile vanished. Massimo ran his hand through his hair. "Quite the little Miss Fixit, aren't you? And not to put too fine a point on it...what if I don't want to leave my own house to suit my bitch of a wife and a nutjob of a father-in-law?"

"Then we have a bit of a problem," I said, nearly giving in to the urge to laugh hysterically and tag "Houston" onto the end of the sentence. I still wouldn't be the maddest person in the room.

He stood with his hands on his hips, eyes narrowed as though he was trying to decide where to thump me.

Any desire to laugh disappeared.

I pretended to kneel down behind an armchair to pick something up. Instead I ducked down and pulled my phone out of my back pocket. I thanked God I still had a shitty pay-as-you-go mobile with no password. I stabbed at the buttons, clattering bits of broken china about with my other hand while it rang. "Anna? Would you mind coming over to Massimo's as quickly as you can? There's a bit of an emergency here and he's got something he'd like to discuss with you."

Massimo lunged around the chair to snatch my phone out of my hand. Anna's voice was still ringing out a shrill "What emergency? Maggie? Maggie?" as it smashed to the floor. Given that it only cost two quid, I wasn't going to hang around to fight over it. I eyed the door, wondering whether I could beat Massimo to it. I could hear little whimpering noises in my throat, the sort Lupo made when he saw a rabbit running across the garden.

Massimo stepped toward me. "You think you're so much smarter than me, don't you?"

Even though my heart was racing, I wasn't going to give him the satisfaction of seeing me scared. I lifted my chin. "No, I don't. But what brains I do have, I try to use for good things, rather than to increase my arsehole ratings." I anchored my feet in case a blow was coming my way.

But Massimo just looked disgusted. "That sassy mouth of yours is going to cause trouble for you one day."

I forced myself to look him right in the eye. "That nasty habit of bullying people and thinking you can get away with it isn't going to do you a great favor either, mate."

I'd forgotten to be frightened with the rush of adrenaline that came from a good old-fashioned slanging match. I wasn't used to the whole nicey-nicey not saying what you really thought that the Farinellis favored. On the estate, my friends and I were always ready with a sharp comeback for anyone who shouted off a balcony or stairwell.

It was almost a disappointment when Anna came rushing in, took one look at the room and screamed, "You've been burgled."

I felt sorry for her, even though I didn't want to be.

"Massimo's got something to tell you. I'll just get Lara." I didn't care about watching the favorite son fall off his sparkly podium. But Lara, she deserved to.

CHAPTER FORTY-SEVEN

LARA

As Anna burst through the front door and charged down the hallway to the sitting room, I realized Massimo wasn't going to be able to wave his magic wand and convince us all that we'd made a dreadful fuss about nothing. Life as we knew it was going to change.

What I didn't know yet was whether it would be for the better.

Maggie shot into the kitchen, beckoning me. "Is Robert okay for a minute? I think you should hear what Massimo has to say. I can stay with your dad if you want. Or do you need me with you?"

Dad looked as though all the drama of the afternoon had taken its toll and he was dropping off to sleep. I took the mug of lukewarm tea from his grasp and wedged him into the armchair with a couple of cushions. "Will you come with me?" I was a coward, but I already knew that.

"Of course. Let's leave the door open, then we'll be able to hear if Robert decides to go for a wander." She ran and put the chain on the front door and, yet again, I wondered how I'd existed before Maggie's arrival, her bohemian aura a front for her highly resourceful nature.

But even with Maggie by my side, I still felt sick at the thought of Massimo's vitriol. Maybe Anna's as well. I couldn't quite piece together how she'd suddenly become part of the showdown. Massimo was obviously still running to his mother to fix things for her favorite boy when the going got tough. But I didn't know how he could bring her on board over his affair with Caitlin. Even Anna couldn't airbrush that into one of his triumphs. Great waves of fear were pulsing through me. Massimo wasn't a man who took to public humiliation well. He'd find a way to make it my fault. He was so clever, so slippery, I'd end up feeling I was in the wrong.

Just before we walked into the sitting room, Maggie squeezed my arm. "I've got this, I promise. You're okay."

I loved her faith when mine could have balanced quite happily on a pinhead.

Massimo was standing looking out of the French windows when we went in. Not defeated or apologetic but defiant. Anna was all peacocky indignant, hands on her hips.

"What on earth has been going on here?" she asked, fluttering her fingers at the array of decapitated ornaments. "Massimo's being ridiculous. Says it's nothing, just a misunderstanding. Doesn't look like a misunderstanding to me. Have you had a fight with Massimo, Lara?"

I felt like the snitch in the playground, the person everyone would turn on later for not keeping their mouth shut. While I dithered, wondering where to start, Maggie took Anna by the arm, sweeping the glass in front of an armchair out of the way with her foot.

Massimo's face was twitching, as though vicious and wounding sentences were distilling at the back of his throat. But Maggie stood there, solid as an oak on a windy day, not stumbling over her words or sucking in gasps of air as I would have been.

"I'm sorry, Anna. There've been a few happenings in the family that you should know about. Have a seat for a moment."

Anna shook her off, as though Maggie had no right to utter the word "family." She frowned and said, "What is all this nonsense about? I've got my bridge partners coming over in three-quarters of an hour."

Massimo piped up. "They're all making a drama out of nothing, things that happened years ago. Maggie in particular keeps sticking her nose in where it's not wanted."

And that did it for me. Suddenly, the dread that had pumped around my body with every bit of me yearning for the unhappy but familiar status quo of before dissipated. I turned toward Anna. "Believe me, we are *not* making a drama out of nothing."

She was still quivering with irritation, her nails tapping an impatient rhythm on her watch face, just in case we didn't realize her time was immensely more valuable than ours.

As the details of what Massimo had done emerged, Anna shrank into the armchair. I'd expected to feel a bit smug at finally having the upper hand, at watching her forced to absorb a few blows after all the times she'd fanned the flames of Massimo's dissatisfaction with me, with Sandro.

But as she said, "Nico, my poor boy," I recognized her need to make things right for her sons. A primeval urge to protect, to defend, to repair. But I couldn't see how she was going to fix things for both of them when the problem was each other.

"Massimo? Is what Lara is saying true?"

"It wasn't like that." But he sounded subdued, none of the usual condescending conviction in his words.

Maggie moved to speak, but I put up my hand to stop her. Standing up for myself might become a habit. "You don't need the gory details, Anna, but it *was* like that."

Suddenly, though, I didn't want to launch in with how he'd bullied me, how Sandro lived in fear of getting things wrong, how every time we thought we'd done what he wanted he'd up the stakes with another demand. Not for Massimo's sake, but because I couldn't face telling a mother what a total bastard her son had turned out to be. No one looked down at a tiny newborn face and thought, "I'm going to teach you to ride roughshod over everyone you meet."

But while I was standing there, hesitating about pulling out the drawer of truths and releasing them to descend like vultures on the corpse of happy families, Maggie frowned at me. She looked almost apologetic, as though she was embarrassed to speak.

"There's something else I need to tell you, Lara." She glanced at Massimo.

"Sandro's got a half-brother."

CHAPTER FORTY-EIGHT

MAGGIE

Anna was the first to react. "Not Caitlin's son?" she asked, her eyes pleading for a negative answer.

"No. Dawn's."

Lara let out an exclamation somewhere between a shout and a scream. "Dawn's?"

She spun around to look at Massimo. "You told me she didn't want any children, that she was too self-centered. Have you told the truth about anything? Did you know about him? How old is he?"

Her distress was so acute, so painful to watch, that I wished I'd never met Dawn, that we'd all staggered on in blissful ignorance. It was like seeing the last stitch attaching a button to a coat finally fray and give up the ghost.

I tried to calm her. "Lara. Lara. I'm sorry. I thought you should know."

But she was beside herself. "Did you carry on seeing Dawn *and* Caitlin behind my back?" Her voice kept petering out, then raging up again as more scenarios and betrayals presented themselves.

Massimo was doing his best to respond but his answers

couldn't break through the molten fury of Lara's torrent of questions.

But it was Anna who took us all by surprise. She stepped toward Massimo, light as a bird skittering over the sand, and slapped him. The noise as her palm made contact with his cheek brought Lara's explosion of questions and accusations to a halt.

It was so unexpected that I nearly giggled. Lara gasped. But most surprising of all was Massimo. He rubbed his cheek but didn't utter a word of retaliation.

Anna, however, still had plenty to say. "I didn't bring you up to lie and cheat!"

I did an internal nod at that. Anna could certainly lay claim to brutal honesty. Never knowingly sugarcoating anything in her life. If I'd been nasty and hard, this would have been my moment to sit back and enjoy the show—the self-important Italian mamma ripping into her arrogant son. Instead I felt sick at the family bloodbath. I'd be devastated if Sam ever hurt Francesca the way Massimo had shafted Nico and she wasn't even my child.

Anna masked her anguish as fury but her words were raw, almost hissed, totally unlike her usual declarations delivered with cold indifference. This was a surge of emotion, erupting straight from the heart.

Reassuring to know she did have one, after all.

"You betrayed your own brother. And you've deprived me of a grandson for—how long?—thirteen years? A boy of Farinelli blood, who doesn't even know his own grandmother. *Vergogna!* You should be ashamed of yourself. Have I taught you nothing? Family is everything we have. Where's your son now?"

Massimo shook his head and looked away. "I don't know. I lost touch with them."

Anna was becoming more Italian, more animated. She waved a hand at me. "You, Maggie, how do you know about the boy? What's his name?"

"Ben."

"Beniamino. Good. An Italian name."

From what Dawn had told me, I didn't think honoring Ben's Italian heritage was high on her list of priorities. She probably stopped eating spaghetti after her marriage to Massimo. But, as always, Anna would see the world through her own personal periscope.

I filled her in, watching her face fall with horror, and then, in true Farinelli fashion, a little lift of pride at the swimming champion bit.

"I want to meet my grandson. I understand responsibility even if my son doesn't. Maggie, can you find Dawn again?"

I glanced at Lara. She looked like she was watching a high-speed car race, where everything was whizzing past her in a blur and she was confused about who was in the lead. I hadn't intended to become a people-tracing service, merely set the record straight so Lara could make the right decisions about her future.

I hesitated. "Maybe. I think Dawn said she lived in the north somewhere." The "north" was a suitably large area. Hopefully, it would take Anna a while to pin him down to Newcastle. I was pretty sure tracking down a county swimming champion on Google wouldn't be beyond me, especially if I enlisted Francesca's help—she was probably already friends with him on Instagram. My brain ached at the thought of trying to fix another family disaster. I'd drop that one off the to-do list for the time being, given that I was supposed to be supporting Lara, not introducing more world-class athletes into the family for Sandro to be compared with. And God knows whether Lara would even want to meet

Dawn—the wife who saved herself, leaving the frying pan sizzling and empty for Lara to jump into.

Thankfully at that moment Robert came pootling down the hallway trying to eat a banana. I was glad of an excuse to escape for a minute.

"Robert, let me just peel that for you."

"Thank you. Who are you?"

"I'm Maggie."

"Pleased to meet you. I'm Robert but you can call me Bob."

Behind me, I heard Anna say, "Massimo, pack a case and get out. You can stay with me until we repair the damage you've caused."

A long pause. "If we ever can."

Then a sound I didn't know Anna was capable of making.

A sob.

CHAPTER FORTY-NINE

Two Years Later

MAGGIE

Anna took a seat on our terrace with its distant view of the sea. Just looking out over the water with the pier silhouetted against the sky made me feel as though I was living somewhere exotic. Anna had begged us not to move from Siena Avenue but Nico had been adamant. To her credit, she'd been very restrained when the "For Sale" sign went up. Thankfully she took herself off to Italy for a holiday a few days before we left forever, sparing us the ordeal of seeing her distraught face bobbing out from behind the moving van. During the nine months we'd lived in Moneypenny Cottage, she'd even managed the odd compliment hidden under a criticism: "You wouldn't think that a dark house like this would be so cozy."

Instead she directed her venom toward Caitlin, or the person now known as *"that first wife,"* at every opportunity. When she saw Caitlin's pastel jugs on a shelf in the hallway, she turned up her nose. "I don't know why you've still got these. *That woman* had such insipid taste in everything. And they're just dust traps anyway."

I'd let Nico decide what to bring with us when we moved. Francesca just shrugged whenever Nico asked her if she wanted to keep various bowls, mirrors and all sorts of other old crap no one had ever needed in their lives. Unless you were a brushing-behind-the-radiators, grout-whitening, lavender-balls-in-your-bloomers type of person.

Today though, Anna was on her big-family-gathering best behavior, snapping open her bag and handing out tubes of Baci chocolates to Francesca *and* Sam.

She hesitated, then passed me a little box, wrapped in the sort of paper that cost three quid a sheet. "Happy birthday, Maggie."

Mum raised her eyebrows at me, Parker-speak for "That looks like it cost a bomb."

I was fairly confident it wasn't a garden gnome to match the one Mum had bought me: "I couldn't resist him. As soon as I saw him, I thought of your new garden."

I wasn't sure what had made me laugh the most—the fact that Mum had spotted a gnome playing an accordion and somehow seen it as a must-have feature for our patio or Nico's face when I opened it. I bet he was bloody delighted that, after all those evenings he'd spent clearing weeds, training a clematis over an archway and faffing about with pots to "draw the eye at the right level," my mum had taken one look and thought, "What this place needs is a gnome."

I picked carefully at the tape, sensing Mum hovering, ready to stash the poppy-print paper to reuse another time.

Inside the box lay an antique silver and sapphire pendant. "It's gorgeous, Anna. Thank you so much."

She smiled. "It belonged to my mother. It was always a sadness to her that I didn't have a daughter, but I know she would want you to have it."

Tears pricked. I gave her a full-blown Parker hug. She

accepted it rather than embraced it, but the fact that I even dared risk disturbing her scarf was such a huge step forward from when I first joined the Farinelli family.

But with the tact typical of a thirteen-year-old, Sam failed to disguise his lack of interest in Anna's big "You have been accepted into our family" gesture and butted into my thanks with a "Can I bring the cake out now?" He was like a steam engine that needed a regular shoveling in of fuel. At least his rubbish father had served one purpose: Sam was already a good few inches taller than Mum and me and showed every sign of inheriting his dad's slim frame. At my lack of resistance, he went running up the steps to our cottage. Anna did a quiet tut in deference to my birthday but that little telltale click of her tongue was still audible. I had failed to fall in with the Farinelli rules about eating—refusing to peel apples, finishing dinner with a big mug of milky coffee and never feeling the need to mop up sauce with a piece of bread. Hence I didn't give a hoot that the kids would hoover up my birthday cake before we'd had a barbecue. Sausages, burgers, chocolate cake…it all went down the same way regardless of scoffing order.

I watched Sam go, glancing over at Nico grinning away, a man at peace with the world. These days he'd lost the tense look he used to have, no longer braced for bad news or another problem to resolve.

He leaned over and squeezed my hand, whispering, "Grow old with me; the best is yet to come."

I wasn't really into fridge magnet romance but since we'd moved into a home we'd chosen together, I'd finally stopped expecting him to realize there was a thinner, prettier, smarter wife hiding around the corner ready to do a better job than me. When I'd suggested my plan for this evening, he'd blown out his cheeks in surprise. "Crikey. That will make it a birthday to remember."

"Do you think I'm mad?"

He'd laughed, kissed my nose and said, "No. I think you're kindhearted and brave." He paused. "And sometimes a little overoptimistic. Which is all part of your wonderful charm."

And now there was no going back. Despite my belief it would all turn out fine, I was jittering about, counting napkins and straightening forks as though it might make a difference to the outcome.

Although Anna had softened toward all of us in the wake of her perfect son turning out to be a complete shit, she hadn't quite lost her desire to get the room to skip to her needs and wants. When Sam appeared with the chocolatey tower he'd made with Mum, she threw her hands in the air and said, "My goodness. Are you going to eat that before dinner?"

Mum got up to light the candles. She acted as though Anna was a small buzzing noise in the corner of a room that no one could identify. I took the stance of "It's my birthday and it's cake before carrots if it suits me."

I nudged Nico. "Where's Francesca?"

He got to his feet. I put out my hand. "I'll go. Just hold the cake pyrotechnics for a minute. Let me see if she wants to join in."

When we moved to Moneypenny Cottage—or as Sam called it "The James Bond Love Shack"—the happy new start Nico and I imagined away from the bad memories of Siena Avenue wasn't quite the party-popping triumph we'd hoped for. Francesca turned in on herself, acting as though she was a guest who'd overstayed her welcome but didn't have anywhere else to go. None of her old posters made it up onto her bedroom walls. In fact, the general skankiness that had driven me mad in the old house—dirty plates, piles of clean clothes mixed with discarded underwear, makeup spilled on the carpet—had given way to a clinical and impersonal bedroom, despite us offering to take her shopping for a new lamp, duvet set and rug.

On the upside, she was no longer downright rude to me. I couldn't deny it was a pleasure to be able to whip out the Bisto without being told that Caitlin made her flipping gravy with the chicken juices and flour. And she'd never brought up the flaming jewelry box again. In fact, Francesca was so furious about Caitlin having an affair with Massimo, she never mentioned her at all.

Nico tried to talk to her but she either blanked him or gave him both barrels, leaving him subdued and distant for days afterward. "You let her do it! How could you not notice that she was screwing Uncle Massimo? Did you even care? She probably wouldn't even have stayed with you for so long if you hadn't had me. I bet she wished I'd never been born, then she could have gone off with Uncle Massimo."

Initially, a small walnutty bit of my mean little heart had been glad Caitlin was no longer the pinnacle of all things wonderful. But when I fished all of Francesca's photos of Caitlin out of the kitchen garbage bin, I managed to locate my inner grown-up. It was a fair bet that, long term, equating your mother's affair with your uncle with proof that she didn't love you would more than likely lead Francesca into the path of unsuitable men, ill-advised cocktails and dodgy substances.

I started up the oak staircase. I suddenly became aware of the sound of my flip-flops slapping on the wooden treads. No music from the landing. My heart leaped. It was all too quiet. With the exception of Sam, none of us had made any real connection with Francesca for months. A great wave of foreboding surged through me. All sorts of horrible headlines about teenage suicide ran through my head until a scream started gathering in my throat. I burst into her bedroom without knocking, my eyes scanning the beams. I nearly fell to the floor with relief when I discovered her sitting on the other side of her bed, flicking through the photos of Caitlin I'd rescued from the bin and put in an envelope in her dressing table.

"Francesca!" I knew by the way she looked so startled I'd shrieked rather than spoken. I concentrated on getting my words out at a normal volume. "Are you all right, love? There's cake downstairs if you want some. We're being very rebellious and eating it before the barbecue." Relief made me rattle on without waiting for a reply. "Anna's doing her nut but trying not to say anything…"

Francesca looked at the photos in her lap. "I'm fine."

I tried again. "I'd love it if you joined us. You don't have to, but I know Anna would like to see you, and Lara and Sandro are on their way. With a couple of special guests."

That piqued her interest for a moment. But it didn't last. "Maybe later," she said, sweeping the photos into a pile at the side of her.

I hesitated but the Parker need to get everything out on the table won the day. "You don't need to feel ashamed of missing your mum, whatever she's done."

Francesca looked at me properly for the first time. "I hate her for what she did. It's just so disgusting and, well, weird. Sleeping with my dad and my uncle." The face she made as she contemplated her mother having sex was so teenage and outraged I struggled to keep a straight face.

I sat on the bed, glancing down at the photos of Caitlin's elfin face, all her features so like Francesca's—the neat nose, the definite chin, the well-defined eyebrows.

"Can I say one thing?"

Francesca nodded.

"It's so hard when your parents mess up because you feel they should be so much better than that, that they should know all the answers and have grown out of making mistakes. And they certainly shouldn't make ones as obvious as falling in love with your dad's brother." I pressed on, hoping that Francesca might feel better if I made out that Caitlin had been caught in some star-crossed lover scenario rather than being some oversexed floozy having it off next door at any opportunity. "But it doesn't mean she didn't love your dad in her own way. It's often not that black and white. It definitely doesn't mean she didn't love you."

She fidgeted but I was sure she was listening.

I carried on, hoping I didn't sound like some cheesy relationship counselor who wanted everyone to "own their feelings." "Grown-ups sometimes don't know what they want. Often they're just bored. Sometimes they're drunk. Maybe they find it hard to be satisfied with what they have. Some people don't take well to being married; they feel trapped even though they love the person they're married to; they still hanker after freedom, adventure, the unknown. It's a big expectation to stick with one person for a whole lifetime and never fancy anyone else ever again."

Oh shit. I didn't want her thinking that a couple of years down the line I'd be walking along Brighton seafront eyeing up the blokes in their Speedos.

I paused for a little backpedal. "Obviously I met your dad when I was knocking on a bit so it won't be so hard for me."

Francesca looked puzzled. Jesus. I was probably putting her off marriage for life.

"What I'm trying to say is that we don't know what made your mum do what she did. We don't know why Massimo hurt your dad like that either. But one thing I *know* for absolute certain is that your mum loved you so much. All she talked about to Beryl when she was ill was how you'd cope without her. She wasn't perfect, but none of us are. You should be proud that your mum loved you so much. And that you loved her. All the other things that happened shouldn't and don't change that. You wouldn't miss her so much if you hadn't loved her. And it's okay to love someone even if they do bad things."

I still had more to say. But Francesca got up and sat next to me on the bed, leaning forward with her head in her hands.

"Thank you," she whispered. "Do you think you'll love me one day? Even though I've been so horrible?"

"I already do, sweetheart. I always wanted a daughter."

CHAPTER FIFTY

LARA

Climbing into my Fiat 500 still made me smile. Maggie had encouraged me to buy a bright red one rather than the silver one. "Make a statement! No more gray and beige for you!" She'd also persuaded me to be adventurous in my new flat near the seafront. We'd chosen some bright butterfly-patterned fabric and she'd made me some curtains for the French doors that led onto my balcony. I loved sitting there after Sandro had gone to bed, breathing in the sea air, listening to the sounds of the city below, secure in the knowledge that a peaceful evening wouldn't inexplicably go awry.

For someone who hadn't had a lot of education, Maggie could have made a formidable divorce lawyer. At her insistence, I didn't let on that I had no intention of fighting Massimo for a house where every kitchen cupboard I'd been pushed against, every cushion I'd rushed to straighten reminded me of how I used to lie in bed in the morning trying to judge what mood my husband was in by the sound of his footsteps on the landing. Anna had been so terrified I'd force him to sell the house in Siena Avenue and he would move away completely, she instructed Massimo to buy me the home I wanted outright.

Whereas Maggie was completely forthright about money, asking the solicitor detailed and unabashed questions, I squirmed, terrified of appearing greedy.

Except when the solicitor told me Massimo was trying to claim he'd had permission to use the money from the sale of Dad's house to pay for the nursing home. Memories of him blocking all my attempts to look into annuities to safeguard Dad's care without relying on Massimo led to such an outburst of invective from me that the solicitor's eyes flew open in shock. A swift letter to Massimo clarifying that any misappropriation of funds belonging to a vulnerable person was likely to result in a lengthy prison sentence led to Massimo releasing the paperwork relating to Dad's finances with all the money intact within a week.

When I mentioned to Maggie my guilt that Massimo had paid out thousands of pounds for Dad, she shook her head.

"He bloody told anyone who listened that he was bankrolling your father, making out he was some Good Samaritan. He can't have it both ways. I'd see it as your due for putting up with him for all those years. You don't owe him anything."

Together we managed to find a little nursing home close to my new flat. It wasn't as posh as the other one but I'd walked in several times and found Dad in the middle of a sing-song and the staff were always encouraging him to play the piano. This time I didn't take any chances with the finances. With the solicitor's help, I set up a special trust to safeguard Dad's care for the future.

On the day I'd left Siena Avenue, I'd averted my gaze from the windows of Anna's house opposite, trying not to wonder whether Massimo was watching as Sandro leaned his cheek on the front door and said, "Good-bye, house. See you soon." I'd never been able to second-guess Massimo while I lived with him, so I had no idea now whether he was full of regret, or just burning up with venom that I hadn't walked away with nothing.

Anna came over just before we disappeared off to our new lives. She took both my hands in hers, which was probably the most physical affection she'd ever shown me. "I'm sorry. I hope you'll be happy. I can't turn my back on him because he's my son, but I'm so ashamed of how he treated you. Don't be a stranger."

I nodded, afraid to open my mouth in case a huge wail of grief came rushing out.

Sandro hugged her. "We won't be strangers, *Nonna*. We're family. You can come and see us at our flat. You can have my bed."

His little spark of bravery nearly finished me off.

Anna forced a smile. "And you'll come back and stay with me so you can see Daddy." She glanced at me. She'd prevented our divorce proceedings becoming any more acrimonious by offering to supervise visits between Sandro and Massimo. Not exactly the cozy granny I dreamed of, but I hoped her despair at Massimo's behavior would mean she would protect Sandro from the worst of his excesses.

I didn't look back once as we drove away.

Now, two years on, I barely recognized myself. I'd never have had the nerve back then to take a gamble and do what Maggie and I had planned for this evening. And it was a mark of Nico's generosity that he was prepared to go along with it. As I made my way through the traffic to Brighton station, I hoped Maggie had been right about tonight. I tried not to think about the pitfalls. What Anna might say. How Francesca might react. Even Nico might not be as sanguine as he thought he would be. Sandro, though, had been asking every five minutes whether it was time to go yet. I'd considered springing it on him as a surprise. However, although he no longer wet the bed or looked at me for permission to ask for what he wanted, I still took our new life one day at a time, grateful that he was finally coming out of his shell. I loved being able to stick up his drawings all over the flat and taking him to practice his newfound swimming skills on calm days at the beach without Massimo banging on about learning the crawl.

We pulled up outside, with Sandro pressing his nose on the car window, peering through the people thronging about. Just as we were getting out of the car, they appeared at the station entrance. I didn't hesitate. It was definitely them. The woman looked exactly as I'd expected, her freckly face full of warmth.

I shouted over. "Dawn!"

I hugged her. She squeezed me back, the honesty and intensity of our phone conversations translated into physical form. When Maggie tracked her down through the swimming club Facebook page and Dawn offered to talk to me, I'd been horrified. "I'm not ready for that. It's bad enough you knowing what a fool I was." But over time, Maggie convinced me it might help me process it all, the only other person who truly understood how Massimo had managed to control two sane, smart women like us.

And it had helped. So much so that we'd agreed to meet. It had sounded so easy on the phone, but my heart was hammering as I prepared to introduce Sandro to his half-brother. I'd tried to talk him through all the eventualities. "Ben might be a bit shy at first. And that might make him seem unfriendly." But I needn't have worried.

Dawn gestured to her son. "This, obviously, is Ben."

Sandro could no longer hold in his excitement. "You're my brother!"

The knot of fear that Ben would rebuff Sandro dissipated immediately as Ben stepped forward and gave Sandro a solemn handshake, saying, "You look a bit like me."

In reality, Ben looked far more like Massimo than Sandro did. The same dark, curly hair, the squarish chin, the thick eyelashes. But he didn't have Massimo's hard edge: Ben's features were rounded and softer. I could see Dawn's cheeriness in him.

"Are you both ready?" I asked, picking up Dawn's suitcase. "Maggie can't wait to see you again."

I drove toward Maggie and Nico's cottage, filling them in on the family, telling them not to mind Anna if she was a bit off at first, that actually she'd turned out to be a great support to me. Ben chatted about sport and school, answering Sandro's tentative questions without sounding dismissive.

As we pulled up outside, Dawn touched my arm and said, "I'm a bit nervous."

"You really don't need to be. I'll look after you." And as I said it, I realized I was so robust, so confident in my opinions and sense of self for the first time in years, that I had enough resources left over to bolster up someone else.

Clearly what doesn't quite kill you makes you stronger.

CHAPTER FIFTY-ONE

MAGGIE

As soon as I heard the bell, I ran to the door. I waved them in. "Lovely to see you again. Was the train okay?"

Ben stood back a bit, shyer than I remembered, but then last time, we hadn't been about to spring the whole Farinelli family on him. Dawn had jumped at the chance when I'd suggested it to her. "Ben's asked loads of questions about his dad's side of the family, but over the years, I just kept sticking my head in the sand. But I'm afraid he'll get chatting to Francesca on the swimming circuit and put two and two together. Even though I gave Ben my surname, he knows his dad's name and that he was from Brighton. As long as Massimo isn't there, I'll give it a go. I'd love to see Nico and Francesca again." She'd laughed as she added, "Not so sure about Anna."

I gestured for them to stay in the hallway.

I marched into the sitting room and clapped my hands. "Right. Got a little birthday surprise. A couple of people who are really looking forward to meeting you all." Nico, who was in on the plan, might as well have had "I bloody hope you know what you're doing" tattooed on his forehead. Sam's cake consumption slowed long enough for him to raise an eyebrow but not long enough for him to stop arguing with Francesca about who *really* needed the orange Smartie. But Anna must have picked up on something in my voice. She straightened up like a dog expecting his owner's key in the door at any time.

I shouted through to the hall. "Come on in!"

Lara led the way.

I kept my eyes on Anna to see if she realized who it was without me introducing them. Her gasp told me she did.

"You brought me Beniamino!"

She was straight out of her seat. I did have a little moment of panic when I imagined her having a heart attack from the excitement and crumpling onto my lovely slate floor, but my overactive imagination had to be content with her walking up to Ben, putting her hands on his shoulders and saying, "My grandson. Thank you. Thank you so much for coming."

Ben was surprisingly tactile for a fifteen-year-old boy, kissing Anna on both cheeks before giving her a heartfelt hug.

Lara put her arm around Dawn as she fought back tears. "I didn't come here to cry."

Mum broke the tension by blurting out, "Lordy, I keep expecting Noel Edmonds to pop through the door in his Christmas outfit! Mags, I think we all need a drink!"

Anna wasn't to be outdone. "Nico, bubbles!"

I shot Mum a grateful look as she clamped her lips together to stop herself imitating Anna.

And then everyone was talking at once, shaking hands, kissing cheeks, commenting on family resemblances.

Nico handed a glass of champagne to Dawn, asking, "So you were already pregnant when Caitlin was expecting Francesca?"

I deliberately wandered off, wanting to give Nico space to talk honestly, to reminisce for a moment without "what came next" spoiling every single memory he had. Despite Anna's wheedling, he refused to have any contact with Massimo. Lara had almost certainly told Dawn about the affair, but I was sure Nico wouldn't rush to discuss it. He must have alluded to it though because I overheard Dawn say, "Your brother was very difficult to resist once he'd set his mind to something."

I wondered if the massive family rift could ever be healed. And whether it would be in anyone's interests. I felt a rush of protectiveness as I imagined Lara and Nico in the same room as Massimo. He'd try and make light of all of it, somehow tricking us into thinking we'd overreacted. I wouldn't be on the *#ForgiveMassimo* team anytime soon.

And anyway, we had our own mini-Massimo in Ben, without the bastard behavior.

Sam was straight in with a hundred questions—"How many swimming trophies have you got? Twenty-seven? Francesca's only got nine," creating an awkward pause while Ben came up with a tactful reply. Francesca seemed rather overawed, but whether that was because she was taking in the fact that she had a new cousin or because he was the god of the swimming circuit and ridiculously handsome, I wasn't sure. I did know that a lot of kudos from her friends angling for an introduction were heading her way.

After a while, Sam got bored with the whole trip down the Farinelli memory lane and demanded that Ben play table tennis with him. I watched them on the patio, loving Ben for tolerating Sam's erratic smash style, which was brilliant when it worked but was let down by its ten percent success rate. Eventually, Ben asked Sandro to have a game. Much to Sam's irritation since we'd bought the table tennis table at the beginning of the summer, Sandro had found his sporting niche. He won the best of three. Ben high-fived him, saying, "Beaten fair and square by my little brother!"

Sandro's face was a picture. His eyes widened and a huge grin spread over his face. I had to clear my throat to stop my eyes welling up as he said, "Can I call you my brother?"

Ben ran his fingers through his hair. "Well, I'm actually your half-brother. But we don't have to tell people that."

Not to be outdone, Sam piped up, "You can be my brother too if you like. And Francesca's."

At a later date, I'd have to help Sam grasp the fact that you couldn't just go around muscling in on other people's siblings and claiming them as your own.

I wanted to capture this moment in time and take a photo of this funny old family but didn't want to intrude on the emotions of the moment—the apologies, the explanations, the reminiscing, the hope for the future. Who would have predicted that Anna, who'd so often sneered at the very mention of Dawn's name, would now be tugging at her sleeve and begging her to keep in touch? That Mum would be belting out "My Way" giving a demonstration of the sing-song she'd had with Robert last time she visited him? That the intimidating Farinellis would turn out to be just like any other family with their secrets but also their strengths—a right hotchpotch of half-brothers, ex-wives, new wives, unlikely friends and even more unlikely allies. It was the human equivalent of Nico's potting shed where bits were grafted on, cuttings taken and planted elsewhere, half-dead twigs watered, fed and given a new lease on life.

Francesca tapped me on the arm. "I forgot to give you your birthday card."

"Thank you." There was something in her face that made me not want to open it. I hoped it wasn't a jokey evil step-mother card I'd have to laugh off but secretly be cut to the quick. She stood there all expectantly. I prepared my face.

I pulled out a picture of a Great Dane. My voice came out all false. "Oh, isn't he cute? That's lovely."

I dreaded opening it up in case it just said a bald "From Francesca" like the year before.

I steeled myself and tried not to make it obvious I was reading through the tiniest corner of one eye.

"To my second mum, have a lovely birthday, I'm so glad Dad married you."

A LETTER FROM
KERRY FISHER

Hello there,

Thank you so much for reading *The Silent Wife*—I really hope you enjoyed it.

When I was mulling over ideas for this novel, I read lots of opinion pieces and internet forums to see what women were talking about, the problems they face, the issues that are important to them. Over and over again, the discussions came back to the intricacies of family dynamics. In particular, I was struck by how much give and take is required—usually from the women—to keep everything bubbling along happily and how devastated they feel when they are at odds with members of their family. Because this is a novel—and at the heart of any good novel is conflict—I was drawn to exploring how much more complicated relationships become when people marry for a second time, finding themselves obliged to weave a delicate path through the established history of ex-wives (or deceased wives), stepchildren and in-laws. I've seen friends weep over the reluctance of other family members to accept them as the new spouse and plunge into despair over the difficulties of parenting stepchildren. But I've also watched patient persistence result in the creation of a new family, still with challenges, but also with its own traditions, celebrations and joy.

As well as exploring how hard it would be to fit into a family where the first wife had died, I wanted to look at how we never know the truth about other people's marriages. Over and over again, I see how much women will endure to protect their children and how hard it is to ask for help when a marriage turns nasty for fear of not being believed, being labeled a drama queen, of repercussions on the children. Because this is fiction, I was able to write a happy—but hopefully credible—ending. I do understand that real life is not always so simple.

Anyway, if you have enjoyed *The Silent Wife*, I'd be very grateful if you would consider posting a short review—reviews are so important to authors in getting the word out about our books. Also, I cannot tell you how much it brightens my day when readers get in touch, so I'd be delighted to hear from you on Facebook or Twitter. Messages from readers are motivational treasure!

If you'd like to be kept up-to-date with news of my next book, please sign up to my newsletter (see below). We won't bombard you with anything else.

All the very best,

Kerry xx

ACKNOWLEDGMENTS

It's only now, with my fourth novel, that I really understand how much hard work is involved in bringing a book to fruition. Which means a lot of thank-yous are required. I'll start with the wonderful team at Bookouture working away on all the things the authors probably never even know exist! Special thanks to Lydia Vassar-Smith for her wonderful editing and general cheerleading, as well as Kim Nash for being a tireless publicity whirlwind. I've also loved working with the brilliant team at Forever/Grand Central Publishing in the US to bring this book to a new audience.

As always, the book bloggers and Facebook groups have been amazing—I daren't mention anyone by name for fear of leaving someone out—but thank you; I really do appreciate the time you take to comment, read and write reviews.

One of the biggest perks of this job is finding a whole new tribe of friends, whom I probably would never have encountered if I hadn't become an author. I have to mention Jenny Ashcroft and Jane Lythell, plus all the members of the DWLC—your support means everything! And I'm indebted to Adrienne Dines for her ability to unpick stories, see what's really going on and send me scuttling off in the right direction. I owe such a lot to Allie Spencer for her friendship, as well as her advice on divorce procedure!

My lovely agent, Clare Wallace, has been such a star. It's

a privilege to be lucky enough to find an agent whose judgment I trust completely. I'm very grateful to the whole team at Darley Anderson for all their hard work on my behalf.

The writing of this book coincided with the lead-up to my son's GCSEs. This threw an extra level of nuttiness into the household mix, so thank goodness for my husband, Steve. He did a great job of plugging the gaps and taking over when I thought my brain was going to blow up.

Finally—a huge thank-you to all the readers who buy and recommend my books. You make my day.

ABOUT THE AUTHOR

Born in Peterborough, England, Kerry Fisher studied French and Italian at Bath University, followed by several years working as an English teacher in Corsica and Spain before topping the dizzying heights of holiday rep and grape picker in Tuscany. She eventually succumbed to "getting a proper job" and returned to the UK to study Periodical Journalism at City University. After two years working at *Essentials* magazine in London, love carried her off to the wilds of the West Pennine moors near Bolton. She now lives in Surrey with her husband (of whisking-off-to-Bolton fame) and two teenagers. She has a very naughty lab/schnauzer called Poppy, which leads to many mortifying moments of whistling and waving pieces of chicken while the dog practices her "talk to the tail."

You can learn more at:
KerryFisherAuthor.com
Twitter @KerryFSwayne
Facebook.com/KerryFisherAuthor